# Fool's End

## A Lesson in Forever Book 1

### ASHLEIGH WOODWARD

# Dedication

*For everyone who loves baby heirs with baby hair and afros, and the ones who love their negro nose with Jackson Five nostrils.*

# Table Of Contents


Acknowledgments i
Playlist ii
The Reliving Invitation iii
Course Catalogue iv
Part I: I'm A Survivor
Prologue 1
1 The Morning After 3
2 How Do I Explain This? 9
3 Wait, What? 21
4 Runaway Love 35
5 Liar, Liar 47
6 Sophomore Year 75
7 Why So Weird? 91
8 Baker's Joy 105
9 Find Your Way Back 123
10 Promises, Promises 135
Part II: Sneaky Little Secrets
11 Oh, No Thank You 155
12 Pray About It 165
13 Dazed And Confused 183
14 Grand Gestures 201
15 Love the Way You Lie 217
16 Busted 225
17 So Not The Drama 241
18 Put a Ring On It 255
19 Okay? 271
Part III: Flash Memory Overload
20 Moments In Time 279
21 Last Tuesday 283
22 Last Thursday 297
23 Oh, That's A Bit Much 315
24 Ready For Love 327
25 Last Friday 339
26 And We're Back 357
27 Do You Remember? 367
Epilogue 375
About The Author

# Acknowledgements

I was obsessed for weeks on end about this story, and I just want to thank every single one of my people who would allow me to yap on and on about how much I enjoyed this entire process. Between FaceTime calls with me in a bonnet and moo-moo, long-winded voice notes in the middle of the night, and ridiculously excited messages with all caps—expressing my joy, it had to have felt like this was going to be the best book, ever!

I mean, it better be to y'all, because it was written by me. Duh!

I woke up one random day and thought about this story. I ignored the other six stories (yes, six. y'all know I can be extra) I was writing, then locked in!

And now it's complete!

Well, book one is. I have about a million thoughts about where to take the story, because I think I opened it up to so many additional things, so while I wanted it to be only two books, I can't make any promithes, promithes. Lol.

I hope you enjoy my characters. I did my best to keep them relatable. I even changed a few things, because I know some people get so sick of me, and well… Some things are still very recognizable. But you love me, so it's fine!

Tell everyone you know to read my book! Seriously, tell them. Now! Or if you hate me, just say that. And if anyone doesn't like my story, they're anti-black woman, so boo! Just kidding, but not really. Maybe a little.

…Or not.

Be well!

https://symphony.to/itsashleightheauthor/foolsend

# C.S. Williams and the Alumni Association
## invite you to participate in:

# THE RELIVING

Please join your fellow Class of 2008 and 2009 students for a two week school experience like no other!

C.S.Williams and the Early College are implementing basic human decency courses in the near future, and we are asking you to be our beta testers for the curriculum. Imagine living as your teenage selves again!
Courses are from December 9, 2024-December 20, 2024.

In recent years, there has been a clear societal decline in the simple behaviors that promote happier lived experiences, and we hope to assist in turning that around with these new course categories.

We understand it is not a simple ask, and we will do our absolute best to accommodate any of your needs for this time.
Thanks to our generous donors and the incredible alumni who have organized this program., we are able to compensate participants for any missed work.
Please contact Dr. Hale for required paperwork on this.

There will be housing available in the Early College dormitories upon request.
Upon receipt of your acceptance of the program, more information will follow.

Attached you will find a list of courses you are asked to take in this condensed study.
We hope it is a success!

RSVP no later than November 22, 2024

# course catalogue

### **Compassion vs Empathy vs Sympathy**

Course instructor will analyze the key distinctions among the three emotional responses and explain how actions and perspectives enhance our ability to care for others in various contexts

### **Logic vs Emotion in Decision Making**

Course instructor will analyze the essential roles of both emotional and logical responses in decision-making, providing real-world examples to illustrate their effective application

### **Know Your Rights (Discussion)**

Course instructor will address legal aspects of human rights, encouraging open discussion on all related topics. (Legal consultation is available if needed.)

### **Acceptance and Understanding**

Course instructor will explore the essential aspects of embracing and comprehending human diversity. Topics will include sensitive subjects such as race, gender, religion, and other key dimensions of individual differences

### **Relationships 101**

Course instructor will examine various relationship categories and explore the intricacies of distinguishing between them, while providing guidance on navigating these relationships with effective boundaries

### **Mindset Theory**

Course instructor will explore influential theories on how mindset can shape personal circumstances and transform one's life

### **Financial Literacy for All**

Course instructor will cover essential financial topics, including budgeting, saving, investing, credit and debt management, as well as retirement and estate planning

### **Combatting Ableism**

Course instructor will examine the complexities of categorizing individuals with diverse abilities, while highlighting the critical importance of accessibility and inclusivity

# Part i : I'm A Survivor

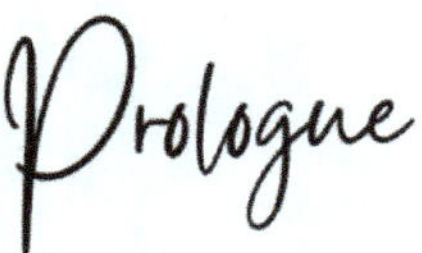

# Prologue

*Summer, 2000*

I stand frozen in terror as the medics surround her lifeless body, blocking her from view.

It was supposed to be a good day.

We were just having a fun time at the pool with all our friends, for the last time before summer break ends.

She never liked being in the water. She preferred watching everyone else swim, while she enjoyed the safety of sitting on the sides. When she felt a little adventurous, she would sit on the shallow steps, but she would never go further than that. There was no amount of convincing that could get her all the way in.

And then she was there.

In the deep end.

I will never forget her screaming. I have never seen someone look so scared before.

I wanted to jump into the water to rescue her, but I couldn't move. I just stood there, with water dripping from my hair down my face, disguising my tears. It felt like time slowed down. I couldn't think fast enough, move fast enough, or even yell for someone else to help her.

She shouldn't have been in the pool.

She can't be dead.

We're just kids. We still have to grow up.

If she wakes up, I will do everything I can to protect her. I promise.
Forever.

# 1 : The Morning After

*December 2024*

I wake up floating in the barely heated pool, with my body lapping on the edge—like the trash I was left as. No panic fills me at the weightlessness the water brings. Gratitude is all I know in this moment. I clutch the wall's edge, raising myself upright. I'm surrounded by green party cups, confetti, honeybun wrappers, someone's lost box braid, and who knows what else. Twisting around, I place both hands on the edge, pulling myself up on weak arms. The moment my stomach presses against the concrete edge, I vomit. The sudden movement was either too much, or my body was simply waiting for me to be conscious of it, as I expel nothing but neon green fluid and stomach acid.

Once I finish heaving, I roll onto my back, laying on the ice-cold pavement to catch my breath. It's still pretty dark, so it can't have been long since the partygoers dispersed. I close my eyes, taking a deep inhale through my nose. The cold air smells fresh. Like welcoming me back to this life with a clean slate. A fresh start.

I release a slow, controlled exhale, opening my eyes to focus on calming my hammering heart. Other than the zinging sound of the broken bulb in a nearby light post, the only sounds are my slow exhales—in an audible hiss, and the soft ripples of water lightly splashing against the edges of the pool. Though these breaths are a little painful, a smile crosses my face. I am so grateful for this new day. Especially knowing I wasn't meant to see it.

I roll back onto my stomach, pausing to make sure I'm not about to hurl again. The ground seems to move a little beneath me, so I take a moment to convince myself that it's solid. Once I'm confident my insides are staying put, I pull up on all fours. The winter temperature has made my body so stiff, that getting up is taking more effort than I'd like. After another deep breath, I finally push myself to stand. Once I'm upright, I have to steady myself, and will away the dizziness.

A dramatic yelp escapes me as the wind blows violently cold, reminding me that it is indeed December. I look down to the unwelcome sight of my black halter mini dress, twisted, with one of my boobs plopped out to the side. I struggle a bit, shifting the drenched fabric back into place, then hug myself around my middle, rubbing my palms over my bare arms. Wearing this dress in the winter was already not the smartest choice, but as I stand here, wet and shivering, I think about never wearing a dress again.

I look down at my bare feet, and notice my left big toe is chipped in a gnarly u-shape. Reaching down to inspect the broken nail, I see that my nail bed is bruised, and there's definitely a cut that bled from the break.

"I really hope this doesn't get infected. Good thing my feet are cute," I sigh through my frown, "who took off my boots?" I ask, as if the air could answer.

I begin to take in my surroundings. My memories are a clouded mist in my mind, struggling to come into focus. I look to the tree line, where I know I left my bag and coat. The extra chairs that were brought out for yesterday's party, remain lined a few feet before the fence to Nowhere, along the largest protruding root of the Initial tree. I remember putting my things in the awkwardly leaning chair closest to the trunk. I walk over, trying to ignore the pains in my body. When I realize the chair is empty, my breath catches. This is annoyingly inconvenient.

I turn my focus to the Initial tree, with its many markings. Like a fool in love, I somehow joined this ridiculous tradition. I was clearly out of my right mind. I crouch down, tracing our initials with my pruned fingers, and my mind replays the moment.

*RHJ + LG*

*"Now, we'll be immortalized here forever. Like something in the movies."*

*His voice has the slightest rasp to it, and it tickles my ear in the sweetest way. He folds his pocketknife back into its cover, smiling at me, with all his teeth showing. Those dimples are like black holes against his milk chocolate skin, and one front tooth is ever so slightly overlapped onto the other. It's the cutest tiny thing. He looks so happy, I can't help but to smile back.*

*"Movies end, Reelin. Nothing is forever."*

*I use the lopsided chair that holds my things as leverage to stand to my full height. Reelin stands too.*

*"You really gotta learn to live in the moment, La," he reaches over, cupping my chin, angling my face to look into my eyes, "you always looking for the end of everything. I always tell you, you could be missing the whole point of the story."*

*"And I always tell you that knowing how a story ends keeps me from being irritated about the inevitable plot twists in the middle. You know I hate not knowing if something's all for nothing."*

*"Well, I still enjoy the twists. Especially the ones where the real bad guy—the one who's been getting away with everything that no one really thinks about—finally learns their lesson." The look in his eyes is so serious, like he's looking through my physical body, to who I am without it.*

*I look over at the pool just in time to see Maliah Harris bellyflop off the diving board. The sharp smack of the water sends droplets flying everywhere, and a roar of laughter erupts across the pool. I turn back to Reelin, and he has not looked away from me, or changed his expression. The heat of his gaze sends a shiver down my spine, as he pushes my hair behind my shoulder.*

*"Well, yes. Lessons are always an important part of life, because they promote growth."*

*He shrugs, placing his hands around my waist, pulling me closer to his warmth, "or the bad guy is just a bad guy. And the lesson, was that being bad means suffering the consequences, and there's nothing they can do to make it better."*

*"Okay, but I don't believe no one is irredeemable. In the end, everyone deserves a chance to be the best version of themselves. No one's all bad, always. I can't believe anyone would wanna be, either."*

*"I love that you wanna see the good in everyone, La. Don't ever change that."*

*"I couldn't if I tried," I give him a soft smile.*

*He kisses my forehead, and his lips linger at my temple, "I'm so glad you decided to come. I really needed you here."*

*"It was a split-second decision. The Reliving is gonna be a cool experience though. When it's over, I think there'll be positive shifts in everyone who participated."*

*He pulls away, giving me a soft smile, with a slight shake of his head. "There you go, thinking about the end. Focus on right now." He lifts his hand back up to my chin, pulling me in to kiss me, as if my lips are his reason, his redemption, and his salvation.*

I reach up, touching my lips, remembering the heat from his.

"That boy, that boy, that boy…" I chuckle to myself.

Turning around, I can now take in the entire scene of the crime against my life. You'd think a green, black and gold bomb went off out here. It's the perfect representation of good ol' C.S. Williams High, and our Python pride.

There are floating balloons tied to chairs and scattered all around. Streamers are still hanging in disarray, and the "Forever Young" banner is half-hanging over the makeshift karaoke stage. The oversized pool almost looks like a solid sheet of neon green, courtesy of Kieran Michaels, and some pool dye. The honeybun vending machine Jessy Rodriguez provided, is busted open on its side. The grill and food tables near the far end of the pool are littered in trashed aluminum pans, and half eaten plates and cups. There's an overturned pan of baked beans in the grass beside the last table.

I shake my head, "wow, the cleanup crew has their work cut out for them."

The gate blocking off what we call the woods to Nowhere, has liquor bottles tied to it with the pool rope. There's silly string stuck to things, weed paraphernalia left around, and literally everything you'd assume would be at a party filled with fully grown adults—living as teenagers again, is somewhere around here. I'm not sure if my eyes are deceiving me, but the air might actually be a giant glitter puff.

The sky is beginning to lighten up, casting a deep purple glow. I really need to get home. Another gust of wind attacks me, and I groan dramatically, turning in place once again, hoping to spot my missing belongings.

"Seriously, where the hell are my things?" I mutter, walking toward the old gym building.

The pool is so large, it runs along the length of the old gym. As I walk around it, my gaze moves from the ground—watching my steps over abandoned glow sticks, beer cans, and whatever else—then back up to the building. The wall is covered in green, black and gold spray-painted names and sayings, commemorating the night. My nickname, "La," short for Lailani, is close to the left end of the wall—sprayed in green with a gold heart around it. Just below, is Reelin's nickname, "Rizz," in black. His name wasn't here when I put mine. I see what he did there, and I can't help but to smirk at the thought.

Carefully stepping around a broken glass, I pause on the final edge of the pool, deciding to look into its surface, "oh! A damn waterlogged birds' nest."

The blurred mess staring back at me, is almost a surprise. The platinum blonde wig I know was laid for the Gods last night, is now a matted mess. I know after floating in the pool for whoever knows how long, my lace is lifted too.

The wind picks up again, and I suppress a scream. I'm half-naked in this wet dress, barefoot, with none of my belongings in sight. I stand upright again, walking quicker towards the building. I wish I could run, but my body would never allow it.

I hurry into one of the unlocked outer doors. Janitor Mike was aware of our party, and was kind enough to unlock them before he left for winter break. It feels like heaven in here. Thanks to Kyler Gaines's tinkering, the heaters in each wall between the inner doors are blasting. These heaters were perfect for the party last night, as a place to come to for a short respite from the frigid air. I lean against one, sighing in thanks. The heat is almost orgasmic as it melts into my furiously stiff, freezing body.

I give myself a moment to focus. I can't quite remember everything that happened. In this moment, I know exactly three things for certain:

One: My life ended last night.

Two: I'm clearly alive to understand why.

And three: I really need a shower.

# 2 : How Do I Explain This?

The old gym vestibule is six feet deep, lined with eight sets of double doors. The inner set of doors open directly into the indoor pool, and the rest of the gym. We didn't bother trying to go all the way into the building last night, when Kyler turned on the heaters, because he was able to make the outdoor pool even hotter, too. The pool's steam kept the surrounding area from being too cold, and the liquor helped keep body temperatures elevated. Add in the heat from the grill that cooked up all the meat, and most of us never needed to come inside at all.

Standing here, warming myself in quiet reflection, images I struggle to make sense of begin swirling through my mind. I try to sort through my thoughts. My things are missing, which means someone took them. No coat, no shoes, no bag—which means no keys, no wallet, and no phone. They obviously didn't expect me to wake up, but were they just going to let the people who volunteered for cleanup find my body? I shake away the uneasy feeling coming over me, because I need to focus on getting out of here.

I reach for one of the inner doors, trying to open it, but it doesn't budge, "come on," I urge, working my way through the other doors.

The school installed phones near the locker rooms. When you have a bunch of reckless teenagers in one place like this, phones often end up in the pools, so they made sure there would never be a time a student couldn't reach their guardians. My sister, Lonayla, was usually on punishment, and the phones in this building were one of her primary means of communication throughout high school. If I can get inside, I know she'll know the number when she sees it, and pick up.

"Oh! Thanks be to Jesus!" I send up my thanks, as I manage to get into the second-to-last-door.

I'm immediately met with a hint of chlorine in the muggy, stale air. This pool was drained when the building officially closed at the end of the summer. Demolition is set to begin next month, so it makes sense that it doesn't have that freshness I'm used to, when coming here. As I walk past the inner pool, the memories of my parents and older cousins trying to teach my sister and me to swim, come flooding in. This isn't the time for a memory reel though. I'm still wet, cold, and in serious need of my hygiene routine.

I walk to the far-right end of the pool, and turn into the hall that leads to the locker rooms. Thankfully the recessed lighting is still functioning, keeping me from walking into complete darkness. Between the boys' and girls' locker rooms, there's a small sitting area, and across from it, is an alcove with privacy phone cubbies. There are four phones labeled 1-4 from left to right, and the last digit of the phone number matches its cubby number. My sister's favorite was the second from the left—the orange handset, because it's her favorite color. I pick up the orange phone, placing it to my ear, and I'm grateful it has a dial tone. Then I realize, I don't know Lonayla's number.

"Come on, La! Think! 404… 404–62… 62—Damn it!"

Plopping down on the built-in seat, I have to nod to myself, hoping the numbers come to me. It's a lost cause. I look up at the digital clock on the wall. 5:47 a.m. is crazy. I know some people are currently on the other side of campus, staying in the housing units that were provided for The Reliving. I think about going over there to see if anyone's even awake at this time, but I look down at myself in this wet dress and no belongings, then change my mind. I haven't really communicated with anyone, so I don't really know who's all over there, and I don't need anyone making a fuss, or someone calling the cops.

"Damn! I have to call the house," I sigh, shaking my head, "Mom's gonna be pissed."

I take a deep breath, then call the only number I know by heart, "please, just don't let it be Mom who answers."

On the fourth ring, the sleepy voice in my ear nearly brings tears to my eyes.

"Hello?"

"Oh my God, Lonayla!"

"Lailani? How the he—? Why are you calling?"

"Lo, are you in bed with the house phone?"

"What?" she groans, "oh, yeah. I lost my phone last night, and Kieran wasn't going for that not-talking-to-me-overnight thing. Just like the old days. He's so excited to pretend we're in high school again. Said he's getting it right this time."

She audibly yawns, and I can hear her voice clearer, but further away from the phone, "what do you want?"

"Oh. I actual—"

"Wait, you're in the old gym?" Lo interrupts.

"That's why I'm calling. I'm so glad it was you who picked up, Lo. I need you to come get me."

She's silent.

"Lo?" I say, holding the phone closer to my ear, leaning in to make sure I can hear her clearly, "you there? I said I need you to come get me. Hello?"

Lonayla's only response, is a deep sigh.

"LO! HELLO?!" I shout, "HELL—"

"I hear you! I'm getting up!" I can hear her moving around. "Bro, it's five in the morning! Where the fuck is Rizz?"

"Lonayla, I'm cold and dirty, and it's a lot going on, so please, just come get me."

I lean my head against the booth wall, closing my eyes. I'm almost ready to cry. I won't though.

"Fine. I gotta pee, and I'm on the way. I'll be there in seven," she hangs up.

I hang up the phone and stand, planning to walk to the front of the gym, so I'll see when she pulls up. Before I leave the booth, I decide to call my own phone. It goes straight to voicemail. I don't know why I called it anyway, it's not like I can hear it in here—wherever it is.

Walking back down the short hallway, to the main connecting hall that leads me to the front of the old gym, I have a sudden urge to vomit again. I rush into the ladies' room, just to my right, then push into the first stall, and bend over to relieve my body of whatever demons are trying to get out. Those demons are clearly made of air, because I'm literally just heaving nonstop. It's awful.

After what feels like an eternity of strained and involuntary ab exercises, I decide it's safe to walk away from here, since nothing's happening. I stand upright, and walk to the sink, to wash my hands. The soap dispenser still has a little liquid in it, which is surprising because when we went here, these were almost always empty, and the building's been closed for months. I press for soap, and turn on the water—finally looking up.

I can honestly say, I've never looked at myself and thought anything negative in life. That changed today. I stare in shock for a few beats, before reaching a soapy hand up to pluck the cigarillo wrapper from the tangles on top of my head. The blurry green of the pool hadn't done this tragedy any justice.

Last night, I decided on a wig for the party. I was going for a sort of ice princess vibe, with Instagram baddie energy. So, I opted for this icy-platinum wig in a half-up, half-down and flipped ends style. This looks like that was a mistake.

Washing my hands, and looking closely at my head, I see that my swoop bang is lifted and flipped back, with the lace frontal, that's pulled up from the left side of my forehead over to the bobby pins just in front of my right ear. The part for my slicked-up ponytail originally started closer to my ears, so the sides of my hair could fall just a little over my shoulders, and now the slick looks like scraggly bunches, raised from the scalp. The rubber band I used to hold the hair, has vanished, and the hair that was down and flipped, is now raised straight up, matted in with the hair that came loose from the ponytail.

I shake my head, and let out a breathy, humorless chuckle, "this is why synthetic wigs get such a bad rep. Never have I ever seen no shit like this. Never have I ever died and come back to life either, but wow." I turn my head to the left and right in the mirror, "a matted bird's nest, indeed—but in a more disastrous way." With a final look, I shake my hands to dry them, and walk out of the bathroom, knowing my sister should be here by now.

I walk through the building, and into the lobby, to look out the front doors. Lonayla isn't outside yet. I thought a lot more time had passed in the bathroom, but maybe my mind was being dramatic. I'm no longer fully soaked, after standing in front of the heaters in the back, but I'm still wet and freezing. My teeth chatter, and I hug myself for warmth, trying not to focus on the biting chill against my skin. I begin bouncing a little in place, hoping movement will create some heat. This building is almost as cold as outside, so I probably should've gone out back. Really, I should've told my sister to bring me a coat and a coffee.

I hear Ciara's *"Goodies"* booming closer, seconds before I see my dad's blacked-out Cadillac Escalade Sport come swerving around the front of the parking lot, screeching to a stop at the curb. The music pulses through my cold world, promising safety only a few feet away. I press my weight into the door handle, pushing it open, and I can't help the yelp that escapes me as the cold air blasts through. I rush as fast as I can to the car.

The window rolls down as my sister shouts, "I almost went to the side expecting you to go out the back! Thank God I didn't have to come find you! It's cold out here!" I can barely hear her over the nostalgia of high school's past.

I open the passenger's side door as Lonayla rolls the window back up, and my legs are so cold and stiff, I can't just hop in. "I'm stuck!" I yell over the music.

Lo just raises her brows in question, and I shake my head. Taking a strained breath, I turn my back to the car and grip the door, reaching for the handle behind the seatbelt, so I can lean back, and angle my body. My sister pauses the music, and I know she's waiting for me to ask for help, but I think I can manage.

I pull up with my arms, hoping to force a response from my legs. My right leg bends just enough to step onto the running board, allowing me to slide into the seat. I reach down and grab behind my left knee to raise my leg into the car. That motion loosens it, and I can twist all the way in. I slam the door, and let out an exasperated shout.

"OH MY GOD!" With a squeal, I hover my hands over the heating vent, then reach to turn up the car temperature, powering on my heated seat, "I hate the winter! I hate the cold! I hate my body! I never want to leave the heat of this car ever again!" I sit silently, eyes closed, focused on the warmth washing over me.

Lo interrupts my seconds of worship, "bitch, you look like shit. It's dead winter, and you're looking like a confused junkie that just did a little too much for a fix!"

I look over at her, and her green eyes are wider than should be possible against her rich hazelnut skin. She's wearing a lime green satin scarf, with rogue dark-brown coils poking out, and a yellow hoodie under her white coat, making her dark skin pop.

"Please, I just want to pretend none of this is happening. I need to get up under the shower, before I do anything that requires thinking." I put on my seatbelt, then return my hands to the heating vent.

Lo chuckles, "Queen of ignoring the important things. We're back in high school, indeed." She takes her foot off the brake, and we make our way out of the lot in silence.

C.S. Williams High School is massive, and has its own roads. When Lonayla turns onto the main road out of the school, she glances over at me, asking, "you want to get Starbies?"

I lean my head against the headrest, looking at her. I'm almost sure there are actual hearts in my eyes, "yes, please," I say in a little voice, "but your treat. I have no wallet or phone, so no monies."

"I figured you were down bad," Lonayla's face scrunches a bit, "when I asked about Rizz, you gave me nothing as to what was going on there."

She clears her throat, glancing over at me, as she stops at the red light, "do you feel as much like *Death Becomes Her* as you look?"

The light turns green. "Breakfast is Daddy's treat, by the way. He came to my room right when we hung up. He heard the phone ringing. He asked why we were using their fossil phone, and I told him I had to pick you up, but we'd tell him about the night later. He only said take his card, his keys were on the hook, and to make sure we eat. Oh, and to get Mom's order from Starbucks, of course. There's a stickie in the glove box to remember exactly what it is, because you know he's cute like that, or whatever."

I can't help but smile. My daddy adores his wife, man. He's literally the perfect example of a husband, "I love him. I love them. I love this car." I'm close to tears again, "I love that this car has heat. I love Kieran for making you talk on the ancient people phone, resulting in you answering my bat signal, and not Mom. I love the old gym for their phones. I love that Mom and Dad never got rid of the house phone, even when we told them they were living like dinosaurs. I love—"

"Okay, yappy pants! I get it! Your night turned trash, and you're grateful it's over. You can tell all the people and objects about how much you love them later."

I give Lonayla my best side-eye, and she presses play, restarting the song. My sister has been explicitly listening to music from our teenage years, since we got back home for The Reliving. I'm so grateful to hear about CiCi and her goodies, as Lo pulls into the Starbucks drive thru.

I shove the last bite of my bacon, gouda and egg sandwich into my mouth, as Lonayla pulls Dad's car into the driveway. I don't know if eating was the best idea, but right now, it feels great.

"I gotta go to the Apple store today. You comin'?" Lo asks, sipping on her caramel hot chocolate, then she grabs Mom's ridiculously customized latte, and opens the car door.

I finish chewing, ball up my wrapper, and take a sip of my matcha, "the way life is starting today, I gotta get myself together first, so I don't know."

"Crazy how so much can change in a few hours. I couldn't get you drunk for nothing. You were barely tipsy, and having a jolly-ole-good-ole time at the party, despite my best efforts."

Something passes over my sister's face, that I can't quite place. I do my best not to let it bother me.

"Yeah, I'm not ready to think too much about it. We'll talk about your night later though, okay?"

I'm not interested in discussing the layers of my life I now need to pull back. Especially because I actually don't know what happened. I shove my wrapper in Dad's car trash and get out, holding my cup close, and tucking my arms to my body. I wince, as my bare feet meet the cold concrete again.

Lo walks around to my side, and we head to the front door. I look over at her expression, but still can't read it, so I decide I don't want to.

"I need to get into my accounts and stuff. I definitely need a phone, so I'll Zelle you before the Apple store, cool? Wait, they don't need ID, right?"

"I don't think so."

As soon as my foot touches the top step of the porch, the door swings open. Mom stands there in her long pink satin robe, fluffy red slippers, and yellow satin bonnet on her head. She immediately tears into me.

"Lailani, what the hell is going on? It's barely six o'clock in the morning, and not only did you not have the decency to let anyone know where you were, you come to *my house* looking *like this*? Is it drugs?" She turns to my sister, "Lo, is your sister on drugs? Tell the truth!"

"Laila, babe, it's cold. Let them in here, woman," my dad's voice drifts closer, before he comes into view. He doesn't even look surprised to see me like this, as he reaches for Mom's hand, and pulls her inside, then gestures for us to follow, "get in here before you get sick."

As we move past him in the doorway, his nose scrunches at me. "Do I even wanna know why you're wet, Lailani?"

"She had a rough night, Daddy. I told her we'd give her time to warm up and shower, before we make her give the play-by-play," Lo shrugs, handing Mom her latte. "She clearly has plenty sins to wash away," she adds to Dad, who has just closed the door, and is looking between us.

I have to remember to thank her for saving me twice now. First, she answered the phone, keeping me from an awkward ride home. And now, when I have no explanation to give, she's just bought me some time. Sisters are *so* necessary.

"I see," is all Dad says.

Mom is not pleased. She walks to the kitchen, saying over her shoulder, "Lonnell, that's *your* child. Walking in here at this time, looking *crazy*. With nothing to say for herself? And of course you're gonna let her."

I don't say anything. I just turn and head upstairs to my room. My mom is already not a morning person, so I don't want to upset her any further. She's right, after all. I started their morning off a little early, by calling the house. I'll make it up to her later. Maybe I'll bake them a cake or something.

I get halfway up the stairs before I hear my sister following me. "I don't need an escort, Lo."

"I know."

I walk into my room already tearing my still damp dress off my body. I set my matcha on my dresser, then immediately walk into my connecting bathroom to turn on my shower, before I toss my dress into the trash bin. After this, I never want to even look at it again. I hear my sister's slippers shuffling to the far end of my room, as I kick off my underwear, tossing them in the trash too.

"Mom's probably regretting agreeing to letting us do this, huh?" I ask, frowning at myself in the mirror.

I hadn't paid attention to my face, when I noticed my hair earlier. My one strip lash is hanging off, my brows are smudged, my eyeliner is streaked down my cheeks, and my eyes look super dark and hollow.

"She's probably just freaked out by how crazy you look. Are you not seeing yourself?"

I look out at my sister, who is sitting up on her knees, in my reading chair. The same strange look is on her face, as she looks around my room.

I turn back to the mirror that's already fogging over, letting out a sigh, "I get it," I reach up to my temple, and tug lightly at the lace of the wig. I have to laugh at just how insane I know my parents think I look.

I wrap myself in a towel, and grab the Vaseline from under the sink, before walking back into my room, "she probably got high school flashbacks from you, honestly. All those times you did something insane, and Daddy had to step in to keep you from going too far?"

I chuckle, pushing the forest green plush rug from in front of my sister, setting the Vaseline on the corner of the chair, then struggle to sit on the cold floor, "I need you to help me get this wig off, without pulling out my edges."

Lo shifts, making a disapproving sound, "I can't understand how your hair went from Ronnie's Player's Club realness to a worse version of the mama from Holiday Heart, in just a few hours. Lean your head back."

I do as I'm told, and she moves her hands to my head, massaging the Vaseline into the hair at my temples, loosening up the rest of the glue.

I try to focus on my breathing, but I'm not enjoying the heaviness in my chest. It must be my anxiety that's making breathing feel like such a task.

I feel the wig start to move away from my head. "How did you even manage this?"

I take another strained breath, "I woke up in the pool."

Silence. As expected. It's another moment before Lonayla reaches her hands to my two braids, undoing them.

"I know, sounds crazy. I wouldn't believe I was in the water either, had that not been exactly where I woke up."

"Lailani, I don't know what the hell you're going through, and I won't pretend to, but if you need to talk about what happe—"

"Not right now. I really have to process everything." I start to move from the floor, running my fingers through my loosened hair. "Thank you for taking out my hair. Throw that in the trash, please," I gesture to the wig Lonayla's turning over in her hands.

"I gotta shower. If you're gonna stay in here, make yourself useful, and Swiffer the floor for me, please," I smirk, walking into the bathroom, and closing the door.

"I'm telling Mom she's right! It's for sure drugs, if you think I'm doing any such thing!" Lo calls through the door, then I hear her making her way out of my room.

After I hear my bedroom door close, I step into the shower to wash away the strangeness I'm feeling. I was going to try coming up with a story that made sense for my parents, but I honestly hadn't had the time to think anything through. I definitely didn't plan to mention being in the pool, but since it was clear I was soaked at some point, I couldn't really pretend otherwise. How do I explain that I came back to life in the one place they know I would never be, without them trying to commit me for insanity? I get the sudden urge to cry, but I don't—I jump out of the shower, because my body is rejecting the Starbucks I just had.

After vomiting like an exorcism, I immediately grab the mouthwash. I pour some into my mouth, then get back into the shower, still swishing. The only thing I want to do, is clean away all of the bad from the night.

# 3 : Wait, What?

The sun is all the way up, shining through my bathroom window, when I finally step out of the shower, rubbing my vanilla body oil over my still-wet skin. I like to air dry, so I open the bathroom door while I brush my teeth, then finish my skincare, and put my hair back into two braids.

My mind keeps bringing me fragmented flash memories of last night, but I still have no idea what happened. I actually don't recall much of anything from yesterday, outside of the things that have been popping up in my head, since I woke up. I close my eyes again, hoping the pieces come together, because I need to decide how I want to approach this.

*Reelin. The Initial tree. Lonayla. Kieran. Classmates jumping in the pool. Karaoke. Reelin. Cake. A toast. The woods to Nowhere. Reelin. Darkness.*

I open my eyes, taking a strained breath. There's something big missing, and I really need to know what it is.

I walk back into my room and pull out an old, faded-black Lil' Bow Wow t-shirt, and a pair of gray shorts from my dresser. Sitting on the edge of my bed, I look down at my ruined pedicure. The fleshy part under my cracked big toe is a little sensitive, but it's not too bad. To be safe, I apply some of the antibiotic ointment I had in my medicine cabinet. I pull on my clothes, and slide into my fluffy black slippers, then study my reflection in the mirror.

For a woman who genuinely adores my melanin, I look a little too pale for my liking. My eyes are so hollow, I look like a candy skull, and my lips aren't their usual rosy pink, but more of a pinkish violet. Hopefully this rights itself quickly, because no one has time to look like the walking dead. Even if I did die. Before I can pick apart my appearance any further, I turn to leave my room, grabbing my lukewarm matcha from earlier, on my way out.

My bedroom is across the hall from my sister's, on the second floor of my parents' house. I walk into her open door, but don't see her. I immediately notice the same Dior D-Dice bag charm I had on my purse last night, now on Lonayla's wristlet, laying on her dresser. I don't remember her having one too, but I don't necessarily notice everything she has. So, if I ask her, that's what she'll say, *"La, you only notice when it's you."* So, I shrug away the question, and turn back out, making my way down the hall.

The stairs are central to this floor, and on the other side of them, is the TV room my sister and I begged for as kids, my mom's private office, and the library. I decide to go into my mom's office, so I can log into my bank to cancel my cards.

I walk into the perfect reflection of the professional diva my mom has always been. The dark mahogany panels are filled with floating shelves housing awards, fashion books, gold-framed photos of Mom with her favorite celebrity clients, and plants that she's kept alive for basically my entire life. Her desk matches the walls perfectly, and sits just in front of the large bay window. The window seat is adorned with a few plush pillows, and her signed Beyoncé and Rihanna photo books—because they deserve their own space. Miss mama doesn't play about Bey or Rih. As she shouldn't.

I sit in her desk chair, and the cool leather is like a calming cocoon on my skin, after that scalding hot shower. I set down my cup, then power on her Mac, just as Lonayla appears in the doorway.

"Why are you on her computer?" My sister asks, with her arms crossed.

"I left my laptop out in Daddy's studio. I was just looking for you."

Lonayla comes further into the office, looking at the walls like she's never seen them before, "I heard you in my room. Why didn't you say anything?"

"I only came to see if you were there. Why didn't *you* say anything? I didn't even see you. I'm finna Zelle you," I turn back to the screen, logging in to my bank.

"I was in my closet. Next time, speak." Her tone pulls my attention. "Don't just sneak around in my space."

Lonayla gives me a strange look, then walks back to the door. "Daddy said to come see him, before you do anything with your bank."

"I lost my wallet. I have to cancel my cards."

"I don't know. I told him we plan to go to Apple, while you were in the shower. I also let him know that you lost your wallet with your phone— that's crazy by the way—and he said tell you to come see him before doing anything else," she shrugs, then leans against the door frame. "Maybe he wants to pay for our phones, girl. Don't block our blessings."

I squint, biting the inside of my cheek, trying to read Lonayla's energy, but she shifts, looking away from my eyes. I thought I was just on edge, but something's definitely off about her today.

"Okay, let's go see what he wants," I log out of the computer, swallowing the last of my drink, then toss the cup in the little trash can under the desk.

"Mm, when'd you get the d-dice charm?" I try not to sound too interested, as I approach Lo at the door.

She shrugs, stepping into the hall, "Ma?"

I step out after my sister, and there's our mom, coming out of my room at the other end of the hall.

"Lailani," she's holding up my green Goyard Saint-Gabriel, and the three of us walk toward each other.

"How—"

"Aht!" Mom interrupts, meeting us at the top of the stairs, "it was left in a brown package at the door when Lonayla came to get you. Your father didn't see who rang the bell. Why the hell is someone ding-dong ditching with your wallet in a nondescript package like a criminal?"

Lo and I exchange confused looks.

"Ma, I don't know. I lost it at the party last night. I was literally about to cancel my cards, when Lo came to tell me Daddy said wait."

"Guess we know why," Lo says, rushing down the stairs, "Daddy?" She shouts, going toward the kitchen.

I take my wallet from my mom, "thank you. I wish it came in my bag, with my boots that were not cheap, but at least I won't have to go to the DMV."

Mom huffs a dry laugh, "that would've been hell. Come on, your dad has questions," she places her hand on my shoulder, nudging me gently down the stairs.

We walk into the kitchen, where my dad is handing a water to my sister, who now sits at the island. I sit next to her, setting my wallet on the surface, and my mom goes to the microwave, pulling out her latte from earlier.

"So, Laila, neither of our very grown daughters has a phone. What're we gonna do about it?" Dad asks Mom, with a small smile.

She smiles back, sipping her drink, "oh, I think we should treat them like they're still in high school, as they requested when they showed up here a week ago. Lose your phone, and you're punished. No phones for the rest of the week, remember?"

"Nah, Ma! That ain't right!" Lo immediately whines, just like she did when we were in school.

"I think that's a great idea, Laila. Remind them how to be responsible. These girls came home, and lost their brains somewhere. Lonayla came in here at almost 2 a.m., crying about using the phone. Lailani never came home, and when she finally called needing a rescue, she walked in here looking like a crazy situation, and had no explanation. What happened, La?"

"Yeah, La? What happened? Thought you had more sense," Mom adds.

"It was just a party. We were all having a good time, and in the midst of it all, I had a little too much to drink. I was mixing brown and light like an amateur, without having much on my stomach. I have no idea what else to say about it right now," I lean over the counter, "it was dumb, and I'm living with the consequences."

"Your wallet was left on the porch in an unmarked package. What's that about?" Mom asks, with an accusatory look.

"I don't know. Really. Sounds insane. Maybe the person who picked up my things just wanted to return it?"

Lonayla scoffs, "yeah, they returned a $1500 wallet in perfect condition. Is there even anything in it?"

I hadn't even thought to look. I open it up, "Looks like it. All my cards, my license, and—" I spot a little polaroid, and pause.

"What?" Mom asks.

My sister leans over to see, then grabs the picture, "oh, these two…" She rolls her eyes, "y'all, La and Rizz were ridiculously adorable last night. Even solidified their love on the Initial Tree."

"Lailani did? Your sister, Lailani? This Lailani?" Mom's dark brown eyes look close to popping out of her head, "Laila and Lonnell's first born, Lailani?" Her shock is almost comical.

"La, you two really put your initials on that tree?" Dad asks, his green eyes wide.

"If I had my phone, I'd show you. There's a video of them right after he carved it." Lo says, passing the polaroid to Mom, "he gave a whole speech about knowing what's important in life. Went on and on about perfect love and second chances, or whatever. La didn't even stop him. She just let him gush for like, the whole night."

"I didn't even realize there were videos," I say, shaking away the image of Reelin's face in that moment.

"I can't believe the two of you immortalized yourselves in that tree. After all the crap you gave me and your father, when you first went to that school?" Mom passes the photo to me, and I look at it again, with a small smile. "La always plays that whole 'forever ends' card, but that's quite the step, if you ask me!"

"Yeah, I can't believe it either. Reelin was so serious last night too," I let out a breathy chuckle, putting the picture back in my wallet, "he kept giving me that super intense face, and said he was putting our initials on the tree. For the record, I did object, because what's the point when nothing's forever? But he kept telling me—"

"Stop thinking about the end?" Dad finishes my sentence.

I sigh, knowing he's going to say the same thing.

"I always tell you that. I don't know why you're so focused on the end of everything. You have such an annoying habit of trying to skip the story."

"Well, the end is what's important. If I expect the end of something, it won't hurt so bad when it comes. If I know whether or not the journey will be worth it, I can decide if I'm willing to keep going or not."

"Okay, well let's get to the end of the part where I still have no idea how you went the whole night being all cute with your man, or whatever, to me picking you up looking like an Atlanta horror story! And most importantly, without my favorite boots you own!" Lo tosses her empty water bottle in the recycle bin, and stands by the counter, placing her elbow on Dad's shoulder.

I stare at my sister, thinking about what she just said. How is the most important thing in all of this my missing boots? That was a weird thing to say, considering the situation. I close my eyes, trying to force the memory flashes, hoping to see something that explains Lo's weird energy, but nothing appears. I puff out a breath, and it feels like someone punched me in the chest. When I open my eyes, my family is still staring at me.

"Guys, it was really just a case of things getting wild and unexpected. I don't even think it's worth talking about right now. I'm pretty sure I wasn't sexually assaulted or anything like that. I just got carried away. I tried *not* to think about the end for once, and foolishly released my inhibitions. If I was thinking about this exact moment last night, I would've been *here* in bed at 5 a.m., not still at the school."

Mom's rinsing her empty Starbucks cup, "well, I don't want to ever wake up to your father telling me some strange package with your belongings appeared at our home again. I don't think I care to hear the details of you going wild, so I'll just be grateful you're seemingly okay. You two are here another few weeks, and I don't wanna worry about you actually being irresponsible enough to get yourselves seriously hurt."

"At all," Dad chimes in.

"I survived y'all's teenage years already, and when we agreed to have y'all here for this, I wasn't expecting my thirty-something-year-old daughters to give me any reasons to worry for your safety."

"Exactly," Dad adds.

Mom tosses her cup in the recycle bin, then looks thoughtfully at me, "I'm proud of you for taking a step towards love though, La. You know we've always adored Reelin, and you two have let enough time pass by. Even if he did let you lose yourself—and apparently all your stuff—then didn't have the decency to bring you home afterwards, I'm still glad you've let him back in."

"I second that," Dad says, patting my sister's back, kissing her cheek, and starting around the island, "Lonayla, I just remembered, Kieran called here when you left. Lailani, I'm glad you weren't hurt, despite this morning's start, and looking like a crazy case," he presses a kiss to the top of my head, "I'll always prefer your natural look. Throw them wigs in the trash." He and Mom start out of the kitchen.

"I'm going back to bed. Don't have no more mess happen in my house, or you're both out of here!" Mom warns, disappearing from view.

I look at the clock. It's only 8:14 a.m. Lo comes around and sits back in her seat. I look at her body language, trying to figure her out. She seems agitated, but I don't want to make it about me. She could've been in a fight with Kieran. Or maybe she's just tired.

"It's so early, Apple doesn't even open till 10, yeah?" I say to her, spinning my wallet with my finger.

"What do you really remember, La?" She asks with a sigh. "I get not telling Mom and Dad, but this is me. Go ahead, fess up."

I pause. I didn't say I don't remember anything. I explicitly stated that I didn't think it was worth the discussion. Lo's weird behavior is going to gnaw at me, but I don't think I should accuse her of anything, until I *do* remember. I focus my thoughts again, but I can only recall the moment Reelin began carving into the Initial tree.

"I think Reelin loves me too much."

"Girl, duh! He has always loved you too much!" She says, smacking my thigh, "that's why he's doing The Reliving in the first place! The man's too busy to just drop everything for two weeks, but he was always gonna do it if you were coming."

"I told him I'd come to his city ceremony thing though. He was gonna see me, either way. I know he's happy I decided to come after all, but he's been a little intense about it. It feels too much like he's trying to pick up where we left off, and I told him already—this ain't that."

"Okay. But you *are* together, yes?"

"I think it's all too much. We've been back in each other's lives all of a solid day, and suddenly we're marked for life on the Initial tree? Did you see the hope in Mom's eyes when she heard about that? She was already designing my wedding invitations in her mind."

"Y'all have been back talking for more than a year now, so don't minimize it. You've only avoided seeing him, because you don't wanna explain it if your body acts out, when he's around. You're actually the only person I know who won't use an illness to get whatever they need out of someone. You avoided him since we got here on some weak excuse, but if Rizz knew about your diagno—" she pauses, shaking her head, "Lailani, you're really a fool. That man will always choose you."

"I know. That's the problem. He loves me too much. I don't think he even gave anything else in life a solid chance. That's insane. After more than a decade apart, he's just all in? Immediately? Crazy behavior. He'd probably murder me, just to keep me from leaving again."

"I wish I had that problem! Instead, I have three baby mamas who love throwing it in my face that they're his baby mamas. I'm actually glad none of them came last night. I can't stand how they get when I'm around more than a day, without it being for the kids."

"Lonayla, it's not like his babies or their moms just appeared overnight. Y'all have been doing this since before you even graduated high school."

"EXACTLY! I was young and dumb, and he used that against me! We were together since what, I was in kindergarten? Then he just decided to be with other people in high school, making babies for *me* to raise. How selfish?"

"You also dated other people in high school. Your junior year, after refusing Kieran, you came with Jessy Rodriguez to *my* Senior prom, because you were in love with *her*, remember?"

Lonayla scrunches her nose, "no. I don't recall that, and neither do you," she gets up, "I gotta go call this fool back. We'll leave around 10, to go to Apple. You wanna watch a movie til it's time to go?"

"Yeah, I'll be up in a minute. I'm gonna make a tea to settle my stomach. You want one?"

"Of course," she walks toward the stairs, "we watching Love & Basketball, by the way. Since niggas always want us to play for their hearts."

"Oh, naturally," I laugh, getting up.

I walk around to put on the tea kettle, then pull out two large mugs, and the tea infusers shaped like little pigs. I pack the infusers with an herbal loose-leaf tea, placing them into the empty mugs, then pull out the agave, slice up a lemon, and grate some ginger. I put everything on a sturdy black tray to carry up. While I wait on the water, I lean against the counter by the stove, and my mind takes me back to three weeks ago:

*New Message From Reelin Houldover Jr.: Babe, before you know it, we'll be in December. You finally decide on coming?*

*Me: I still dunno. Lo's excited about seeing everyone, but I've seen Facebook. I'm not missing anything.*

*Reelin: It's about the in-person experience, La. Lol.*

*Me: I still don't understand why they chose to do this in the dead of winter, either. I don't do the cold, if you recall.*

*Reelin: Of course I remember. I could never forget the way you complain about it being below 70 degrees, every single winter. I'll keep you warm, though* 😊

*Me: No.*

*Reelin: Damn, straight like that?*

*Me: Straight like that.*

*Me: No, but for real, I have to have a few things in order before I can say yes, for sure.*

*Reelin: You're really gon have me ask you again, huh?*

*Reelin: You always play this game, Lailani.*

*Reelin: You want me to sound crazy, trying to spend time with you.*

*Reelin: I'm cool with sounding crazy, but baby, you gotta give me something.*

*Reelin: It feels like you got me as a secret side nigga just waiting on the day you decide to let me in again.*

*Reelin: Why haven't I seen you in the last year, Lailani? You never give me a reason.*

*Reelin: You always just shut me down.*

*Reelin: Shit gets old, La. I ain't into this distance.*

*Me: Reelin, chill before you piss me off.*

*Me: I said I have to handle some business, that's all. I can't just leave for weeks at a time without making sure someone's here to handle my day-to-day. Especially because my sister's coming. She's who I'd usually have run my shop.*

*Reelin: Aight, my bad.*

*Reelin: It would just be really nice to have you home with me.*

*Reelin: Especially since you like to sneak into town without so much as a text.*

*Reelin: Oh, I already put in the deposit for the dorm thing, too.*

*Me: Dorm? Deposit? What the hell? You're local, why would you need a dorm.*

*Reelin: Ain't even read the invite through, huh?* 

*New Audio Message from Reelin Houldover Jr.: They're providing housing all month for The Reliving participants in the apartment complex they built for the early college. They got people who need the additional time, and others who need space for their small kids and stuff. They even asked to use my youth center a few hours a day, and K had some of his teens volunteer to shuttle back and forth, to help with the lil' ones. It was gonna be hard having a bunch of 30-somethings drop everything for this, but they did what they could to make sure everyone's comfortable, with somewhere convenient to stay. I reserved a spot for you, because I knew it would be work convincing you to stay at my crib.*

*Reelin: You at least know they're compensating people, right?*

*Me: Yeah, I know that part. That's cool. I'm sure if Lo and I come, we'll stay in the comfort of our parents' house. I didn't even do dorms in college, remember? That sounds dirty.*

*Reelin: Lol, a bougie princess forever*

*Me: And am*

*Reelin: Lol, Hurry up and figure out what you're doing, so other people can plan accordingly.*

*Reelin: I miss you more than I can even say.*

*Me: You talk to me literally every single day in some form or another, Mr. Rizzy. You'll be fine if I don't come.*

*Reelin: I'll be so much better with you near me, though. I have always been better with you, than without.*

*Me: yeah, okay.*

*Reelin: I'm for real. I keep telling you, I still love you, Lailani*

*Me: Stop.*

*Reelin: Come home. I'll show you*

*Me: [Blank bubble]*

*Reelin: I'll take your lil bubble as a "yes, daddy rizz. I'll finally return to your arms in just a few weeks, and we'll live happily ever after." 🔒🖤🥰*

*Me: You're insane. Lol*

*Reelin: You make me better, so come fix me*

*Me: I can't fix your crazy.*

*Reelin: you ARE my crazy.*

*Me: Lol*

*Reelin: You never take me seriously, but I know you wanna spend life with me, too. You gon promise me forever when it's all said and done*

*Me: boy, you know forever doesn't exist*

*Reelin: We're older this time around, and your whole outlook on forever is gonna change.*

*Reelin: I am your happy ending.*

*Me:* 😜 *You think so?*

*Reelin: I've always known. I feel like you have, too.*

*Reelin: but just in case you need reminding, come home. Lemme show you. It's been long enough*

*Reelin: This is the perfect opportunity*

*Me: You're a trip.*

*Me: I'll let you know about The Reliving soon though. I gotta go.*

*Reelin: Yeah, aight*

*Reelin: I love you*

*Me: Goodnight, Reelin*

*Reelin: Call me first. Lemme hear your voice.*

The tea kettle brings me back to the present.

I smile to myself, while I pour the boiling water into the mugs, "that boy, that boy, that boy…"

I pick up the tray, then head upstairs to watch the movie with my sister.

# 4: Runaway Love

*Reelin. The Initial tree. Lonayla. Splashes. A toast. Reelin's smile. Honeybuns. Kieran's laugh. Tequila shots. Reelin. Lonayla gives me another drink. The woods to Nowhere. Some strange feeling comes over me. My reflection. Reelin's emotionless face. Darkness.*

I gasp, coming back to the moment, then reach a hand up to massage my chest. That image of Reelin's blank face makes me feel even more unsure about all of this. In that moment, I remember feeling disbelief, but I have no clue why. These flashes need to become whole, because I need to know everything. Who all was involved in the attempt on my life?

I casually mentioned that I thought Reelin would kill me earlier, and Lonayla didn't even react to it. Aside from her weirdness today, she used to joke about how my detachment would be the death of me. But would she ever knowingly be part of something so terrible? Would she think I deserved this? Would she have helped? I really don't like thinking like this, because it's making breathing feel like a foreign concept.

I look over to the other side of the couch, where my sister is focused on the movie. Quincy's breaking up with Monica, and Lo always hated this part. I watch as her eyes water when Monica says, *"So you messed around to prove a point?"* and decide I'm being ridiculous. There's no way someone who still cries at the same scenes in movies they know the ending to, would help someone else to take out their only sister.

I move from under the dark navy heated blanket, and massage behind my knees. "Lo, you want more tea?"

"Sure. And bring me some of those soft pretzel things."

"Okay," I get up, grabbing both mugs from the coffee table, "back in a flash."

I head down the stairs, and see Mom coming around from hers and Dad's room. Their bedroom used to be the TV room upstairs, but when Lonayla and I were in middle school, they decided to add another wing to the house. Mom said she wanted an escape from our raging pre-teen hormones, and Dad said a private wing was the answer. Just beyond the formal living room is the entrance to their quarters. Their bedroom, bathroom, and personal sitting room, rival anything I've ever seen. Everything Mom wanted in there, Daddy made sure she got it.

"Oh, Lailani, I was just coming to get you," she stands at the landing with her perfect brows furrowed, wearing a gorgeous yellow two-piece pajama set. "When's Reelin's ceremony? Your father said the invite said Tuesday, and I wanted to be sure, but I don't know where to look for it in this damn iPad."

I let out a small laugh, as I reach the last step. Mom tucks her iPad into the crook of her arm, and takes the mugs from my hands, raising her brow at me. My parents are weird about me and things that can break, especially if those things can hurt me when they do.

 I sigh, smiling innocently at her, "it is on Tuesday."

Mom purses her lips, turning toward the kitchen, "I still need to see the invitation."

"Your email is the envelope icon at the bottom of the screen, remember?" I ask, following her.

"It's empty, La. It says there's no messages," Mom sets down the mugs, and opens her iPad.

I let her try looking for herself again, while I fill the infusers, then go to the walk-in pantry to pull out the pretzel bites, a ginger ale, and a pack of gummy worms—setting everything on the counter.

"I clicked that envelope, and ain't nothing from Reelin," she hands me her iPad, then sits on the stool closest to the stove. "I always click that one, and the green one, because y'all always tell me that's where my mail is, but it's not there."

"The green one is where your text messages go. Reelin sends you email invites," I press the back button out of her trash bin, then click her inbox.

I place the iPad on the counter in front of her, "you were in your trash. See the top? You want it to say 'inbox' when looking for emails."

"How did I get to the trash?"

"You clicked it."

"No, I didn't. I wouldn't go to the trash, Lailani," she says with a little attitude.

"Okay," I shrug, turning to the kettle that's now ready.

"I don't care how senile you think I am, I wouldn't go to the trash." I look back at Mom's confused face as she focuses on her inbox, and I smile fondly at her.

I pour the water into the mugs, then turn back to look at her screen, pointing to the email from Reelin, "it's that one."

She frowns, reading the invitation again, "you kids and your electronics are gonna send me to my grave. But you just wait till you get older and don't understand anything."


Mom gets very frustrated with technology. My parents are a bit older, so some things just don't make sense with how technology progresses. In the early days of their retirements, Dad took some online classes for seniors with the library. He said it would help him to expand his mind, keeping up with the times. Mom refused, saying it didn't make sense to learn technology online, when the online part is what she doesn't understand. Dad tries to help her, but she gets even more upset when she doesn't grasp something after he breaks it down. Dad always tells her she doesn't have to learn, because she has us. She still gets really irritated though.

Our parents are still pretty cool for their age, and they're such a beautiful example of lasting Black love. They've been together since Mom was a cute-little-sixteen-year-old, in her junior year of high school. Dad was a skinny fourteen-year-old freshman, who played the guitar. They met in the after-school program at C.S. Williams High School, in 1966. Dad walked over to Mom in the original version of the old gym, and told her he liked her yellow paisley ribbons. Mom asked If he wanted them. He thought the question was crazy and made to walk away, but she stopped him, explaining that she could make him a case for his guitar with the same fabrics. She had seen him play, and knew it was his passion. He told her that was the coolest thing someone could ever do. The two became inseparable from then on. Even when Mom graduated and went to college, they always found time for each other. They married shortly after Dad's undergrad graduation. He still has that yellow paisley guitar case today.

For years, my parents tried and tried for a baby. They did every natural and medical thing they could, but it wasn't happening. Mom and Dad struggled emotionally, building their careers, while their peers were growing families. They were so disappointed in themselves for not being able to do the one thing they felt they were supposed to do. It took quite a toll on them. My parents thought themselves failures, despite Mom being a designer, who often worked with every iconic star of multiple generations, and Dad being a lawyer, who has never lost a solo case in his career. Dad decided that for financial stability, law was a safer bet than pursuing music, in case mom ever wanted to stop working. He said she deserved to be taken care of with guaranteed benefits, so he put his all into building an elite portfolio. They had incredible success in life, but they still felt like they were missing the best part.

After years of heartbreak, Mom and Dad accepted that having a family was not meant for them. They were both exhausted from the never-ending negative results, and Mom was starting to feel like she wouldn't survive another letdown. They leaned into their love for each other, letting go of the pressure of it all, and they finally got what they were praying so hard for. As soon as they stopped trying, they got pregnant. I came the year Mom turned forty, and Lonayla the year after. Mom and Dad always say, God rewarded them for sticking it out together, through those tough years of feeling hopeless. That's the reason our names are literally a play on theirs:

**Lonnell and Laila**

**Lai (Laila) + Lani (Lonnell) = Lailani**

**Lon (Lonnell) + Ayla (Laila) = Lonayla**

Cute and ghetto, I know. Some people think they're misspelled Hawaiian names, but nope! Just the names of two beautiful people, and the culmination of their love.

Our parents did their best to give us absolutely everything we could ever ask for. They raised us to be good women, who could do everything on our own if we had to, but they also made sure we knew it was okay to let others do for us. We aren't like the Carters or anything, but we have money, and they've never penny-pinched with us. Dad always told us we were princesses. Like Lori Harvey said her daddy told her, we are the prize. And as Black women, that we are.

Mom huffs, closing her iPad case, "La, I think you should tell Reelin to send us paper invites from now on. You know the only reason we missed his last event was because I never got the email. His gala for the suicide thing this past summer? It was themed, and you know I love a good theme."

"He knows y'all aren't great with technology. I think he just sends the invites to everyone in his contacts, so I'm sure he ain't hurt about you never responding."

"Well, I wanna support my future son-in-law in all his endeavors. I really love that he's back in the picture."

Telling her I still don't want to be a wife anytime soon is pointless, so I don't say anything.

Mom cocks her head to the side, squinting her eyes at me, "you ain't slick keeping him away from here last night, either. We want to see him too."

"I told y'all you can do whatever you want. I never kept him from you. You and Daddy have his number."

"Mhmm. You know you don't want us talking to him without you controlling the conversation. But you keep pretending otherwise, baby."

Mom walks over to the counter, picking up the tea mugs, "where's the tray, Lailani? I don't like you carrying this porcelain up the stairs by yourself. The tray will keep your other hand free, so you can hold on. That's why we got it."

I try not to roll my eyes as I pick up the snacks, starting toward the stairs, with Mom following me, "I am fine, Mom. I do everything by myself at home. I promise. Y'all are starting to make me feel like an invalid every time I'm here. It's a wonder I come home at all."

We get up the stairs, and around to the TV room, where Lonayla is still focused on the movie.

"Whether you accept it or not, look like it or not, or act like it, Lailani… We just want you to be safe." Lonayla looks over at me, with wide eyes and a shrug. Mom sets down the mugs, then looks at her, "you're supposed to be making sure she's careful, too. Why is she bringing *you* tea?"

"She asked! She's capable, Ma. She prefers doing things herself." I hand Lo the pretzels. "I can't force her to act disabled. She asks for help when she needs it, I swear! Don't worry, she's still very much a weak and dying girl on paper. She just refuses to let it control her. You should love that for her! I do."

"Please, let's keep talking about my disease, because y'all know how I love that," I roll my eyes, plopping down on the couch, pulling the blanket over my legs, then I squeeze a lemon from the tray into my tea, "y'all actually gotta stop talking about me like I'm dying or something."

Dad comes in, and stands behind the couch, grabbing the gummy worms from the pillow next to me, "every time we talk about this, you pretend it ain't real. It's very real, and it feels like you're the only one who don't accept it."

"Guys, I know I'm sick, and this illness isn't going anywhere. But my faith and my mindset have more power than whatever these doctors choose to believe. I prove that daily," I take a sip of my tea, "please, I hate this topic. I promise, the day my body decides it's more powerful than my God and my mind, I'll let y'all be as dramatic as you wanna be about it. Until then, I'm fine with navigating through life just as I have been. This works very well for me."

"La, I love that you keep going like it's nothing. Faking-it-till-you-make-it or whatever," Lonayla says, picking up my ginger ale off the table, with a frown, "I hate that you drink these room temperature, though. Are there any in the fridge?"

"I told you to put them in the fridge in the first place. Your bad," my voice breaks, and I wince at the sudden tightness in my throat.

I collect myself, taking a slow breath, then go back to sipping on my tea. I can feel everyone staring at me, but I ignore it.

Lo scoots closer, raising the honey, and I let her add some to my mug.

"I'm fine, Lonayla. It was literally just a spasm, you know this. See? It's already gone."

"I just want to help." Lo's mouth tugs into a half smile, but her eyes are filled with concern.

"Ugh, fix your face! I said I'm fine. Let's get over this already. Move on!"

Dad sets the candy back on the pillow beside me, puffing a breath through his nose, "Laila, that's *your* daughter, always pushing the uncomfortable things to the back."

"She definitely didn't get that from me. That comes from *you* spoiling her."

"What's that say about Lonayla? She makes everything bigger than what it should be, and she's the real spoiled one," I mumble into my tea.

Lo yanks away my blanket, "hey, nuh unh!"

"Let's not start this, you were both given the same of everything," Dad insists, walking over to stand by Mom. "Lailani, we get it. We don't like it, but we get it. You feel good when you convince yourself you feel good. We'll try to leave you alone about it."

He pauses for a beat, and I take another sip of my tea, savoring the way the hot liquid coats my dry, cracked throat. My body needs all the good sensations today, so this is perfect.

"Anyway, I came up here to tell you two, I'll buy your new phones."

Lo and I look at each other with mischievous smiles. Mom clears her throat, and Dad adds, "but you have to take your mom's car to get it washed and serviced, while you're out."

"Okay!" Lo and I both respond.

"Spoiled in your thirties. It's just sad. My keys are by the stairs," Mom laughs, then winks as she leaves the room.

"Lo, switch the card you took earlier, for the one by your mother's keys. La, make sure you go get those braces for your legs, please. The representative at that mobility store said they should help you in the cold. I told you the research has been promising, so I'm happy you're here to finally see for yourself."

"Fine," I say, swallowing the rest of my tea.


I really don't want to wear some big ugly braces. Especially for The Reliving. I can already imagine the unwanted attention. I've been diagnosed for a little over a year now, and while it's been incredibly challenging, my main focus has been maintaining my peace through this disease. Pretending to be healthy isn't a perfect solution, but it keeps me feeling like I have a little bit of control, again. I've gotten pretty good at being out without any sort of visible mobility aid, so I haven't had to endure the stares and strange comments about how I'm too young to need a walker or a cane.

The unsolicited advice and never-ending questions bother me the most. People always ask questions directly related to situations with simple fixes, but that's not my path. So many people ask what surgery I'm recovering from, giving me suggestions on healing faster, without even letting me respond to the question. Others suggest I let go of the assistance, and put weight on whatever they assume was broken, so I *"get used to it."* Some even decide that I have mobility aids because I want to park in the disabled persons spaces, even though I rarely ever do. Apparently, looking good, smiling, and minding my business, is too *"normal,"* and I can't possibly have any medical conditions. The few times I did decide to share that I was simply cursed with a rare and incurable illness that affects my ability to control my body, I only got more questions, and a whole lot of *"God cures everything, when you pray about it"* comments. It was all too much, so I decided to stop letting people see my struggle.

"Lailani, if you come back here with a phone and no braces, you will owe me for the phone," Dad's tone is serious. "I know you got it, but I also know you don't want to pay that kind of money, when you don't have to. Just do the things to keep me and your mother from having to worry about your safety. At least while you're here."

"Okay, I'll go to that store," I get up, walking over to hug him, "I'll do my best to be my best. As always."

"Me, too!" Lo turns off the movie and stands, stretching, "La, make sure you do your stretches! It'll keep your muscles warm," she smirks very childishly, "see, Daddy? I'm doing my best to keep La at her best."

"You two are a trip," he laughs, turning to leave, "but La, listen to your sister. It's chilly out, so warm those muscles."

I pout, bending toward my toes.

When Dad leaves, I shake my head at my sister, "Lonayla, you are such a suck up."

She laughs, starting past me, "we get free phones, though. And I can even bet your pink Kelly, that if you wanted to buy a new coat on him today, Daddy won't care. He'll think about his *sick little girl*, and how it'll keep you healthy!" She smiles, walking backwards out of the room and I follow, toward our bedrooms at the end of the hall.

"See? Use your illness, Lailani. Use it for the betterment of our lives!"

"Yeah, you can use it, sister. I'm just fine."

Lonayla rolls her eyes, "you're ridiculous. You basically survived death a second time, and as crazy as that is, here you are. You don't believe in forever, but your lifeline seems to be eternal. You don't even realize how good you've got it. In all of this, you still haven't learned to stop being so… *you*." She scrunches her nose, then turns into her room.

I turn into my own room, thinking about what she just said. I didn't even tell her I died. I only said I woke up in the pool. I guess one could only deduce that I died in that situation, but it's still strange that she said it so casually. The weird energy I'm getting from her, is throwing me off. I have no idea what she meant by me being *me*, but I also feel like I'm supposed to figure that out. Maybe I need to make some lifestyle changes. I had to be given this chance for a reason, so I need to make it count.

I walk over to my mirror, and frown at the person staring back at me. It's probably just me being extra, but I look a complete mess. I start to kick off my slippers, but my right leg decides to stiffen halfway through the movement, making my body stagger. I grab on to the bookshelf beside my mirror, catching myself.

"Don't start this shit, Lailani. You are strong. You are steady. You are fine." I affirm myself.

I focus my attention back on my reflection. Thankfully my lips seem to be brightening up a little. I still don't like this paleness, but I think I look a little less gray than I did earlier. Maybe. Hopefully the hollowness around my eyes goes away soon, too. I need to look like myself when I figure out what the hell happened to me.

On Monday morning, The Reliving begins, so I'll be around all the people who were at the kick-off party last night. Someone there, tried to end my life. I mind my business and quite literally live in a completely different state, away from everyone, so I can't imagine who has it out for me, honestly. When I piece together who it was, though? I'm going to make them wish they had succeeded.

I decide to stretch for real now, preparing to go out in the cold. I really need a phone, because I need to talk to Reelin about last night. I have to know what happened with us, because from what I can recall, things were going okay. Our initials are in that damn tree for Pete's sake! He begged me to do that since we met, and I finally gave in, by not stopping him. I think that means we were good, no?

But somehow, I woke up completely messed up, and alone, which makes no sense. The flashes that have come to my mind don't explain anything, and I have this weird feeling that I'm just not remembering because my mind refuses to. There was something that hurt me so bad, my brain seems to have locked it away. As much as I don't want to believe it has something to do with Reelin, my gut says it does.

*Reelin.*

*Lonayla.*

*Kieran's frown.*

*The Initial tree.*

*Reelin's blank stare.*

*My Disbelief.*

*Someone's laugh.*

*The woods to Nowhere.*

*My reflection.*

*Splashes.*

*Reelin leaves.*

*Pain.*

*Darkness.*

That rush of flash memories stops me in my tracks, "slow-motion? Really?" My heartbeat gallops into my chest, and I lean on the wall, trying to steady myself, "he really left me?"

I shake my head, feeling even more uncomfortable than before. I suck in a sharp breath, wincing at the pain, then slowly start to move down the hall again. When I reach the stairs, I have to pause, nervously grasping the banister. Heightened emotions are a trigger for my stiffness, and I don't want to tumble to my death. I've already survived twice, but I shouldn't press my luck.

Giving myself an internal pep talk, I decide to brush off my panic until I can ask Reelin about this. I don't think these images are popping up in order, so I'm just going to believe that there's an explanation, and it's not what it seems. It can't be, or everything is about to get very dramatic, and I'm not letting anyone get away with anything.

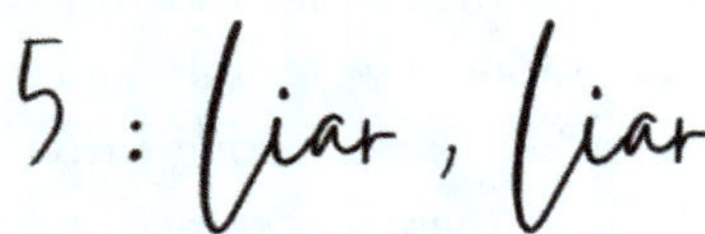

We're not even all the way out of the Apple store, and my sister has already cussed Kieran out twice, since we activated our devices.

"Lo, we've not even had these phones on a whole five minutes, and you're already on that man's head. This is why you have so many issues already. You have to find some chill."

"Because he's being sneaky, and I don't have time for the bullshit!" She's already FaceTiming him again. He answers as FaceTime audio, "oh, hell no! I swear you ain't neva gon be shit! Why you ain't answering on video, Kieran? Who you with, that got you playing games with me? We was supposed to be past all this shit! I come home for an extended amount of time, and this is when you decide to be dumb?"

When Lo's grammar goes, so does her filter, and she doesn't care where we are, or who can hear. Thankfully, it's too early for there to be many people in this mall. I'm already too nauseous to listen to these two bicker about nothing, so I'm ready to go.

"Gimme Daddy's card, so I can go get those braces." Lo pulls her wallet out of the bag for our phones, and passes the card to me. "I'll meet you outside in 10. Pull the car up to the food court for me?" She nods, then walks off, screaming into her phone about one of Kieran's baby mama's.

I walk into the mobility store, and a gorgeous, dark skinned South Asian woman greets me, with a bright smile, "hello, Dear. You have the exact same eyes as the sweet old man, Mister Grander, who comes here every Wednesday morning. He called about an hour ago, and said you'd be stopping by."

I smile back at her, but I'm also taken aback. Did she say every Wednesday? My dad coming into this store weekly was not something I was expecting to hear. I only knew he had been here once, because he teaches free guitar lessons in the music store, on Wednesday mornings. He called on his way home about two months ago, saying he found some cool braces for me to try. He was walking through the mall after his lessons, and stopped because there was some sort of demonstration. He was very excited to tell me about it, then when he heard I may come home for a few weeks, he said he wanted to bring me by to try them.

"Every Wednesday? As in weekly?" I ask, as she reaches behind her, to a box on the shelf.

"Oh, yes! And your mother has come a few times as well. She tried on a few sizes," she pulls out a pair of thick black braces that look to be made of some sort of compression material, but with boning that has a sort of technology, allowing the sides to bend in a smooth robotic motion, "she said you two are the same size, and these were the most comfortable. Your parents were not sure you'd come, and they really wanted you to have these. When they came this week, your mother said you were asleep, so your father planned to schedule shipping for after the holiday, just in case you couldn't make it during your visit. They say your syndrome is incurable? Are you okay, Dear?" She asks in a nice, noninvasive way, but I really don't like being asked about my illness.

"Oh, I'm fine. Thank you," I smile awkwardly, shifting my weight, "so my dad said there's a video I'm supposed to watch, something I sign, and that these are actually still in trials?"

"They have actually been in trials for three and a half years, and are starting to market for patients with weakness in their limbs. We currently have a few ambulatory wheelchair users, who have had much success and comfort with these helping them to feel more confident on their legs and feet," she turns the braces over in her hands, offering me one, "feel how light they are."

I shake my head in apprehension. She smiles, placing the braces back into the box, "there's a link on the brochure inside. You can also take them to your doctor if you want, and give them the link for their own questions. Your father paid over the phone when he called earlier, so take these, Dear! No signature necessary. That is for the physical therapy sessions you can request with the link, as well. If you want. I hope they help. You can always come back here with any questions as well!"

"Awesome, thank you. I will!" I reach for the box, and she stops me.

"Wait, let me give you a bag to carry it easier, Dear. The receipt is in the brochure. I stapled it inside," she puts the box in a paper bag with handles, walking it around to me.

"Thank you, so much," I look at her name tag, "Ms. Veda. And thank you for being so kind and professional with my parents as well," I add, as she walks me out.

"You are very welcome, Dear. Stay safe. And please don't hesitate to ask questions," she smiles, leaning against the store entrance, presumably to watch me walk off.

I turn to walk away, but my legs and back suddenly feel like they're not part of the same body. I take a few uneasy steps, but I'm having a hard time. There's something strange about knowing someone's watching me walk, that triggers something in my brain, causing my legs to be both weaker and stiffer. I hate when this happens.

"Damn it," I whisper to myself.

I take a deep breath to focus, and even that's harder than it should be. My legs are fighting me, and I know I look like a wobbly tin man. I usually keep a collapsable cane in my purse, but that's gone. I keep spare canes in my parents' garage, but with them decluttering, that's where everything that didn't have a home, is currently piled up.

I stop trying to force it. Feeling defeated, I turn around to go back to the mobility store.

"My treat," Ms. Veda is already walking up to me, with a beautiful sage green collapsable cane, already extended to its tallest height. She winks, also passing me the package it was in, "and it matches your eyes."

"I was just coming back for one. Thank you, so very much!" I could cry. I won't, but I could.

I slip the packaging into the other bag.

"Of course, Dear. Take your time," she reaches for my forearm, but stops before touching me, "I want you to be safe."

I roll my lips inward, literally wanting to explode in gratitude. The warmth in Ms. Veda's smile threatens to open the floodgates to my tears, despite my best efforts. I give her my best nod-and-smile combo, before turning from her kindness to keep myself from sobbing. Now, with the cane's assistance, I can make my way to the food court and head outside.

I get to the doors, and look out into the cold ugliness of December. I asked Lonayla to pull the car up in 10, and it's been about that long now. I wait another minute or so, but when I don't see my mom's navy blue C300 4matic coupe, I text my sister.

**Me: where you at? I'm at the doors by the food court.**

**Sissy: stay inside. gimme a second. Kieran's here. We're in the back of the lot.**

**Sissy: he said mom's car can get serviced over here. I'ma call daddy to see if that's cool.**

**Sissy: you hungry? we can eat here. Kieran said his treat.**

**Me: find out about the car first**

**Sissy: kk but stay out the cold. I don't want something weird happening and mommy blaming me for letting you be outside. Find a seat, I'll come find you.**

**Me: cool**

I go into the ladies' room off to the side, because I feel like I'm going to vomit. A weird fuzzy feeling keeps coming over me too, but I chalk it up to me being so anxious today. I still have so many things to sort through, and the random images from the party that appear when I close my eyes, don't help at all.

When I get back into the food court, I sit at one of the tables closest to the doors, so my sister can find me easily. I look around aimlessly for almost ten minutes, before I decide to text Reelin.

### Me: So… 👀

My phone rings almost immediately. I stare at it a moment before answering, but I don't say anything.

"Lailani?" His voice raises the hair on my arms, even through all my clothes.

"Why?" I croak around the lump in my throat.

"Lailani? Where are you?" His voice sounds insistent.

"You left me, Reelin."

He clears his throat, before speaking, "La, a lot happened last night. All I know is, I woke up at Aunt Kira's house, instead of with you."

"Hm. Aunt Kira's, huh?" I shake my head, annoyed. "That's interesting, especially since I know you reserved the dorm for The Reliving."

"I reserved that for you. I was never planning on staying there without you. I told you that. Where are you right now?"

I see he's trying to FaceTime me, but I decline. The audacity of this man.

"Does it matter?"

"Yes. Answer your FaceTime."

"No. You left me for dead. FaceTime privileges are eternally revoked."

"Lailani, you left that party without saying a single word to me. You, Lo and K was just gone, and I ain't know shit!" His tone is a little on edge, and too aggressive for my liking.

"That's the story you're going with, Reelin? Nah, you ain't finna lie like I just went home or some shit. I woke up in the pool. THE POOL. ME!" I look around, making sure my aggression isn't bothering anyone nearby. I switch my phone to my other ear, and hunch over the table, lowering my voice, "I was with you one second, while you pretended to care about me. Then the next, I woke up floating in a fucking pool that had long since stopped heating in the middle of December. I had no shoes, no coat, no phone, no purse with my wallet and house keys, nothing, Reelin! Nothing!"

A low frustrated growl comes through the phone, "Lailani, you left that party before me. What the fuck do you mean you woke up in the pool?"

I look up, seeing my sister and Kieran walking through the doors from outside, "delete my number, Reelin," I hang up just before Lonayla and Kieran get close to me.

"The car's getting serviced, they wash and detail here, too. Who was that? Your man?" Lo asks me.

"Only one with a man here, is you," I say with a sigh, declining Reelin's call.

"Don't do my boy like that, La. Y'all were the it couple of our lives last night, all reunited and shit. Where that fool at, anyway?" Kieran wraps his arms around my sister's waist from behind. Lo rolls her eyes but leans into him.

"That's none of my concern," I snark, declining Reelin again, putting my phone in my jacket pocket, "Lo said you're feeding us. I want Din Tai. Let's go."

I get up, grabbing the cane from the table's edge. I collapse it, then put it into the bag with the braces. Without caring about the look on Kieran's face, I turn and start walking through the food court, back into the mall.

"You good, La?" I can hear the questions Lonayla isn't asking. What she means is, *Why do you have a cane? Why are you pissed? What did he do? Do we need to call Daddy?"*

"I'm fine, Lo. Just hungry."

I am not in the mood to talk about Reelin, or my body betraying me today.

"What's with the cane, La? We're literally twins, and I ain't nearly old enough for that shit," Kieran jokes.

"Seriously?" My sister pushes away from him, walking closer to me, reaching for the bag, "let me, La."

"Wait, what I do?" Kieran questions.

I let the bag go, still walking with purpose on angry but surprisingly steady legs.

The hostess at Din Tai greets me, "how many?"

"Three," I immediately feel sorry for my tone, and give her an apologetic smile. She smiles back grabbing menus, and telling us to follow her.

"Give me a second, I'll be right there," Kieran turns away, placing his phone to his ear.

My sister holds my hand as we walk to our table. We thank the hostess, and I sit.

"What just happened?" Lo pushes the mobility store bag under my chair, and walks to the other side of the table, sitting diagonal from me, with her face twisted in what looks like concern.

"Did Kieran tell you where he slept last night?" I ask, just as our waitress comes to greet us.

I smile, "I'll take two lychee martinis, please," I pull my wallet out of my dad's Baltimore Ravens racing jacket, that I wore in place of my missing coat, to give her my ID.

"I'll have the same. And we'll start with the cucumbers and green beans. Thanks." Lonayla pulls her ID out of her orange Prada Saffiano leather wallet. The waitress checks the IDs, then walks away with a kind smile.

"You know, I need a new wallet. Since you're definitely about to get some fire ass bag from some man or another, to replace the one that went missing, get me one," she shoves her wallet back into her jacket pocket.

I roll my eyes, "get back on topic. Kieran? Sleep? Where?"

"Kieran was at his mamas last night, Jammy was up when I called. You know she lives there now. So, about this wallet?"

"No," I pull my vibrating phone out of my jacket pocket, swipe away Reelin's call, and place my phone face down on the table.

Lonayla huffs, "so, what's happening with Rizz? Should I worry for his safety?"

I cross my hands on the back of my neck, releasing a breath, "he's a liar."

"Aren't they all?" She lets out a humorless laugh, "but that one is a good man, Lailani. This is Rizz we're talking about. It can't be all that bad."

"It is, but I'll handle it."

We sit silently for a few minutes. Lo takes off her coat, keeping her attention near the hostess stand, where Kieran is still on his phone. I keep on my jacket, finding comfort in the warmth, then decide to take a few deep breaths. It really feels like my chest is way too tight, but I guess that happens when you die and come back to life.

"It's been at least ten minutes. Who do you think he's talking to?" Lonayla looks so worried, massaging her temples.

"Probably one of the kids. Relax. I doubt it's something to worry about, girl. Y'all get so crazy, and it's always for no reason."

"You don't get it, because you never had to worry about the kind of shit Kieran has done to me."

"You choose to be with him though. If you can't get past it, then stop stressing and let him go," I keep my hands on my neck, massaging, to relieve some of the tension.

"It's so easy for you to just pretend people don't matter. That ain't how I operate, Lailani. It's not as simple as just ghosting him, like he doesn't mean the world to me. I actually have real feelings I can't just shut off." She looks so defeated.

"Then meet him in the middle, Lo. He's been doing so much to prove himself to you."

"You're one to talk."

The waitress returns with our drinks and starters, as Kieran sits next to me, across from Lo, "one of those mine? That's that liki-liki thing?" He asks, reaching for one of my drinks.

"Lychee, and absolutely not," I take both drinks and immediately down them, not caring about how it looks.

"Damn, La!" He looks at me in surprise, then to my sister, "she aight?"

Lonayla shifts in her seat, "she's fine. What were you doing out there? One of your lil' hoes call or something?" Her squinted eyes and accusatory tone, give away just how much the idea of him doing wrong gets under her skin. I hate that for her.

Really, I hate that for me, because I probably look exactly the same, right now. Reelin-the-liar is currently all the way under my skin. How can he just act like he didn't leave me for dead? I close my eyes, taking another deep breath.

*Reelin. Lonayla. The Initial tree. Kieran. Reelin*—I push the memories away.

When I look up, Lonayla is watching me with the same odd expression from earlier. I roll my neck, and give my shoulders a little shake to push away the thoughts swirling in my head.

"Lailani?" Kieran leans into me, "you cool? What's going on?"

"I'm fine. Niggas ain't shit, but I've always known that. Only man I can trust is my daddy," I shrug, and my sister nods in agreement. I reach for one of her drinks, downing it, too, "don't act like you care, Kieran."

The waitress nears us, and before she can ask, I hold up a martini glass, "can I get two more, please? And a green tea? Thank you."

"And I'll take an old fashioned. And another one of those for her," he motions to Lo's glass. She's aggressively chewing on the perfectly crunchy cucumbers, doing a little dance of happiness in her seat.

Kieran glances at his phone, "actually, make it two old fashioneds. Thanks."

"Actually, I think we're ready to order. Um, we'll take another order of both of these," I point to the green beans and cucumbers, "and the broccoli, the bok choy, sweet and sour ribs, two orders of the chicken bao, chicken dumplings, shrimp dumplings, two of the black pepper beef, and a shrimp fried rice. Anything else, Lo?" My sister shakes her head, and I smile up at the waitress again, "that'll do it, then! Thank you."

The waitress smiles, takes the empty glasses, to leave.

Kieran, who was texting someone while I ordered, turns to me, "La, I'll always care about you, you know that. I don't know what my cousin did, but I know he ain't mean whatever it was," he checks his phone again, "and ay, I know y'all are princesses and all, but everyone ain't rich like your people. You ordered the whole damn menu," he shakes his head, looking at Lonayla, "is this my punishment?"

Lo scrunches up her nose, "you said it's your treat. Don't offer if you suddenly can't afford to feed us the things we eat. This ain't your first rodeo, so whoever is keeping you occupied on that phone, must have your mind gone," she shrugs, shoving the last of the green beans into her mouth.

Kieran just chuckles, "y'all are funny," he checks his phone again, "it's cool, order what you want, baby."

"Don't *baby* me! Who the hell is on your phone?" Lonayla's annoyance is all over her face. Her hair is in two tight buns on top of her head, making her look exactly like she did when she was little, and always had to give a good neck roll. She was the sassiest little chocolate drop. I smile inwardly at the thought.

"Lonayla, it's nothing like that," Kieran looks down at his phone again, responding to a text.

She reaches her hand across the table, "let me see your phone."

Kieran looks at her with a smile, then shrugs, "okay, let me handle this, first."

"If you clear your history, I swear—"

"Chill, baby. It's nothing like that. You gon see!" Kieran insists, locking his phone screen, "I have nothing to hide from you, Lonayla."

"I don't believe you," Lo twists up her face, sitting back in her chair.

They're now staring at each other, having some silent conversation. In an attempt to not feel awkward, I check my phone.

**New Message from Reelin Houldover Jr.: what the fuck Lailani?**

**Reelin: Where you at?**

**Reelin: Pick up**

**Reelin: LAILANI???**

**Reelin: I love you**

I lock my screen, turning my phone over on the table, then close my eyes to take a few calming breaths, but I don't allow my mind to drift away from the sounds around me. I don't have time for that right now.

"Seriously, La he's playing in my face right in front of you! I alre—" my sister's griping stops short.

I decide to stay in my quiet breathing to let them figure out whatever their issue is without me.

"He ain't playing in your face, Lo. He was texting me."

My heartbeat skips. That voice—the one that feels like the perfect note in my life's favorite song—was not what I expected to hear right now. I keep my eyes closed as the chair in front of me scrapes against the floor, and his familiar scent wafts over to me, suffocating my senses.

"See, woman? I was just tryna help a man in love," Kieran insists to my sister.

"You clearly forgot about her temper, I see. You might never wanna do that again," Lo warns in a low voice. I think to both of them.

The waitress has returned with our drinks, but I don't want to open my eyes. As childish as it may seem, I don't want to see this man. I inhale and hold it, hearing two glasses slide in front of me. I exhale slowly, hoping the pain leaves with it. I feel the waitress close behind my left shoulder, placing the hot tea pot and a mug in front of me.

"Lailani, open your eyes, please."

I'm a cluster of conflicting emotions. I wasn't ready to face him in the flesh. I needed to figure out my feelings without his closeness pulling me in, making me forget myself.

"Lailani, please."

His voice is warm and soothing. Like a fireplace burning in a cozy room. He says my name in a way that feels like a plea I can't ignore. I open my eyes, and it's like for that first moment, the entire world is him.

To make it worse, he smiles, "there she is."

I could die.

"La, you good? You want us to give you two a moment?" I look at my sister with all the purpose I can. She pulls back like I struck her.

"No? Okay! Don't turn your wrath on me, sister! Have another drink!"

"Shawty's already three in! I'm shocked she ordered two more!" Kieran is clearly just making sure Reelin knows how much I've had to drink.

I reach for my next martini, and look at Reelin again. His dark eyes are focused on mine, and the hairs on the nape of my neck rise.

His head tilts in question, "you've already had three of those? They virgin?"

Lo lets out a half-snort half-chuckle. I roll my eyes gulping down both drinks, then turn my attention back to the liar across from me. His fervent gaze makes my ears heat, and I shift in my seat. Even after all this time, and his disappearing act, he still affects me physically. I look down at my hands, suddenly very interested in the freckle on my finger.

"Lailani, are you gonna tell me what's wrong with you?"

I cock my head, squinting in confused annoyance. He knows damn well what the issue is. I hate when people play dumb.

He raises his brows, "talk to me."

This fake obliviousness only raises my irritation, "why are you here, Reelin?"

Without a thought, he responds, "you're here. Where else would I be?"

"I don't know, wherever you were when I woke up alone in the pool, I guess."

"Oh shit," something about the sound of Kieran's concern catches my attention. I look at him, then at Lonayla, who shifts awkwardly.

The waitress returns with someone else to help her lay out our food. I watch them set everything out as a welcome distraction from the topic at hand, but I can feel Reelin staring at me. I wish I could run away, honestly. I have no idea where we go from here, if he's only going to lie to me. Doubt swirls through my mind like a cyclone, tearing through all the goodness he's ever filled my life with. I pull on a shaky breath to calm my nerves, unsure if this pain is real, or if it's just the echo of his goodness leaving my head.

When the waiters leave, my sister clears her throat, then starts excitedly swiping her chopsticks together.

"Your woman ordered all this food, by the way. So, it's only right we split the check," Kieran says, reaching for a rib, "they got forks in here?" He goes to find the waiter.

"I really don't know why I deal with that fool," my sister says, more to herself than anyone else.

Reelin responds anyway, "you love him. Just like your sister loves me. Y'all just don't like feeling it, for whatever reason. I don't get it, honestly. The feeling of looking into someone's eyes, and your soul recognizing itself, is priceless. Can't deny that kinda love."

I meet his gaze, masking my emotions, but the look on his face does something to me. My heart suddenly grows unbearably heavy, plummeting straight through me, crashing into the floor.

"Oh, I know I love him, but I don't always like him," Lo takes a bite of her rice, "and La still ain't into all the true love stuff, Rizz. That hasn't changed, but more power to you for trying! I hope it works out, bro."

Kieran sits back down, "they're on the Initial tree, baby. Only couples in love go on the tree. Look at them. They can't even look away from each other.

"No, he won't stop staring at me, and it's weird." I gesture to Lo's second martini. She hands it over, with a shrug.

"I love what I see, I can't help it. So, are we getting drunk today?" Reelin takes a sip of the second old fashioned Kieran ordered—which was clearly for him, and winks at me.

I gulp down the drink, then reach for a dumpling, ignoring him, "Lo, how long till the car's done? I think I do want to get a coat when we're done eating."

"They said an hour or so. I gave them your number."

I check my phone.

"A coat?"

I ignore Reelin's question.

"She lost hers last night. The rest of our jackets are somewhere in the garage, but we can't get to them," Lo shrugs, "you get your car serviced here? My dad said if we come home, and they fucked mom's car up, Kieran's a dead man."

"Yeah, I always get mine done here. Rallo's cool peoples."

He directs his attention back to me, "I love your hair in your lil' braids. The white hair last night was cool too, but the natural you is forever my favorite."

I turn to Kieran, "pass the rice, please."

He scoops rice onto my plate, then onto his own, "I like both y'all's hair in the lil' piggy-tail things."

"Of course you do," Lo retorts.

I feel my face heat under Reelin's focus, "I missed you. I feel like I can finally breathe again."

I puff out a breath, then look at all the food, "Lo, pass the broccoli, please."

Reelin takes it from her, scooping some onto my plate, "your pops stays fly with the Ravens gear," I pretend not to hear him, "that jacket you got on is still one of the coldest ones I've ever seen."

"Daddy will be eternally fly," Lonayla answers, while I take a few bao onto my plate, "it helps that his team has the best colorway, too."

The waitress comes to check on us.

"I'll have two more, please," I gesture to my empty glasses.

"No, she won't," Reelin says, a little too forcefully.

There may be literal daggers in my eyes when I look at him. He looks at me in challenge.

"Yes. I will," I emphasize.

"Yes, she will, please," my sister says, trying to keep Reelin and me from going back and forth, I'm sure, "and we'll also take an order of chocolate buns."

The waitress takes the empty dishes, and leaves.

Lo shakes her head, "Rizz, I suggest you slow down, man. She hasn't been in the best mood today."

Reelin lets out a small laugh, "I can handle her moods, but thanks, Lo." Then says to Kieran, "do me a favor, switch seats with me."

When they switch seats, Reelin moves the chair to my left much closer, and Kieran does the same by Lo.

"Uh, no! Move yo ass over!" She exclaims, swallowing the rest of her martini, "why didn't you sit over here in the first place?"

"I don't know, I like sitting across from you, so I can see you clearly," Kieran smiles, and she smirks, shifting closer to him.

I push the food around on my plate, ignoring the fact that Reelin's into me.

"You're beautiful. Even when you're mad." His voice coats my brain like honey.

"Stop it. And please move over, you're in my personal space," he moves closer, putting his arm around my shoulders. I frown, "wow, you are on one, today."

He leans in, his breath tickling my ear, "stop acting like this. After too much time apart, you're finally here with me. Don't be pushing me away. What's your favorite thing to say? 'Nothing lasts forever,' right? You can't be upset with me forever, Lailani."

My frown deepens, "you're right, Reelin. I can't stay mad forever. But in this moment, I am. The more you try to force me not to be, the more it's gonna irritate me."

"Okay," he moves his arm from around me, but doesn't move over, "I accept that you're upset, but at least tell me what I did."

Lonayla, grunts and sits up higher, swallowing her food, "I've been waiting for this all morning!"

"La, you have been a little weird, so what's up?" Kieran actually looks concerned.

I look from Kieran to my sister, then focus my attention back on Reelin. He looks at me so intently, it gives me pause. He truly has the kindest cocoa eyes I ever did see, and I'm often caught off guard by them. The allure in his gaze holds me steady, grounding me as if he were the roots to my tree. But then he left me, like he was only an autumn leaf, and winter has come early. How did we get here?

I look away, feeling slightly disoriented. I need to focus on anything else, "I'm fine," I say to Kieran.

We sit in awkward silence for a while, and I move the food around on my plate again. Reelin's presence is so inescapable, I'm acutely aware of each breath he takes, while my sister and Kieran have a hushed conversation across the table. Reelin never touches the food. He only continues staring at me.

"Quiet game's over, Lailani. I need you to tell me the problem, so I can fix it," he angles his body a bit more, so his knee is pressing into mine. I move mine away, and he blows out an annoyed breath, straightening back up.

I know I'm being difficult, but what am I supposed to do right now? I woke up how I did, where I did, and now I remember him leaving me there. I focus my thoughts, and close my eyes, hoping my mind fixes that memory. It would be so much less complicated if that one was a mistake.

*Reelin. The Initial tree. Lonayla. Glow sticks. Kieran. The food on the grill. Reelin's smile. The woods to Nowhere. A toast. Lonayla gives me another drink. Reelin's eyes. A strange look on Kieran's face. Disbelief. Laughter. Reelin walks away. Darkness.*

I look down at my food again, my stomach souring. He really did leave me.

Kieran shifts, clearing his throat, "La, we gonna talk about what that cane was?"

"What cane?" Reelin asks Kieran, who just got popped in the arm by my sister. "Lo? What cane?" He asks her, before turning to me. I can feel the question heating my face.

No one speaks, so Reelin looks around me, spotting the bag under my chair. I reach my hand under, moving it closer to the wall, then return to picking at my plate.

The waitress returns with my drinks, and the chocolate buns. Kieran says something else to Lonayla, and I just know it was something freaky, because she looks so embarrassed.

"La?" Lo raises her brows at me. My face must give away my anxiety, but I shake my head.

"What are you keeping from me? I need to know why I'm getting the cold shoulder," Reelin persists.

I look at him, and the sincerity in his face actually irritates me. "You left me, Reelin. You left me for dead. Literally. What am I supposed to feel?" My head shakes in disgust, "and in the pool, of all places. You left me for dead in the pool, and you're acting like nothing happened," I gulp back the first of the two new martinis, and Reelin takes the second, holding it away from me.

"Lailani, what the fuck are you talking about?" His voice is once again too aggressive for my liking. "*You're* the one who left *me* at the party."

Kieran cuts in, "I thought you left together?"

"He says I left with you, actually. Anyone wanna explain?" I look at all of their confused faces.

"You did. K, when I got to your mom's, Jammy said you had just dropped them off at their crib," Reelin has the strangest look on his face.

"Um, No. Kieran didn't take me home," Lonayla sits up, looking at Kieran with an accusation I know is going to come up later. She turns back to Reelin, "he only walked me out front to the parking lot, but he went back into the party. I saw him walk back inside. I went with Jessy and Kass to get weed from Kass's cousin. Jessy took me home," she frowns, "I picked up the crackhead version of Lailani this morning."

I squint my eyes at Reelin, who's focused on Kieran. Then I look back at Kieran. They have some sort of silent conversation that I can't pick up on.

"I saw Lailani leave the party, right behind you," Reelin's sticking to his lie.

Kieran clears his throat, "oh, yeah. I had to use the bathroom, and when I went back to the pool, La was gone, too. I thought she left with you, babe," he swiftly kisses my sister's neck, then chugs the rest of his drink. His body language is off, though. He reaches for his hair, then stops himself. Lonayla catches that gesture, too.

"But you just said you thought Rizz left with her?" Lo presses.

"I was high. I just remembered, I left with Rizz," he chokes out, taking a sip of water.

Reelin shifts again, "nah, you left first, I saw you at the house. I came there, because I didn't feel safe driving home. Man, you gotta stop smoking." Something in his tone bothers me, but I shove it down.

He turns to me, eyes soft, "you must have had more to drink than you remember, Lailani. I don't know who you left with, or how you got back to the school, but you left me there, I swear. I saw you leave. You said you were going to the bathroom, and I went to see if they had the pineapple on the grill because you mentioned wanting some. When I turned back, I saw you walk out. You had on your coat, and everything. I even called you. You picked up, hung up, then sent me to voicemail for the rest of the night."

He's lying through his teeth, but something about him looking so convincing, makes me feel a little uneasy. I'm not in the right mental space for this conversation. My heartbeat is racing, and my mind can't process what I'm feeling.

"Okay," I shrug, holding out my hand.

Reelin raises his eyebrows, then looks at the martini still in his hand. He scoffs, "you've had enough. You're mad for reasons no one knows, you're blaming me for something that didn't happen, and the confusion is most likely from you drinking last night. We don't need these problems."

"Give me the drink, Reelin."

He seems to think about it for a second, then lets out a huffy sigh, passing me the glass. I drink it in two gulps as my phone vibrates on the table.

I check the message, "car's ready, Lo. Let's take this home," I gesture to the food, then look at Reelin, "I need to get up, I have to pee. Also, we promised our parents we'd chill with them today, and we have church tomorrow, so we gotta get going."

"I thought you wanted to get a new coat?" He reminds me.

"Nah, I'll just wear one of my mom's. Can you move, please? I need the bathroom," I shift uncomfortably, waiting for him to move.

Lo gets up, "me, too, I'll come with you."

Kieran sits back, clearing his throat.

"I told you, La can't drive!" She exclaims.

I freeze, looking at her in shock. Did she tell him my business?

She shifts her weight, answering my unasked question, "you saw how many martinis she had!"

I didn't realize I was holding my breath until I exhale. Reelin stands, reaching a hand to help me up, but I don't take it. As I stand, my sister reaches for me, then puts her hand down, when Reelin looks at her, confused by the gesture.

Kieran blows out a breath, "Rizz can take her home."

"Not leaving my mama's car! You're out your mind!" Lo scrunches up her face, then looks at me.

I step around Reelin, placing my hand on her shoulder, hoping she sees the silent plea in my eyes. I feel overstimulated, and she catches on quickly.

"You really took those martinis back, huh? Hold my hand," she takes my hand in hers.

"Thanks, I didn't think they were that strong. I feel a little weak in the knees."

"I would say it's probably Rizz got you that way, but I feel like you would jump across the table and whoop my ass. Good thing you got that cane!" Kieran smiles nervously, raising his hands, "I was kidding, I ain't even say it, I said I wanted to, but I didn't. It was a joke, La."

Lonayla sighs, "my goodness, that cane you're so concerned about, is something my daddy sent her here for. Learn to mind your business!" She crosses her elbow with mine, then smiles at Reelin, "we gotta pee out some of that liquor. Be right back."

When we get far enough away, Lo looks back, then whispers, "why does it feel like Daddy Rizz is about to give Kieran a whoopin'?"

I look back, and Reelin's still standing, with his back to us and shoulders squared. Kieran's looking up at him, apologetically. As silly as Kieran looks, I still can't help but to wonder why Reelin's acting like Kieran's the problem right now, when I know he left me. The look on his face before he did, was serious. Expressionless. Like the man that I know wasn't there. It makes my stomach hurt even now, remembering how I felt in that moment. I learned something, couldn't believe it, he left, and then nothing.

"I want to go home, Lo. I don't think coming here for The Reliving was a good idea after all. Let's get on a plane, and get back to life," I beg, "and thank you for not telling my business. I almost passed out thinking Kieran knew, when you said I couldn't drive. You promised I could tell him in my own time, but I get so nervous about you slipping up."

We get to the bathroom, and I rush into the stall. Relief washes over me, as I empty my bladder. I feel my mouth watering, like I might throw up, but I take a few slow, painful breaths to stop it.

Lo is in the stall beside me, "I know you don't want to talk about your illness. And as much as K has kept from me? I can have a secret. Even if it's not my own. Rizz deserves to know though. You really can't keep it secret forever."

"I know. I'm just not ready for more people to look at me like how Mom and Dad do. You do it too, Lonayla. That look when you saw the cane, today? That shit eats away at me. I really don't need Kieran's unserious ass being all sensitive and worried. He'll be all weird, and afraid to joke around. And can you imagine Reelin? Because I can. He will get ridiculous, and that's the last thing I need, especially now."

"I get it. But also, that man has loved you for so long, La. While I know you aren't in the same space as he is, I do know that even when you wouldn't talk to him, he cared. He wants nothing more in this world than to see you be happy. He'll do anything to keep you safe. I don't think you can go wrong with him."

"I know something isn't right, though. He can't even get his lie from last night straight."

I come out the stall, and wash my hands. Lonayla does the same seconds later.

"Girl, it sounds to me like his story's straight. Kieran's ass is the one who doesn't even know who the hell he went home with. He's so freaking lucky Jammy was up, when I called. Because if she wasn't, we'd have some serious issues right now."

I smile at my sister, "everyone keeps talking about Reelin and me, but you two are the ones who've literally been fighting like an old married couple, since you were beefing on the playground as kids. The most in-love-people-with-issues I ever did see."

"That *could* be you and Rizz, though! If you would just spend the time with him. You refuse to let him come to Miami, and you never let him know when you're home. You've been here four separate times since y'all started talking again. That's the most you've been home in years, mind you. Kieran and the kids basically live with us, so we spend a lot of quality time."

She frowns, still drying her hands, "La, I got baby mamas with grown kids, still secretly trying to push up on my man, just because they can. Rizz ain't got kids. A man in his 30s with no baby mama drama, is the dream! You have a man who's waiting for you, Lailani. You know how many of us wish we had us a him? With everything he got going on? The man is basically perfect."

"Just because he seems perfect to everyone else, doesn't mean I'm supposed to give him all of me," I take her outstretched hand, and we walk out of the bathroom.

Lo smacks her teeth, "I guess. Daddy be right when he gets on you about being weird with love. That control thing is too much. Love is way too beautiful for you to run away from it like you do."

As we get closer, I can see that the food is now boxed up, and there are two more martinis on the table. Reelin's moved into my seat, sitting sideways in the chair, with his back against the wall. Of course he's watching me. I'm pretty sure he has some sort of sensor that alerts him of my presence—like some kind of evil sorcerer, or something.

"I figured you two wanted one more for the road," he says, as we sit.

Lo pushes the glass to me, "I'm driving, but thanks."

I look at Reelin through squinted eyes, "you just watched my sister have to hold my hand to go to the restroom, after already telling me that I had too much to drink. You quite literally attempted to keep that last drink from me. Now I'm just supposed to think you ordering me another, is what? Cute?"

"I was wrong for tryna tell you what you should have or what to do. You're a grown woman, and if you say you're fine, I respect that. If I'm supposed to make sure you know I love you, that means I also trust you, right?" He leans forward, bringing his face closer to me, looking into my eyes.

I feel like this is a trick, but I turn, toss back both martinis, then smile, "cool."

I turn to Kieran, "thank you for lunch. Next time it's on me."

"Your man paid for it. He's big money today, Princess."

"Of course he did. The man ain't eat a bite, but of course he did," Lo mumbles.

"Well, Thank you, Reelin," I give him a quick glance, then turn to my sister, "ready?"

"Yep," Lo claps once as we get up, then smiles wide, "we'll see y'all, Monday! I can't believe we're really gonna be reliving our school days for two whole weeks. This should be fun!"

Reelin reaches under the chair for my bag and stands up, grabbing my hand to get my attention. When I look at him, the hope in his eyes weighs me down.

"Can I come see you tonight?"

It's so hard to say no when he looks like this. His serious face, with the sweetest eyes, beneath gently furrowed brows, split evenly by a permanent wrinkle, deepened by his hopeful expression. His nostrils are slightly flared above his soft lips that are naturally, just slightly pouted. I can't imagine wanting to look into another face every day, when every version of his exists.

"We can sit by the fire pit like we used to. You can even read to me, again." That smile, with his almost perfect teeth and those crater deep dimples, ruins me.

This is what I wasn't looking forward to, being around him again. It's been so easy to pretend he doesn't affect me, since we mostly communicate over the phone these days. Being here, this close to him, I feel like a teenage girl all over again. He has this ability to consume me, making it hard to focus on myself. I fall into him so effortlessly, because it feels like coming home—being wrapped in all that he is.

But he's a liar. He's lied more than once today, and he's done it so easily, it makes me want to question everything.

He's always been so open and honest, from what I know. He has a level of integrity people don't usually get to experience in another human being. I always loved that. Even when we were just kids, it was so important for him to remain solid in his own moral high ground. Trust was always one thing I never had to think twice about with Reelin. That was all I ever knew, until he left me at the pool.

I'm now standing here, feeling so conflicted. This honest man has lied so well, anyone else would've gone for it. He's maintained his story, and he seems to genuinely believe what he's saying. What am I supposed to think? How do I just ignore what *I* experienced, because *he* has convinced himself, that he experienced something different?

"Maybe. I told you, we're bonding with our parents. I'll let you know," I'm glad I managed to get my words out, with his thumb rubs circles over my hand.

I pull my hand away, taking my bag from him, then take a step back. My mind already feels clearer outside of his body heat. We stand, staring at each other, and it feels like we're suspended in time. I don't know how to feel about this man right now, but looking into those eyes that look like when fresh earth and sunlight combine, to create life, I'm at a loss for any feeling other than the comfort his presence brings.

I hear Kieran's muffled talking, while still maintaining eye contact with Reelin. And then Kieran's voice becomes clearer, "and y'all got here almost a week ago, but last night was the first time we seen you. When we talked about this, Lonayla said we was gonna make it be like the old days, but that ain't normal. I asked her to stay with me, but she wanna stay where you stay. That's why we need to stay at the dorm. The Reliving's our chance to get shit right."

I finally pull my eyes away from Reelin's, realizing Kieran's talking to *me*. Lo's not standing next to him anymore, though. I look around, confused.

"She said she left her phone in the bathroom. I figured y'all didn't notice her panicking. I almost forgot how y'all be so focused on each other, nothing else exists," he shakes his head.

"Oh," I pat my own pockets, and my eyes widen as I pat harder, not feeling my own phone. We haven't had these phones a whole two hours yet. "Oh, shit," I mumble.

Reelin holds my phone in front of my face, "you left it on the table." I take it from him, avoiding his eyes.

"I don't remember your phone being this new last night," his statement is more of a question.

"We just got them before we came in here to eat," I put my phone in my pocket, as Lo comes closer.

"Girl, I almost had a heart attack. I got it though!" She laughs, waving her phone.

"La, what you thinking?" Kieran asks.

Lonayla's eyes move from him, to me, then back, "thinking about what?"

"Letting us come over, like we used to. Chill by the fire pit. We'll bring treats, just like the old days. Y'all always loved Saturdays in your backyard. Even when it was cold, that was our thing. We're supposed to get back to that. Or the dorm. I like the dorm better, but the house is nostalgic for today."

"Oh," she looks at me, "what did you say?"

"I said we'd let them know. Let's go," I tilt my head toward the exit.

The four of us walk out of the restaurant, to the far end of the mall, where the car is. Reelin is silently walking beside me, while Kieran and Lonayla are already arguing about why we're being difficult about spending time with them. We get to the counter and the mechanic, Rallo, is super happy to see Reelin. He even gives us a discount for Mom's car. We walk outside, and Kieran storms off to his car that's parked only a few spaces away from the doors, while Lo climbs into the driver's seat.

Reelin opens the passenger door for me, and I get in, thankful my body didn't try to fight me in the cold. "Y'all be safe. Let me know when you get home, aight?" He leans in, pressing a kiss to my cheek.

I roll my lips inward, nodding, as he closes the door, then steps back. Lonayla waves to him before we pull off, and I look in the rearview, seeing him walk back into the mall. He must've parked by the restaurant.

"I hate Kieran so much, man," There goes my sister, being dramatic, "he's so spoiled! It's that only child thing. He needs everything his way! I'm gonna rid myself of that man, and find myself a husband, La. This shit is for the birds!"

"Girl, please. You'll probably have him at the house before we even get there. You two are the most ridiculous people, ever. Even the kids are over y'all acting crazy. Everyone wants y'all to just get it together. Y'all want each other to get it together! One of y'all just has to actually make it clear that it's time to be serious," I look pointedly at her, "be serious, Lonayla."

Her phone rings, and of course it's Kieran. I laugh, and look out the window, while my sister screams into her phone, telling him to make the leap to seriousness. As we turn onto the highway, my phone vibrates, and I already know who it is:

**New Message from Reelin Houldover Jr.: I promise you, everything will be okay.**

**Reelin: I don't know what else to say about this confusion, but I need you to trust me**

**Me:** 

I lock my screen, and stare out the window, closing my eyes for a moment. When the flash images from last night start to come to me, I immediately shake them away, deciding to watch the clouds instead. I don't know what to do about this liar, who has a voice that alters my brain chemistry in ways I can't explain or escape. And he has eyes that look into the deepest parts of my very being, existing in spaces he shouldn't have access to. Reelin's the only man who's ever affected me this way.

Still watching the sky, blocking out my sister's conversation, my thoughts go to the first time I met him.

# 6 : Sophomore Year



C.S. Williams High School is a lot of things, and "innovative" has always been one of the first words people use, when making selling points about the school. Last year, they began expanding, to create a more technology-friendly space. There's a lot of wealthy parents and alumni who love to keep things evolving, so there's a lot that's changed over time. Parents from all over Atlanta have transferred their kids here, since C.S. Williams started the scholarship program. With everything the school offers, there are plenty roads to success after graduation, and the goal is to help students choose the best one for them. Along with upgrading the classrooms, computer labs and library, we now have a new building dedicated to the magnet program, and we also got updated gym equipment, affording more collegiate level training opportunities. The more successful Black youth in whatever career field they desire, the better.

The school is almost done with its latest updates. This summer's focus was the gym, and creating an additional layer of comfort, for the students who would be spending more time here, than at home. There's now a massive outdoor pool that's under a glass half-enclosure, that's not quite ready. It's way bigger than a standard Olympic sized pool, and goes from behind the old gym, all the way over near the woods to Nowhere. The pool has diving boards, and slides, and it goes up to fourteen feet deep. So naturally, I will never enter that dome.

There are now restrooms between the inner and outer doors of the gym, and we have new indoor basketball, volleyball and tennis courts, plus small rooms for things like racquetball and yoga. The new locker rooms inside are huge, with comfy seating areas, that have phones for when we need to communicate with our parents. The administrators also added a lobby up front, for us to safely hang out before pickups. It's so cool, now.

Today is my first day of tenth grade, and I'm currently wearing my gym clothes. I'm all glistening warm hazelnut skin, in a mint green tee, black Sophies, and no-show socks with my pink trainers. My dark brown hair with faded blonde ends, is in two buns on top of my head, and my mint green and pink headband is keeping my edges from coiling after my morning workout on the volleyball court. I'm sitting outside on the side bleachers by the football field, watching the boys' varsity football team do early morning drills.

There are other students spread out, resting and stretching, after their own morning workouts. For it to be the first day of school, there have only been a handful of people in actual first day of school attire. My parents told me before I even came to C.S. Williams, that the first few weeks are when the coaches for all sports, no matter what season, pay the most attention to who is dedicated to their goals. Every athlete who wants to be taken seriously, comes to school early, even when they're not scheduled to, and some coaches host open workout sessions.

"La, there's a new boy out there. That brown skinned one with the box top," Lonayla says to me, while she finishes rewrapping my knee.

I have weak knees, but I'm determined to still play volleyball this year. I can't run to save my life, but I've always been good at the sport, despite that. My knees aren't a fan though.

"Yeah, I saw him at orientation. He was talking to Daddy by the music display, when I came out of the bathroom. I think it was when you and Mom went to the freshman photo op."

I look back over to the field, at the mystery boy. He has on a gray ripped C.S. Williams gym shirt, black joggers, and some black cleats.

My sister looks at me from the bench in front of my legs, checking the wrap on my left knee again, "did you speak to him at all? He looks cute!"

I stand, doing a little bounce, to test my knees, "I think the right one is a little loose, Lo," I sit back down, and she gets to work fixing my wrap.

"But no, as soon as I walked up, he looked at me like I was a ghost or something. Big dark brown eyes popped out his face, and he just stopped his conversation, apologized to Daddy, then walked away. It was weird, but maybe he's shy?"

"He's kinda fine to be shy, but okay," she pats behind my leg for me to test my knee again, "better?"

I bounce on my tip toes, and nod.

"He was with Kieran and his mom this morning. I wonder why? Think they're related? K always has cute cousins coming around. Remember that one, what was his name? MJ, or something? He came like every summer, and was obviously obsessed with you, but never actually asked you to be his girlfriend, then he just disappeared? He kinda looks like him, yeah?"

I think about it for a minute, looking over at the boys, who are now huddled together around Coach. The new boy and Kieran are leaning on each other at the back.

"I think he might have the same eyes, but I mean, they're brown eyes? They all kinda look alike in that family, don't they?"

Lo shrugs, reaching into my bag for my lotion, then kicks off her black ballet flats, and lotions her feet, sending the scent of Love Spell over to my nose.

"You think I should've worn the wedges today?" She stands up and does a full spin, so I can assess her outfit.

Lonayla looks almost exactly like me, our daddy's green eyes, and all. People often think we're twins. She's just a half shade darker than me. She's wearing a cute white cowl-neck sleeveless top and a long A-line denim skirt. Her accessories include a silver sparkly slouch bag, chunky bangles in green and gray, and a long gray beaded necklace, tied in a knot halfway down her chest, with a big green heart that matches her eyes.

Her hair, which is currently an auburn color, is straightened, and hanging down her back, with a gray headband holding her swoop bang in place.

"No, I like the flats better with that skirt. Plus, I hate when you look taller than me," I reach for my lotion that she left on the seat, putting some on my hands, then I put it back into my bag.

"I love feeling taller than Kieran, though. It gets under his skin, since I'm a year younger than y'all," she lifts up on her tip toes, posing for me.

I laugh, "Kieran's only what, 5'11? Which means he's really 5'10, because boys lie, so you're probably always kinda taller than him, with any shoes, because we're 5'10."

"Please don't say that out loud around him. He tells people he's almost 6'1," she rolls her eyes, as she sits, reaching into my bag for my lip gloss.

Kieran runs over to us, after the coach releases them. The new boy hangs back, talking with coach.

"Lo, you gonna get breakfast with me after I get dressed? I'll walk you to class after," he pulls my sister up, and kisses her cheek. She pushes him away, playfully. Then he looks at me, "hey La. What's up with your legs?"

My sister hands me my gloss, and I put it in my bag, zip it, and pull it onto my lap, "nothing, I was in the gym doing some drills with Maliah and Jessy, for volleyball, and I think I overdid it. I'll be fine by practice later," I shrug, turning to my sister as I stand, pulling my bag to my shoulder.

"Lo, I'm gonna go get changed. I'll come get you from your third period, and we'll go to lunch together, okay?" I start walking down the bleachers and say to Kieran, "we have the same homeroom, Kieran. You better be in class."

"Okay!" Lo responds to me, and Kieran just smacks his teeth.

Lo asks him, "who is the new boy, and why did he look at my sister like she was the enemy at orientation last week?"

I stop my descent, and turn back to them.

"Who? My cousin? I told you he was staying with us. You met him before, Lonayla. When we was kids. He used to come all the time for the summers, he just hasn't been back in a while. La, you don't remember him?" Kieran looks at me in question.

I shake my head, "I have never seen that boy in my life. What's his name?"

"My name is Reelin."

I'm startled by the voice behind me, but play it off as if I was shifting my bag, then turn around.

"You can call me Rizz, though." He's staring at me like I'm a bone, and he's the dog trying to be a good boy, waiting for it.

"Rizz? Like that singer, Ralph Tresvant? Are you a fan?" My sister laughs.

"Nah, Rizz is because my sisters said I have a lot of charisma. It just stuck with me from middle school," he smiles, and the deepest dimples I have ever seen, appear in his milk-chocolate cheeks.

"This fool always gets all the girls, and his sisters think it's charisma. I think it's the dimples. I got the charm in the family," Kieran chimes in, as he leads Lo down the bleachers to the one I'm on—the second from the bottom.

"Be careful, he uses them dimples for evil, La," He says to me with a sly smile before addressing Reelin, "you remember Lo, my lady love," he squeezes her closer, nodding his head at me, "and La, of course. I'm gonna go get dressed, then we're going to breakfast. You coming?"

Those eyes never left me.

"Are you going with them to breakfast, Miss La?" His voice has a little rasp in the back of it, and it's doing something to my brain.

"I wasn't planning on it," I breathe out, almost embarrassed by how I know I sound.

"Well, I wanna go wherever you go," he smiles again, and I swear, the dimples in his cheeks are literal holes to the other side.

"Oh, like that?" My sister asks with eyes wide, and a smile as she looks from Reelin to me, "okay!"

I don't know what to say. I'm stuck staring at this boy, with what I know is the dopiest face. I wobble a little on my feet and sit, pretending to get something out of my bag. I can still feel him staring at me, and it's making me nervous. What is this? A boy, making me nervous? Send the rapture, because this can't be.

"So, are y'all coming or what? I gotta get changed, and it's baby Lo's first day of her freshman year. She got Ms. Hightower for homeroom, so you know she gotta be on time, La. Ms. Hightower takes the morning blitz very seriously," Kieran insists.

"Blitz?" Lo asks me.

Kieran responds, "every morning, they do trivia for each grade. You write your answers down on your paper, and they get collected, and checked by the administrators, to be fair, or whatever. The eight homeroom teachers who have the most students with the right answers by spring break, gets to go to the faculty war games. They do, like, field day things. If your class was a winner, you get two full days to skip classes to watch the competition, and just do what you want. You get to like, chill on the football field with pizza, and stuff. It's cool."

"But homeroom isn't a class. How is that fair?" Lo questions.

"You didn't pay attention to your schedule, huh?" Kieran laughs, "your homeroom teacher is also your first period teacher. I hope your sister warned you about how Ms. Hightower gets about the mornings. She's a cool English teacher, but a psycho warden for homeroom."

He turns back to me, "La, we need an answer."

I take a deep breath, looking at my sister, who's staring at me a little bug-eyed. "Um, sure. I have to get changed, too."

What is this breathlessness?

"I'll come with you, La," Lo pulls away from Kieran, and tells him, "y'all go get changed. We'll meet you by the cafeteria."

"Cool," Kieran steps down off the bleachers, next to Reelin, "Rizz, you gotta blink sometime, man."

Reelin, who has indeed been staring at me as if he's seeing in color for the first time—and doesn't want to look away—finally does. He looks to my sister, "I'm sorry, I don't think I properly introduced myself. Hello, Miss Lo. I'm Rizz. Thank you for dealing with my cousin."

He looks back at me, "Miss La, was it? Is that short for something?"

I think I can see my life in his eyes.

"Lailani," Lo blurts, plopping down next to me, "she's Lailani, and I'm Lonayla. They're not Hawaiian, our parents made our names out of theirs! It's a long story about God's plan, and stuff. We go by 'Lo' and 'La,' because when we were little, La couldn't say my name, and I never even attempted hers! But please just call me Lo, I like it better. My sister doesn't seem to have a preference," I'm surprised by my sister volunteering so much information, but she keeps going, "people always think we're twins, too! But La is a year older. Eleven months, actually. She's April of '90, and I'm March of '91! Aries and Pisces. What's your si—"

"Lo, what are you doing?" Kieran looks so annoyed, stepping up, between us and Reelin, "are you flirting with my cousin right in front of me? Seriously?"

"Boy, what? I was telling him about La, because she—"

"You just gave dude everything but your phone number! Is that next, Lonayla? You know what? I gotta get changed," he steps down, and storms off.

"Kieran, you are A CRAZY PERSON!" She yells after him, but stays seated, and then she looks at me, "what am I supposed to do with that?"

"I'll handle him," Reelin smiles, and I feel like the world is spinning. "It's very nice to meet you, Miss Lailani. Lo," he nods to her, before fixing his gaze back on me, "I would still very much like to meet for breakfast. If that still works for you."

"Um, sure, Reelin," I say.

"I like the sound of you saying my name."

He smiles with all his teeth, and I notice his front one is slightly overlapping the other. It's such a tiny flaw; I am immediately obsessed. I love the little things. An adorable mini flaw, those dimples, obvious charm he knows how to use? Oh, he's going to be a problem.

"Okay, we'll meet you! Thanks, Rizz," Lo says nicely.

"Of course," he keeps his eyes on me a second longer, "see you in a few," he has the nerve to wink at me as he walks off, and I feel like there's no air to breathe, even though I'm outside.

I watch him walk away, and I might as well be drooling. His gym shirt has sweat stains on his back, and under his arms. I didn't even notice the front, because I was so focused on those dimples. He's tall, with an athletic build, so his muscles are defined, but not bulky. His walk is so confident, like he knows exactly who he is. He turns the corner, and I feel like I can breathe again.

"I gotta get changed," I finally say.

"Mhmm. I gotta figure out how to hang Kieran from the flagpole," Lo scoffs, then gets up.

"Rizz was looking at you like you were a triple stack of pancakes, with extra syrup. You said he ran away the other day? He sure ain't shy, now. I've never seen someone try to look into someone's mind before, but if they did, I'm sure it looks like what he was doing."

"Yeah, I don't think I like that. It's weird."

"I think it's hot."

My sister pulls me up by my arm, and we walk off to the gym locker rooms, so I can get changed for the rest of the day.

We have about fifteen minutes until the first bell for homeroom, as Lonayla and I make our way into the main building, to go to the cafeteria. I changed into my low-rise light-wash jeans, yellow satin handkerchief shirt with rhinestones across the top, a white cropped shrug with short sleeves, and white flip flops, showing off my yellow toes, with a pink heart design. I have on a bunch of yellow, white and silver bangles, two beaded white necklaces, and my hair is still in two buns on top of my head, but with a yellow headband now, and white flower earrings.

"You think Kieran is still gonna have an attitude?" Lo asks, looking down the hall, toward the cafeteria.

"Nah, you two have been weird like this since elementary school. He'll be fine."

"He's been getting very bold since last year, though. Remember when he decided to take that girl, Kennedi, to y'all's spring fling? Talking about some, 'I had to go with her, Lonayla. She was the freshman class representative, and she asked' like I was stupid?" She stops walking, "wait, what if she's in there with him right now?"

I look at my sister, shaking my head, "Kennedi *was* the freshman class representative, Lonayla. And she *did* ask him, because he was the only freshman on the varsity football team. She wanted to have the best date, and there was no one more popular than Kieran. Also, I heard she's not even coming here this year. Her mom is making her home school, which is actually annoying, because she was my best outside hitter on the volleyball team last year, and her mom's still my coach, so who is homeschooling her? But whatever, I guess. He ain't with her, relax."

I lean against the lockers, giving Lo a second to calm down.

"Cafeteria or class? Where are we going? I don't feel like walking all around the world."

She chews on her lip, then finally decides, "cafeteria. Rizz is gonna be there, and I think he likes you," she teases, grabbing my hand, to keep walking.

"I think he has the makings of a potential serial killer, just with his weird stare alone."

Kieran comes out of the cafeteria.

"There's your boyfriend," I point my yellow French manicured finger at him.

Lo rolls her eyes, then looks back at me, "I hate him so bad, I could die."

We're closing in on Kieran, when she asks him, "Where's Rizz?"

"Really, Lonayla? Really?"

His body language screams confrontation, and it's only the first day, so I cut in, "Kieran, don't." Kieran scowls at my sister, and then checks his phone. "She's not interested in your cousin, and I'm hungry."

"I guess it's perfect timing, then." That little rasp. My goodness. I turn my head, and there's Reelin, standing behind me in True Religion jeans, and a plain white tee that's so crisp, it rivals his sparkly white Air Force 1s.

"Miss Lailani? Shall we?" I try not to seem too eager, and glance over at Kieran, who's looking at Lonayla through squinted eyes. He's dressed almost identical to Reelin, except with fresh straight-back braids, and black and white 10s.

I purposely avoided looking into Reelin's face right away, but my eyes move up past that single gold chain around his neck, to the circle beard around moistened pink lips, that are neither thin nor thick, but plump and pouty. His nose is broad with a very slight downward point in the middle, and he has little freckles that are just a tad darker than his chocolate skin. Then there are those eyes. His irises are a deep brown that reminds me of dark chocolate fondue. His brows are naturally perfect, with a cute little baby wrinkle in the middle, and his hair is expertly lined, and tapered into his box fade. His hair texture looks like tight coils, that he picks out. He has virgin ears, clear skin, and he smells like Irish Spring soap.

Why is it suddenly so hot in here?

"Uh, yeah," I say, looking away from him, "Lo and I will find a seat for us. I'd like a chocolate muffin, and a cranberry juice, and I can give you cash."

I turn around to find a table, but find I'm suddenly on unsteady legs. I reach for my sister., and she holds my hand, turning halfway between us. I hear Reelin let out a little laugh, and I close my eyes to focus on sound. How does that little crackle wiggle in my ear like that?

"I don't want your money. What would you like, Lo?"

"Kieran, what do I want?" She questions.

I look over at her, and she's nailing him with expectant eyes.

"You want a banana nut muffin, a blueberry muffin, and an orange juice. Yeah, I know. Same thing you got every morning we went to the rec. You always split the blueberry one with La, but somehow, I always pay for it, knowing it's really for her, and you only split it because she saves the chocolate one for her afternoon snack. Every. Time."

I roll my lips between my teeth, suppressing a laugh at his irritation. And then he goes to the line, with Reelin following him.

"Good boy," Lonayla shouts after him, and we head over to a table close to the doors.

"La, that Rizz is something. All like 'I don't want your money,' putting those dimples on display, while you literally refused to look! You seem nervous, sissy! Is Lailani Grander gonna let herself actually like a boy?" She's smiling at me like a cheshire cat, as she sits across from me.

"Lonayla, I don't know that boy. I can't like someone that doesn't even have a last name."

She snorts, "It's probably Michaels, like Kieran's. Anyway, he's cute. You're cute. It's gonna be cute."

She looks around the cafeteria, then frowns, "I don't like sitting this close to the doors. I feel like everyone has to walk over here to leave, and that gives Kieran way too many chances for attention. Can we move?"

I look at the time—7:53 a.m. Then I look to the line, and see the guys are still waiting, with at least nine people in front of them.

"First bell is at 8:05. People will be clearing out more by the time they get over here. We won't even have time to eat, especially since you have to get to Ms. Hightower's class. Is Kieran walking you to all your classes, today?"

"He said he would, but I did the walkthrough with Mommy at orientation, so if he doesn't, I'll be fine."

She sighs, looking to the line, then looks at me with a smile, "guess who's staring over here?"

"A creepy killer?" I bounce my right leg, nervously, "that's so creepy, Lo. I don't like that. I'm not some zoo animal, but he's already watching me like I am."

"Come on! This is normal for you. The boys always fall for you, without you even trying. Girl! Remember when summertime-boy-toy Reece said Beyoncé wrote *'Hip Hop Star'* for you, because the lyrics match? Ha!"

I bark out a laugh, "oh my gosh, he really went crazy about that song! Beyoncé will always be my mood." I settle my anxious leg, and look in my bag for my lip gloss, "Lo, you have my pink lid?"

"Ah, come on, That's my favorite one! Your green one is in there! Let me keep the pink one!"

"Ew. Stop whining, you're in high school now," I scrunch my face, "I like the pink one, too. You had your own, it's not my fault you lost it." She pouts, and I roll my eyes, "you know what, whatever," I pull out another gloss, as the guys come over to the table.

Kieran plops down to Lonayla's left, texting someone on his phone, and Reelin sits to my right, sliding my muffin and juice over to me. He has two blueberry muffins, a cranberry juice, and a sprite. I put my gloss back in my purse, without using it, and open my juice, taking a sip.

"Thank you," I smile, without looking at his eyes.

"Um, where is my stuff?" Lo asks Kieran.

"Oh!" He looks up from his phone, then stands, taking off his backpack to take out their things. He pulls out a sprite, some powdered donuts, a bag of skittles, a banana nut muffin, and finally an orange juice. He slides her the muffin and the juice, "here," looking back at his phone.

"I know you have about three seconds to produce my other muffin!" Lo leans back, pushing her hair behind her shoulders, rolling her neck.

Reelin slides her one of his blueberry muffins, and she pushes it back to him, "oh, no! I don't want your breakfast." She looks back at Kieran, who's focused on his phone, "Earth to Dumb-Dumb?"

"He bought the muffin, because it was for La, anyway. Chill, man." He responds to her without looking up, then sighs heavily, closes his eyes, and puts his phone in his pocket. Lo stares at him in bewilderment. When he looks up at her, his face sours, "he wanted to buy it. I wasn't finna tell the man he couldn't. You gotta relax sometimes. Be grateful about things, you spoiled ass lil' girl."

I immediately interject, "oh nah, we ain't doin that, Kieran, I don't know who has you so bothered, but don't you ever talk to my sister like that again." I look from Kieran to my sister, seeing her eyes mist over, and I want to throw a chair at him, "you've been pushing it, lately. I let y'all do you, but don't get it twisted, I'll whoop yo ass about this one right here, so try it again."

I can feel Reelin's stare, but he stays silent. Smart move, pretty boy.

Kieran's face falls, "I'm sorry, La. I got a lot on my mind. My bad. The bell is finna ring, we should go," he stands, "Lonayla, I apologize, I shouldn't have reacted to you like that. Come on. I'll buy you another muffin, and bring it to your second period, aight?"

She looks at me, and I ask her, "want me to walk you?" She nods. "Okay."

Lo reaches into her purse for nothing, most likely trying to distract the tears that are threatening to fall.

"Lo, I'm walking you. I said I was sorry, man," Kieran moves closer, and puts his arms around her, and kisses the top of her head, "it's fine. Come on."

She shrugs him off, and blinks her eyes a few times, then looks up at me through her lashes. I'm trying to read her expression, but then she looks at Reelin. I look at him too.

He addresses Kieran first, "we'll all walk her to class, then I'll walk Lailani." He stands, reaching a hand over to me. I look at his hand in confusion. "Is that cool with you, Miss Lailani? I heard we have the same homeroom."

I look at my sister again, and she nods, then flips her hair back over her shoulder, standing up, "that's fine, Rizz. Thank you for being a gentleman." She looks at Kieran, and he doesn't say anything.

I stand without taking Reelin's hand, and then I put my muffin in my purse, "yes, thank you, Reelin. And please, call me La."

He smiles, and my insides catch fire, "okay, La. And please, call me whatever you want. I'll always answer you."

"You're so corny, man," Kieran complains, while my sister puts her juice and muffin in the bag, on her shoulder, and she moves closer to him.

"Lo, I'd really like for you to have this muffin," Reelin holds one of the muffins out. She takes it, smiling, "I did ask him to let me pay for it."

He puts his things in his bag, then grabs my bag from the table, and we all leave the cafeteria.

Kieran's holding Lonayla's hand, ignoring anyone who speaks in the halls. Reelin and I follow behind them, my arms crossed, and my purse bumping against my hip. We get to Ms. Hightower's homeroom just as the first bell rings. Kieran says something to Lo, and she nods, but doesn't say anything back. She looks at me, and winks, then goes into class.

Kieran turns to Reelin and me, as we turn to heat to class, "y'all, the day started great, then turned to hell. La, I'm sorry, again. I got some news that I wasn't expecting. You know I care about your sister, I didn't mean to be disrespectful."

"You gotta think before you speak, for real," Reelin swats at the back of Kieran's head, "you make it seem like we weren't raised right, sometimes."

"I don't know what my sister does to you, or what you do to her, but y'all gotta keep the disrespect away from me. You know we were raised to not accept anything less than we feel we deserve, just like you know I'm not afraid to handle you, if I have to."

We walk into the classroom, and I make my way to the seat in the front row, closest to the window. Kieran sits behind me, and Reelin sits to my left. I turn to Kieran.

"If you keep playing with my sister, you're gonna have to be reminded just how much I don't play about her. Last year, you did all that playing, because we were here, and she wasn't. I ignored your foolery, because you told me you weren't going too far, and you were just having fun. If things are different, let Lo know now, or I swear, Kieran, she'll have to help me hide your body."

I turn back around in my seat, and notice Reelin is staring at me, with a strange look on his face. I'm stuck staring back at him, like someone said, "Simon Says," and my brain listened. The final bell rings, and he looks down, releasing me from his spell. He passes my bag to me, and I take it, pulling out my notebook.

Kieran clears his throat, "things have changed, Lailani, but not how I feel about your sister. I know we're gonna be like your parents one day—

married and happy. I just have things happening right now. I need you to help me keep her. She's my forever." His voice sounds so sad.

I turn, "we're so young, and nothing is forever, Kieran. If my sister is hurting in the end, the middle and temporary feelings don't matter. The whole story is a compete waste, if she was never truly happy. You can't be hurting her feelings and being mean, then expect her to just be okay with it."

"We're in high school, man," Kieran groans, "mistakes are what being teenagers is for."

"If that's how you feel, I can't change that. But don't make your mistakes, and think I'm gonna let my sister waste her young life praying for a future with you. Yes, teenagers make mistakes, but I won't let Lonayla's be wasted time. She doesn't deserve that," I shrug, and turn around.

"La, I can't be perfect. I wish I could be."

"Kieran, no one is perfect. In the end, it's about the effort. You just have to try," I say, as the teacher closes the door, and greets us.

I look at Reelin again, and I don't know what that look on his face is, but he seems to have some thoughts. I hate that I'm wishing I knew what they were.

# 7 : Why So Weird?

Lonayla abruptly hangs up on Kieran as we pull up to the house. I look over at her, trying to read her energy, because I wasn't paying attention to their conversation. She sighs, climbing out of the car, so I decide to leave her to her thoughts.

"La, you need anything?"

"Nah, I'm good. I don't feel so great, so I'm gonna go chill out in my room for a bit." I focus my attention on her as we walk to the front door. I can't help myself, so I ask, "y'all good?"

"Yeah, he's just annoying."

Lonayla has the food, our phone bags, and my bag from the mobility store in her hand. When we step into the house, her phone's already ringing, again.

"I'll put the food up. Hello?" She starts to the kitchen.

I hang Dad's jacket in the closet by the stairs, and change from my Dr. Martens into my slippers. I hear my sister greet my dad, as I walk into the half-bath beside the closet, to wash my hands from the outside germs.

"Hey, Daddy," I chirp as he appears behind me, in the mirror, with my laptop in his hand.

"You get the braces?" He waits while I dry my hands, then steps back, making room for me to come out.

"Yeah, I did. The lady was very nice. I didn't know you went there every week. Have you met any of the people who've used them before?" I turn off the light and close the bathroom door, then we walk to the stairs.

"Not personally. I met a couple whose daughter had a skiing accident a few years back. She was paralyzed, and had to learn to walk again. They said she loves how confident she feels with the braces. That's why I keep telling you they're worth a try."

He gestures to the stair rail, that I was not going to reach for, "I know you aren't about to go up without holding on."

"Of course not," I give a half smile, grabbing the rail, then start up, with my dad following me. "I'll try them out, and let you know if there's any noticeable difference. I know you're hopeful, Daddy. I think it's so easy for everyone to want to find some magical option that makes everything perfect, but I think I'm doing just fine."

"You're doing great, but if something makes things even a little easier, I think it's worth a shot."

We walk into my room, and I go straight to my bathroom, taking off my earrings in the mirror.

My dad sets my computer on the dresser. "I brought this in here so you wouldn't have to go out for it. You get everything you needed?"

"Yes, thank you," I smile, and he moves to the door.

"I'll be in the studio, if you need me," he walks out, and I hear him tell Lo the same thing, before I hear her bedroom door close.

I don't like outside clothes in my bedroom, so I pull my phone from my back pocket, and set it on the bathroom counter. I remove my black jeans and cream-colored sweater, draping them both on my changing stool, then turn to stare at myself in the mirror.

My face is still a little puffy. My eyes are slightly less hollow than they were before, but they still look very tired. My skin is still very much on the dreary side, giving me that slight gray tint. I feel like I look. Maybe worse, really. I had quite a few drinks earlier. Not enough for it to really affect me, but I feel pretty yucky.

My phone vibrates.

**New Message from Kieran Michaels: La, tell your sister to chill, pls**

**Me: I can't make her do anything more than you can.**

**Kieran: She's being so difficult! Ma dukes asked to have her over for dinner, but she ain't wit it. She acting crazy**

**Me: Idk, maybe have Jammy ask her?**

**Kieran: Jammy won't be here, she's helping put some stuff together for Rizz's ceremony.**

**Kieran: I think she's only acting like this because Bianca stopped by the house earlier**

**Me: To your mom's? For what? **

**Kieran: She was just dropping something by, but it pissed Lonayla all the way off**

**Me: Because you know sometimes the mothers of your kids play weird games. I told you y'all need better boundaries.**

**Me: They pretend everything's all good and they respect y'all's situation, then one of them starts doing weird shit, trying to get close to you again.**

**Kieran: I swear, La, I ain't even on that type of time. Bianca was dropping off something important, that's all. I wasn't even supposed to be at mom's crib, but I stayed there last night because I was a little too wavy from the party.**

**Me: What time did you leave the party anyway?**

**Kieran: idk, whatever time Lo left, I left right after**

**Me: Why can't you remember who you left with? Reelin's under the impression that I left with you, so where is that coming from?**

**Kieran: La, leave it alone. idk**

**Kieran: Y'all gotta stay with us for The Reliving. It'll help in so many ways.**

**Me: I don't think so**

**Kieran: man, tell Lonayla to pick up her phone, please**

I set my phone down, and take off my bra, hanging it on my doorknob. I go to close my bedroom door, then return to my bathroom, thinking about taking down my two braids, to blow dry my hair.

My phone vibrates again.

**Incoming call from Reelin Houldover Jr.:**

I answer on speaker, "I'm home, my bad."

"You okay?"

I see he's trying to FaceTime. "Pick up."

"No. I told you your FaceTime privileges are revoked."

I squeeze my shoulder blades together, to expand my chest, wondering if it's harder to breathe today, or if I'm just being dramatic from the trauma of it all.

"I have a few errands to run. You want to come? I can be there in like, twenty minutes."

"Absolutely not. I told you I'm doing family things."

**New message from Kieran Michaels: On some real shit La, I'm glad you're okay**

**Kieran: some of us really need you**

I'm thrown off by Kieran's message, so I reply.

**Me: What do you mean? Why wouldn't I be?**

Reelin's still on my phone, "Lailani? What are you doing over there?"

"Nothing, I was thinking about doing my hair, but changed my mind. You with Kieran right now?"

"Nah, I had to swing by my crib, but I'm heading back to his mom's in a few. He should be there. You sure you don't want to come with me? We can go to that dessert spot."

**Kieran: no reason, just glad you're good, is all. I care.**

I set my phone down, already overthinking this message, and I want Reelin off my line, "Nope, family time. Be safe."

He lets out a small laugh, "okay. I'll take you saying be safe as you caring."

"Yes, Reelin. Everyone knows I care," I roll my eyes, and stretch my arms over my head, taking a sharp inhale. It hurts way more than it should.

I push out my breath, "I gotta go."

"Call me when you're free."

"Bye," I hang up.

I pick my phone up to look at the messages from Kieran again. Why would he say that he's glad I'm okay out of nowhere? That's weird.

I look back at my reflection, and my discomfort has my vision blurring. I refuse to cry, when I don't even know what I'm feeling, for real. My chest feels like it's tightening, so I stand up straighter. That triggered something, and now, I'm rushing to the toilet, so my body can relieve itself of everything I have ever eaten in life.

When I finish brushing my teeth again, I walk back into my room to put on some lounge clothes. I throw on a pair of dark purple sleep shorts, and a pale-yellow tank. Grabbing my computer from my dresser, I go to sit in my reading chair to Google drownings.

I can't swim. I never wanted to learn. I literally hated it every single time I was in the water. Voluntarily getting in a pool is not something I would do alone—especially in my current physical existence. Waking up the way I did, means I had to have drowned. There's no other explanation for the flashes of the night making me so uncomfortable as they come to me. I know trauma can cause memory loss, and my mind is clearly trying to protect me from reliving something awful.

I scroll through pages and pages of drownings, but don't find anything about someone dying and coming back to life. It's actually frustrating me to no end. Everything says it's not possible to survive a drowning, but I'm sure that's literally what happened to me.

I set my computer on the side table, and close my eyes. The flashes of last night begin again.

*Reelin. Lonayla. Kieran. The initial tree. Reelin's eyes. Some random chick I have never seen before, is staring straight at me like she knows me. The pool. Glow sticks. Reelin. Classmates toasting. Spray painting my name. Reelin's smile. That same random chick gets closer. Reelin. Kieran. Lonayla. Reelin's laugh. Random chick smiles, with the most perfect teeth I've ever seen, and dimples almost as deep as Reelin's, appear in her cheeks.*

I open my eyes, to get her away from me. My heartbeat is ringing so loud, and so fast, I have to focus my thoughts on not believing my very essential organ is about to jump out of my body. I don't know who the hell that ridiculously stunning mystery woman was, but I didn't like whatever she was making me feel last night.

In an effort to be productive, I think about what to do for my parents, as a way to make up for the morning. I scroll my notes app, looking at the last few things they've both requested I make them, that I haven't yet gotten around to, yet. I also want to thank them for this past week, because we've been doing a bunch of nothing in this house, and it's been great. I've mostly been asleep, outside of checking on my shop, and Lonayla's been binging *The Wire,* in the TV room. Mom and Dad have left us to ourselves.

Our parents take a lot of things literally. When learning about The Reliving, they took it as they were supposed to live with us as teenagers again. They get to spend weeks with us in the house, and we get to live like people with no real responsibilities. Only thing they really required, was making sure we didn't give them anything to worry about. Our teenage years were not the easiest on their nerves, so we agreed to be as low-stress as possible. I messed that up by coming in here looking like the star of a horror film, this morning.

I look at the picture of the four of us on my bookshelf, and smile. Mom and Dad have always been the best. No matter how old or ridiculous we get, they will always be the most supportive people we could ever know. It was actually not even hard to convince them to let us do this.

*Last Sunday*

### *Incoming FaceTime Call from Daddy:*

*"Hey Ma! You look so cute!" I hold my phone up at an angle so they can see Lonayla, too. Mom's sitting at the kitchen table in a gorgeous blue and yellow dashiki, that makes her rich mocha skin look even more radiant. Her hair is free in loose, dark brown coils, that sprout out from her graying roots, framing her face.*

*"Thank you. Your dad walked over there to get his glasses, can you see him?" Mom turns the computer, but all I see are the flowers on the table.*

*"No, Ma. It's fine, turn the screen," Lonayla laughs.*

*Dad walks over, turning the screen with him.*

*"Ooh, you look extra handsome sir!" Lo says, as Dad adjusts into view.*

*"Yeah, Daddy! Let me have that sweater!"*

*Our dad is a nice warm honey complexion, with the same green eyes as Lonayla and me. Mom always says she loves that we look so much like him, but she's happy we didn't get his tiny lips and sharp nose, because we're so much cuter with hers.*

*Mom laughs, "everything green belongs to her in her head, Lonnell. You know that."*

*"Daddy, do you have the email open on the second screen, like I showed you?" Lonayla asks.*

*Mom frowns, leaning in, "Lailani, are you driving on video time?"*

*"No, Ma!" Lo and I say at the same time.*

*"You know I don't drive," I add.*

*"Sweetie it looks like Lonayla's driving, see?" Dad points to the screen, and I move the phone to emphasize the steering wheel in front of my sister.*

*"The mail is open. So, for this Reliving, you want to come here for the two weeks, and be teens again?" Dad asks, with his glasses down his nose, his face close to the screen.*

*"Yeah, we figured it would be cool. I decided to close the shop for the holidays. Even gave the employees a little bonus on top of their bonus, so the energy in the shop was extra cheerful today," I smile, thinking about the extra happy energy.*

*"Pays to have rich niggas trying to buy your cat," Lo jokes.*

*Mom's face twists, "who bought a cat?"*

*I bark a laugh, "no one, Ma. Your daughter is weird. No cats of any kind have been purchased."*

*"So, this says they're compensating for attendance?" Dad's reading through all the details, of course. "And you two made sure they are? Is there a contract for me to review?"*

*"I had to wait for La to decide if we were doing this first, because I wasn't doing it without her. I never looked that far into it, since I didn't need to ask her for time off, but I'm sure there's paperwork," Lonayla parks the car.*

*"I sent an email today, but it's Sunday, so I'm assuming I'll hear back tomorrow." I get out the car, "The original deadline was the 22nd, and we missed it, but Lo said they were gonna let us in anyway, since we're coming from out of town. Apparently they've made exceptions for a few others."*

"*Yeah, and since the alumni committee loves how much the two of you still donate, we're for sure gonna have it all taken care of,*" *Lonayla walks to the back of the car, and I follow.* "*And if anything, Daddy, you can talk to them for us.*"

"*Yeah, Daddy. And if they play with the pay thing, I'll need your help, because I am the owner of my establishment, so I don't know how that works without me having hours and a rate to pay. And since I'm closing the shop, that might get sticky,*" *I move, as Lonayla pulls out our bags.* "*I have the numbers for how much pay we're missing out on for three weeks, and if they're willing to pay half of that, I'm good with it.*"

"*Three weeks? The letter says two,*" *Mom's face is very close, as she reads the flyer herself.*

"*This says the campus housing is available. Are you trying to get in there? You're doing the full experience? Or you want to come all the way home?*" *Dad asks.*

"*That's the best part!*" *Lonayla says, taking my phone. She turns and holds it up, with me and our luggage in view behind her,* "*We're on the way to live with you!*"

"*Oh, Lonayla, you said you were coming next week!*" *Mom laughs,* "*I just asked you last night!*"

"*La literally only said she was willing to do this when I woke up today,*" *My sister looks at me with fake disappointment.* "*I had to book our flights and everything in like an hour! And then, I packed for both of us, while she was at the shop giving the employees their bonuses.*" *She pauses,* "*which I didn't get, so she needs a whoopin', Ma!*" *I huff a laugh, and Lo shakes her head,* "*by the time she finished telling them the limited shop hours for this week, and that they get three weeks off with their holiday cards, I was helping her close up for the day, and we came straight to the airport.*"

*Dad squints at the screen,* "*Lailani, your shop has limited hours this week, and you closed for the rest of the month?*"

"*Yeah, they'll open two hours late, and close an hour early through Friday, and then they're off until the fourth. I figured it made the most sense for everyone, and we've been so busy, they deserve a break. I'm still fulfilling online orders, with delayed shipping, so I think I'll be fine.*" *I give my best believable smile.*

*Lo takes my larger bag from me as we make our way across to the main terminal, "it's gonna be great!"*

*"We figured being home for the holidays would be nice. Lo hasn't even told Kieran and the kids. It's all a surprise! When they find out we're home, they'll be so happy. They won't even know we're staying for Christmas, so they'll get another surprise, when we do!"*

*"And you can afford this? I thought two weeks was pushing it," Mom says.*

*Lonayla snorts, looking at me with a ridiculous expression, as we get to the Delta digital bag drop.*

*"Yes, it's already taken care of," I say, passing my bag to the agent, then walk over to pre-check. "Trust me, I wouldn't be coming if it wasn't handled. Hold on, let me put my phone through the scanner."*

*I walk through the security scanner, and we wait on the other side. When our things get to the end, Lonayla grabs my phone, smiling wide at the screen.*

*"We know you're not worried about money. We wouldn't let you fall apart, but you like to do everything yourself, so it was a valid question," Dad says, leaning back, and grabbing mom's hand.*

*"So, to be clear, you want to be teenagers again? Same rules as when you were in high school?" Dad's brows rise.*

*"Yep!" Lo smiles, holding the phone up so they can see us both.*

*"It'll be fun to be a kid again!" I pause near the entrance to the Sky Lounge.*

*"Okay, so same rules apply. We don't want no issues!" Dad warns.*

*Mom frowns, "You're here a whole month as teenagers?"*

*Lo and I both laugh.*

*Lo smirks, leaning on my shoulder, "No Ma. We only want to be kids for The Reliving. You can even have the weekend before, so we can prepare. I don't know if we can take it than that."*

*"Okay. I think it'll be fine. The courses look interesting, too. We'll get the details together when you get here," Dad says, while mom nods.*

*"Okay! We'll call when we land!" I smile with my face close to the screen.*

*"Okay, have a safe flight. We love you."*

*"We love you, too!"*

*When we get seated in the lounge, Lonayla turns to me, "La, we're really finna be teenagers again. How crazy are we?"*

*I laugh, "I think it's Mom and Dad who are the crazy ones. You? As a teenager? That was a lot."*

*"You were no walk in the park yourself, sister."*

*We cheers our drinks, and we chill out until our flight home for the Teenage Winter Dream.*

There's a knock at my door.

"Come in," I don't look up, expecting it to be Lonayla complaining about Kieran, or something.

"This was left on the porch," Mom says, placing a large brown package in front of me, "what did I say about these packages, Lailani?"

I sit up in my chair with a confused frown, then open the package.

My heartbeat skips. I reach in and pull out my long black Dior D-Town heeled boots—the ones I wore to the party last night.

"This is the second random thing of yours arriving at this house in unmarked packaging, today," Mom eyes me suspiciously, "I heard the bell, but I didn't see a person. I don't like this stuff showing up here like this, Lailani."

"Mom, I don't know what to say." My voice is thin.

I really don't have an explanation, and I know this looks crazy.

"Say you know who's showing up here, leaving your things without any words, so I don't have to believe you're involved in anything crazy," Mom's distrusting expression is making my chest hurt.

"She's not up to no good, Ma," Lonayla offers from my doorway, "you know some people are just good people. Plus, we were with people we know, and even then, her wallet had her ID, so they had the address. You know we never change it."

I look at Lo, and can't help but wonder if she was listening in, or if she came to my door by chance. She looks back at me with that same expression that's appeared on her face all day, and I still don't know what to make of it.

Mom turns to her, "and how do you explain the boots?"

Lo shrugs, "I don't know. Maybe they were gonna keep the boots, but realized they were too big or something?"

"Mhmm," Mom looks back to me, "you better not be in no shit, La," she walks to the door, and Lonayla walks further into my room. Mom looks back at us both before she leaves, "I don't need any problems."

Lonayla comes over, and sits on the ottoman to my reading chair, picking up my boots. "I always wanted these, but every time I try to get them, they don't have our size," she wipes at a small scuff, "literally my favorite boots of yours."

"Have them," I say, getting up from my chair.

"Really?" She jumps up, hugging the boots to her chest, smiling like a kid in a candy store.

"Yep," I walk out of my room, and Lonayla follows.

"I'm gonna bake a cake for Mom and Dad. I think I owe them something nice for dealing with things like mystery packages, and spending thousands of dollars on new phones."

"Oh, hell yeah! I thought today was gonna be fucked, when it was you calling here this morning, but it just keeps getting better!" Lo rushes into her room, with her new boots.

I walk down the stairs, thinking through things. I don't know what the point of delivering my things to my parents' house is, but it's giving me the creeps. My wallet was one thing—like Lo said, my address was in there. My boots, though? That doesn't make sense. Why not wait for someone to accept them? It's obviously one person doing this, so why not drop my things off at one time? Why make it seem like some psycho stalker, with the unmarked packages? Why even take my stuff in the first place?

My chest is so tight, I feel like I can't breathe. I take a moment in the pantry to center myself, before I pull out the mixer. I need to clear my head, and the best way to do that, is in the kitchen.

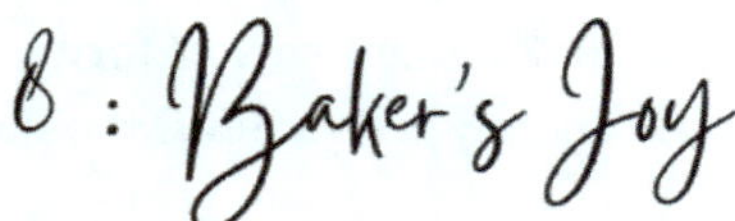



"Lonayla, ask Daddy where the piping bags are, please," I say to my sister, who's sitting on the counter, while I put away the cake pans I just washed.

"He's in the studio. It's too cold to go out there!" She complains.

"I moved them to the bottom left drawer in the pantry, La," Mom says, as she emerges from her sewing room that's just outside of the kitchen, across from the formal dining area, "Lonayla get off my counter," she asserts, swiping her finger on the side of the bowl of icing I just finished coloring a pretty blue, "I can't believe you started today looking like you needed to sleep in a padded room for a month, and now you've blessed us with your baking! Thought you lost your mind this morning, but I'm glad you didn't lose this. When was the last time you even made a cake?"

"I think not since I was here last," I guess, walking into the pantry for the piping supplies, "was it Father's Day?"

"Yeah, and I begged her to make cupcakes for the shop anniversary, Ma. She pretended she didn't have time," Lonayla whines from the other side of the island, licking the frosting off the spatula.

"I did cookies for the employees and their families, for Juneteenth! They all had special cookies with their favorite add ins, in addition to the dinner I made, to celebrate! It was a lot of work! I'll start baking more often once I open up the next spot. I am busy!" I defend.

I'm adding the light blue and white fondant stars onto the three-tiered cake. It looks like day fading down into the night sky. Lo eyes the star, cloud, and moon-shaped sugar cookies I have cooling, to my left.

"I didn't get any specialty cookies, though. Some sister you are!"

"You literally get something every time I'm in the kitchen. The staff doesn't. That was to show my appreciation." I laugh when she sticks out her tongue. "I can stop cooking and baking for you completely, if you want to play, sister. You can only get whatever the staff gets, if that's how you want it."

Lonayla's eyes widen in horror, and she shakes her head violently.

Dad walks in from his studio that Mom had built for him on the other side of the backyard, "I love seeing you destroy this kitchen again." I smile, now piping fluffy clouds on the top of the cake. "But I really love that you clean it up after," he comes and kisses my cheek with cold lips from the outside air, then moves around to do the same to my mom and sister, who are on the other side of the island, watching me create the sugary art they get to devour.

"Did you notice? She made it the night sky," Lonayla's smile is huge, Mom tilts her head in happy recognition, and Dad just smiles and nods.

"I think he finally got to her," Lo laughs.

"I only did the sky because the blue food coloring was the first one in the box that had the matching glitter," I shake my head. I hadn't even thought about it, honestly. I just started, and this is what happened.

"Mhmm, everyone knows y'all's weird thing with the sky. You hate the idea of the sea, so he wants to keep you above the clouds, so you never have to worry, blah blah, cuteness, or whatever," Lo teases.

I pretend to ignore her. Reelin and I do share a love of the sky. It's not just about me and hating the idea of the ocean, though. It's the idea of the unknown. The expanse of the universe and life beyond earth, is super interesting to me. It's the only topic I enjoy theorizing about, and the one thing I don't feel the need to know the end to. I can stare out at the stars, and never have an anxious thought. The infiniteness is so beautiful to me.

Reelin and I would spend hours just watching the clouds pass by. The calmness of those massive fluffs would be the background to a lot of our deepest conversations. A random fact about the weight of a cloud actually turned into him planning our first date—a cute little take-out dinner under the stars, at the park near our high school. He was such a little gentleman, he actually asked my dad for permission to date me, beforehand. To my complete and total surprise, during the date, my dad came out of nowhere, playing *"Sweet Love"* by Anita Baker, on his guitar.

I think my dad has loved him ever since, really. I smile to myself, blinking away the memory, and move from the cake to start icing the cookies with simple blue and white frosting.

"Daddy, Lo attacked me for not opening my bakery just before you came in here. It was so rude!" I whine, like a dramatic child.

"Nuh Unh!" Lo jumps up, "Ma was right here! Mommy, tell him she's lying!"

"My name is Bennet and I ain't innit!" Mom laughs, swiping a cookie.

"I thought we were thinking about that again, though? The boutique with the bakery? Is that not happening anymore?" Dad asks, taking a cookie for himself.

"Yeah, *Grander's Goodness* is still a thought. I have to make sure *Grander Things* is good without me being there every day, first. Lo is great, of course," I offer my sister a cookie, and she takes it and smiles.

I take a calculated breath, hoping she doesn't take my next statement wrong. "But Lonayla, you're not ready. I don't want to force you into those responsibilities before you are. You hate how busy I can get, and you have a freedom you wouldn't have if you ran the shop. You come back home way more frequently than I do, because you have that luxury. You aren't ready to give that up, I know you're not! When Kieran's in Florida, you never have to be at the shop. I give you that, because I know what it means to you. You, Kieran, his kids—that's important to you! Whether you admit it or not, you might not want to even stay there when you two stop playing and settle down. With me, it's just me. I don't have a man and kids to think about. I'll find the rhythm and get back to this," I point to the cake, "I know it's coming, but it has to be at the right time. You know I have to know how to make it all work out in the end. For now, it just has to wait a while." I bite into a cookie.

"La. I didn't know you were waiting on me," Lo frowns. "I thought when we did all that paperwork to add me to the shop, you just freaked. I thought you figured you couldn't take on another business since your diagnosis, honestly."

"Lo, no. You know I'm not even thinking about letting anything I can't explain stop me. I keep telling you guys, I understand my diagnosis, but I'll also defy whatever odds are against me. They don't even know enough to be definitive, so I won't live like they are, either."

"Lailani, I admire your strength. And you know if you need to come home, and open your shop here, you can always do that. You have more help here," Mom looks at me with concern.

I smile, "I'm not asking for help, though. I'm literally fine."

"Would you move back here, though? If you needed help? What if you had to close Grander's? Could you?" Dad walks around to stand at my side. I realize it's because I've begun leaning against the counter more, when his hand finds my elbow.

I wave him off, "yes. I'm not so stubborn I would kill myself for work. I would close my shop, and see if it could run virtually, or figure it out with Lonayla, if that's what I had to do."

Mom stands, taking another cookie, "I'm sure Reelin would help, too— If you wanted to relocate here. I know it's not the same foot traffic, but we could always figure out a way to do pop-up shops every so often and maintain the Miami anticipation. You could have them every month or so, and that means people will look forward to Grander's coming, every single time you go out there."

"I have employees, too. It's not just about me," I shake my head, and Dad nods in agreement. "I just need my sister to know how to run the shop, and to show me she can handle it, before I think about another venture. It'll come in time, guys. I have time." I let out an awkward laugh, "I'm not dying tomorrow."

Dad squeezes my shoulder, "La, we're here to figure this out together. We'll always support you in every way we can."

"Lailani, if you need me to grow up tomorrow, I will. I genuinely thought when the shop's officially mine, I could hire someone to run it, and it would be cool. If you really want me to learn the other stuff, I can. If it means you might actually start taking real breaks, and letting Rizz in— I'm all for it. Life's too short to keep playing with him."

My sister looks at me with eyes I can't take. I look from her to Mom, who's still standing with a cookie in her hand, a crease between her brows, and her lips pursed to one side in contemplation. I can feel my dad's concern beside me, and avoid looking at him, knowing the same eyes on Lonayla's face will be on his, too.

My family still doesn't know how I broke Reelin's heart for my shop in the first place. I don't know if they would ever look at me the same, if they knew how wrong I was in the situation. I pick at another cookie, and ponder if I should tell them the whole story.

I currently own a boutique in Miami. I was never interested in fashion beyond doing little projects with my mom, but things shifted very quickly for me. My senior year of college, I woke up one day and decided I no longer wanted to pursue law. It was a difficult thing to come to grips with, because I thought my dad would be disappointed. It came as a surprise to me when he said he was proud I decided, before I spent the time, and his money on law school.

When he and my mom asked what I wanted to do, I really didn't know. I was good at a lot of things, but I couldn't decide on one. My parents didn't press the issue. I think they expected Reelin and me to get married, and for me to just be a housewife.

My last year in school, I enrolled in some additional business classes and told my parents I wanted to open a bakery. They were ecstatic. Ever since I was allowed to, I learned every little thing I could about cooking. I experimented often, enjoying every moment of being in the kitchen. I specifically loved baking, though. The entire process, all the way down to cutting a cake I spent hours on, made my soul happy. My family was very excited for me, because it was something I truly enjoyed. Reelin was, too. He was super supportive, and even helped with a lot of the research for locations, contractors, cost and everything in between.

My mom's business was doing so well at that time, and with Lonayla—the fashion student—always busy with Kieran's kids, while in school herself, I helped my mom with her fashion needs, during the evenings and most of my off days from classes. Along with her designs, Mom started styling more for high paying customers. They'd shop with her, and also learn how to shop for themselves. I baked when I had free time, but I fell in love with seeing how people reacted to understanding their body types, learning color theory, and how to dress themselves to feel their best. I really enjoyed the ins and outs of design and styling, more than I ever expected to. It was a lot more than just throwing stuff together, like I originally assumed.

When I graduated, Reelin took me to Miami on a celebratory trip. He kept bringing up me opening my bakery, and telling me about business things we could look into, but I wasn't interested in the topic. We got into a little argument the first night, after dinner, because he was pressuring me to look at spaces he found online. He was being way too pushy, and I understand that he just wanted to help, but it was a lot, and I was in a different headspace about what I wanted. I hadn't told anyone I was more interested in fashion yet, because I didn't want to seem like I was all over the place, after already deciding to change paths the year before.

The third day of our trip was the worst. Reelin brought up the day he tore his ACL during yet another argument about my shop plans. That topic had been a tough one for us since right after his second surgery. The doctors said he would likely never play football again, because of permanent nerve damage. He took his anger out on me, and I broke off our engagement. He promised to never bring it up in that way again, so when he did, in Miami, I knew that I needed to leave, before the argument got out of hand. I went shopping, to clear my head, and while I was out, I walked past a beautiful space that was becoming available soon on the South Beach strip. The real estate agent was inside on a random stop by, and it felt like fate. She gave me a tour and a price, and I took her information.

I decided to get my own hotel room that day. When I went to get my things from the room with Reelin, he wasn't there. I took that as another sign to just follow my gut. When he called me that night, he was even angrier than earlier, because I got my own room. I was not in the mood to fight for four more days, so I also changed my flight. I left the next morning, leaving him in Miami. I never told my parents about why I was home early, or that Reelin hadn't flown back with me. For four days, I obsessively looked for apartments close to the space I toured, I figured out a plan, and decided to sit my family down to let them know I wanted to move.

Almost two weeks later, after receiving a phone call a day, with weak apologetic voicemails, and 60 or so ignored texts saying nothing except, "I'm sorry," and "I love you," I asked Reelin to come over, so we could talk. He still had no idea I was leaving soon, and I didn't know how to tell him. We sat in my parents' backyard, eating tacos, when he told me he put in an offer on a place he knew I'd love in Buckhead. I was very confused, but I felt more annoyed about him doing something without me, that was supposed to be for my business.

Where there should have been gratitude, I only felt suffocated, and I needed to do whatever I could to keep him from sucking me in. I had originally planned to ask him if he would like to spend the rest of the summer in Florida with me. I hoped we could figure everything out before he started his medical school journey in the fall, because Reelin's dream outside of football had always been child psychiatry, so he had to continue his education. I changed my mind about asking him, though. I needed to get away from him.

That day, next to the lemon tree in my parents' backyard, standing above him with a taco still in his hand, I told him I needed him to let me go. I told him I would never love him the way he wished for me to—no matter how much he loved me. I told him that I didn't think he would ever get over the loss of football, and I refused to have him resent me for the rest of my life. I told him I'd rather learn to swim in the deepest depths of the ocean, than continue pretending like we were never going to end. I told him it was just better to let go, because he looked forward to forever, but I always knew better. When he stood up to protest, I blurted out that

I was leaving that month, because I finally found a love I was willing to chance, and it was never going to be him. I watched his heart shatter behind his eyes, thinking I meant another person, and I let him believe it. I needed him to let me go, so it was better that he thought something awful, and didn't fight for me. I turned and walked inside, then asked my dad to make sure he left.

Three weeks later, I was relocated to Miami. Almost three months after that, Grander Things opened—with my fabulous mother, Laila Grander, being the main designer I showcased. My shop was basically an overnight success. Four months after that, Lonayla's plans to join me became real. She still had a semester left of school, but flew in on the weekends, when she could. When she graduated, Kieran moved her down to Florida, by way of a romantic weeklong road trip, and he stayed for the summer.

That was in 2013, when my sister came. I had left Reelin almost an entire year prior. Until 2023, I hadn't spoken to him since that day in the back yard. I also hadn't eaten a taco since then. That's the closest I think I could ever come to knowing heartbreak.

**New Message from Reelin Houldover Jr.: I'm outside.**

I'm on the couch in the family room with my parents and sister. We had the rest of our Din Tai for dinner, then decided to watch some crime documentaries together. Empty glasses of wine and cleaned plates of cake litter the coffee table. I text my sister, who is sitting on the other side of our sleeping parents:

**Me: Why the hell is Reelin texting me he's outside?**

I see her smile.

**Sissy: I might have told him we were okay with them coming over when Kieran asked like an hour ago. Kieran ain't text me, though**

**Sissy: wait, yes he did. He said they brought treats**

**Me: I didn't okay this. Y'all have fun, though**

Lo looks at me, then our parents, and back at me.

**Sissy: I'll wake them, and you know it. I'll tell mom Rizz is outside and she'll invite him in here. you know she will. Is that what you want? Because I think it's great**

**Sissy: outside! now! or I'll do it**

My turn to look at her.

**Me: You really are a brat, bro. It's sad.**

We both get up.

**Incoming call from Reelin Houldover Jr.**

I press decline, and slip on my black house slippers. Lonayla's hurrying out of the room.

**New Message from Reelin Houldover Jr.: you do know your read receipts are on, right?**

I lock my screen, walking into the kitchen. I hear Lo behind me.

"I told Kieran they can just walk around back, and to start the fire pit," she's holding one of the black Snuggies from the hall closet out for me, with a white beanie. She snatches out her two buns, then pulls an orange beanie over her hair. "Hold on!" She sets down the black Snuggie she had for herself, running out the kitchen, and up the stairs.

A few minutes later, my sister walks into the kitchen wearing a black Nike hoodie, plain purple sweats, with green and brown ski sock in her black adidas slides. She hands me a black Nike hoodie, some thick red adidas sweats, and pink ski socks. I shake my head smiling at her, and then sit in one of the kitchen nook chairs to put on the socks, before I step into the sweats, to pull them up.

I pull the hoodie over my head, with a small chuckle, "You were too cold to go to get Daddy for me earlier, but now that it's dark and colder, you wanna go outside? You're insane." I shake my head, sliding on my slippers, then pulling the beanie over my braids.

Lo flares her arms in a dramatic fashion, "your husband is here, Lailani. He's by the fire on a cold winter night, waiting for you, desperately! I am doing this for LOVE!" With that, she hands me the Snuggie I set on the island, and opens the back door, so we can walk outside.

It is so cold, I instantly regret this. I've already been feeling unwell all day, so I'm not pleased. I want to go back into the comfort of the heated house, but Lo takes the Snuggie out of my hand, shoving it over my head, while my arms hug my middle. I look across the yard at the burning flame, then look down to watch my steps, as I follow after my sister.

Reelin walks over to us almost halfway, and wraps his arms around me, "stop leaving me on read." He pulls back, noticing my arms aren't through the sleeves. "Let's get you warm." As he moves beside me, his arm finds my waist, and he kisses the side of my forehead, walking me the rest of the way.

The fire-pit in our backyard is a beautiful one. It's gas operated, and set in black sandstone. The pit itself is round, and about six-feet wide. There's a raised bench made of the same black sandstone—with thick deep-seated Sunbrella cushions, and a high back that wraps almost the whole way around the pit, leaving a three-foot gap to walk in and out of the space. Lonayla is sitting on Kieran's lap already, and I stand as close to the pit as I can, loving the heat from the blazing fire.

Reelin reaches into the small compartment of the bench, pulling out one of the electric blankets. I forgot he knows where everything is here. Once he plugs in the blanket, he comes over, and wraps his arms around me from behind, pulling me close.

"That blanket should be warm enough for you in a minute." That little scratch in his voice is so much clearer when he speaks in hushed tones. I stare at the flames, trying to steel myself against the way the sound tickles my brain. "Or I could hold you right here all night."

He presses a kiss to my ear lobe, "I love you wearing these earrings again." His breath is hot against my neck, making me shiver.

I'm wearing the same earrings I wore last night. Tiny gold studs shaped like the letter L. Reelin bought them for my 16th birthday. I wore them last night for the first time since high school, and he immediately noticed. I close my eyes when he leans his face further into my neck.

*Reelin. The Initial tree. Lonayla. Kieran making fun of me. Random chick staring at me with her perfect smile. Reelin's smile. Classmates in the pool. Lonayla gives me a drink. Random chick cupping Reelin's cheek—he gives her a strange look.*

I open my eyes and shift, trying to shrug him off.

"That blanket should be warm, now," I try to turn, but he holds me steady. I feel trapped with my arms being held down, unable to push him away.

"Reelin, I want to sit," he loosens his grip, and I turn to the bench, but he takes hold of the Snuggie. "What are you doing?"

"What just happened?" He searches my eyes for the answer.

I look back at the fire, trying to decide if I have the energy to get into this right now. I keep seeing that girl, but that was the first time I recall her touching him. I don't know if I should care or not, but now, this memory flashing to me only reminds me that he really left me. Was it for her? Who is she? Why have I never seen her before? I look back at Reelin, and I feel like he'll only lie to me, if I ask him.

I shrug, "It's cold, and I'm tired."

He looks unconvinced, but let's me go. I sit on the bench, a few spaces from Lonayla and Kieran, who are making out like teenagers. I put my arms through the Snuggie, and immediately reach for the blanket. Reelin lifts it before I can, wrapping it around me from the front. The warmth is wonderful. I give a tight smile, and look back to the fire.

Reelin goes to the other side of the fire pit, and I watch as he lifts a box, then turns round. I look at his face, and the orange-ish light from the fire is highlighting his jaw. His eyes home in on me, and I can feel my temperature spike. His smile that comes immediately after threatens to end my resolve. I could almost forget every bit of discomfort, looking at him.

"Ooh! Presents?" Lonayla cheers, moving off Kieran's lap. Kieran looks like he needs a minute, with his hooded eyes focused on my sister.

I look back at Reelin, as he stands in front of me. "It's not my birthday." I hear how nervous my voice is, and I want to jump into the fire.

Last year, I told Reelin that it was too soon to fall into old habits. It was the holiday season when we reconnected, and he always loved gifting me, so I asked him not to. Then for my birthday, it really bothered him that I told him he had to wait until next year.

"It doesn't have to be your birthday for gifts," he sets the box on the ground at my feet. It's a decent size, and wrapped beautifully in green velvet paper, with a simple mint-green bow.

I stare at the box, then lift my gaze back to Reelin. He looks so innocent, but so serious at the same time. I know I'm supposed to be upset with him, but that little reminder of the sweetest man I've ever known, is staring straight through me, holding on to my lifeline in the slight natural pout of his lips. I suddenly feel like I'm free-falling.

I look from his lips down his body, that has somehow only improved over time. Under his black puffer jacket, is a black thermal top, that hugs his broad chest, and clings to his perfectly defined abs. My eyes continue downward to his maroon sweats, hanging off his hips in a grown man kind of way. Not too low, but just on his hip bones. I exhale, not realizing I was holding my breath. My eyes dip a little further, against my best efforts. I know exactly what is just beneath the fabric of his pants, resting comfortably on his big, strong thigh. It naturally favors the right, and I can see it from memory.

I say a silent prayer to myself, "Lord, please keep me."

"Lailani?" His voice is my undoing, and I put my face in my hands. I don't want to close my eyes though, because I don't want to see that stranger right now. I can feel Reelin come sit beside me, and then his hand comes up to mine.

"Look at me, Lailani." He pleads.

He gently peels my hands from my face, holding both of mine in one of his. I stare at our hands, trying to remind myself that he is a liar. I try to tell myself not to let him get to me, because he really left me, like I was nothing to him, and I can't just let that slide. He cups my chin, turning my face to him, but I keep my eyes down.

"Look at me. Please," the almost-whisper scratches that spot in my brain a little harder than before.

I give in.

His eyes are on me, assessing. Questioning. His intensity is taking over the air. I feel like I'm trying too hard to breathe. I keep focused on him, seeing every tiny detail of his face that I had committed to memory, and things that are new. He always had a tiny wrinkle between his eyebrows, but now, there are two more—like he frowns often. The thought of him frowning permanent wrinkles into his face makes me sad, and my eyes meet his again. I want to melt into him. I know he would love nothing more, and I have this sudden urge to give him whatever he needs, if only to keep him from frowning again. Please, Jesus, save me before this man reels me in for good.

"La, open the box!" I hear my sister's voice, and pull my chin out of Reelin's hand to look at her. I don't know what she sees in my expression, but she smiles, pursing her lips like she just saw the cutest puppy, ever.

Reelin's hand falls away from my face, and I look at my hands as he gets up, returning to standing on the other side of the box at my feet. Lonayla moves closer to me, and Kieran moves in too, crossing his hand over her legs to reach the blanket I'm under, pulling it over her. I smile, appreciating the gesture. Lo smiles, too.

"Open the box," Reelin insists.

I bite my cheek, looking at the box, "I hate surprises. You know that." I don't look at him, but I can see his body shift, causing my eyes to wander back to his thighs. I immediately catch myself, and turn to my sister, who looks at Kieran.

"Don't look at me, I mind my business," he lets out a small snort, leaning back on the bench, pulling my sister's hand to his lips, holding it there.

Reelin chuckles, "It's not a big deal, really. It's just something I knew you needed."

"Then why is it wrapped like it's important?" I look back at the ribbon.

Reelin squats in front of the box, and waits for me to look at him. When I finally do, I might as well be floating through space.

"It's wrapped because I have had pre-wrapped boxes, with these two greens—your favorites—since you left me, waiting on the day you let me in again. I remember how you would open gifts and wrap them again, just so you could use the boxes for something in your room. I know you. Still. I want to gift you with purpose for the rest of my life, so anything I gift you will be wrapped. And just so you know, I also have wrapping paper that matches your eyes. The sage green, because it's the color they are the most often. I use it for every single gift I give to anyone."

He softens his gaze, "it's wrapped because you deserve to be gifted, thoughtfully. It's wrapped because you deserve to unwrap gifts as often as possible, even for the just because of it all. It's wrapped because little things like gift boxes and wrapping paper bring you joy, and your joy, especially when it's because of something I did, makes life that much more meaningful. The way you appreciate little things like wrapped gifts for no reason, gives me even more reason to adore you. If this box were empty, I know you would still love it just because it's wrapped. It's wrapped because things like this matter to you, and what matters to you, will always matter to me, too. Is that sufficient enough?"

Swear, he wants me dead. I knew it already, but who says things like this to someone and doesn't expect their heart to give out?

I finally lift the lid, "Reelin," I gasp, pulling a Burberry fossil check bouclé coat from the box. "It's beautiful!" I pull it up to my chest, and run my hands down the front.

"I know it's not the exact one that went missing, but I went to Burberry today, and it felt like you," he moves the empty box to the side and stands all the way up, taking the coat and undoing the buttons.

"Kieran, have you ever cared about me?" My sister swats at her man. "You don't buy me nice things!"

"I don't know if you forgot this, woman, but I'm not rich like your people!"

"Rizz is *your* people!" Lo moves closer to me, "I'll try it on for her!'

"No, I don't need you to. I'm sure it'll fit," I look at Reelin's face, he raises his brow in question. "I know it'll fit. Thank you, Reelin. I was not expecting this. I appreciate it. Really."

"Of course. Couldn't have you walking around here without a coat," he folds the coat, and puts it back into the box, then sets it to the side.

He sits next to me again, grabbing my hands in his, then nuzzles his nose between my ear and neck, whispering, "I will always do anything for you," he releases my hands, and leans back.

I lean into him, and he takes this as his opening to wrap his arm around me, so I move my head onto his shoulder. We stay like this for a while, just breathing together. The crackling of the fire, and the warmth of this cozy situation makes everything seem so peaceful. I stare up at the stars for countless minutes, and then look at Reelin's face. He's doing the same, as always. We would sit out here, just like this, when we were younger. It feels so natural, like we're those people again.

Reelin's other hand cups mine on his chest, and I find myself wondering what all of this means. Why am I so comfortable with a man who I know is somehow part of the reason I died last night? I know he left me, and he keeps lying about it. And who is that stranger? Why was she there? What else am I missing? I close my eyes, deciding I want to force the flashes. They don't come. For the first time today, last night is not invading my mind. I can feel myself getting anxious, so I look back to the stars. They always ground me, somehow.

My sister removes herself from the cover, and stands by the fire. Kieran joins her, pulling her close. Their noses touch in a sweetness I know she appreciates. They were having a hushed conversation before she moved, but it seems like it was a good one. They actually look happy. The four of us here like this, would probably qualify as a super cute moment. Lo looks at me with an adorable smile, and I know she's thinking the same.

Time seems to stand still.

"I haven't been here since that day, La," Reelin interrupts the silence. "It's been over a year, and we still haven't talked about it."

I close my eyes, and take an uncomfortable breath. I don't want to do this right now.

"It feels like both no time and too much time has passed."

He's going to take it there. I can feel my back stiffening at the discomfort.

"Lailani baked a cake and some cookies, today!" Lonayla blurts, and Kieran looks at me with a huge smile. "Y'all want some?"

She doesn't even know that in trying to save me, she might have just made it worse. I should've told her how I ended things with Reelin, because me baking might be a sore spot for him. I sit up, removing the blanket from my body, suddenly feeling too warm.

"It's been so long since I've had anything your sister made, I'd love a slice," Reelin answers, and Kieran nods in agreement.

I know Lo feels accomplished by the shift in topics, "okay! Mom and Dad are asleep so," she looks at Kieran, "do not get inside of this house, and act out. My mama will murder you, and my daddy will keep her out of prison. In case you forgot, she don't play about her sleep."

I stand, but Reelin grabs my hand, "hold up a minute," his thumb rubs circles over my palm. "I just need a minute."

I guess I have to do this. I bite my cheek, and look at my sister's questioning expression, "we'll be in in a few." I nod, giving her a half smile. She grabs Kieran's hand, and they walk to the house.

I sit, and reach for the blanket again.

We don't speak for a few minutes. I can feel Reelin's stare burning into me, but I stare across the yard, through the kitchen's glass doors. I watch Lonayla hop onto the counter, and Kieran sits at the island. I would love to be either of them right now, so I don't have to have this conversation. With everything I have to sort through already, how can I truly sit here, and rehash the day I broke this man's heart?

I calm myself, focusing on my breaths, then twist around, so I can cross my legs. It takes a little more effort than I wish it did, but once I get comfortable, I look into Reelin's face. He looks like he does in my dreams. Heavenly. Pure. The flames are dancing in his eyes as he looks into mine, and I suddenly feel so heavy. My mind takes me back to the day we reconnected, after more than 11 years apart.

# 9 : Find Your Way Back

*I'm scrolling Facebook, seeing all the pregnancy announcements, marriages and divorces, job anniversaries, and whatever weird drama the people who never left the immaturity behind are sharing. I check this app every other month or so, in case there's anything I should care about. Every time I click my inbox, it's the same kinds of messages: someone's hitting me up about party promotions like it's still the early 2000s, group threads from extended family members sending rage-bait posts, and boys from as far back as elementary school trying to holla with eight or more kids, and just as many baby mamas. I always click them just to clear the notifications. If someone really wants to talk to me, it wouldn't be on Facebook.*

*I click all but one very specific thread, every time. I haven't clicked a message from him since the day I told him to let me go, leaving him without a chance to talk me out of it. This latest message is timestamped for 57 minutes ago. I don't know why, but I decide to finally click his name.*

***New Message from Reelin Houldover Jr.:*** *Lailani, I feel so good about today! The kids were so excited about the youth center. I really am so grateful for the way this all came together! After so many years of wanting to do something like this, it finally happened! I was nervous as hell, thinking people would think a black man being so hyper-focused on kids was weird, but you know how important this was, so I pushed through, and here we are!*

*I've been so busy these past few weeks, I couldn't even sleep, but it was worth it. It IS worth it. Today was the day! Opening the week of Thanksgiving was K's idea, believe it or not. He said with the schools being out on break and people being off from work, it would pack the grand opening. It did, La! It was packed! We signed up almost 100 kids in total! So many kids will have a positive space to grow and flourish with people who can help to nurture their young, brilliant minds.*

*I'm sure I'll have to expand in the next couple years to accommodate them all at once, but for now, we got 47 boys signed up for Gracefully Growing Guys and 49 girls signed up for Lovely Little Ladies! We'll have the counselors and mentors do shifts so it doesn't become overwhelming with there being so many kids. All that'll be worked out by the official start date for the programs in January. We have some fun winter activities for them to start getting to know everybody coming in the next month, so I'll lock everything in during that time.*

*Outside of their growth mindset groups, they have a place to be together, and to just be kids. These kids weren't afforded all the things some of us were, but I want them to feel like anything is possible despite that. They can do it all! Today, they made dream lists as an ice breaker, and I could see the hope in their bright eyes! I feel like Iron Man or some shit. We always talked about how important it was for the underprivileged kids to have programs where they could spend time with people who fuel their dreams. I know this is gonna be exactly that.*

*I know I'm rambling on, and you never read these, but I can't wait for you to see it, Lailani. For you to see these young faces, and how inspiring you are through the eyes of kids who wish to grow up to be just like you. Shit's cool as hell, having them tell you they want to be you for real. They got so many dreams! I can't even express how it feels to see so many young lives that can change for the better because of me. By extension, it's all because, of you, too. You believed in me. We went through some shit when I lost football, but you consistently encouraged me, helping me to stay focused on my other dreams. When I felt like everything was impossible, or when I was in a funk, you forced me to get it together. I can never forget that. I will always give you your credit in my success. Sometimes I can hear you telling me why I gotta keep going. Even without talking to me, baby you make me better. Thank you.*
*Forever.*

*I miss you, so much. I wish you were here. This grief journey ain't been easy, but I know it's because I'm not supposed to grieve you. I know God will bring you back to me, soon. I hope you'll be proud to do life with the man I grew into, knowing I will always keep striving to be better. For myself, and for you. Until then, I love you.*
*Eternally.*

*I scroll up the thread, and there are so many messages like this. Every idea, every accomplishment, every random little thing. I would hear about these things from my sister and Kieran, but from his own point of view, it feels so special. I sit and read them for over an hour, soaking up his words that tear me apart and put me back together again and again, before I have to stop myself. I can't believe this man really found a way to include me in everything.*

*I blow my nose and take a deep breath to calm my nerves. Through the tears that are still streaming down my cheeks, I press reply.*

**Me:** *Dear diary…*

*I press send, and get up from my computer chair in the back office of my shop. I suddenly feel naked and exposed, but also embarrassed, thinking it was crazy to say something so foolish after all he poured out to me.*

*"Dear Diary, Lailani? Really?" I mumble to myself. It's a Facebook message, so I know he won't see it until he's online. Thankfully no one keeps Facebook notifications on.*

*It's nearly 1 a.m., and I'm just leaving the shop. I stayed late, to handle some last-minute payroll things. I lock up, and walk outside into the fresh air that helps me to shake off my jitters. I get into my forest green Mercedes G-Class, then lean my head on the steering wheel. Why would I respond like that? Would that upset him? Should I say something else?*

*After a few breaths, and some serious internal regrets, I decide I'm going to delete the message, and mark his thread as unread. If I'm going to say something to this man after all these years, it needs to be more than something so silly. I prefer he not even know I saw his messages until I decide what to say, if anything. It was clearly a moment of weakness, and I need to think this through.*

*I open Facebook again, click my messages, and the world spins three times faster.*

**New Message from Reelin Houldover Jr.:** *Lailani, call me. Number's the same.*

*I look around the car, to make sure I'm not being Punk'd, and it's not actually closing in on me, and then I look back at the message. How the hell did he see it so fast? Was this dumb? Am I dumb? What is happening? I close out, and immediately call my sister.*

*"Hey, La."*

*"Lonayla, Is there a retropage thing happening right now?"*

*"Girl, what? You mean Mercury Retrograde?" She laughs, "no, you're in the clear. Why? You do something silly?"*

*"I don't know yet. I either just pulled the clip off a grenade, or I cracked a window. The latter feels too simple," I sigh into my phone. "You home?"*

*She laughs again, "we're pulling in now, their flight was a little late. Kieran brought both Jazmynn and Payzlie, so get excited for a much-deserved girls night this week. What did you do?"*

*"Aw, I love that the girls are here," I start my car. "I'll let you know when I figure out if it's the grenade or the window. I'll be home soon. Be safe."*

*"No, YOU be safe, Lailani," she pauses, "For the love of God, just get home." The concern in her voice causes my eyes to roll.*

*"I am. See you in a few!" I hang up, shaking off my sister's fear about me driving. Nobody has time for that weirdness. I know I shouldn't be driving, but I was gifted this car, and I'll be damned if I don't get to drive it.*

*I roll down my window, in need of fresh air, then pull onto the street. I wish Publix was open, because I need to get things for breakfast. I tell Siri to set an alarm for 7 a.m. so I can go for groceries in the morning. Whenever Kieran visits with any of his kids, I try my best to make sure they feel special—even though they try to act too cool, since they're all basically adults now.*

*I don't hit a single red light, and pull into the parking garage to my apartment ten minutes later. I turn off my car, give my thanks for making it without losing control, then sit in quiet reflection.*

*After giving myself time to settle my heartbeat, I reach for my phone, and go back to Reelin's thread. I start typing and backspacing so many times, but I don't know what to say. How do I start a conversation, now? And he requested a call, so should I call him? I close out, go to my contacts, click his name and unblock him, then I hesitate. I really don't know what to say to him, so I lock my screen.*

*"There is no way you are calling this man," I assert to myself. "Not yet, La. Figure out how to approach the situation first. Sleep on it."*

*I nod my head coming to grips with not calling. I grab my things and get out of the car, then go upstairs to the gorgeous apartment I share with my sister.*

*"Honey, I'm home!" I shout, kicking off my shoes.*

*I walk past the empty kitchen and front room, then turn left to go down the hall to my room. The first door on the right is the guest room, and I peek my head in, waving to Kieran's daughters.*

*"Hey Auntie La," Payzlie says, from the reading chair by the window.*

*Jazmynn's laying on her back across one of the two full-sized beds, "Auntie La, the Wi-Fi ain't connecting."*

*I smile, and shake my head, "hello to you too, Jammy. The password is Yonce184090. I had to change it."*

*I look at Payzlie, "Pooda, those chips you like are in the pantry. I got them when I went to Germany last month. I'm happy to see y'all. I gotta get in the shower, see you tomorrow."*

*"You flying back with us on Thursday? We're doing Thanksgiving at Grammy K's, and since Kayde couldn't come, Lo said we're doing brunch with the Grandys, then Black Friday shopping." Jazmynn says.*

*I shrug. "I'm not sure. I wasn't planning on being in Atlanta. I think prefer the warmer weather, and I'd even like to lay out on the beach, if it doesn't rain."*

*"Me, too! Tell my dad to let me stay with you!" Payzlie pleads, and Jazmynn laughs.*

*"My name is Bennet and I ain't innit!" I laugh, turning back down the hall.*

*Lonayla's room is between the guest room wond mine. Her door's closed, and I don't bother knocking. She hasn't seen Kieran since he was here in late September. They usually see each other at least twice a month, but the shop's been hectic, and Kieran's been extremely busy with his own work. He has a master's in social work—focusing on teen parental rights—and he's been working with a lot more kids than usual, these past few months.*

*I walk into my room, turn on the light, and close my door. My room is my favorite place in the world. I have wall-to-wall floor-to-ceiling windows, giving me a panoramic view of the beach on two full walls. My queen-sized bed is so cozy, and all nineteen of my pillows stay on it while I sleep, like I'm on a cloud. I set my phone on the nightstand, connecting automatically to the wireless charger, then walk into my bathroom to shower.*

*I turn on the light, and look into the mirror that covers the full wall to my left. I take off my pearl earrings, and grab the mouthwash to gargle. I put my auburn waist-length boho braids in a bun on top of my head, strip out of my black midi dress, and step out of my panties, tossing them into my hamper. After I turn on the shower, I sit on the toilet to pee.*

*I suddenly feel my chest flutter, and I know it's my subconscious, thinking of Reelin. All these years later, and in just a fleeting moment, he's back under my skin, filling every part of me with something I can never explain. I opened myself up to this, and I have no idea why. With Reelin, everything is so intense. Every single feeling is amplified, because he has a powerful energy that calls and responds to the very root of my own. I finish my business, and walk back to the sink to spit and wash my hands, before I grab my floss and get to work on my teeth.*

*I hear my bedroom door open, "I'm naked. So, if you're Kieran, turn around or you're gonna fall in love with me, and that would be so unfortunate for you."*

*"Ah, boo!" My sister answers back as she appears in my bathroom doorway, "so, what did you blow up, today? You finally bust it open for that begging ass Panamanian billionaire?" She leans against the door frame.*

*I huff out a laugh, looking closer at my teeth, making sure the spaces are clear. "Nah. I may or may not have messaged a certain man, who may or may not have done something really cool that he always wanted to do today, though. Then, I may have gotten bold and unblocked his number, and I may or may not have almost called him. But it could have also been a fever dream. I'm not sure, really."*

*"Oh my God, Rizz?" Lonayla sounds way too pleased. I look at her through the mirror, and she is indeed way too smiley. "They had such a successful day, La! Kieran was beaming when I picked him up! But why almost call? Why not call call?"*

*"I don't know, Lo. It feels crazy. I opened his messages for the first time, and he's been sending me literally every little thing! I felt like I was reading his personal journal or something," I take a deep breath, and go to the shower, "so, I messaged him 'dear diary…' and I felt like a fool for not saying something more, but when I went to delete it, he had already replied, telling me to call him. I panicked. I don't know, I'm gonna sleep on it."*

*"Lailani, he always asks about you. I told you, he's still waiting. He never gave up hope. I think this is a sign. It could really, finally be time. Let it be." And with that, she leaves.*

*I spend a good amount of time in the shower, just thinking about Reelin and the things he shared with me in his many messages. I also think about how much I've hated all the pointless dating I've done since him. He said he knew I would find my way back. I can't imagine being so hopeful, if things were the other way around. I would've hated me into oblivion if I were him, but I sensed nothing but love and kindness in his words.*

*Has he really been waiting for me to come back? But back to where? We were so young, and I was so incredibly sure of what I needed. I wasn't looking for forever, and I had already banked on the end of us. I thought the end would come later, but I definitely knew it would come, so I brought it about sooner. I had to, before he could get too much deeper into my soul, because the longer he loved me, the harder the end would become. Am I supposed to just jump back in, and look forward to the end coming again? I know it will. That's the only way our story goes. Can I handle that, though? Can he handle that? I don't know what to do, or why I'm even thinking about this.*

*This would require changes I'm willing to make, and I definitely can't share certain parts of my current life without him trying to find a way to make it all work. Reelin has a habit of needing to find the answer to everything, but some things just aren't possible. Some things aren't as simple as his White Knight tendencies wish them to be. This is probably not the best idea. I should leave him where he is, and keep on like I have been.*

*I get out the shower, moisturize, brush my teeth, and do my nighttime skincare routine, then walk into my room. I slip into one of my oversized sleep shirts, and do a few quick stretches, before I turn off my light, and climb into bed. I lay, staring at the ceiling, just thinking about my current dilemma, when my phone vibrates. I lean over to pick it up, seeing who it is.*

### *Incoming Call from Reelin Houldover Jr.:*

*"There's no way," I say to myself, then press the green blimp, and place my phone to my ear, "hello?"*

*"My God, I have waited for this for so long." That slight rasp in his voice still affects me the same. It's been so long since the last time I heard him speak. I inhale sharply, trying to accept the weight of emotions that just plowed into me, while the ringing in my ears continues to sing some song from the heavens only his voice knows.*

*"Hello, my love. I've been needing you. I didn't know if you'd answer."*

*"How did you even know your call would go through?" I exhale the words out, and lay back against my pillows.*

*"Honestly? Lo and K called me. Lo said I wasn't blocked anymore, but that you weren't sure you were ready to talk. But then she told me to call you as soon as they hung up."*

*"Oh." I don't know what else to say.*

*"Are you okay?"*

*I close my eyes, holding on to the sound of his voice, "mhmm." I try to calm my heart.*

*"Do you feel up to talking?"*

*"Umm. It's late, and I'm not sure what to say." No sense in lying.*

*"Say you're willing to try. Say this means I didn't lose you forever," he sounds so hopeful, I feel like the room is spinning.*

*"I answered."*

*"Thank God," He sounds muffled, like his phone's between his head and his pillow.*

*We're silent for a few breaths.*

*"Dear diary…" His sleepy voice sounds almost playful, and that deep scratch sends heat through my every muscle.*

*I blush, embarrassed, pulling my duvet over my head. "I know, oh my gosh. I felt so stupid for sending that, I tried to delete it, but you had already responded."*

*His laugh ripples through me, and I know in this exact moment, I'm going to end up giving in to him again. "It was a very Lailani response. Leave a nigga on delivered for more than eleven years, then pretend he ain't said shit, even though he sapped out, and poured his every emotion into words on a screen," he laughs again.*

*"Okay, don't do me like that. I had just finished reading a million freaking diary entries, and I didn't have any idea where to begin with a response. I haven't had to use that English degree in years, and words were lost at almost 1 a.m. My bad, sir." I'm smiling like an idiot, and the energy feels light.*

*It's quiet for another minute.*

*"I think it was the perfect start, actually. Especially because you already tried to race to the end. It was like a smooth, light-hearted Segway to a new beginning," he responds with a pleasantness that makes me smile.*

*"Maybe that's it," I muse.*

*Silence again.*

*"Fall asleep with me?" His voice seems so far away.*

*I think I mumble something, but I can't be sure because next thing I know, my alarm is going off, telling me it's 7 a.m., and I need to go to the store.*

Reelin tugs the blanket tighter around my knees, bringing me back to right now. His eyes are still burning into mine.

"I have never felt pain like that in my life, Lailani. Everything I have experienced, the people I have lost, even the parts of my body that have broken—all of it pales in comparison to you leaving me the way you did."

"Reelin…"

"No, Lailani," he shakes his head, and sits up taller, grabbing my hands in his. "I just need you to listen, please." He tilts his head, making sure I give him the space to speak. I nod.

"I wanted to die that day. I was so fucked up, I wanted to end my life, because I thought there was no way I could ever live without you. Your dad came out here not even a minute after you ripped my heart out of my chest, telling me I had to leave." He takes a breath, and the wrinkles between his brows deepen, "When I looked at him, I saw your eyes looking back at me. I know they're the same, and it might sound crazy, but I only saw you. The stars burned out, the sky fell, earth's core exploded, and all I could see was you, telling me to let you go. I couldn't handle that."

He pauses, and looks over to the opposite side of the yard. I follow his line of sight, and realize he's looking at the lemon tree. The exact spot where I told him to let me go, and left him there.

"Your pops must've seen it. He must've seen that I was gonna end it all, because right then, I don't think he was looking at me as your father. I think he was looking at me as someone he needed to save. Then he told me not to give up on you."

I jerk my head back to him at that. I didn't know my dad even spoke to him, outside of making sure he left, when I went back inside—let alone told him not to give up.

Reelin's eyes come back to me, "he told me that whatever it was you had just said, it was your own fear, and not to take it personal. He said it was you running away from me, because you didn't know how to accept us yet, and that you needed time. He told me so many things in those few minutes."

He pauses, squeezing my fingers. I concentrate on his face, and I realize that his hands are shaking, "I was listening to his words, and I could tell he meant them. He wasn't just saying shit to say it, or because he knows my history. I could feel him trying to reassure me, because he believed what he was saying. Your dad talked me off that ledge. He took me from locking in the image of you, and nothing else, as I decided to end my life in a single second, to a solid place of knowing I was gonna fight for you, until the end. He made me realize I had to hold on, because giving up would not have been worth it. He made me see that it was necessary to allow you your space, while making me feel like it wouldn't be forever."

His voice softens, "I was never gonna let you go. I didn't care how long it took. You tried to force our end, and no matter how much it hurt, I had to let you that day, because I knew it wasn't forever. You didn't yet realize that I am your end, Lailani. You are my end." He moves closer, his face a breath away from mine, "there is nothing past us."

I shiver, and hug my arms, trying to will away the tears that are threatening to turn this yard into something vaster than the ocean itself. Reelin pulls me into him, placing his chin on the top of my head.

"I know you don't like difficult conversations, so we don't have to talk about it anymore. I just needed you to know how I felt. I need you to understand that whatever this is that has you pulling away from me right now, I will always keep trying to show you why you don't have to." He presses a kiss to my forehead, "I just got you back. As long as you live, I will love you more than life itself, and there's nothing that has ever or will ever change that."

His arms squeeze me tighter, "you're cold, let's get you inside."

I nod against him then pull back, looking into his face. When his eyes find mine, I want to let go of every question, every doubt, and every bit of discomfort I've felt since I woke up in that pool without him this morning. I want to forget it happened more than anything.

I move the blanket away from my lap, and Reelin stands, unplugging it from the outlet. I uncurl my legs, and turn to stand, but my legs rebel against me. He sets the blanket back into the hidden cubby, and with a little extra effort, I stand, wobbling a bit, splaying my arms out for balance.

Reelin grabs my waist. "You okay?" His eyebrows are knitted together, and his fingers tighten around me. I can feel the warmth of his hands through my layers.

"Mhmm, just cold," I nod, looking toward the door to the house. He keeps one arm around my waist, and guides me to the opening of the pit area, then releases me to turn off the fire. I look over my shoulder, watching him. I don't want to tell him I don't feel comfortable walking by myself, because I'm not ready to explain why to him just yet. This day has been heavy enough, already.

The fire is off, and he picks up the gift box and a big tote bag I didn't even notice before. When he turns and comes back to me, he smiles, "you should've gone ahead." He shifts the box to under the crook of his left arm, with the tote in his left hand, then places his right hand on the small of my back.

I pull his hand around to hold, moving closer to him as we walk, "No point in leaving you out here, when I could walk in with you."

The way he smiles, squeezing my hand tight, makes me want to explode. He's so pleased by our closeness. I really only needed to hold his hand for safety, but this little bit of comfortable affection makes him feel good, and I feel like I'm supposed to keep him this way. His happiness feels worth anything, right now.

# 10 : Promises, Promises

When we walk in, Lonayla and Kieran are perched by the island, their faces plastered with grins as wide as the horizon. Kieran winks at Reelin and gestures to our clasped hands. Reelin releases my hand to set the box on one of the stools, then lifts the tote bag onto the countertop. As he shrugs out of his coat, I grab the counter's edge pretending to mindlessly trace it as I walk to a seat. Lonayla notices the action for what it is and looks at me expectantly. I shake my head and sit, pushing the Snuggie off my arms, and draping it over the back of the stool.

"We brought your favorite, I just forgot about it out there," Reelin pulls out three bottles of Veuve Clicquot, yellow label, setting them on the counter. "I'll put them in the fridge." He also pulls out a large bag of Hi-Chew candies, a box of zebra cakes, a family pack of almond Hershey's bars, a big bag of jumbo marshmallows, a box of both cinnamon and honey graham crackers, a package of Starbucks hot chocolate, and a pint of peppermint schnapps. The perfect fire-pit snacks, if you ask me.

"The cake is way better than all that right there, Rizz," Kieran says, reaching for the plate he left on the counter, gesturing to Reelin to give him another slice. Reelin ignores his silent request.

"La has always known how to make everything taste like it was actually made in heaven," he smiles at me, then starts picking up the snacks to take to the walk-in pantry. He really just remembers everything, it seems.

"Indeed, she has," my dad's voice comes in from the other side of the kitchen. "Reelin, Kieran, it's nice to see you two here," he gives them both a head nod, then goes straight to the cake.

Mom is beaming, "oh, I thought this one"—she jerks her head to me, as she walks up to Reelin, who sets the snacks back down on the counter, to embrace her—"was going to make sure we only saw you at your ceremony. We know she likes to keep you to herself." Mom winks, pressing her perfectly manicured pointer fingers into Reelin's dimples that are deepened by his cheesy smile.

"I'm very grateful to be welcomed. Sorry it's so late, I know y'all were bonding today. Heard it was a bit of a morning." He turns to my dad, patting his shoulder gently.

"We had a very interesting day for sure. But when the kitchen looked like the bake shop horror stories, it made it all better." Dad jokes, with blue frosting on his mustache.

Mom walks over to Kieran and Lo, squeezing Kieran's shoulder, "we should do Christmas Eve here, like when the kids were little, since both the girls are here. What do you say?"

"Jammy's meeting her boyfriend's family for Christmas Eve, and Kayde and Pooda are supposed to be doing some music thing in Florida. I don't think they even get back until Christmas morning, right?" Lo asks Kieran, who nods at Mom apologetically.

"Well, remind me to get their Christmas money to them before they leave, then. Just in case. I haven't seen any of them in a while." Mom gets herself a slice of cake. "So, are you two spending Christmas over here?" She looks between Kieran and Reelin.

Kieran looks at Lo, before answering, "of course. You know I love Christmas over here. I thought y'all were leaving on the 22nd, though?"

Reelin looks at me with a curious expression, then picks the snacks back up, taking them into the pantry. Lonayla and I look at each other, then I look at our dad, who looks back at our mom. Mom shrugs, taking another bite of her cake. We already told our parents they didn't know we were staying, because it was supposed to be a surprise.

Mom lets out an excited sound, "well, we're happy to have you! Reelin, it's been too long since you spent quality time with us!"

"Yeah, son. We're glad you're back in the family. Only you show up with champagne," Dad lifts a bottle in salute.

Reelin comes around the counter, standing beside me, "I can't begin to express how much I love being back here," without looking at him, I can hear his joy, and it makes me smile.

"We'll take this bottle, and see you kids later," Dad winks, and turns to leave, with Mom in tow. "We'll pretend my daughter didn't walk into this house looking worse for wear, and then worse than that, for now. Don't let it happen again."

"Or that's your ass!" Mom adds, now out of eyesight.

"Damn, I love them." Kieran smiles, and goes to the cake.

"Everyone does," I add, as my phone vibrates on the counter by the stove.

Reelin looks at the name on the screen, "who is Mario, and why's he calling at 11:30 p.m.?" He hands me the phone.

I press decline, then place my phone face down on the counter, "Literally no one."

Feeling a little warm all of a sudden, I pull the beanie off my head, and set it on top of my phone. I catch the look on both Lo and Kieran's faces when I shift in my seat, but I don't let our eyes meet.

"I thought ol' dude moved to Dubai or some shit. Gone forever." Kieran's tone is obvious. I look up, and his eyes confirm his irritation.

"He did, back in January," Lo says, eyeing me in question.

"Who is he, though?" Reelin looks at Kieran, "I ain't never heard about anyone named Mario."

"Literally no one, as I've already stated," I get up, and go to the pantry, surprisingly on steady legs, despite my sudden nervousness. "I've met a lot of people over the years. That was probably just a butt dial." I return to the island with the marshmallows.

Reelin has taken my seat, and is now looking at me with a weird expression, making the hairs on my neck rise. "What?" I ask, looking away from his face.

"Rizz, it probably was just a butt dial. I don't think we've even heard from him since before he moved. Right, La?" Lonayla walks around to me, taking the marshmallows I'm struggling to open.

"Umm..." My phone vibrates under the beanie, right in front of Reelin—whose eyes don't leave my face.

Kieran snatches it, answering, "ay, man. It's K. You know what time it is?" Lo passes me the open marshmallows, then walks over to Kieran, who's watching me with a look I'm not a fan of. "Nah, she ain't available. What's up?" I take a short breath, and shove a marshmallow into my mouth. Reelin keeps his eyes locked on me, and I avoid meeting his gaze.

Lo has her ear pressed against the other side of the phone. She looks over at Reelin, then back to me, then grabs the phone from Kieran, "hey, its Lo. Thank you for reaching out, but no. We're with family. You have a great time! Bye!" She hangs up, glaring at me, and I want to disappear.

Kieran walks over to me, eyes blazing, "Lailani, can we talk for a second?"

Without letting me answer, he grabs my elbow, guiding me through the hall between the back door and the refrigerator. If he weren't holding me so tight, I know my stiff legs would have given out, as I roll up on my toes with each step. He nudges me into the laundry room, and I immediately press my hand to the wall for balance, facing him as he closes the door.

In a very aggressive whisper he asks, "Why the fuck is Blacky Martin calling you about New Year's plans in the Swiss Alps? You fuckin' him?" I stare blankly at him, mouth still full of marshmallow.

Kieran raises his hands to his head, pulling the hair tie off his locs, then he runs his fingers down his face, stopping in his beard. "La, are you fucking dude?" His voice is just above a whisper, and I can feel the anger radiating off of him like a furnace, as he tries to keep himself calm.

I swallow, shaking my head. The marshmallow was way harder to get down than it should've been, but I manage, "no, Kieran. But that's none of your busine—"

"No!" He interrupts, leaning in, with brown locs falling into his face. He catches himself, lowering his voice again, "no. My cousin is sitting in there with his fucking heart barely beating—because he loves you, and you been trippin' on him all day. And now that sassy ass, fifty-year-old, wannabe-Puerto-Rican-Chris-Brown ass nigga is calling you, for an international booty call?" He pulls back, "of course it's my business!"

"Watch your tone," I warn, eyebrows raised, my head tilting, "I said no. I don't know why he called inviting me anywhere. I haven't heard from him since Labor Day weekend."

"Labor Day? When Lonayla was here? You were with him for Labor Day?" He paces the small space, hands on his hips. When he faces me again, he flicks his hair back aggressively, and then exhales, "you spoke to him, or you were with him?"

I don't say anything.

"Fuck, La!" He pulls his hair tie off his hand, turns around, and puts his hair back up.

When he faces me again, he sighs, leaning on the dryer, arms crossed over his chest, looking like a lost little boy. "So, you are fucking him? Is Rizz finna get his heart shattered again, Lailani? Because he thinks y'all are possibly starting over."

"Reelin's a complicated matter," I turn my body to match Kieran's, leaning against the washer with my own shoulder. "I'm not with Mario, though. Labor Day weekend was a one-time thing. He flew in that Friday, and popped up at the shop. We hung out for a bit, and then Sunday, when we went to dinner, I had a little more to drink than I planned. Next thing I know, I was leaving his hotel room, carrying my clothes and wearing his."

Kieran shakes his head in disgust, scrunching his nose at me, "but Rizz said he was talking to you that whole weekend? How was you on dates with Negro Iglesias?"

I shrug, "because it wasn't that deep. Can you relax? Us being in here is already making it seem like I'm doing something wrong—which I'm not.

It was once, that's it. I'm not interested in anything that man has." I push off the washer, tapping Kieran's cheek playfully. "Perk up, buttercup! I'm not whoring myself out to the highest bidder, or getting married to anyone just because they saw me naked."

Kieran twists his face further, then huffs a humorless laugh, "yeah, aight. But Rico-no-suave needs to never call you again, or I'ma have to handle that. I told yo ass he was gonna be a problem last year, when he bought that damn car. Niggas do too fucking much, and you just let 'em. Shit's sick."

I shrug, giving him an innocent smile. I can already feel the tension leaving his body.

"But seriously, Rizz ain't been as happy as he was last night in a long ass time. You did that, La. Pretty sure them dumb ass dimples got deeper, somehow," he pulls me into a hug, and kisses my forehead. "Don't be playing with him. You and me, we promised each other we'd keep it a buck, remember? We was just kids making that promise, but it's permanent. No takebacks. I don't care about your beef with forever either. This shit?" He pulls back, and gestures between us, "me and you? Our promise is forever. We locked in."

"Have I broken that promise yet?" I move to the door, my eyes wide, staring into his. "Hmm?"

He laughs again, and shakes his head, coming to open the door, "nah. So don't start now." We smile in agreement.

When we walk out, Lonayla's standing at the far end of the counter, by the back door. She looks at us, biting her cheek, nervously. After a few more steps, Reelin comes into view. He sits in the same seat, but now with his coat is on. His eyes are on me the second I see him, and his expression startles me. My body stiffens, halting my steps, and I splay my arms out for balance.

Kieran grabs my elbow, and his other arm smacks against my back. Lonayla's in front of me instantly, looking into my eyes, with my outstretched arm in her hand.

"What the hell? Is the floor wet?" Kieran looks around our feet.

"Nah, it's probably her slippers. She be putting them in the washer and the bottoms loses their grip." Lo looks at me for my confirmation, then takes my elbow from Kieran, guiding me the last few steps to the island. She releases me once my hand finds the counter, and looks at me to make sure I'm okay.

Reelin stands, "It's late. I didn't want to leave without saying goodnight."

Those wrinkles between his brows deepen, and I want so badly to run over to him, to reassure him that I'm not interested in another man. I don't know if I want to explain everything, though. Opening the conversation to our sexual partners, will only take me back to the random chick from the party, and if he lies to me again, I might make things very ugly.

I nod, "okay. See you Monday."

He looks at Kieran. "You riding?"

Kieran looks at Lo, and she looks back at me. I shrug, and look back to Reelin. His jaw is tight, and his lips are turned down. He seems to look at anything but me.

Kieran walks over to the cake, "yeah, Gimme a second." Reelin nods, reaching in his pocket for his keys.

Lonayla finally steps away from me, and walks over to Reelin, "I'll walk you out. La's slippers are gonna break her damn neck, and I might have to fight her to walk barefoot on this cold floor. I'll get her to bed safely, though." She looks back at me with a lopsided smile. Reelin doesn't acknowledge me again, and he and Lo walk out. That stings a little.

I let out a breath, and look over at Kieran.

"Lailani, that man will do whatever you ask of him. I know y'all have shit I don't know all the details of, to work through, but I do know he's been so hopeful since y'all started talking again. He was sure you'd come back, so he always had hope for real, but now it's like he got his spark back. He's moving different, and smiling more. Everybody's noticed it. All because he got access to you again. He gave you your space. He's done all the things, respected every boundary, no matter how ridiculous. The way you've kept him away? I wish Lonayla would have tried that shit. If I were him, I'd have been in your apartment waiting, when you got home, because ain't no game when I love you. But he's so serious about making sure you understand he just wants to do right by you."

He picks up his plate, looking thoughtfully at me, "your exact words to me all those years ago were, 'the end of the story can only be great if you make it so.' I got the shit tatted, so I never forget it. And while I fucked up a few times, you always made sure I remembered what I wanted in the end. You act like you don't know it, but that man's your end, La. Everyone seems to accept it, but you. You gotta be the one to make it great, though." He raises his plate in a salute. "You really can have it all, sis. You already know how he's moving behind you. All these chances are coming to you for a reason. Surviving life is better when you enjoy it, too."

He winks, walking toward the front door, "thanks for the cake, you really gotta bake more."

When Kieran leaves, I lean over the counter, with a groan, then walk around to sit. What all chances is he talking about? Reelin and my second chance? But what else? Is he referring to my life? That's the second time today he's made me feel weird—like he knows something more than me. I rub my chest, and focus my attention on the mostly eaten cake, but my mind takes me back to the first day of tenth grade, again. That's the same day Kieran and I made our promise to each other.

*New Message from Sissy: La, Kieran just showed up early to walk me to second period with a little bear and single red rose! I'm in looooooovvvvveeeeeee <3333*

*Sissy: and the muffin he didn't buy earlier! Even the teacher looked jealous. Lol*

*Me: oh, that's why he missed the whole first period. He left right after the homeroom blitz.*

*Sissy: he's so cute. mister rizz walkin' you to class? Kieran said you have almost the same schedule.*

*Me: I'm in the office right now, I got pulled right before the end of first. Coach V pulled me and Maliah. Something about practice changes. And that boy was in my class, but he didn't say a word to me the whole time. He's been looking at me funny since right after we dropped you off.*

*Sissy: looking like he's in love? Lol*

*Me: nah. Looking at me like my face was sliding off.*

*Me: like he's grossed out by me.*

*Sissy: not possible.*

*Sissy: Jessy's in my health class. Coach V didn't need her?*

*Me: idk, guess not. But get off the phone and pay attention. Jessy took health last year, and is sitting there with you because she wasn't paying attention. Don't be her! ttyl*

*Sissy: lol, I could neverrrrrrrr*

*Sissy: ttyl*

*I put my bag on the empty chair and lean back, as the final bell for second period rings. Maliah Harris sits next to me with her black leggings, orange satin cami, denim jacket and black flip flops, with her red kinky twists bringing out the freckles against her caramel skin. She's bobbing her head to no music.*

*"Maliah, why do you think coach pulled us?"*

*"When you left the gym this morning, Jessy said Coach was on a call, and she sounded upset. She mentioned roles that had to change or something. I don't know for sure though. She probably called you here because you're her prized setter, the*

*captain, and obviously her favorite, so she wants you to be cool with the changes." Maliah guesses.*

*I think for a second, "hmm. I don't know who would be switching roles, but I guess." I shrug, fidgeting with my bangles. Maliah's logic is lacking. If it's because Coach favors me, why call Maliah, too?*

*Coach V comes through the door a few minutes later, holding her keys and purse like she was out, "Grander, Harris, walk with me."*

*We gather our things and follow her. She takes us to the conference room at the end of the hall, then walks around the table and sits, squeezing her phone between her hands. Her green cardigan is open, and she's wearing a billowy white blouse, tucked into a black pencil skirt with pantyhose and black pumps. Her blonde hair that brings out the yellow in her hazel eyes, is tied up into braided up into a bun. Her usual warm caramel complexion seems a little dull, today. She never gets dressed to come to school, so wherever she was right before this, must have been important.*

*"Coach, everything okay?" I ask as Maliah and I sit.*

*She squares her shoulders, letting out an exasperated sigh, "The two of you are only being informed of this because you," She motions to Maliah, "Will find out through your mother this evening. And you," she looks at me, "will hear about this soon, too. I've asked your father to look into some legal things, and I'm aware of your close relationship with Kieran Michaels."*

*Maliah and I look at each other, then back at coach.*

*Maliah sits up in her chair, "What does my mom have to do with anything?"*

*I add immediately after, "my dad's a professional, so he wouldn't share your business. And Kieran is just a childhood friend. Wait, is he okay?"*

*Coach V lets out a heavy breath, "Miss Harris, your mother will be seeing a lot of me in the coming months, and because you frequent her workplace, I don't want you to be surprised at what you learn." She pauses. "You're aware I've decided to pull Kennedi from this school."*

*We nod. Coach's phone buzzes, and she looks at a message, with her brows bunching together.*

*"Coach, I'm just a little confused. My mom's a pediatric physician. Why are you seeing her?" Maliah asks, but my mind is already putting the pieces together.*

*Kennedi. Kieran. Coach's sickly pallor. Kieran's sudden bad attitude this morning. Mrs. Harris works at a private practice. Kennedi being taken out of school. Kieran talking about mistakes. Kieran. Lonayla. Heartbreak.*

*"Oh, God," I breathe out. I feel sick. "Kennedi. Oh, God."*

*Maliah looks at me, confused. I look at Coach, shaking my head, and she just nods, then looks down at her phone.*

*Maliah still doesn't get it, "what about Kennedi? Is she sick?"*

*I take a deep breath, and look to Coach for permission to say what I think I know out loud. She nods.*

*"Kennedi's pregnant, Maliah. She's having a baby, and your mom will be one of her doctors. My dad is—"I pause, because I actually don't know what my dad's doing.*

*"Your father will be assisting me in terminating paternal rights, and taking legal custody myself," Coach says in a matter-of-fact way.*

*Maliah's mouth opens and closes twice, like a fish. I slide down further in the chair, and let out a hard breath. I want to turn back time. I want to keep my sister from having to learn about this.*

*Coach sits up, clearing her throat, "I'm sure you both realize that this is a very important matter, and I'm trusting that neither of you will share this information." She looks pointedly at Maliah. "This is extremely sensitive, and no other student is aware of this situation. I don't want my daughter to be judged and ridiculed for the irresponsible actions of being a young teenager acting on foolish impulses, and peer pressures. This has already been tough enough. Your parents are aware that I pulled the two of you for this chat, so you may share your thoughts with them, and no one else.*

*Coach rolls her shoulders back, "This season will be a little different for me with practices. Grander, you will be running the Tuesday practices without me. Harris, please assist Grander in any additional needs for the team. We still want to have a winning season and that means we have to work together, even with me being a little less available."*

*"Yes, Coach," Maliah nods.*

*I can't believe this is happening right now. I also have so many questions.*

*"Okay. Are we dismissed?" I say, picking up my bag from the chair beside me.*

*"Yes. Have a nice day, ladies," We get up, and head to the door. "Grander?" She stops me. Maliah shrugs, and keeps going. "I take it you understand why this is so important? Why it has to be this way for your friend?"*

*I do. Coach is about to yank away Kieran's rights to his child, and there's nothing he can do about it. Kieran's life is changing no matter what happens, but with Coach taking custody, his life is ruined twice. Kieran will have a baby that he can't be a father to. Even if he is just fifteen years old, this isn't fair. They can't just strip his rights without giving him a chance. I have to talk to Kieran.*

*"Yes, Coach. Of course." I nod, and walk out.*

*I walk as quickly as possible back towards the office, reaching in my purse for my phone, and bump straight into Reelin.*

*"Oh, sorry" I say, as he says, "Excuse me."*

*He takes a step back, his eyes homing in on mine, "You okay?"*

*I feel a weird chill go down my spine, as he focuses on my face. I want to look away, but I feel pinned under his gaze. My cheeks, ears and neck heat.*

*"Junior, you can go back to class." Ms. Michaels, Kieran's mom, comes from inside the office. Thankfully, that distraction breaks Reelin's spell on me, and I can finally blink and look away.*

*"Hey, Lailani, baby. Nice to see you."*

*Kieran comes up behind her, and he looks so tired. His mom places her palm against his face, before she turns to leave. Reelin's still staring at me, but I try not to look at him*

*I turn to Kieran. "Can we talk?"*

*He nods, and turns down the hall that takes us outside. I follow him, and look back to see Reelin retreating down the other hall, back to class.*

*Kieran and I walk out to the picnic tables that are just outside the cafeteria. I sit on a bench, setting my things on the table at my back. Kieran sits on the table beside me, his feet on the bench.*

*We sit silent for a few minutes, then I ask, "You gonna be okay?"*

*"I gotta be the one to tell her, La," he places his elbows on his knees, and cradles his head in his palms. "I don't even know how this is happening."*

*"Kieran…" I want to say he knows exactly how, but stop myself.*

*He raises his head, looking at our reflections in the cafeteria windows, then starts talking, "It was the spring fling. Kennedi was all over me, and we were having fun. Remember how Gabriel Jackson was talking about how those apartments up the street had those open models with the fancy furniture?" I nod. "When Coach V left the dance, Kennedi said we should go see them. It was me, Kennedi, Gabriel and Yesenia, and Jessy brought that girl Kia. We walked over there, and it was just like Gabe said. The doors were unlocked, so we went in. We was all chillin at first, then we kinda started moving into separate areas."*

*He scratches at his head, stands on the bench, then jumps down, to stand in front of me. I lean back and cross one leg over the other, preparing to hear the story I know ends badly for my sister.*

*"It was so fast, La. It all happened so fast. I didn't even think about what was happening until it was happening. Then it was over. Everybody else was gone when we came out the back room. And when we came back to the school, we both acted like nothing happened, because that was what it felt like we should do." He sighs deeply, shaking his head. "Then, the last day of school, Kennedi asked me to come over."*

*"So, you did it again?" I ask, with my face scrunched up.*

*"What?" He shakes his head at me, in disgust, "no. When I got to her house, her dad was over there. He was standing at the door with Coach V, and Kennedi was looking all scared on the porch, then my mom came up behind Coach from inside, and I was even more confused. Coach told Kennedi to speak up, and that's when she said she was pregnant. I almost passed out, La."*

*"So, you've known this whole time? The whole summer?" I stand up, placing my hands on my hips, and walk around the table, trying to keep my cool. "So, my sister*

*was supposed to never know that you have a baby? You're a teenage father, and you thought no one was gonna know?"*

*He swipes his hands down his face, "no. By the time my mom and I left, we were told they were gonna take care of it. Mom told them she didn't believe in abortion, and Mr. Morris said he didn't believe in teenage pregnancy. How could my mom tell them what to do with their kid? She had no real say so, so we left. I figured that was the end."*

*I sit down, placing my forearms on the table, "so, if they were gonna take care of it, what happened?"*

*He sits across from me, grabbing my hands. His palms are so sweaty, and I can feel that he's shaking.*

*"I don't know, La. I spent the summer thinking it was a done deal. I hadn't heard from Kennedi. We heard she was being homeschooled at orientation. Both me and Mom assumed it was because her parents were punishing her for having sex. Between Rizz moving, and all our football stuff, we been mad busy. I ain't even think anything else about it, or I would've reached out. It's not right that she gets punished for something both of us did, you know?" I squeeze his hands, and he squeezes back, then pulls away.*

*"My mom got a call from your dad this morning, sometime after we got to school. He told her Coach V asked him to help her strip my rights. Mom texted me when we were at the cafeteria, to let me know what was happening. She came to get me, and we met up with your pops to discuss my options, during first period. He said we can talk some more once he figures out how far into this Coach V has already gotten."*

*"My dad is representing both you and Coach V?"*

*"Nah, he said he's only giving all of us our options. He said he didn't feel comfortable getting too involved. He gave us a few social workers to call, and some lawyer contacts he thought would be a good fit."*

*Kieran sighs, and his face looks so sad, "I didn't know this was still a thing until today, I swear. My mom said she'll figure out what to do next, and we'll go from there. But La, I ain't know. I would've never kept this from you, and I definitely wouldn't have kept it from Lo. You know that, right?"*

*I nod. "I'm sorry, this is a lot."*

*We sit for a moment. Kieran is looking at his hands, and I can tell he's seriously troubled by this.*

*"I gotta be the one to tell Lonayla. Your pops said he won't say anything, but I know he can't keep it to himself for too long. I know I have to tell her, before anyone else can."*

*"So, do you want to give up your rights? Or do you want to be a father to your baby?"*

*"I want whatever's gonna be best for the baby, so if that means I have to let Coach raise it as her own, okay." He pauses briefly, and the smallest sad smile comes across his face. "But if I get to be a dad? I would be the best one I could be. I'll get a job, I'll learn how to do everything, and I'll take them everywhere with me. Anywhere I can. I will love them so much, La. And I'll do whatever I have to do for my kid. You know my dad ain't a dad for real. Yeah, he makes sure we got money, but he chose his dreams over me. He doesn't understand that I would prefer him being here. He had a dad without money, so it doesn't make sense to him that I don't care about his."*

*Kieran looks me in my eyes, "but kids just want you to love them. So, I would want my kid to know that even without an active father myself, I did my best, no matter what. I'd want them to know that I'll always choose them, over anything else, and that I love them more than I could ever express. I'd want them to feel that every single day. I'd want my kid to grow up and be able to say that even at just fifteen years old, I still became the best damn daddy they could ever know."*

*I search his face, and I know he's sincere in wanting this. I want this for him, too. I can feel how much he means what he's saying. But what will this do to my sister? She's just a fourteen-year-old girl. She has so much life ahead of her, and she can't alter her own life for someone else's choices. This is going to break her young heart, but I won't let it ruin her. However this story is supposed to end, I'll do my best to make sure they're both okay.*

*"Kieran, I hope all of this works out in your greatest favor. I don't know what the future holds, but I do know my sister has cared about you since she was a little bitty girl. We were raised not to judge others, and to be as compassionate as possible, so Lonayla might still want to be your friend while you figure life out. I don't know*

*how she's gonna immediately take this, but she's young, and she will heal. You and Kennedi have to go through life differently now, and that's just y'all's cross to bear. I can't predict the future, but the end of the story can only be great if you make it so. I'm here, I got you. I'll still be here to keep it real with you, okay?" I reach across, and squeeze his hand.*

*"Yeah. I'll keep it straight up with you forever, too." He looks at his phone, and gets up.*

*"Let's get to class, Rizz told Mr. Lightly we're his lab partners."*

*"He in all my classes for real? Also, your mom called him, Junior,' just now?" I shake my head, "wait, you weren't in chemistry with me, when I looked at orientation."*

*"Ha, yeah, his pops' name is Reelin, too. Nobody in the fam calls Rizz that, though. We never have. He had different names growing up, but this one stuck. My mom wasn't with his new nickname for real. She said it sounded wrong, so she stuck with Junior. And nah, I think you still got a different fifth than us. Mom had them fix me and Rizz up, so we got the same classes. She said this way she can keep up with our homework easier."*

*He grabs my bag. "But for real, promise me you'll always stay solid, La. No matter what, promise we got each other. Always."*

*"I promise." I give smile, and pinch his arm. "Now fix your face, ugly lil' boy. You got this!"*

"La, you want me to walk you up?" Lonayla walks into the kitchen, bringing me back to the present, "you seem real shaky, tonight."

"Yeah," I stand. "Think we can hop on that plane, now?"

"So, you can get to the Panamanian Billionaire that ruined the evening? Absolutely not!" She jokes. "It's all gonna be just fine, Sunshine," Lo grabs my hand, and we walk to the stairs. "If Rizz is still looking all sad by Monday, I'll give the last of the cake to him. It'll be like a Band-Aid, but for his heartache."

She holds my hand all the way upstairs, watching my legs, and looking at me with too much concern. I try to ignore the pity.

When I get into my room, I'm immediately hit with exhaustion. It's been quite a day.

**Apple ID Sign In Requested**

**lkgrander@granderthings.me**

**Your apple ID is being used to sign in to a device near Atlanta, GA**

**Don't Allow      Allow**

I press don't allow. Whoever took my phone must have just turned it on.

I strip out of my clothes, do my hygiene routine, and fall into bed. When I close my eyes, those flashes start again, but I don't see any new ones this time. Maybe I'm overthinking things, assuming I know what's what without the full story. But I still need to know who the hell that girl at the party was, so I know what I'm supposed to do.

I woke up today when I know I was dead. I was given another chance at life, but I can't decide if it was to figure out why, and confront my would-be-murderer, or if God wants me to take this chance to finally let go of control, and fall all the way in love with Reelin.

I hope to gain some clarity by the time we get to church in the morning. If it's one thing I can't stand, it's uncertainty.

# Part ii : Sneaky Little Secrets

# 11 : Oh, No Thank You

*I kick and scream against someone who carries me away from where I was seated, safely on a solid surface. The fear that takes over me is an angry demon, laughing in the face of my pleas.*

*And then, I'm in the air.*

*There is no worse feeling than my limbs flying in every which direction, and my booming heart trying to escape my body to save itself.*

*Until I hit the water.*

*I am sucked under immediately. The fiery sensation that attacks my nose and throat makes my head sting. My ears are ringing, my eyes are burning, and I know that the tears in my eyes are only tiny drops in this blue hell I have been thrown into.*

*My body comes up, and I gasp with everything I am, begging the air to rescue me. It answers both in kind and with a rage that cannot be calmed. Oxygen invades my lungs with a vicious scratch, clawing at my throat chasing the racing waters that went down before it. The air is scorching my windpipe, not wanting this fluid intruder to leave anything behind.*

*The force of the wind expanding my lungs urges me to beg my furiously unrelenting captor to release me from its weightless wrath. I can see blurred images of the human figures in different colors of swimwear, but none of them move to help. I cannot form words, but I pray with all my might, that these brutal walls of chlorine madness have mercy on me.*

*The sudden realization that no one is going to save me, wraps me in an icy wall of sadness, then heats me with a feeling of pain I can never explain. I only hear my own screams echoing back to me, before the boundless monster takes me over once more.*

*This is how I die.*

*The deep is sucking me down, no matter how hard I try to rise. Kicking and peddling like I've been told so many times before, is not helping in the slightest. It's like I'm in a jar of molasses, losing my strength in a fight I never had a chance at winning.*

*Finally, the world goes black, ending the torment of existing in my suffering.*

I jolt awake, gasping for air with my eyes already filled with tears, and my heartbeat filling my ears. My sheets are soaked, my body is clammy, and every breath feels like there's molten lava filling my lungs.

I have only had the nightmare of the first time I knew I died in a pool once before. It was my freshman year of high school, when I would be returning to C.S. Williams for the first time since the summer before fifth grade. I never thought much about it after it happened, and I never mentioned the nightmare, either. I had a child psychologist who was supposed to help me cope, but the sessions were not all that useful. My mind chose to remove that day from my memory, and I never had a reason to want it back. Everything that led up to the moment I was thrown into the pool, completely left my head. Most of that summer did, actually.

When ten-year-old me woke up in the hospital, my parents were a mix of anger, sadness and gratitude. I couldn't recall anything that happened, but I knew who I was, who they were, and that my head and throat hurt. They told me that I panicked myself unconscious in the indoor pool at the high school, and that sometime after, my heart stopped. I never wanted to know more.

The doctors said I didn't suffer any serious brain damage or anything, and it was so lucky that I was pulled from the pool when I was. I handled the news of what happened rather well, joking about how black people don't swim for that reason. Lonayla had nightmares for months after the incident, but I was fine. My parents and doctors felt it best to let me deal with it however my mind felt necessary. I was more upset about having to miss the first few days of school than anything, but my family did everything to make sure I was okay.

I look around my room, focusing my energy on the calm the greens in my space bring me. The light of dawn is just barely creeping in, giving my walls a muted silver glow. I move to the edge of my bed, and sit with my feet planted on the floor. Taking a few shaky breaths, I shift to stand, and stretch my arms high over my head, concentrating my breaths and movements on each part of my body. After a few pulls and shakes, I can feel the tension release a little, so I walk over to my window. It seems the rest of the world is still sleeping.

I walk over to my bathroom to look at myself in the mirror. My eyes are still hollow, and my mouth seems to be leaning towards a permanent frown. My bonnet is drenched, so I remove it from my head, tossing it onto the counter. I shrug my shoulders a few times, then roll my neck. Everything seems too tight for comfort. I lift my boobs, hoping the missing weight will help with my weird chest pain. It doesn't.

"Lailani, what are you going through, girl?" I sigh, rubbing my hands over my eyes, then walk back into my room to change my wet sheets.

When I finish with my bedding, I grab a silk scarf from my drawer, and sit back on the side of my bed, taking my phone off the charger to check the time. It's almost 6 a.m. I walk back into my bathroom, thinking to put some oil on my edges, hoping my sweaty sleep didn't make them too terrible. I've already washed my hair in the last 24 hours, so I don't need to do it again. Surprisingly, my edges look fine, so I might just straighten my hair before church. Just need to make sure I don't want to lay back down first.

I check my phone again, disappointed there are no notifications from Reelin. I don't know why I expected there to be. I don't know how to feel about this shift in what I'm used to with him. I know we spent a lot of time apart, and we have probably become so many different versions of ourselves, but that doesn't make it any less uncomfortable. I hate the way he left last night. That look was one I have never seen before.

I want to say something to him, but what would be sufficient? How do I explain that a man I met while we weren't speaking, just so happens to want to buy me the world, and he wants to take me to beautiful places, and sometimes I let him, but as friends? And how do I even tell him that yeah, we slept together once, but it literally meant nothing, and won't happen again? We are definitely in complicated territory here.

I chew on my lip, and walk into my closet to figure out what to wear to church today. I stop short and grab one of my shelves, because my chest feels like it's being pressed through a woodchipper. I close my eyes to concentrate on my breathing.

*Reelin. Lonayla. Kieran. Classmates toasting. Reelin's laugh. People stripping down to get into the pool. Honey buns galore. Reelin's carving our Initials. Kieran's bragging about the pool dye. Random chick with her perfectness being perfect. Reelin's smile. Lonayla gives me another drink. Random chick reaches her hand to Reelin's cheek. Reelin's strange look. Cake. My reflection. Reelin and the random chick over by the woods to Nowhere, in a heated discussion. Kieran's discomfort. Pineapples. Someone's laugh. Random chick pulls Reelin's cheek to her lips, and he does not move away.*

I open my eyes. That was a new one, and I didn't like it. I decide that my mind just made that up.

When I turn, my eye immediately catches my computer on the small table to my reading chair. I think about opening it up to look into my first drowning incident as a distraction from my current thoughts, then decide against it. No sense in looking now, when I've never wanted to before. There were interviews when it happened, but they never made it to print, and the police reports were not made public. My dad did everything in his power to prevent me from being triggered by a kid at school with information, because I didn't remember. When people asked me or my sister what happened, my response was always, *"I told y'all I can't swim,"* and I would leave it there. Lo would usually just start crying. It took a long time for her to be okay again. I felt so bad for her, even though I couldn't understand why she was so dramatic about it, since I was alive. But she knew what actually happened that day, and I didn't.

It's becoming clear that I'm awake for the day, so I should get a head start, and go make my tea. I walk out of my room and see that Lonayla's light is on, underneath her door. I knock, but she doesn't answer. I knock twice more, and then let myself in.

"Lo?" I call out, not seeing her. Her main light, her bathroom lights, and her closet are all on. "Lonayla?" She still doesn't say anything, but I hear movement in her closet, so I walk over, looking inside. She's putting a large black box into the corner, then turns.

"Oh My God!" Lonayla yells, then rushes over, nudging me away, and closes the closet door behind us, "what the fuck are you doing sneaking into my room like that?"

"I saw your light was on and knocked multiple times. I also called your name. Twice." I raise my eyebrows at her angry face, "what are you doing up?"

She looks me over, and her nose wrinkles, "why do you look like that?"

"Why do you?" I hold her stare.

"I was looking for something, but you look kinda sick," Lo walks over to her bedroom door, "you up for a reason?"

"Had a bad dream. I'm gonna go make my tea, then I might straighten my hair." I look around her room, at the clothes piled all over the place, "why is your room a disaster?"

She clears her throat, grabbing my attention, "you gonna straighten your hair before church?"

"Thought about it," I move closer to her and she shifts, so now, I'm in the doorway.

"I feel fat. Wanna get in a quick workout before we gotta get ready?"

I think for a second, feeling the tightness in my lower back and behind my knees, "yeah, actually. I think the cold has me a little more messed up than usual."

"Cool, I'll meet you out back in 10. Mommy goes in there before church, too."

"She ain't gonna let me work out, Lo. She freaks out when I stretch too far for her comfort."

Lonayla laughs, "she thinks pilates is the answer to everything. She'll be fine, especially if we only do floor."

I shrug, "okay. Let me change, I'll meet you out there."

Lonayla starts closing her door, making me back away, like she's rushing me out of her space.


In my room, I walk back over to my phone, thinking about texting Reelin. I don't know what to say, but I feel like even in my current confusion about why he left me—and why he keeps pretending it didn't happen—I need him to know that I'm not giving any other person my attention.

Since we first started dating, it was clear that neither of us were interested in anyone else. Reelin's as intelligent as he is gorgeous with a dope personality, and he's always carried himself exceptionally well. There was never a shortage of admirers for that man. Some would even try their luck, doing any little thing to get his attention, but he never once wavered. I'm cute and all, but I'm very standoffish as soon as someone shows too much interest in me. I've always been this way, even with Reelin. He somehow managed to woo me out of my personal pact to wait until after college to date.

When I left him all those years ago, I had my mind set on being single and celibate for the rest of my life. Naturally, my sister and other people I knew would make me feel insane for not getting out there, but I wasn't into it. One night, about two years after I left, I thought about reaching out to Reelin. I was feeling so good about my business and life in Miami, and I felt like it would be even better if I could share my joy with him. But Lonayla was on the phone with Kieran, and he and Reelin were out somewhere. I heard her say she hoped they both caught something they couldn't get rid of, and it made me feel silly for thinking he'd just be available for me after two whole years of radio silence. I didn't ask her any questions. I just changed my mind about calling, and told her we should go out that night too.

I started hanging out with a guy who owned the apartment building Lonayla and I used to live in. He was a constant for a little while, but it was never that serious for me. He wanted a wife, and kept trying, but I told him that would never be me. I actually introduced him to the love of his life, though. She was a sweet girl from Oregon who had been coming to my shop for a while. She and I built up a nice rapport, and I told her I knew a man she would like. I tricked him into meeting her at my shop one day, and they really hit it off. Once they married, he relocated so they could raise a family in her hometown. He bought me a boat, as a thank you.

I don't know if me telling Reelin about the people who came into my life during our time apart would make things better by opening the lines of communication further, or if he would have issues with it. I feel like as single people, we could have done anything during that time, but I also know I don't want to know everything he's been up to. I only want to know who that ridiculously beautiful girl who's been popping into my memory is, because she came to our party, and I don't know why she would be there. She was clearly not someone else's significant other, if she was so focused on me and Reelin, so I need to know if I came home and interrupted his life with someone else. But also, for more than a year now, he's been telling me that I'm supposed to be with him. There's no way he'd be that scummy, right?

Whatever he did while we were apart, wasn't my business, and I didn't care to make it so. When we started talking again, I made it very clear that we had to take things slow, and he seemed okay with respecting that. Neither of us asked about private affairs. We have to learn each other again, and because I decided we had to be completely no contact, I don't feel like I deserve to ask any invasive questions about his personal life.

I will say that I know he's been giving people every reason to fall in love with him, and I can only imagine how much more intense he's gotten over time. I know all too well what it's like to be with him. He gives all the feels of those 90s love songs, without even trying. His focus, his intention, and his consistent effort go to levels people write about in romance novels. In every way, Reelin is everything anyone could ask for.

Or at least he was, before he left me for dead.


I set my phone down, deciding I can't think about the "what if's" or play the who's-been-in-his-bed game. I can't help wondering if I'm going about this all wrong. His mood shift from last night really bothers me, but I was supposed to keep him at a distance until I figure out what to do about my would-be-murderer, so I really shouldn't care how he feels. Should I? Because Lord knows I do, and I hate this for me.

I shrug off these feelings that are trying to weigh me down. If I stay in this headspace, I'll either end up on the floor sobbing for the foreseeable future, or in bed. Whether it would be mine or Reelin's, is up for debate. This whole mess has me all over the place. There's no time for this when I'm supposed to work out with Lonayla. I pull on a pair of compression leggings and a sports bra, then head down to our home gym, seeing Mom is already inside.

"Hey, Ma! Can I join you?"

She smiles up from the rebounder, and motions to the yoga mats on the side wall.

I grab a mat, then get positioned in the open space, "Lo's coming down, too."

Lonayla walks in, and Mom winks, "your father's coming in here too!"

"Okay! This can be a thing! We can call it "Fine Ass Family Fitness, or whatever!" Lonayla laughs, setting up a yoga mat for herself.

"Lailani, take it easy please," Mom side eyes me.

Dad walks in with a smile plastered across his face, "well, ain't this a sight to see? My Grander girls up well before church to get in some movement. I love this." He walks over to the treadmill, powering it on, "Lailani…"

"I know, Daddy… I'll take it easy." I shake my head.

Mom starts her instructional video, and we begin our workout.

# 12 : Pray About It

"Lailani, let me have it!" Mom is standing in the front room, hugging the coat Reelin gifted me last night, when I reach the bottom of the stairs, carrying my shoes.

"You can literally buy your own! I'm just the poor little sister who works in La's store. If anyone deserves it, it's ME!" my sister whines, with her arms crossed, beside our mom.

I shake my head, and the corner of my mouth turns up. "The way this family plays broke is crazy. I literally just got it as a gift. It hasn't even been a day. I lost my coat, remember?" I drop my black slingbacks to the floor to put them on.

"Not my fault you're irresponsible!" Mom quips with a little laugh, hugging the jacket tighter. "I think the color makes it prettier than the other one."

"I said the same thing to Kieran! I didn't even see this color way when we went and got our last ones." Lonayla walks over to me, handing me one of the dainty gold watches she was holding, "Daddy said these were getting cleaned last time I was here, and we should wear them today."

I put the watch over my left wrist and my sister clasps it, "I haven't seen this watch since Granny-Gran's funeral."

"He said they were in the file cabinet out in his studio, and he didn't know how they got there," Mom is walking around the stairs to the closet beneath them. "La, your dress will go better with my cranberry peacoat, today. You wear that one, and I'll wear yours." She walks back to me, extending her jacket that is almost the exact color of my midi length, long sleeved dress.

"Nice try," I say taking my jacket from her other hand to put it on. "I happen to want to wear the one I was so nicely presented with."

"Ah, boo!" Lonayla takes mom's jacket. "I'll wear this one, just gonna go up and change my shoes." She says as she races up the stairs in her black midi dress that has short puffy sleeves, her low ponytail flopping behind her.

"You ladies ready?" Dad comes around the corner in his navy suit with an ivory top, forest green tie and navy dress shoes, matching Mom who has on her forest green midi dress, ivory, green and navy scarf tucked in at her neck, and navy kitten heels.

"Lo went to change her shoes." I say, putting my second small gold hoop into my ear, then fluffing my hair. I didn't have time to straighten it this morning, but I felt cute when I took out my two braids.

My sister comes down the stairs and we start out the front door. When I step onto the porch behind my mom, who is looking in her purse for her offering pouch, I immediately spot Reelin, getting out of his chocolate brown Mercedes GLE coupe, in the driveway. I reach for my mom's hand that's holding her purse open, gripping it tight. She looks at me, then follows my gaze.

"Oh, Reelin! Coming to church with us?" She shouts. He nods, walking toward us, smiling at my mom like an innocent little boy. "How lovely!"

Mom looks back at me with a questioning look, gesturing to our hands, wondering why hers is in a vice grip. I feel her try to pull away. I tighten first, but then release her to grab hold of the banister.

Lonayla steps outside now, "Rizz, I didn't think you'd be ready in time!" I jerk my head to her, and she passes me down the porch steps, "I also told you to meet us at the church." She hugs him, then answers her phone, walking to my dad's car.

I hear Dad chuckle behind me as he's locking the door.

Mom steps down and walks into Reelin's hug, "This is such a treat!" she pats his cheek and walks to the car after Lo.

"I take it you'll be driving Lailani?" Dad asks Reelin as he passes me, too. I continue to hold the banister, as if my life depends on it. "You want Lonayla, too? I won't be mad! I know she's arguing with Kieran already, look at her!" He nods his head to where my sister is standing just past the cars, whisper-yelling into her phone.

Reelin laughs, "I would be happy to drive both of your beautiful daughters to church, if they'll let me." Dad pats his shoulder lovingly, then walks over to open the door for my mom to get into the car.

Lonayla comes around to the passenger's side and Dad opens her door, too. He looks back and smiles, shaking his head, then gets into the car himself.

Reelin looks at me and steps closer to the bottom step. I'm feeling more nervous now, without anyone able to hear what he's about to say. The face he gave me last night is in my mind, and I'm a little worried about why he's here.

He extends his arm to me, "May I?" I take his hand, praying I don't lose control of my body with this man.

"I wasn't expecting to see you, today," I say, stepping down at last.

"Does it bother you?" He asks, guiding me to the car.

My dad toots his horn, and Mom's window rolls down, "y'all be safe!" Dad shouts, before they pull off and out of sight.

Reelin opens the passenger's side door, and waits for me to get in. Thankfully, we did pilates this morning, so my muscles are warm, and my legs don't stiffen. As the door closes, I put on my seatbelt and take a nervous breath to calm myself. When Reelin gets to the driver's side, he stops at the back door, removing his gray suit jacket. His button down is crisp white, and his tie is the same color as my dress. Lonayla clearly told him what I was wearing. I bite my cheek and look straight ahead. Reelin drapes his jacket over the driver's seat headrest before getting into the car himself. He reaches behind my seat, pulling up a beautiful bouquet of pink peonies and white roses.

"These are for you."

I take them into my lap. "They're beautiful, Reelin. Thank you." I stare at the flowers with my brows furrowed.

"Why do you look so pained?" I look at him, and his eyes look so soft. I'm not sure what changed from last night to today, but his expression is such a stark contrast, it feels like a trick.

"I thought you were mad at me?"

He lets out a small sigh, putting on his seatbelt, and starts the car. "Lailani…" A pause. He shakes his head, then pulls out of the driveway and starts down the road, "whatever that was, it doesn't change anything for me. I didn't like it, but I love you the same, regardless."

I frown and look back at the flowers. I don't know if I should try to explain, or if I should leave the subject alone. My phone vibrates. I reach into the little crossbody bag under my jacket to pull it out.

**New Message from Sissy: Mom said ask Rizz if he wants to do dinner**

**Me: No.**

**Sissy: She said don't be difficult.**

**Me: I'm not**

"My bad, it's Lonayla." I say to Reelin.

"Do ya thang. I ain't trippin'."

**Me: When did you even talk to him?**

**Sissy: Right after pilates. When I was on the phone with K, Rizz was pulling up to the house with Jammy. She had her lil' boyfriend at his house yesterday, putting together the centerpieces for the ceremony on Tuesday, so she stayed the night.**

**Me: Oh.**

I lock my screen and look out the window. Reelin's car notification goes off, and it takes everything in me to not look at the screen in the dash.

No matter how weird it feels to think about, it's not my place to know who's on his phone. He presses a button, and the car voice tells me anyway.

**New Message from Lo: Mom said do you wanna do dinner?**

I immediately text Lonayla.

**Me: REALLYYY??????!!!!!!!!!!** 

Reelin is frowning, but straightens up and taps reply, speaking into the car, "I have to make sure your sister's good with that. Plus, I think I have to pick Payzlie up, but I'll let you know."

I look at my phone. Lo left me on read. The car notification goes off again.

**New Message from Lo: Mom said what if we pick up Pooda, and to see if Jammy and Kayde wanna come to dinner, too?**

I look at Reelin as he stops at the red light. He stares ahead for a moment, with a contemplative look on his face, "what are you thinking, La?"

"I'm not thinking anything," I answer a little too quickly.

"Are you good with dinner?" he looks at me with hopeful eyes.

"Sure. Do what you want."

"I want to do what YOU want." The light turns green, and he turns his attention back to the road.

"If dinner makes you happy, I'm good with it." I look back at the flowers on my lap.

Reelin speaks into the car again, "can you text the group to see if they're all available?"

"Y'all have a group? And what happened to Payzlie's car?" I ask.

Reelin smiles, "yeah, we've had a group a couple years now. We had to have one place to communicate since they always got so much going on, especially with them being so grown now. Pooda's been scared to drive since her first accident, so we been taking turns taking her to and from her job on the weekends. And you know Jammy is spoiled as hell. We want her to do anything, we gotta drive her 9 times outta 10." He chuckles lightly, "and that boy Kayde, he be busy with his basketball and all the lil' girls, just like his dad."

"Oh, my nephew is nothing like his pappy," I laugh out, "and Jammy always wants to drive when she's in Miami."

"That's because Jammy likes your car. She has a Nissan, and that ain't good enough for her. Babygirl is just as bourgeois as Lo. It's still wild she wasn't the one who gave birth to her."

We both laugh.

While Kieran and Lonayla were already complicated, things only got crazier after he told her Kennedi was pregnant. Lo never even shed a tear about the situation. Kieran told her everything, right after school the day we found out. Lo was so understanding, and she even offered Kennedi her support. She tried to throw a baby shower and everything, but Kennedi was against it. She insisted she didn't want Lonayla trying to pay her way into her child's life, especially when Coach V was originally supposed to raise the baby as her own.

Kennedi thought she was going to get back to her teenage life after she gave birth, but Coach decided not to take custody after all. Kieran's first statement at the court-ordered paternity test was what changed Coach's mind. She was surprised by Kieran's sincerity and all the steps he took to do the right thing.

Jazmynn was born that New Year's Eve. Lonayla was in the hospital waiting room with Kieran, his mom and our parents. Laila and Lonnell Grander are going to support their kids no matter what, so they were along for the ride with my sister and this complicated situation.

Once Kennedi took the baby home, she started treating my sister like she was the enemy. Anything Lonayla bought the baby went to the trash, and she would say Kieran needed to replace those things. It was two full weeks of chaos; I felt so bad for the baby. Kennedi started threatening to kill herself if Kieran didn't break up with Lo, and when that didn't work, Kennedi took it even further. Lonayla learned that Kennedi told Kieran she would make up whatever story gave her full custody, if Kieran didn't break up with her. That's when my sister decided to date other people. She refused to come between Kieran and his daughter, and she didn't want anything happening to Kennedi after doing her own research on postpartum.

The next few months were like a battle of who could make the other more jealous. Lonayla or Kieran?

Kieran won the war.

Near the end of March, we learned that both Alexa Davenport, a senior, and Bianca Levy, a junior, were pregnant. Lo cried this time, especially because both girls shared the news during her birthday weekend, while she and Kieran were in a fight. Lonayla was a wreck because Kieran was having two more babies, and she was still a virgin freshman, trying to prove to him that she was better than all the other girls.

I could've killed him myself. I hated the whole situation and tried to write Kieran off. Lonayla was adamant that I didn't pick sides, because Kieran and I were always friends, but I do not play about my sister. By the time both girls started showing in May, Lonayla was trying hard to be their friend, and Kieran was right back to trying to win my sister over.

Bianca gave birth to Payzlie in October, and Alexa had Kayde in November. All three baby mamas hated my sister, because Kieran still wanted her, and he made sure they knew it. Because my family could afford to help them care for their kids, they stopped with the threats of keeping their babies away, and would accept our assistance. By Jazmynn's first birthday, Lo was allowed to spend time with her at Kieran's, as long as his mom was there. By spring break, Lo was baby-sitting Kayde, and by summer, Kieran and Lonayla were taking all three kids to the park together, like a little family.

Lonayla and Kieran would break up and get back together so often, Lo started going through his mom to see the kids. Jazmynn, in particular, became very attached very young, and soon, Lonayla was keeping her on weekends at our house.

During the second semester of her junior year, during one of their many breakups, Lo started dating Jessy Rodriguez. Her "lesbian phase" was very odd, to say the least. Kieran then made it so Lo couldn't see the kids if she wanted to keep throwing her relationship around. That only made her act out more. She took Jessy everywhere, made sure everyone knew she was in love, and would pretend she never even liked Kieran at all.

Lonayla went the whole summer before her senior year without seeing the kids, and she hated it. She gave in and broke things off with Jessy in a messy, public way, to prove herself to Kieran. She changed her relationship status to single on Facebook, and made a picture of Kieran and all three kids her banner.

When Kieran started college and Lo was a senior, they decided to call a truce. No more fighting, no more keeping the kids away, and no more games that could hurt each other. But because they had major trust issues, they would end up in messy places again.

Coach V reached out to Lonayla shortly after the first week of school, asking if she'd like to start keeping Jazmynn a few nights a week. Lo begged our parents to allow this, because no matter what, she was a mother—even if she didn't birth these kids. By January, she would have at least two of the kids at any given time, and Kieran would only visit when Lonayla had them, to avoid the drama. Lucky for them, she had the kids more often than not.

By the time Lo started college, Jazmynn was with her Tuesdays, Wednesdays, and every weekend. Naturally, the other kids started joining more often, too. When I moved to Miami, Lonayla had already put it in her mind she would follow. She sat down with Kieran, his mom, and all three baby mamas to discuss being able to visit when she moved away. They all agreed, after crazy negotiations that were, in my opinion, not in Lo's favor. She and Kieran would pay for their after-school daycare at places of Kennedi, Bianca and Alexa's choosing. Lo would do back-to-school shopping in August and January, as well as pay for any school related expenses. In exchange for this, Lo got them for every spring break, and as long as she could in the summers. She went home for holidays to be with them, and even when Kieran could not travel because of school or work, Lonayla still got the kids. She did this all their lives, and now Jazmynn has graduated and is in college, and Payzlie and Kayde are high school seniors.

Kieran has asked my sister to marry him about a thousand times, but she always says she knows he isn't serious. They raise these kids together, and they seem to be unable to live without each other, but it's like she doesn't believe he'll ever be serious. She loves those kids like they're hers, though. They basically are.


The car notification goes off again:

**New Message from Lo in FamBam:  Y'all all up for dinner with your Grandys?**

**Kayde: what time?**

**Jammy: Can Micah come?**

**Lo: 5:30, and yeah. Is he driving?**

Reelin and I both keep glancing at the display, as the messages come through.

**Lo: Pooda?**

**Kayde: she at work**

**Jammy: he can. where we eating?**

**Lo: Grandyla is cooking**

I smile at that. Mom loves making big meals.

**Jammy: Oh, absolutely**

**Kayde: I'll be there. Grandypa gon play for us?**

**Lo: You know it**

**Lo: Rizz we at the church, y'all close?**

**Jammy: Who is y'all?**

**Lo: wrong thread**

**Jammy: too late! Who is it? 👀**

"How long has it been since the kids have been over?" I ask Reelin.

"I think not since Easter. I'm not sure, but I feel like that's the last time I heard they were there. Everybody be busy."

**Lo: he's driving your auntie La**

**Jammy: ooh, that's cute 🥰**

**Kayde: bout time**

**Pooda: My bad, it got busy. Dinner? Fasho! Auntie La making some desserts? 😛**

**Kayde: I feel like she owe me some cherry turnovers now that I think about it**

**Lo: she baked a cake**

I laugh, "I don't think there's enough cake left for them."

**K: y'all blowing up my phone. Lo, why you ain't answer? Where u at?**

**Pooda: Daddy you goin' to church? 👀**

**Jammy: you want the church to catch fire?**

"They ain't right!" I laugh.

Reelin laughs too, "But are they wrong?"

**K: y'all ain't right. And I'm in the church, for your information.**

**Lo: stop lying 😓**

**Kayde: ain't no way**

**Jammy: *FaceTime screenshot of Kieran in church***

**Jammy: Y'all, hell has frozen over**

**Kayde: Tell everyone to take cover!**

**Pooda: STOP DROP AND ROLL!** 🥵

**K: only flames is my fit. Y'all know y'all pops is HIM** 🕺🤮

**Jammy: If y'all could see his face, rn. You'd be embarrassed.**

**Pooda: bro, who got you to church?**

**Kayde: auntie La done made pigs fly? She came home, baked, she wit uncle rizz, pop's in church, what else?** 🤔

**Pooda: next, y'all gon tell me auntie La is pregnant** 🧕

"Oh, hell nah. They're crazy," I scrunch my nose, and let out a breathy laugh.

**Lo: lmao! I wish! I'm ready to be the auntie!**

**Jammy: Lo, daddy's by the bathroom**

**Lo: I see him**

We stop at the light that turns into the church.

"They get started in there and can go all day," Reelin shakes his head.

"Teenagers," I smile.

**Kayde: where is uncle rizz at? Respond! We having a baby?**

The light turns green and we turn into the church lot. Reelin presses the car button to speak his reply, "we're pulling in, y'all still by the bathrooms?"

**Jammy: uncle rizz you got a baby?**

**Lo: yeah**

**Pooda: YEAH?!!!** 🤣😍🤗

**Jammy: WHAAAATTTTTT??? OMG!!** 😩😍 **Don't play with me right now!**

**Kayde: hell yeah!** 😏

**Lo: no! yeah, we're by the bathrooms!**

I shake my head in quiet laughter.

Reelin responds, "Just parked, be there in a sec."

**Kayde: be careful with my auntie, bruh. she's walking for two**

**Pooda: I'm crying** 😂 **what if it's twins?**

**Kayde: walking for three then! Make it four, for fun**

**Jammy: Ha! Imagine her having triplets with them green eyes for real! Aw. I'm so excited! it took entirely too long!** 🥹

I gasp. "Oh my."

Reelin pulls into a parking space.

**Kayde: a boy name is Kayde, I call it! for a girl, Kadyn.**

**Pooda: Man, you know they prolly gon have R names**

**Kayde: Rayde, or Radyn, then**

**Jammy: LMAOOOOO!** 😂 **Rayde gives roach spray, brother.** ❌ **Sounds dirty** 🙅🏿

Reelin turns off the car, so I can't see the messages pop up anymore. I suddenly wish I was in their chat.

"They're a mess," I say, as Reelin takes the flowers from my lap, placing them in the back seat.

"They get it from their mamas," he laughs. "All four of the mamas and their daddy, actually." He looks at me and I swear his eyes sparkle. "Shit, their Auntie La, too!"

I squint my eyes behind my smile, "Whatever, mister." I take a look in the rearview mirror at my hair, then put my phone into my bag. "I think it's cute how close y'all are."

He looks at me from outside of the car, putting on his jacket. "I knew y'all were close, but the way they talk to y'all, I love it. I thought it was just Lo and Kieran because of how they grew up. They talk to them like friends. I always loved that comfort."

"I think it's best to be as friendly as possible with the kids, but to be parents when it's time. I think they have a good balance," he walks around to my side of the car, helping me out, like a gentleman, and we walk toward the church entrance. "With me, it's a time and a place, but for the most part, they're respectful kids. You remember when they were younger, they spent more time at your parents' than anywhere else. That time is what shaped them, for real. They had that old-school influence from your mom and pops. A lot of kids their age don't have that."

"Yeah, I love that they grew to be such good people. They're so fun, too." I smile. We're almost at the doors. "And they just keep getting better with time."

"That's partly because of all the time they spend with you, too," he places his hand on the small of my back, guiding me through the open door to the church. "You look beautiful, by the way." His voice is low, and the little crackle in the back of it lingers, radiating through me in a way that is very inappropriate in the Lord's house.

I blush. "You don't look so bad yourself, Uncle Rizz."

The smirk that appears on his face makes me feel like I need to repent. "I don't know, the kids seem to like the idea of "Daddy Rizz" better." I freeze, looking at him in shock. I could have fallen out right then. Had his hand not been firmly on my back, I probably would have.

Lonayla comes up behind me, "Hey! Mom and Dad saved seats." She's all smiles with Kieran at her heels.

"Let's enjoy a beautiful sermon today, my beautiful brother and sister," Kieran winks, and we follow him and Lonayla into the sanctuary.

We're walking out into the lobby when Reelin reaches for my hand, squeezing it intently, "I feel like that sermon was for us."

I felt that way, too. Halfway through his sermon, Pastor started with Colossians 3:13 out of nowhere, then finished off with 1 Peter 4:8. I don't remember his initial message, because I was distracted by my mom reaching over in tears, and squeezing my hand. She was obviously thinking the same thing once the messages turned into what they turned into.

"I think any time someone misses church for a while, the day they return, it feels like the message was specifically for them," I smile and look to the door, where Kieran is standing by himself.

I look around, "Did you see where Lonayla went?"

"I think she was talking to the first lady." He leads me over to Kieran, who seems to be buzzing in place.

"Y'all, I'm gonna propose to Lo again today," he removes his hair tie, shaking his crinkled locs free. "No sense in waiting. I know that sermon was for us." I wink at Reelin, and he jokingly rolls his eyes.

Kieran shifts his weight, looking past me, "Lonayla did, too. She literally couldn't stop crying. She's in there with Pastor and the first lady, probably telling them about how much she wants to be released from me, but I love her. I need her to finally say yes."

"Stop it. Ain't no releasing. She is clearly in it with you, forever." I pat his shoulder.

Reelin's hand squeezes mine again, "I'm sorry, did Lailani Grander just reference something being forever?"

"Oh, shit," Kieran's shoulders hunch. "She's definitely leaving me, if Lailani is talking about forever." He turns, walking outside with his hands on his head.

I call after him, "Because Lo believes in forever! Also, Language!"

I shoulder-nudge Reelin, "Go after him."

"It's only been a little more than a day, and you believe in forever, now?" He smiles, "Maybe all that drinking has been a good thing."

"I wasn't even drinking that much, thank you. And no. Lonayla believes in forever. That's what I was saying," I insist with a firm nod.

"But you said it like you did, and that's a step in the right direction." He gives me a smile that says a million beautiful things, and I feel that familiar flutter in my chest. When he releases my hand to go after Kieran, it's like he took my breath with him. I try to suck in the air, slowly.

"Where they goin?" Lonayla says to me, as she crosses our elbows.

"Kieran thinks you're leaving him," I shrug. We walk towards our parents.

"I've been leaving him my whole life. It never sticks," her eyes are puffy.

"The sermon got you, huh? It got your man, too," I lean into her.

"It was a lot. But I was thinking more about you," she looks over her shoulder. "La, you literally defied death, and it was obviously for him. Please stop acting like you don't love that man."

"I am not acting," I rush out the words then smile as we reach Mom and Dad. "Beautiful sermon, yeah?"

"Where are the boys?" Mom looks over our shoulders, "we still doing dinner?"

"Ma, it's only 11. We have plenty time before dinner." Lo lets out a little laugh. We all turn to head out the doors.

Reelin appears at my side, "will you go to brunch with me?" Lo loosens her grip on my arm, but doesn't let go. Reelin addresses her, "Kieran is at his car. He would like you to join him, as well."

"See y'all at home," My dad tosses over his shoulder, walking mom to their car.

"Wait! I didn't even answer him, and you're just leaving me?" Dad laughs, throwing up the deuces. I shake my head.

Reelin holds his elbow out to me, and I slide mine into his. Lo is still on my other arm.

"Lo, you good?" Reelin asks her.

"Yeah, just thinking," we get to Reelin's car, and she sees Kieran parked a few spaces over. "He really came to church. I can never get him here. Every time, he refuses, so what's different?" she looks at me, now in the car. Reelin is holding the door open. "You think it's the end, La? Like he's throwing me a bone because he's officially over me? A little 'Here ya go' kinda goodbye?"

"That makes absolutely no sense. He did something you want him to do, and you think it's a bad thing?" I twist up my face, "you two are actually insane."

Kieran comes over, "who's insane?" he reaches for Lo.

She takes his hand and moves close to him, "Apparently we are. What made you come to church?"

"I thought it would make you happy," he pulls her closer, kissing her temple. "Are you happy?"

My sister's eyes mist over, "yeah."

She gives me and Reelin a soft smile and they walk off to go to Kieran's blacked-out BMW X7. Reelin closes my door and gets into the car a moment later. Just before we pull out of the parking lot, his car notification goes off.

**New message from K: Tell Lailani.**

**K: She deserves to know.**

I probably shouldn't have read those messages, because now all I'm thinking about is what he has to tell me, and if I don't like it, I can't escape unless I decide to jump out of the car. I look at Reelin, and he just looks at me with an unreadable expression.

He runs his hand over his beard, then blows out a breath, "we need to talk. But first, let's get your favorite." We pull out of the parking lot onto the main road.

The car notification goes off again:

**New Message from Lo: I think today is the day. It makes sense, and I can't keep this secret much longer.**

His fingers flex on the wheel. When I look at his face, his bottom lip is curved into his teeth with his eyebrows bunched. This was the face he always made when he had something to say, but didn't know how to say it. Just before I ask what's on his mind, the car notification goes off again.

**New Message from Stacee: I want to see you today**

Reelin turns off the phone-to-car connectivity, and I shift in my seat, staring straight ahead. My chest feels both heavy and hollow, and I don't know if it's because I'm feeling unwell, or if it's because my mind is reeling, coming up with questions. What are my sister and Kieran talking about? Why do they have secrets? Am I allowed to even care, when I'm keeping things from him, myself? More importantly, who the hell is Stacee? Is she the girl from the party? Another woman he has been dealing with, while acting like he's all about me? Should I even care? I look out the window and convince myself it's none of my business. The car volume is low, and I hear Usher's *"Confessions Pt. 2"* playing. How ironic.

As we ride down the road, my stomach starts to tug at me. I didn't even realize how hungry I was until now. He said we're going to get my favorite, so I know we're going to Richie Bros, and they have an incredible brunch menu. I'll feel better once I'm filling my stomach with waffles, and a mimosa… Or four.

# 13 : Dazed And Confused

We pull into the parking lot of Richie Bros, and as expected, it's busy. This is one of those places that will always have a lot of business, because it was created with good intentions and remains a welcoming space. The Richie brothers created this space to honor their late mother, who they described as Black luxury personified, with a southern heart. The vibe is exactly that. This place opened during our senior year of high school, and for a while, Reelin and I had a standing date here at least once a week. Just thinking about eating here, gives me all the feels.

"I haven't been here since the last time," Reelin confesses.

"Daddy requests this place for Father's Day, every year," I smile, but feel the need to elaborate, "we don't come, though. Then he pouts most of the morning about it, so I end up cooking whatever meal he has in mind, because I have to make sure he feels the love." I chuckle at the thought. "I think he might actually request it on purpose, just to get me into the kitchen."

When I look at Reelin, he's staring at me with those eyes that suck my soul from my body. It unnerves me. I can feel myself wanting to stay here, in the warm embrace of his full attention. "I never do anything you and I did without you, honestly."

He leans closer to me, his gaze pulling me in. His tongue passes over his lower lip, slow and deliberate. "Anything?" The low timbre of his voice sends that one word vibrating through me. The air between us is buzzing with shared desire. His deep brown eyes are smoldering, taking in every bit of my existence.

His phone vibrates, ruining the moment. Something like guilt passes over his eyes, and I almost miss it. He sits up straight and checks his phone. Against my better judgement, I let my eyes wander to the screen, hoping it's not that chick named Stacee.

**New Message from Lo: I have it here, in Atlanta. After that sermon, I feel like she needs to know, so y'all can figure out your shit.**

I feel cold, now. I almost forgot about the secrets, just that fast.

**Lo: We just parked.**

**Reelin: ok**

He locks his screen and looks at the restaurant, releasing a slow breath. "Lailani, I love you. I hope you know that, and have never doubted it."

I'm not sure why, but that just made me nervous, "I know," is all I say, then Lo is knocking on my window, startling me.

"Oh shit! I thought Rizz saw me! I didn't mean to scare you! You okay?" She's opening the door Reelin just unlocked. Startle triggers my stiffness. "You okay?" she asks again, this time more hushed, bringing her face closer to mine.

"I'm fine," I look over at Reelin, who's getting out of the car, "something you want to tell me, sister?" She takes my hand, helping me out.

"No, why?"

Reelin comes around the car, and I don't miss their shared glance.

Lo turns and starts walking, "K already walked in to get us a table."

Reelin reaches for my hand, and we follow Lo inside. I'm trying not to be annoyed that she's also keeping something from me. She's been a little weird and cagey, but I've been trying not to give it too much thought. I'll figure it out, though.

Reelin rubs the back of my hand with his thumb as we walk into the restaurant, "your energy shifted."

"Did it?" I shrug, pursing my lips, "I'm probably just cold."

"Hmm," He sounds unconvinced, but he doesn't say anything.

Kieran waves us down from the table. Thankfully we got one near the fireplace that takes up an entire central wall, because I really am cold. Reelin pulls out my chair, and helps me out of my coat, then I sit. He takes Kieran's and Lonayla's jackets, and gestures towards the coat check, then walks away.

"You good, La?" Kieran's face is neutral, but he's twisting one of his locs above his shoulder, which is one of his anxious tells.

I raise my eyebrow in question, "Fine. Why?"

"No reason," Lo interjects before Kieran can reply, taking his hand from his hair, holding it in her lap. "Just making conversation." The smile she gives is annoyingly awkward.

I already felt uncomfortable, but my unease is reaching a boiling point. Whatever they're keeping from me, it needs to come out soon. The weird vibes only bring more questions to my mind. How long have they been keeping secrets? What did I do to deserve to be lied to? Is there more than one thing they're collectively keeping from me? Is this thing the real reason for my chance at life? Will it break me or build me up? Will these bonds be severed? Should I just run away from it all?

And then, the questions cycle through to: Am I even allowed to feel bothered by whatever they have chosen to hide, when I have my own secrets? Only, Lonayla knows mine, so shouldn't that count? I decide to hold off on my interrogation, though. I'll wait until I can't take it anymore, and I stop doubting my feelings. Once I get to that point, I can question the three of them together.

I look around the restaurant. It's been so long since I last came inside this place, but it's still the exact same. There's soft, romantic lighting no matter the time of day, thanks to the fire wall two feet to my right, and the gorgeous black sconces that are placed every few feet. There are beautiful round-edged light fixtures placed perfectly into the mirrored ceiling that cast a warm glow. The floors are a matte-finished porcelain in toasted taupe with deep brown veining. The walls are a dark stacked wood-illusion tile that adds a cozy texture to the room. The seating is a mix of high and low tables with matching brass chairs topped with thick black cushions, and along the walls furthest from the flame wall, are booths on raised platforms with thick quilted benches to match. The tabletops are all the same glossy calacatta-gold quartz on swirling brass legs.

Just past the hostess stand is the coat check, and the hall to the restrooms and a private party room. There is a small alcove just beyond that that leads to the kitchen and prepping area. Next to that entrance, the ground drops down about two feet, spanning the length of the wall, with steps that lead to the currently curtained-off patio. The curtains stay closed until sundown, to maintain the ambiance. The full bar is on the opposite end of the room, and beside it is a raised stage for musicians to play. Right now, there are two older gentleman doing their own cover of Janet Jackson's "That's the Way Love Goes" with their instruments: one on bass and one on keyboard. There are gorgeous art pieces the Richie brothers created themselves, hanging on some of the wall space, and vintage brass instruments placed in glass cases every so often. This place is so beautiful.

I look back by the hostess stand and don't see Reelin. I only looked away for maybe twenty seconds. I try to stop myself from thinking too hard, but where did he go?

Lonayla stands, "I'm gonna run to the ladies room, if the waiter comes, order me the kale thing I like, please," she says to Kieran, then grabs her phone, and walks away.

My eyes follow her. She makes a call before she gets into the bathroom. Did she walk away just to make a call? Since when is she so private? I look at Kieran, who's texting someone, and his hand is back to twisting his hair by his shoulder, and I feel a sudden urge to scream. Why is whatever they're all doing alone, or with each other, freaking me out?

"Kieran?" He looks at me and I take a quick breath. "Is Reelin seeing somebody?"

He finishes whatever he was doing on his phone, then looks back at me through squinted eyes.

"What?" He releases the hair he was twirling, and shifts in his seat, giving me his full attention.

"Is he seeing anyone?"

Kieran blinks like he doesn't understand, "yeah, you. That's a strange question."

"No, I mean, is he dating? Has he had… like…" I sigh, annoyed with myself for asking, "serious situations? More than just casual sex, situations? Possibly seeing a future with someone for the long-haul situations?

He gives a firm nod, "yeah. You."

He leans onto his elbows over the table, " What's up, Lailani? Where is this coming from?"

"It's just… I get it if he has some other things going on. I mean, I was gone out of his life for eleven whole years, so naturally, I expected it. The man's got it going on, so of course I can't assume he was just lonely. I haven't thought to ask him in the year that we have been speaking, but I feel like I might be missing something. I would hope you would let me know and not have me looking crazy out here, though. Because we promised, remember?" I hate how desperate my voice sounds.

Kieran shakes his head, "Lailani, Rizz loves you. Whatever y'all need to discuss, y'all need to discuss with each other." He leans back in his chair. "You tell him about ol' boy who bought you that car, since he's calling you again?" I frown. "Exactly. How about the one who took you to Bora Bora? Or the one who bought you the boat you pretend not to have? How about that one fool who bought you that phat-ass diamond and literally begged to build you a house? Hell, even that scammer nigga who broke into your shop! You tell Rizz about him? Was I supposed to? You expect Lo to?" I lean back in my chair with a sigh, and Kieran chuckles. "It was never my place to tell him about all the many suitors you had over the years, La. Just like it ain't my place to answer these questions for you, either. Just know, Rizz loves you. He has always loved you."

I look near the hostess stand again, still not seeing Reelin. I huff a breath and run my hands through my hair. "Okay, but it was never serious, though. None of them. It was never serious."

"Let you tell it, neither was Rizz," I felt that in my chest like a physical blow, and reach my hand up, like I can massage the comment away.

Kieran returns to his phone, and I look over at the fire wall, counting the flames that reach my eye level to soothe myself.

"You okay?" Reelin's voice pulls my attention. Lo stands beside him, her brows raised in question.

"Fine. Where'd you go?" I move my hand from my chest, while they sit.

"I had to take a call."

I nod, ignoring the look on his face as he puts his phone back into his pocket. Then I look back to the fire wall. Inside the flames, the memories flash again.

*Reelin. Lonayla. Kyler informing everyone he turned up the pool temperatures, and the heaters in the old gym vestibule are on. A bunch of classmates come out of their clothes to jump into the pool. The initial tree. Maliah bellyflops into the pool. Reelin telling everyone about his love for me. Kieran gloats about the pool dye. Jessy comes in with the honey bun machine. Reelin's laugh. Kassidy asking to work for me. Gabriel showing me his kids photos. Reelin. That random chick and her perfect teeth and dimples, smiling like she knows me. Lonayla laughing at me. Spray-painting my name on the wall. Random chick and Reelin by the woods to nowhere. Random chick talking to me, but I can't hear her. Lonayla. The initial tree. Reelin and the random chick by the initial tree. Kia and Jessy bringing out a cake. Reelin. Kieran teasing me about being cold. Someone announces there's pineapples on the grill. Lonayla passes out shots. Random chick talks to me again, repeating what I could not hear: "I said I can't believe you don't remember me! My name is Stacee!"*

I blink her away just as I hear the waitress greet our table.

I turn my focus to my menu, and speak my drink order without ever looking up. "I'll have an orange-cranberry mimosa and a pineapple-kale smoothie, mimosa style."

I feel nauseous all of a sudden. I can feel a lump in my throat, and my eyes sting with tears I refuse to let fall. I tell myself I'm just panicking, making the person I don't know into the person Reelin has been communicating with, because I don't know what else to do with her. I reach into my purse for my hand sanitizer, needing something to do so I don't ask right now.

By the time everyone is finished ordering their drinks, I have settled on my mind playing tricks on me. I sit and watch the three of them, wondering how everything went from so simple at the party to me questioning if I trust any of them? How long have I not noticed the little things? Is Lonayla right? Do I only notice things when they happen to me? What all have I missed? Is my memory from the party even accurate? Did I even see what I think I saw? Or could my mind be trying to ruin things, because I don't know how to restart something I've already ended? Was it really the end if we're here again? Did I really leave the party early? Is Reelin telling the truth, and I'm not letting myself trust him, because I'm afraid of getting too close?

If this is the case, how did I wake up in the pool? Who had my things? Why is all of this so insane? Why is this my life? Am I being punished for something, or am I just not taking the chance I was given the right way? Do I just move on from it? Should I?

I look at Reelin. His mind seems occupied, but he nods as Kieran makes small comments about the changed menu options since Reelin and I last came. Lo and Kieran still come, of course. Our parents do, too. I never felt comfortable enjoying this place without Reelin, since we had only ever come here together. I look down at the menu. I always ordered the same thing during brunch hours, but I decide I'll try to look at other options today.

When the waitress returns with our drinks, I try my hardest not to immediately chug them down, because of all these questions circling in my head. I'm the first person the waitress asks for their order, and I up look at her for the first time. Her caramel complexion, and the freckles across her nose in tandem with her red weave, reminds me so much of how Maliah Harris looked when we were kids. I lose my train of thought, and my mind flashes back to that first day I met Reelin again.


### Fourth Period

*A squealing Maliah Harris rushes into class just as the final bell rings, to sit right next to me in the front middle row. I raise my head from my notebook in interest.*

*"La, the new boy totally likes me!" Maliah pulls off her backpack and her cheeks flush in excitement.*

*"What new boy? There's a lot of newbies this year," I put my pencil down, giving her my attention.*

*"Umm, hello?" she scowls and smacks her teeth, "obviously the very hot, very dimply one! He kinda looks like Kieran? I know you've seen him."*

*I squint my eyes, "hm. That's nice," I go back to writing down the things I need to have Mom get from the store. I want to make a crumb cake tonight, since Lonayla is going to probably have her heart broken about Kieran and Kennedi.*

*"La, seriously!" Maliah presses, flicking a pencil at me, "he just walked me to class, AND he said he thought it was so cool I play volleyball! Even said he plans to see us practice sometime!"*

*I shrug, "I said that's nice."*

*"Oh my gosh, you're supposed to be excited! This will be the best year ever, La. Guess why?" I finish my list and close my notebook, looking at Maliah's huge smile. She lowers her voice, leaning in, "we don't have to worry about you-know-who always taking the attention for herself and her boobs anymore!"*

*I immediately stand, now leaning over Maliah. Her shoulders cave in at my sudden approach. I look into her eyes and say I in a menacingly low voice, "If you ever mention anything about that situation out loud to anyone, you. are. over. If your flat chest is ever puffed up in confidence because you're speaking down on that girl, I will make you wish you could disappear from this planet. If you even whisper her name and it has to do with what you and I know, I will make it my personal business to ruin every little thing you think is good, for the rest of your life. And you know I won't even blink, before I act, so don't play with me. This is real life, you low self-esteem-having-weirdo. You're so jealous of anyone else's attention, and it's all because you don't get any, yourself. It's because you don't know how to shut up. If this gets out, I'll know it was you, and I promise you, Maliah, I will wreck your entire world."*

*I pull back and smile at her worried face, "Okay?" I chirp, lightly smacking her cheek.*

*Maliah nods and turns to the front of the room. I return to my seat and roll begins.*

*I sit through class, bouncing my leg in anticipation, hoping this foolish girl hasn't already told anyone. I know it would destroy Kieran if he couldn't be the one to tell my sister.*

*Class dismisses and Maliah rushes out before anyone. When I get into the hallway, Reelin is walking in my direction. I quickly turn to go the other way, even though my class is behind me now. Seconds later, Kieran is at my side.*

*He grabs my elbow and turns us back toward class, "class is this way. Why you look at me and run?"*

*"I didn't see you." I mumble.*

*Reelin is now in front of me, "your new girlfriend had to hurry along, sorry you missed her!" I snark, walking around him and his stupid confused expression.*

*"Wait, what are you talking about?" Kieran asks.*

*"Maliah said he walked her to class and told her he's coming to watch our practice," I walk into the classroom. "I think that's great. First day of school, and already, he has a girlfriend. Guess he really does have the 'Rizz' after all." This jealous tone is so unlike me.*

*I sit in the first row at the far end of the room, and Kieran sits in the desk beside me, then leans over, "I'm so confused." He looks around, "where did he go? We got the same schedule."*

"Probably to find his little high-yellow girlfriend," I shrug. "Also, I may have had to threaten her about that situation. If anyone finds out, it was her. If you don't want anyone beating you to Lo—"

"I already know," Kieran leans back in his seat and pulls out his notebook. "I'm telling her right after school. I want her to at least make it through her first day of high school before she decides she hates it and me."

Reelin walks in with the last bell. I focus on the wall as if the tiles hold the answer to solving world hunger.

"I have not asked anyone to be my girlfriend," Reelin says in a low voice, standing directly in front of me.

I look to where our teacher clearly has no care in the world outside of her computer. "that's not my business." I reach into my bag for my books.

Reelin moves beside me and says to Kyler Gaines, in the seat behind mine, "ay, let me have that seat."

"No!" I whirl around, but Kyler has already stood up.

Kyler shrugs and moves a seat behind him. Reelin sits, smirking at me. I look around and half the class is staring.

"Miss Grander, is everything alright?" Ms. Petty asks, finally rising from the chair behind her computer.

"Yes, ma'am." I smile and push my bag under my desk, then open my notebook.

After roll is called, Ms. Petty says she has to print the syllabus again and leaves the room. I feel Reelin tap my shoulder, but I shrug his hand away. He taps me again. I shake my head. The third time he taps me, I turn in my seat.

That was a mistake. Reelin is smiling so big, the dimples in his cheeks look like someone pulled two Milk Duds straight out of his face, leaving missing spots in the perfectly smooth chocolate. His eyes are like bright white ponds of milk with Hostess cupcakes someone licked the swirls off of, making the center look darker. He's so beautiful, I hate him already.

"I got you something," his voice wiggles in my ears, making me feel all fuzzy inside.

*I scrunch my nose, "I don't think that's appropriate."*

*His smile gets bigger, and I don't know why, but I feel like the floor is now the ceiling. He pulls out a blueberry muffin and a cranberry juice, "I heard you and your sister split one of the breakfast muffins, because you like to save yours for the afternoon."*

*I don't have any words. I frown. Kyler laughs behind Reelin, and I scowl, "shut up, Ky."*

*I look back at Reelin, then at the muffin in his hand, "I already had my snack muffin, but thanks."*

*When I turn back around, I feel like the butterflies in my stomach have somehow morphed into pterodactyls with fluffy feather wings. Reelin shifts in his seat, and it sounds like he put his bag beneath his desk, but it felt like it went under mine. I don't dare look.*

*"Lailani?" He says my name like a one-word poem. Wow, he's going to be trouble. I school my expression to appear uninterested, before I turn around again.*

*"I like that you care about who I date," he leans forward a little, and the depth of his dark brown eyes seems endless, "even though I'm not officially dating anyone yet."*

*"I don't care."*

*"I think you do," he raises an eyebrow.*

*"You can have however many girlfriends you want, Reelin. I really couldn't care less, I literally don't even know you," I turn back to the front.*

*Once Ms. Petty returns and passes out the syllabus, she tells us to familiarize ourselves with the quiz schedules and to start our reading, then she turns to her computer. I look over at Kieran, who is drawing something without actually focusing on whatever it is. I refuse to look at Reelin, so I open my book and start reading the quiz one lessons. I read until the bell rings.*

*"One more class until my life falls apart again, today," Kieran stands with his shoulders hunched. He looks so tired.*

*"I don't even know what to say. Lo had lunch with Jessy and some other girl from their health class, so I don't even know how her day's going so far," I lean down for my bag, but it's not under my desk. I look up to see Reelin holding it.*

*"I'll carry it to class, don't worry," he smiles. I scrunch my face and look away.*

*"She's having a great day. She said they did a pop quiz in her math class and she got a 98 on it," Kieran half smiles, "my smart lady love."*

*I sigh, picking up my book, "I really wish I knew what to say to help."*

*"He'll figure it out," Reelin takes my book out of my hand, and I roll my eyes.*

*"Careful, wouldn't want those gorgeous green eyes to get stuck in the back of your head," he extends his arm for me to walk forward, "let's get to class."*

*We get into the hallway and start towards our next class.*

*"Kieran, I want the best for you, I really do."*

*He tugs at the end of one of his braids, "I do, too. And the best for me happens to look exactly like you. Only prettier, of course," he shrugs.*

*I playfully shoulder bump him.*

*Maliah rushes past us and Reelin calls out to her. "Hey, Red!" I suddenly feel the urge to punch him in his face. Maliah looks at him.*

*"If anyone asks," he raises my bag, nudging his head at me, "this is my girlfriend."*

*I stop in my tracks, and I think my eyes pop out of my head. Maliah looks sick and rushes down the hall. Other students are all looking at us, smiling and laughing.*

*"La?" Kieran moves in front of me, "Lailani, breathe."*

*I focus on his face and exhale, not knowing I was holding my breath. He backs up a step, allowing Reelin to move into the place. All I can see is him.*

*He smirks under his wink, "care now?"*

*I'm too stunned to speak.*

Reelin's hand gently squeezes my thigh, and snaps me back to the table.

"She'll have the double waffle with the strawberries on the side. Two egg whites scrambled with avocado thinly sliced on top, grits with American cheese, and maple-mint bacon crispy, with an extra order of turkey bacon as well, the Greek yogurt with a dash of honey, the fruit cup without the banana, and a hot herbal tea with a few lemon wedges, please."

The waitress smiles then looks from him to me, "any granola?"

"No, thank you" Reelin and I say together.

I look at him while my sister orders, "you remember my exact order?"

"I remember everything about you," he looks into my eyes, squeezing my thigh again, "literally, everything." His smile makes my heart ache. How does he affect me like this?

After all of our orders are taken, Kieran laughs, "one thing we can always count on, is Rizz showing off around Lailani Grander." Lonayla nods, laughing in agreement.

Reelin shrugs and laughs along with them. We sit without speaking for a while, enjoying the musicians' selections. They have such a good sound. They're currently playing a cool cover of Erykah Badu's *Rimshot,* echoing each other and the instruments.

I don't know what comes over me as I blurt, "men keep trying to buy me!" I wince, feeling Reelin's hand retreat from my leg.

"I'm not trying to buy you," he almost sounds offended.

I sigh and look at him, "no, *other* men keep trying to buy me. It seems like every time a man is interested in me, he goes to crazy extents to get me to like him back. It always starts with me telling them we can get to know each other, and it usually ends with some lavish gift, massive wire transfers, or trip as a last effort. And a few times it ended in a ridiculous marriage proposal."

I look at Kieran and Lo's surprised expressions, then back to Reelin, "Mario, the one who called, he's one of those men. He bought my car for my shop's 11th anniversary last year. He wasn't able to attend my celebration, but a week later, my car was in front of my shop, with a card saying it was in my name, fully paid, and insured for a year with no strings attached. There have been a few of these men who I dealt with for months at a time. Usually out of boredom. I didn't sleep with all of them of course, but I did give in to Mario this past September, when he came to the states to wrap up some business."

Lonayla is choking on her drink, and Kieran leans over to rub her back. I look at my hands, "other than him, there was only one other that I've slept with, since you. That one was around off and on for almost three years, but he has been out of my life since 2019. I feel like it's only right you know, since you have no idea what kind of situations I've been in all this time. Now that we're going to be in each other's physical presence, it felt right to share," I reach over, pouring the champagne into my smoothie, "Oh! And I have a boat. A yacht, really. But I never take it out. For obvious reasons." I start sucking down my drink.

Reelin reaches over, and takes my drink, setting it down. He cups my chin, turning my face to his, "Lailani, whatever happened before this very moment, it doesn't matter. Nothing and no one else matters," he leans in and presses a gentle kiss to my lips, then lets my face go, to lift his drink, "but know this: no one else will know what it's like to experience you in that way again. I fucked up letting you go before, so that's on me. Now that you're here, that shit's dead." He sips after a small huff and a nod.

I bite my cheek in contemplation. I can't tell if he just gaslit me into not asking about his other partners or not, but I need to know who the hell Stacee is, or I'm not going to be okay. I look at Lonayla. She presses her lips together and raises her glass to me in cheers. I look at Kieran and he gives me a half shrug and smiles. I reach for my drink again, deciding to leave the questions alone for right now. I'll for sure come back to it, though.

Kieran and Lonayla keep the conversation focused on the kids. To everyone's surprise, they didn't go overboard with their Christmas wish lists, so Lo and Kieran are surprising them with a trip to Japan for three, next summer. They're so proud of their young adults, and the way they seem to be maturing. During our meal, I steal glances at Reelin, watching him eat, as we listen to the two parents gush about their children.

Our waitress comes to clear away our plates, and Lonayla's face lights up. "Mom and Dad are gonna have a ball with the kids today! They don't see them enough!" She looks at me, widening her eyes, "let's get them all matching pajamas! They can take pictures tonight after dinner! And they can have a slumber party like the old days, before everyone got so busy."

I give her a half smile, "I mean, that would be great, except it's technically a school night."

"Your mom and pops didn't play about school night company," Kieran lets out a small laugh as the waitress sets down the check and walks away. "So that means you gotta be in bed by 11, for real?"

"Yup! Just like the old days." Lo smiles, "the kids can still stay! They're not our company, they're there with their Grandys."

Kieran snorts, "good luck getting that past Attorney Grander, babe."

"I will!" She finishes the rest of her drink.

"I think we should ask your parents what they would like to do, and make sure the kids want to stay the night," Reelin adds, "They could have other plans. Y'all the only ones we know who are being kids for real, so it ain't a school night for them."

That makes sense, but I don't say it out loud.

"Pooda just texted the group, should I ask?" Lo questions, checking her phone.

Kieran sighs, "sure. I actually vote we stay on campus and they can do what they want. If y'all are serious about being teens, your moms and pops would probably prefer that." He laughs a little, reaching for the check.

"They probably would feel better about us not being home. We might have taken this a little too far, and they may or may not regret agreeing to it. But I mean, we make life more exciting! Our teenage selves were so much fun!" Lo and I share a smile.

"Y'all were spoiled as hell, too." Kieran says passing the bill to the waitress with his card inside, "they doing everything, then? Pickups and drop-offs? Or are we coming to get y'all?"

Reelin has not spoken in a while. I put my hand on his, and he jumps, "you okay?"

"Yeah. I'm gonna get our coats," when he walks away, both Lonayla and I watch after him.

She stands, "no, I'll be driving us, that's why we had to get Mom's car serviced."

"You're driving? Not La?" Kieran looks at me, and I look at Lonayla.

"La became a passenger princess the moment Rizz got his license, so I figured why change that?" Lonayla shrugs.

 "Between the three of y'all, it's a wonder I still know how to drive at all."

Reelin returns with our coats, followed by the waitress who thanks us and wishes us a great holiday. Kieran helps Lonayla into her jacket, and Reelin does the same with mine. When I turn back to him there's a strange look on his face.

"Hey," I place my hand on his chest, "what's wrong?"

He shifts away from my touch, "nothing. Just thinking."

I frown, but I don't press further.

"So, I vote y'all stay at the dorm," Kieran insists, while signing the check and leaving the tip, "It's a whole apartment with two rooms that should fit your needs."

Lo looks at me. I look at Reelin.

He sighs, then guides me around the table to walk to the exit, "I told you it was reserved for you. It's not like the regular dorms, I made sure. It's the independent living styled ones. I don't have to stay there with you, but I wasn't staying there without you, either. My house is further, so I'll stay at Aunt Kira's."

Kieran chimes in, "we're both staying at Mom's, so we'll be close. You know Micah, Jammy's boyfriend? He's staying at my house, so I wasn't gonna ask you to stay over there."

"La, we can at least look at it," Lo gives a half shrug, "If we don't like it, we go home."

When we get outside, the wind is blowing furiously. Lonayla immediately grabs my hand, and I squeeze hers back in thanks.

"You good?" She asks with her voice low, walking me to Reelin's car.

"Yeah, thanks. If you really want to stay on campus, you can stay there, Lo. You don't need me."

"I know. But we're doing this together, remember?" She smiles, and Reelin opens my door, so I can climb in. "We should all ride over there together! Rizz, you wanna drop off your car at our place since we're doing dinner anyway?

Reelin and Kieran exchange a look I can't read.

"I actually gotta run a quick errand. I thought you ladies might want to change and stuff. We can swoop you by the dorms, and see if it meets your standards, then go get Pooda from work on the way back to your house." I put on my seatbelt.

Reelin closes my door and walks to the back of the car with my sister and Kieran. They chat for a minute longer, then they get into the cars to leave. Reelin's phone automatically connects to the car. As he puts on his seatbelt, the car notification goes off:

**Incoming call from Sta—**

He immediately declines and disconnects his phone from the car.

I look at him and he winks at me, "what you wanna listen to? We got that playlist Monica Cooper sent to The Reliving chat. It has our song on there," he smiles.

"Who is Stacee?" I ask with a frown.

His body stiffens for a split second. I would have missed it if stiffness weren't something I literally battle every day of my life.

"I don't know what you're thinking Lailani, but trust me, it's nobody and it's nothing."

"Is that where you're going?" I challenge.

He takes a deep breath and pulls out of the restaurant parking lot. "Lailani, please. Leave it alone," his jaw locks, and his hand grips the steering wheel tight, the other hand runs his fingers along his beard.

I look down at his phone on his lap. I think about reaching for it, but stop myself. I feel like the air is thinning, so I turn to look out the window, cracking it open. I need to get home. I need time to really think about why I'm losing myself in these opposing emotions.

There's no way God gave me this chance to fall in love with Reelin, if this is how it's making me feel. Maybe it's my fault, though. It was hopelessly foolish of me to assume things were supposed to be easy after he left me. Especially because I wasn't even supposed to make it out of that pool alive.

But I did.

# 14 : Grand Gestures

"I'll be back soon," Reelin says, walking me to the door of my parents' house. He didn't say another word to me the whole way here. "No more than an hour or so."

"Okay," I walk inside and turn to look at him. He stands just outside the threshold with his lower lip tucked into his teeth, and his hands are in his pants pockets. I can't help but think that while I thought it was just me being overly cautious with him, he may be being careful with me, too.

"I'm sorry, Reelin."

He frowns, "for what?"

"I don't know. Leaving you when I did? Giving you too many boundaries when we started talking again? Not telling you that you matter enough?" He looks away, and it pains me. "I guess I can understand if you feel like I took you for granted. I guess I can't really be all that upset that you left me, too. The other night felt a little too perfect, and it can be scary when you don't trust someone."

His jaw hardens, and he comes closer, pulling my hand into his, "Lailani, stop." I raise my brows. "Please, just stop. I'll be back soon." He kisses my hand and leaves me standing in the doorway.

I feel a rush of sadness come over me, watching him pull off, and it's so confusing. Friday, I was wrapped up in possibility. Yesterday started with knowing there was no way I could possibly trust him again, but the moment he was in my physical presence, I questioned that. I don't know how to accept him leaving me like he did, but do I owe it to him to try? After all, I left him once, even though I didn't leave him to die.

I close the door, and take off my coat and shoes, then start to my room.

**Incoming Call from Kieran Michaels:**

"Hello?" I get to the top of the stairs and turn to my room, but don't hear anything on the other end, "Kieran? Hello?"

I hang up and walk into my bathroom to turn on my shower. I look in the mirror, and my eyes look so sad behind the hollowness that remains. Just when I reach for my shower cap, my phone rings again.

**Incoming Call from Kieran Michaels:**

"Yeah?" I answer on speaker, "What's up?"

"Shit." Kieran hangs up.

That was weird. I text him.

**Me: You okay?**

**Kieran: yup**

**Me: You called.**

**Kieran: accident**

**Me: twice?**

The response dots start and stop a few times before they disappear. Whatever that was, it only adds to my current confliction. I hear Lonayla go into her room and I feel compelled to talk to her.

"Lo?" I knock on her door.

"Hey!" she calls out. I jiggle the handle, but her door is locked.

"I'll come find you in a little bit!" She sounds odd.

"You okay?"

"Yeah! I'll come find you!"

I shake my head and I can feel the deepest frown on my face. Why the hell is everyone being so weird? I don't understand. I go back into my bathroom and I have to vomit before I get into the shower.

I didn't mean to wash my hair again, but now standing in my mirror, brushing my teeth with my dark brown coils dripping all over the place. The same images were playing in my mind, and I kept thinking about the little things that have been bothering me, and I felt absolutely insane. I wanted to wash that uncertainty away, so I scrubbed my body. Maybe a little too hard, because my brown skin now has a red tint. But I think I've successfully convinced myself to relax.

Sitting in my reading chair, with my fluffy gray robe, I open my hidden photos album and scroll through memories of Reelin and me. He was always so perfect for me, even when I literally refused to acknowledge it. He was honest, attentive and always so respectful. He was so intelligent and loved to carry on stimulating conversations. He was thoughtful, consistent, and gentle with me. He was all of the good things. I felt like a princess with him. We had our issues, but it was never because he wasn't everything I needed. It was me. I started pulling away when I came to terms with the fact that I couldn't give him what he deserved. I couldn't pretend I believed in forever, and he needed that, no matter how much he said it didn't matter.

**Apple ID Sign In Requested**

**lkgrander@granderthings.me**

**Your apple ID is being used to sign in to a device near Atlanta, GA**

**Don't Allow      Allow**

I press don't allow, "let it go, weirdo."

I lean my head back, looking up at the decorative boxes on the top of my bookshelf. Reelin remembered that saving gift boxes was something I enjoyed. He even said he was intentional about having boxes made for me. How is he still so perfect, and why does it feel so wrong, at the same time?

I hear a knock at my door, "come in."

Lonayla walks in, wearing a dark brown oversized long sleeve shirt, and her orange slippers. Her hair is also wet, her coils hanging around her shoulders. I lock my phone screen and move from the chair to my bed.

"You wanna do some stretches?" I shake my head, but she persists, "You need to do some stretches, La."

"I don't need to do anything but stay Black and die." I shift into a lounging position against my headboard, one leg crossed over the other, hands on my lap, holding my phone.

Lo's phone dings in her hand. She looks at it, looks at me and blows a breath through her nose, "Don't move," she rushes out to her room.

When she returns, she's holding a flat courier package and a little box the size of her palm, "I have to share something with you."

I sit up and move one of the pillows to keep my lower back comfortable, "what is that? You buy me some earrings?"

Lonayla smiles, "first, you know how I always tell you about the things Kieran stresses about, and how whenever I do something I think is nice, he gets a little offended?" I nod. "Well, you and Kieran have the same weird reactions to nice gestures. Must be that weird twin Aries thing." She sits up higher and sets the little box behind her, "so, I didn't want to bother you with any of this stuff, because it was a lot going on, and you were busy. Plus, I had to do a lot with Rizz and you weren't ready to see him yet, but I made a big decision, and I think I want to let Kieran know today."

"Okay, what is it?"

"When Rizz originally started the plans for opening the youth center, he was super stressed out. Kieran and I tried to help as often as we could, but neither of us fully understood just how much he had to do. I would let him vent about all the things whenever he needed to, and I actually liked learning so much about the process. Kieran started helping him more and more, and I loved seeing how much he loved working on it, too," she takes a deep breath.

"Remember how I missed the opening of the youth center for an appointment?" I nod. She looks down at the package in her hands, "I think Kieran felt like I missed it because it wasn't important to me. But the truth is, I missed the opening because the developer I had been hoping to meet with, happened to be in Florida on a layover."

She pulls out a large stack of papers with smaller, labeled manilla envelopes on top. "I purchased a business."

I blink in shock, "a business? What kind of business? For what? You have Grander's?"

She pushes the stack to me, "I purchased land, originally, and built on it over the last year. Rizz has been helping me." I look up from the papers. "Kieran was so excited about having a place to send the kids he works with to, with the youth center. Some of the teen parents are doing good things for themselves, and because of the programs with Graciously Growing Guys and Lovely Little Ladies, they get to be mentors, like big brothers and big sisters and they get additional work credit. Kieran loves the way these young parents respond to the opportunity, and they do it for free. So, I had an idea. I looked into some things, and I asked Rizz to sell me part of his business, for Kieran."

I set the papers down, "wait, you bought part of Reelin's youth center?"

"No. He actually had a better idea," Lonayla clarifies, reaching for the papers, flipping to a business proposal from Reelin. "I bought the land, and built a second youth center location—"

"Wait, you bought Reelin a second location? Lo, why wou—"

"No, La," she stops me before I tell her this is weird, "I built the youth center for Kieran as an extension of the one Rizz owns. Only now, there will be a way to pay those teenagers who work for the extra hours, as real part time and full-time employees. Bigger than that, there is a separate building for those teens to have a safe visiting space with their kids.

These kids aren't criminals, they're just young and in need of help. Instead of parks and office buildings, they'll have a comfortable environment to bring their little ones to. They deserve this.

Daddy and Rizz helped me to do all the work with permits, licenses and everything. Mommy helped with design and furniture, and we stocked up on necessities. Rizz has been working overtime to find more counselors and people who can work, so it can open as early as January. If that's what Kieran wants to do, it's ready for him. He has been so busy this year. He took on nine of these cases at the same time! Nine young people are struggling the way he would have when Coach V said she would strip his rights."

Lonayla takes a deep breath, pulls photos out of one of the envelopes, and passes them to me. "thing is, K has no idea, because I have been terrified of how he'll react."

I look at the images in awe, "Lonayla, this is so cool. I can't believe you did all this!"

There's a full recreation center with a pool, basketball courts, tennis and volleyball courts, and two smaller activity rooms. There is a fitness room, nicely sized bathrooms with showers, a theater, and both indoor and outdoor play areas. There are two rooms that look like classrooms, and a sitting room that could double as a library, along with a full kitchen.

The second building has an open space with bookshelves and café style seating around a food service area in the center, giving a coffee shop feel. Beyond that is a hall leading to bathrooms, storage closets and a full kitchen. The best part is, just on the other side of the hall, there are four decently sized rooms, made to look like individual living rooms. They're fully furnished, decorated and stocked with everything anyone could need.

"Can you think of any reason he'll be upset?" I look up from the pictures, and Lonayla has tears in her eyes, "I mean, I know you've accepted a few gifts, but they always just appear, and you can't really say no. But would you accept this, if you were Kieran? Would you understand why I did this? Or do you think I overstepped?" she looks so small in this moment, so helplessly concerned.

I can't deal with the nervousness in her sad eyes. Reelin probably did all of this with her, and felt the pain of his own grand gesture all over again. I literally left him after he told me he did something for me that was for my future, on his own. I felt so trapped, because I needed him to let me do my things my way. He didn't talk to me about my needs when he thought getting me a space for a bakery was a good idea. At the same time, I was already feeling like things were too much. So many things were shifting in our lives, and I started to panic about how my life with Reelin was supposed to be. As someone who needs to know how the story ends, I couldn't give myself any definitive reason to not let him convince me of forever, so I used that gesture as my escape. I was a coward, and right now, I feel like I never deserved him.

"Kieran is so blessed to have a love like you. You have always given him so much grace, and you continue to move through life with more and more love, as time presses on—even when you act crazy. Kieran could never feel negatively about this. I'm so proud of you for putting yourself into such a responsible space."

Lonayla wipes at her eyes. I set the stack of pictures down, and move to the bottom of my bed beside her.

"Lo, I have a hard time accepting gifts from people who are only trying to convince me to choose them. They think giving me things is enough to win me over, and I value myself more than that. This is probably the most thoughtful gift I have ever heard of, and it's so clear you did this for Kieran, because you love him so very much. You created something for him that might take up more of the time you don't get to spend together, and this is so beautifully selfless of you. This has nothing to do with you or what you need from him, and everything to do with him and his goals, without a personal stake in it for yourself."

I get a little choked up, and smile at my sister through my tears, wiping hers away, "you really let me basically tell you that you weren't ready to grow up yesterday, and the whole time, you had this big grown-up project. Also, Lonayla Grander spending big money on something for a man? No way!" She laughs with me, "This is why he keeps proposing to you. I'm ready to see y'all finally take that leap."

"About that," Lonayla pulls out the little box, from behind her.

"My earrings?" I say with excitement.

"Better," she winks, passing me the box.

I open it, and it's a timeless three-stone marquise cut diamond ring with exceptional color, and clarity.

I gasp. "Kieran proposed again?"

She looks at me like I'm crazy, "La, you don't remember this ring?"

I look closer, and I remember it vividly now.

*April 9, 2011, My 21st birthday.*

*"La, don't be too much, Today is Kieran's birthday, too," Lonayla teases from across my room as we get ready for the club together.*

*"No one cares about Kieran. Today and every other day in April is all about me," I wink at her. "Plus, you're already doing too much with the sparkles, white dress and crown. Lo, It's MY birthday. Tone it down."*

*"Okay, but it has to look like I'm also the birthday girl, according to YOUR ID." She winks. "Best part about looking like twins? You turn 21, I turn 21. Where is your ID, anyway? Put it with your license so we don't forget." She turns back to the mirror to fix her lashes.*

*"I think it's already in there, I keep them together. Lo, remember, you have to let the guys go between us in case they read the name," I rub more body oil on my legs.*

*"Okay, just check again, please!" Lo says, running to her room for her shoes. "They're here!" She yells back as the doorbell rings.*

*I get up and look myself over again. I'm wearing a short nude bondage dress with sparkly gold strappy heels, and gold chunky bangles. My bangs swoop over my forehead, held in place by a gold tiara that says, "I'm 21," sitting perfectly in front of my light brown, small barrel curls that are flowing down my back. I have on long wispy lashes and nude lipstick. I didn't want to put on too much makeup and not look like myself in any of the pictures. I give myself an approving nod, and reach for the gold "Birthday Bitch" sash and my little gold clutch, checking that I have both my ID cards, gum, and my lipstick before walking out my room.*

*"La, come on!" I hear my sister before I see her standing at the bottom of the stairs, now in silver shoes that match mine.*

*Kieran walks over to the bottom of the steps to meet me. "dang, birthday girl, don't hurt 'em now!"*

*I laugh, giving him a hug, "You don't look too bad yourself, birthday boy."*

*He has on a pair of white jeans, a light gray button-down with the sleeves rolled to his elbows, a navy belt and navy boat shoes.*

*"You kids please be safe," Dad's voice comes before I see him, coming from the kitchen with Reelin behind him. "Don't come stumbling in here at crazy hours like hookers in those little dresses, either." He kisses our foreheads, gives Reelin a head nod, and walks away.*

*Lo's fluffing her soft curls around her tiara in Kieran's aviators, "La, you brought your lipstick, yeah?"*

*I nod, and Reelin reaches for my hand, pulling me close and wrapping his arms around me. "Seven hours felt way too long. I missed you." He speaks into my neck, making me shiver, then he presses a gentle kiss just beneath my ear before he pulls back.*

*"I feel like I blinked, and you were back." I laugh, tossing my hair back dramatically, "my hair basically took this whole time!"*

*His eyes roam over my body. He takes all 5'10 of me in with a warmth I can feel from the two feet he has stepped away, to assess me, "you look phenomenal."*

*I roll my eyes through my blush, "you say that when I look insane, too."*

*With a smirk I gesture for him to spin around. He laughs but obliges.*

*"You look very handsome too, Mr. Rizzy."*

*He has on tailored camel-colored dress pants, a white button-down, with the sleeves rolled to his elbows, a brown belt with gold hardware and brown dress shoes. His single gold chain, watch, and pinky ring finish off his look.*

*"Well, you picked everything out, down to my drawers, so I better meet your expectations." He laughs coming close again. "Let's go get your first legal drink, my love." And with that, the four of us walk out and head to the club.*

*Club Bourgeois Beat is in the heart of Atlantic Station. People always come here for their 21st rite of passage, so it was only right we come here to keep with tradition. Once we get stamped and let in, Lo immediately walks over to the bar. Kieran makes a face as he's pulled along with my sister, and I laugh. We've had drinks before, but she's so excited to order her own—never mind that it's only because of MY age, and not hers.*

*"I actually have another gift for you," Reelin says to me over the music. I nod. "We gotta go back outside, though." I raise my eyebrows, and he just smiles, making me smile, too. He is so gorgeous.*

*We walk back to the door, and he says something to the attendant that I can't hear because a group of girls decide that right next to me, is the perfect place to scream their adoration for one of their boyfriends for dropping them off tonight. When Reelin walks me out the door, I realize one of the ladies who was checking out IDs, walks out with us. Then I'm confused when we don't go to the car.*

*"Okay, so where are you taking me?" I whisper, "You signed up for some secret freaky room or something?"*

*Reelin smiles, and I see the lady laugh a little. I guess I didn't whisper quietly enough.*

*We turn at the back of the building and go inside a different door that leads into a dark hallway with blue string lights. I can barely see a few feet ahead of me. The lady opens up a door, and lights come flaring into the hall. I close my eyes at the sudden brightness.*

*When Reelin releases my hand and moves his arm to my lower back to guide me into the lit room. I can hear the door close behind us, and Beyoncé's "Satellites" starts playing. I blink, giving my eyes a moment to adjust, then I lose control of my legs. Reelin holds me steady as I take in this room.*

*There are multiple shades of shimmering blue curtains in a gradient from dark to light, with stars projected over them making it look like the twinkling sky. The ceiling is covered in white fluff, made to resemble stratocumulus clouds, and there are hanging iridescent stars at different heights, spanning the entire space. Scattered around the room are glowing balls of blue or white, fading in and out in a lazy pattern. There is a giant white cloud in the middle of the room that looks to have light bursting from it. And a dense white fog is floating around our feet, giving the illusion that we're in a cloud. It's gorgeous.*

*"Reelin, what is this?" I'm in awe.*

*The lights dim as Beyoncé sings, "We're always on display, let's run and hide." Reelin guides me toward the giant cloud, and as we get to it, I see the moon projected on the back wall, and there are images of us inside of it. The giant cloud has steps on the side, and Reelin helps me up. There's a seat built into the cloud, and he waits for me to sit. He presses a button, and the dim lights around us fade a little more. Above us, a small satellite, flashing a little light every so often. Reelin sits beside me, watching my face, while the song finishes. I continue to admire how perfect everything is.*

*"No matter what happens in this life, Lailani, I never want to leave your orbit. I know it's not the easiest thing for you to accept that my love is eternal, because you need to know the end to a story before you can truly enjoy it. I have so far been unsuccessful at changing your mind about forever, but you have let me stay here, completely in love with you. My heart, my mind, my body, my soul, everything I am—is drawn to you. I will gravitate to you in every lifetime."*

*Reelin pulls my clutch from my hands, setting it on the seat, "you don't even understand the gravity of what I feel for you. The very first time I looked into your eyes, I felt like I saw the only reason for my entire existence, right there, staring back at me. That day your eyes were more sea green than your typical sage." He smiles at that, and I try to remember to breathe. "You know I learned all the shades of green that I could because of you? Your eyes change according to your moods. But they also change depending on your appetite, your energy level, your clothing, and sometimes, in the winter, they might go to that tea green that looks like all the color has drained away, but that is when you are the happiest." He leans forward, "Right now, they're* closer to an aquamarine, which means you're confused, or nervous." He lifts my hand to his lips, kissing it gently, "don't be nervous."

With a smile, he lifts me to stand with him, then, without giving time to prepare, he drops to one knee. "I have been floating in your world for so long, and I want to stay here for the rest of my life. I could never minimize you to being a satellite that's simply flashing by, because you are more vast, more wonderful, and more powerful than even the sun could ever be. I am yours, though. I will orbit you for as long as life lets me. I love being just a tiny speck of existence, remaining close to you. I want to give you every little thing that you require, so that I am by your side, in the end and beyond it. There is nothing in this world that could ever pull me away from you, and I pray that with God's grace, you can love me even half as much as I love you. Lailani Kiersten Grander, would you do me the honor of being my wife?"

I feel like I'm going to pass out. I feel myself wobble a little, and Reelin reaches his other hand to my waist.

"Reelin," I breathe out, "I—"

His beautiful brown eyes are staring into mine and I feel like my body has been set on fire. I have no idea what other thoughts cross my mind, but I can feel my head moving. Nodding. "Yes," I whisper. "Yes, I will be your wife." I don't know the voice leaving my body, but I keep nodding as he slides the ring onto my finger.

"I love you!" He stands and pulls me into him, kissing me like he's never kissed me before.

When he pulls back he asks, "Are you okay?"

I nod, pretty sure I'm in shock. I look at my finger through my teary eyes, and back up at the man of my dreams. He pulls me close again, whispering his thanks to God, the universe, and whoever else is listening.

I don't know how much time has passed, but I pull back and blurt, "I have to tell my sister! My mom! My dad!" He smiles, pulls out his phone, and sends a text as I reach for my bag. "Let's go! I have to tell Lo!"

He grabs my hand and takes me back down the steps of the cloud, pressing a button to bring the lights up to a brighter level.

*Just as I reach the bottom, the door opens, and in rushes my mom, "My Lailani! It took everything in me to keep this from you!" She pulls me into an embrace, and Dad and Reelin hug.*

*"Wait, you knew!" I squeal out, pulling away, immediately pulled into my dad.*

*"Of course we knew. Reelin isn't the kind of guy to ask you to marry him without our blessing," Dad winks, kisses my forehead and gestures to Mom. "This one has been crying all week about it, that's why you haven't seen much of her."*

*"I'm just so happy for my baby!" Her eyes mist over, and she hugs me again.*

*"We should probably let Lonayla in on this now," Reelin says through a light laugh to my dad.*

*"Wait," I look at my parents, "Lo doesn't know?"*

*"It was too much of a risk." Reelin shrugs and comes close, swapping places with Mom. He puts his arm around my back, kissing my temple. "I needed you surprised. Forgive me?"*

*"I'm not the one you should be asking. Lo might kill you for keeping her out the loop," I laugh, shoulder bumping him.*

*We go back into the club to tell my sister, with my parents joining.*

*My 21st birthday celebration was even better than I could have wished for.*

"Wow, I don't know how I almost forgot," I look at the ring a little closer.

"Yeah, me neither. The ring is everything you wanted. He always paid attention to you and your ridiculously expensive tastes. I still want to know how he was able to afford you. They did well for themselves with Mama Michaels and the money from Kieran's dad, but Rizz would spend BANK. I still need to know his secrets.

I let out a small huff, "why do you have this?"

Lonayla looks thoughtfully at me, "I've had it since that day in the hospital, when Rizz came out of the second surgery. You weren't there when I arrived. He was a mess, Lailani. He told me you called off the engagement, and that he didn't mean whatever he said to you. He asked me to hold on to the ring and give it to you when I thought you were ready." She frowns, "Back then, you just pretended the engagement never happened. Like the whole year of looking at dresses and venues never happened. Whenever he called you his fiancée, you immediately shut it down. You wouldn't let anyone mention it. Then, after months of pretending, y'all went on your grad trip, and when you came back, you were alone. And then you moved."

"And then I moved…"

I turn the ring over in my hand. "But why are you giving it to me now?"

"Today? Church. That sermon started with not judging others, and turned into a full-on speech about why you two belong together. I know y'all caught that, too."

Lo smiles, "And because you laid everything on the table, telling Rizz about your personal life while you were apart. I felt it even more, then. I almost gave it to you last year, when you drove home from work that day and the next, decided you couldn't drive anymore. You cared about what happened to you, without a second thought. I know it was Rizz making you feel like your life meant something more, again."

I shake my head, "I stopped driving because I didn't want to hurt anyone else, not for me. You know I wasn't even driving before that! That was my first time driving my car, and I had had it for two months by then. I got my one drive in, and decided it wasn't safe by the time I parked, because I didn't lose control, and I shouldn't press my luck. It wasn't Reelin."

"Yes, of course you cared about other people, but that day, you explicitly stated that you didn't want to 'die driving when there's still more life to live.' And I knew you were open to him again. It's okay to have someone who makes you want to live, La."

She reaches for the ring, "let's see if that finger can even fit into this dainty ring, miss I-eat-Cuban-food-twice-a-week."

When my sister pushes the ring onto my finger, it feels so right, I want to cry. But it also feels wrong, because I have no idea what is even happening with Reelin. He went to do whatever, with whoever, and I still feel so betrayed by him. I feel like he has some resentment lingering there, too. I don't know what we need to do to move forward, but I hope we can figure it out, soon.

Lo's phone dings, and she excuses herself.

I sigh and lay back on the bed, holding my hand up in admiration. I chuckle at myself because I thought my sister could be keeping something crazy from me. I've never even had a reason to doubt her or her intentions. This is probably Kieran's secret, too. I've been so worked up for nothing.

Maybe the answer to my survival is both options. Maybe I'm supposed to deal with death, while also learning in rebirth, that love is worth the leap.

But first, I have to know who the hell Stacee is.

# 15 : Love The Way You Lie

**New Message from Reelin Houldover Jr.: I know I took a little longer than expected, I'm omw.**

**Me: okay.**

**Reelin: I'm sorry I didn't clarify where I was going. It was nowhere important.**

I look at the time on my phone screen, then at the ring still on my finger.

**Me: it's fine. I'm not your owner, it's not my place to question you.**

**Reelin: You can always question me. It will always be your place. I just wish I always had the answers to give you.**

**Reelin: The answers you want**

**Me: so, if I ask who is Stacee again?**

**Reelin: Please, leave that alone.**

Lonayla and I are in the TV room, watching *Living Single*. She's lounging on the couch, and I'm on the floor, closing up my hair box that I have had since I was a kid. We just finished straightening our hair, and it smells like burnt hair follicles—just like when we were teenagers.

"La, Kieran said they're close. You want me to take your hair box back to the closet?" Lonayla gathers up her things.

"Yeah, thanks," I stretch my legs and lay back on the large pillow behind me.

Lo lifts my box from the floor, shaking her head, "you should've stretched, bro. You've been skipping stretches and meds. I haven't seen you take anything since we got here." She carries our boxes down the hall.

I take a few short breaths, then use my hands to pull my knees towards my chest. Sometimes, my body lets me pretend that sitting in one spot for too long isn't the worst thing. Most times, though, I struggle to get back up.

I hear Lo's slippers shuffling back.

"You gonna take the muscle relaxers at least? I know you don't like the pain stuff, but what about everything else?"

I sigh, and my chest feels like someone just kicked me in it. "No, ma'am. I stopped all of my medication weeks ago, and I have been able to do more, since."

"That sounds stupid and dangerous, Lailani."

My brows pinch together involuntarily, "okay, so don't do it. It sounded great to me, and it has been working just fine."

"Whatever. I know you're stuck." She comes in front of me and reaches for my hands. I take hers, begrudgingly. "You gotta tell Rizz. It's been long enough. He still has no idea that less than a month before you rekindled, the doctors' news ruined our lives."

"Your life is just fine, girl. So is mine." Now standing, I bend my knees a little, still trying to hold her hands. "If I can help it, he'll never know."

"They said you're dying, Lailani. He's gonna know" She releases my hands, once I'm steady on my feet, "It's not like there aren't signs and symptoms."

"I was always clumsy. He's always known me to be a little anxious, and for my body to be reactionary to my feelings. It's normal. If he doesn't know, he doesn't have any worries he can't fix for me, and I'd like to keep it that way." I walk out of the room to go downstairs.

"You sound so crazy. Things progressed so quickly in just that year before your diagnosis. That shit was not normal. You never fell like that before, Lailani."

Lonayla follows me down the stairs and into the kitchen where Mom is prepping dinner. I signal for her to hush, but she keeps going. "I'm serious! You had those weird episodes where you basically blacked out time, you kept finding random bruises, and then, you literally fell like a board in front of us! This is REAL, Lailani!"

I sit at the island, and Mom has stopped peeling the potatoes, "Lailani, your sister is right. Things are different now. We know the problem is more serious than when you thought it was just anxiety."

"Exactly! She doesn't want to tell Rizz, but he deserves to know."

Lo goes to stand by our mom, "Look at her finger Ma, then tell me he doesn't need to know!"

I put my face in my hands.

"Your engagement ring?" I can hear the joy in her voice, wrapping around me. "I thought you gave it back! He asked again?"

"She did give it back. Then he gave it to me to return to her when I thought she was ready." Lonayla opens the fridge, "I was hoping once she put it on, it meant she trusted him enough to let him know she has a terminal illness. But I was clearly way too hopeful for my insanely selfish sister."

"What's this about selfish?" Dad comes and sits next to me,. After a moment, he says, "Lailani, your finger looks very cold. Icy, even."

I remove my hands from my face with a snort, "It's not a big deal. Lo had it, she put it on me, the end."

"And yet, it's still there," Lonayla rolls her eyes and takes a sip of her apple juice, "Daddy, tell your daughter that Rizz deserves to know about her diagnosis, please?"

"I think that La has to figure that out for herself," he responds, and Lo rolls her eyes.

"Thank you, Daddy," I smile, and Mom shakes her head.

"I think that if your sister wants to keep such an important thing away from Reelin, she must be doing it for a reason. I think that young man has proven that he cares about her, and he's worth the truth. She knows that. It's a sensitive topic, so just give her some time."

"It's been more than a year since they rekindled. How much more time?" Lonayla looks at me in question.

I tilt my head to one side, raising my brows, "why do you care so much, Lonayla? It literally has nothing to do with you."

Lonayla's face twists, "It literally does. Unfortunately for *me*, *you* are my sister, *sister*. The man you're consistently trying to downplay, is a very good friend of *mine*, and he just so happens to be the *blood-related* cousin of the man I have been raising a family with, WHO, BY THE WAY, ALSO DOES NOT KNOW BECAUSE YOU ARE SUCH A SELFI—"

"Okay, Ladies. We get it," Mom interrupts. "Lailani, while this is your situation, it does directly affect everyone else in this family."

"Their family, too," Lonayla puts her juice bottle in the recycle, "Kieran loves you, and when he finds out I kept this from him, it's going to hurt. But when he realizes you made me keep it from him, that will hurt more and you know it."

"Lailani, you do plan to let them know at some point, right?" I nod at my Dad. "Okay, at least a week more feels acceptable, right Lonayla."

My forehead wrinkles and my mouth falls open. *A week?*

"Fine. By Friday or I'll tell him for you," Lo raises one eyebrow in challenge.

I return the expression, "I'll do as I please, when I please, and you will mind your business."

The doorbell rings, and I get up.

"I'll get it," Dad says, passing me by.

Mom sighs, and goes back to peeling her potatoes, "Lonayla, you said Jammy isn't coming till seven, now?"

"Yeah, her boyfriend picked up a shift at work, so now Kayde's picking her up, and they'll get Pooda.  We'll be back at seven, too." Lonayla walks around me, as Reelin comes into the kitchen, behind our dad, who sits back at the island.

"Hi," Lo pats Reelin's shoulder, but keeps walking.

"It's just after four, Ma. If you need me to do anything, I can. We're just running up the street to look at the housing for The Reliving," I say as Reelin hugs her.

She pokes her knuckle in his dimple, "no, y'all be safe. We'll see you at seven."

She winks at me, and Reelin follows me toward the front door.

"I like your hair," he says, reaching for my coat to help me into it.

"Thank you," I turn to the door, where Kieran and Lonayla are.

Lonayla's nose scrunches when our eyes meet, "Look at her hand."

Reelin does.

"What's wrong with it?" He asks us both.

Lo looks at my ringless hand, as I wave them together. She shakes her head in disgust.

"What's wrong with it? Are you hurt?" The wrinkles between Reelin's brows deepen.

I shake my head, giving a small smile, "no, Lo's just being a brat. High school version, remember?"

Kieran looks at me with wide eyes as Lonayla says something only he can hear. His brows furrow and one side of his mouth turns down. I shrug.

Lo rolls her eyes and walks outside, "Let's go see our home for the next two weeks."

Kieran smiles, following her, "so, we're really thinking about it?"

"What was all that about?" Reelin asks, "am I missing something?"

"Not at all, Reelin. Leave it alone," I wink.

When we walk outside, I absolutely hate how cold it is. The wind is angry, and my freshly straightened hair is blowing over my face. Reelin's warm hand is on my back, while he walks me to Kieran's car. When he opens the door and Lonayla is in the back seat.

"Lo, get up front."

"Why would you get back there, lady?" Reelin asks as I get in.

Lo smiles sweetly at him, "you need the leg room. We're fine back here."

He gives a half shrug, "you good?" I nod, and he closes my door, then gets in, himself.

"Need me to move my seat up?"

"I'm good."

Kieran's watching me in the rearview mirror. I widen my eyes in question, "Kieran, are you deejaying?"

He shakes his head and pulls out of our driveway, "Lonayla, you want the aux?"

"Nah."

Lo digs into her purse, and my Fenty gloss bomb tumbles out onto the seat. My heart skyrockets, and I pick up the gloss.

"Lonayla, how did you get this gloss?" When she looks at my hand, she shrugs, and continues her digging. "Lo, answer me. I know it's mine, and I know it was in my bag last night."

She pulls out her phone, and ignores me, but I press on, "the bag that's now missing? The one from the scene of the crime against my life?"

"I don't know, Lailani. You sound confused. You might need a nap."

Who the hell is she talking to?

"No, Lonayla. Stop playing with me. This is my gloss. You don't even like the heat bombs, so WHY do you have this? This specific one? I used it AT the party, so explain."

I can feel my body vibrating, and I'm pretty sure my heartbeat has reached the cardio zone. What the hell is my sister up to?

She sends a text to someone, then looks at me with an annoyed head shake, "I said I don't know. You've been a little lost these past few days, girl. You clearly got it mixed up somehow." She shrugs and shifts in her seat, looking out the window.

I know for sure I had this gloss, and my sister just lied to me. The gaslighting alone is enough to make me break into hives. I try to calm myself, so I close my eyes. That was a mistake.

The flash come again.

*Reelin. Lonayla. Kieran laughing at me. Reelin and the initial tree. Random chick smiling at me. Lonayla hands me another drink. Kieran jumps into the pool. Reelin at the grill. Monica announces her pregnancy. Jessy hands me a honey bun. Random chick approaches Kieran, and he looks at her like he's seen a ghost; he pulls away from her. Reelin and the random chick are in a heated discussion—she reaches for him, and he doesn't stop her.*

The pain in my palm from squeezing the gloss so tight, makes me look down at my hands, bringing me back.  It's not the first time I saw that last memory, but it was the first time I saw that girl talk to Kieran. His reaction doesn't help calm my nerves about Reelin's opposite one.

So, he knows her, too. Why did *he* look so unhappy to see her?

Lonayla says to Kieran, "Play some music."

A moment later, Rihanna's voice comes through the speakers, singing *"Love The Way You Lie."* I look at the rearview mirror to see Kieran's looking at me again. I chuckle in annoyance under my breath and turn to look out my window, too.

What the hell is going on?

# 16 : Busted

"What the actual fuck is wrong with you, Lailani?" Lonayla asks, just before Reelin and Kieran open our doors.

We get out and start toward the mall.

We were only about a block away from our house, when Kieran and Lonayla decided it made sense to get the matching pajama sets for our parents and the kids before going to the dorm. Reelin jogs ahead to getting the door for two elderly ladies.

"No, what is wrong with you, Lonayla?" I side-eye her, walking into the entrance.

Reelin is still holding the door for the large family coming in behind us, when Kieran comes in front of me, "really, La?" He demands, with his eyebrows pinched in.

I look back, and the last man walks through the door, freeing Reelin up to join us. "It's nothing. Chill," I mutter, then I smile at Reelin, who takes my hand in his.

Lonayla rolls her eyes, and starts walking towards Bad Mamma Pajamas, a seasonal pajama shop that was created by an adorable elderly couple who wanted to provide more options for colors and prints during the holidays. This will be their third year in business, and the shop has been a huge success. They have something for everybody and keep all of Atlanta from looking exactly the same.

Right inside the entrance, both Lonayla and I gasp. We walk right up to the rack of mint green, pastel orange and white plaid pajama sets.

"Immediately, yes!" I smile.

"How crazy is this?" My sister squeals out, "The first pair we see? Oh my God, I want them, too! We should get some! It's a sign!" She looks at Kieran.

"Yeah, babe. That's cool with me," Kieran pulls out a pair of the pants to look at the size, "Pants, onesies or shorts?" he asks her.

Reelin squeezes my hand, looking from me to the rack.

Just when I realize he's asking my thoughts on the pajamas, Lo declares, "Onesies for Mom and Dad, shorts for me, La, Jammy and Pooda, and pants for you, Rizz and Kayde!" Her smile gets bigger, as she starts checking sizes, "So freaking perfect!"

I smile and start looking for my size.

Reelin points to a sign on the wall, "Look, hey add on-the-spot personalization."

"That's so cute," I smile again, as we finish gathering the pajamas. "We should get slippers, too,"

Lo starts towards the slipper shelves, with a bounce in her step, and Kieran follows her, with very full arms.

I hold the pajamas up in the mirror, trying to decide between a long sleeve and short sleeve top. Reelin comes up behind me with his PJs over his shoulder, and wraps his arms around my middle.

"Why are you and your sister beefing?" He presses a soft kiss to my neck.

"We're fine, she's just dramatic."

He presses his nose into my cheek, "I know it's something. You've been a little on edge." Lonayla calls his name and he pulls away, turning to her.

"What size?" Lo is still by the slippers, and her face is beaming.

"Twelve and a half," he calls out.

I hang the short sleeve top back on the rack, deciding on the long sleeve, then look up at Reelin just as he looks back at me. I search his face, but I don't know what I'm looking for.

"I guess I just didn't know you kept so many secrets from me." His mouth starts, but I press on, "even with my sister, you two share things that I didn't know about, and I just—" I take a short breath. "I have no idea what else you're hiding from me, and I don't like the way that makes me feel."

Reelin's face twists in a way I've only seen once—when we were in high school, and I thought Maliah Harris was his girlfriend. A mix of annoyance and confusion. I quirk my lip and look to Kieran, who's waving us down from the counter. I give Reelin a shrug, then start over there, too.

"Mom's gonna cry when she sees these!" Lo is so excited she's still bouncing on her toes, "and these, please!" She points to Reelin and me. "Oh, and we would like the customizations, too! La, write the names. You have best handwriting."

The salesperson hands me a pen and pad.

"So, it's Grandyla, Grandypa, Daddy, or K—you want yours to say pops?" Kieran shrugs. Lo mimics his gesture and then continues, "do Pops. Then, Mama Lo, Uncle Rizz, Auntie La, Jammy, Pooda, and Man-Man. Kayde is too formal, and he's still my little man, I don't care," she nods definitively.

Kieran pays for everything, and we move off to the side to wait for the names to be embroidered. Reelin checks his phone, Kieran and Lonayla are hugged up, and I lean against the wall in the corner, watching them all.

Looking at them, I'm reminded of all the lies and the secrets, and I start feeling hot. I know I don't want to talk about it right now, and ruin the evening, because this is for my parents and the kids. I move a little closer to the window, because there seems to be a slight breeze, even though it's inside of the mall. I take a slow, annoyingly painful breath.

Leaning against the glass of the window, my eyes catch on the mobility store. I can see Ms. Veda inside, and I feel a rush of emotion come over me. I think about my illness, and how I was going to tell Reelin about it the day we started talking again.

## November 21, 2023

*I turn off my alarm, and shuffle into my bathroom, to prepare myself to go to the store. I'm so tired, I could sleep for a week, but I always make breakfast when the kids are here. I audibly yawn and reach for my toothbrush, when I suddenly remember that I spoke to Reelin for the first time since the summer of 2012. I freeze, toothbrush midair.*

*"There's no way." I say to myself, then start on my teeth. When I finish tongue scraping, I pause in the mirror again, looking into my reflection. I can hear his voice so clearly in my head—"I've been needing you."*

*"Was that a dream?" I ask myself out loud, then walk back into my room, to check my phone, seeing there's a new notification.*

**New Message from Reelin Houldover Jr.: Please tell me it wasn't a dream.**

*I stare at the message, thinking to close out, then lecture myself, "don't be dumb, La. Use your words." Then, I reply.*

**Me: Your message says delivered, does it not?**

*I'm immediately annoyed with myself, "Lailani, I said use your wor—"*

**Incoming Facetime call from Reelin Houldover Jr.:**

*I panic and press decline. I'm still not sure what to say.*

**New Message from Reelin Houldover Jr.: Good morning.**

**Me: Good morning, Reelin.**

**Reelin: Why didn't you pick up?**

**Me: because I just woke up and I'm ugly.**

**Reelin: impossible**

**Incoming Facetime Call from Reelin Houldover Jr.:**

I answer with the phone facing the ceiling. His face appears and I have to sit. I feel like looking at him in real time, is stealing all the air from my lungs.

I shudder a breath, "Hi."

He laughs, and the sound nearly brings tears to my eyes.

"Why am I looking at the ceiling?"

I've missed seeing those dimples that look like tiny suction cups are inside of his cheeks. His eyes are like chocolate-colored coals that could warm my entire world for many more lifetimes. His smile truly outshines the beauty of the moon, high in the night sky. I can feel every one of my nerve endings respond to the sight of him.

I swallow, "I told you, I'm ugly."

He laughs again, "I'm in a durag, Lailani. Shit, I probably got eye boogers, but I risked you seeing me like this for the first time on the off chance that I get to see you before I start my day. I haven't even brushed my teeth yet, if that makes you feel better."

I laugh, "I did at least brush my teeth before reaching for my phone."

"You could've answered with slime strings coming out your mouth, and I wouldn't care. Let me see you."

I huff another laugh, picking up my phone, "happy?"

"Overwhelmingly."

I can't help my smile.

"There she is."

"You look good, Reelin."

"You're just as perfect as you've always been. Bonnet and all."

I laugh again, then get up to go back into my bathroom, propping my phone up.

"So, what's on the agenda for today, Ironman?"

"Loving you."

*I reach for my facial cleanser, "sir, get out that bed and bump your gums before you start yapping like some fool."*

*He laughs, but gets up, "yes, ma'am. I know you don't play about hygiene."*

*"At all," I work my face into a lather, "so, I want to know everything about the youth center. You going there today?"*

*Reelin's brushing his teeth when I look back at the phone, so I use the time to rinse my face. When I look again, he's smiling so wide, and I swear my bathroom got brighter.*

*"How about you come here this week, so I can show you?"*

*"Umm," I roll my lips between my teeth, so I can apply my toner and SPF, then reach for my moisturizer, "So, we gotta take baby steps. I can't just come to you because we've had a few words."*

*"I can accept that," He starts sharing his screen, "I'll show you now, then."*

*I watch him scroll through images and videos of the youth center, and he explains which rooms are for what, and tells me about the processes. He also shows me some of his counselors, and a few of the volunteer mentors. Most of them are from notable families, and are people with large influences in Atlanta. All black. All very positive role models.*

*I can feel Reelin's excitement, and I'm swelling with pride. He has wanted to do this his entire life.*

*I pull a pair of sweats out of my closet, holding up my phone, "this is truly so incredible. I love that you made this happen. I always knew you would."*

*"You definitely did. You never once told me it was too big of a dream." I look back at my screen and see he's putting on clothes, too. "I was so nervous, La. I didn't know if I could pull it off the way I saw it in my head."*

*Before I can respond to him, I hear a loud noise outside of my window and it startles me. I suck in a gasp as I fall straight back, and my phone flies away from me.*

*Reelin is calling my name, when Lonayla rushes in, "La? You okay?" I roll onto my stomach. "I think that idiot popped their car, again," my sister keeps her arms out as I steady myself to get up.*

*"Hey? Lailani?" Reelin's voice is worried. I sit on the edge of my bed. "Lonayla, what's going on?"*

*Lo picks up my phone, "hey, she's fine," she looks at me, but I'm still a little shaken, and I shake my head, "she'll call you back, Rizz."*

*"Wai—" Lo hangs up on him.*

*"You okay?" She asks me. I nod. "I hate this, La. I hate that this happens to you. I hate that all of this is happening to you."*

*"It's just the way the cookie crumbles."*

*I look at my sister, and her hair is all over her head. She has sleep in her eyes, and dried drool is going straight across her cheek.*

*I laugh, "did I wake you? You look like you were getting that good sleep."*

*"The noise startled me awake! I jumped up and came straight in here for you," she frowns. "That same car did that shit the other day, when you weren't here. That's why I know it was them. It's too fucking early for that shit."*

*"People have to find their joy somehow."*

*Lonayla stands, stretching up high, then she walks over to the door, stopping to look at me, "I'm glad you and Rizz are talking again. Especially now. It's only been a few weeks since your diagnosis was confirmed, and you deserve some happy."*

*"Yeah."*

*When Lonayla leaves the room, I pick up my phone, checking my notifications.*

**New Message from Reelin Houldover Jr.: Are you okay?**

**Reelin: why did Lo hang up on me?**

**Reelin: Call me back, please.**

*I think about it for a moment. I know he won't accept that I just fell and Lonayla freaked about it. So, what do I even say? The truth? That I'm literally supposedly dying, and my body likes to remind me by literally taking me down for any random reason?*

*I call him back.*

*"Hi," I can see that he's driving, now.*

*"What was that?" His frown is so deep.*

*"I fell, it's nothing. Fix your face."*

*"You hurt?"*

*"No, I'm fine. It happens."*

*I shrug and try to ease my way into the topic of my illness, "you know some people have weird reactions to existence. Sickness, weird incurable diseases, and that kind of stuff."*

*"You're not some people, though."*

*The sureness of his tone takes root in me. This is going to be hard for him to accept.*

*"What if I am?"*

*He seems confused by the question, "Lailani, if you were one of those people with some incurable illness, I would find you the cure. Your life is worth more than anything else to me, and I will do everything I can to make sure you live it."*

*I knew he would say something like this, but it still makes my heart fall into my stomach, "you have to focus on your own stuff, Reelin. I have to focus on mine."*

*"Yeah, well. Thankfully, I know you're okay," a pause, "right?"*

*I nod.*

*I know that if I tell him now, he'll only push everything he has to the side, trying to figure out what to do for me. I don't need him trying to take over my worries, and stressing himself sick because he can't fix me. If I am supposed to have him in my life, I know I'll have to tell him somehow. But if he can't handle this, it will only ruin what he has going on, and I won't do that.*

*"Hey, I'm making breakfast, so I have to go to the store. I'll call you later, okay?"*

*"Okay. I look forward to it," his smile could have broken me.*

*Me: Lonayla, can you take me to the store? I need to get things for breakfast.*

*Sissy: You don't wanna drive? I am shocked!*

*Me: No. I don't want to die driving when there's still more life to live*

*Sissy: amen, sister. Give me 10.*

I shiver coming back to the pajama store, moving away from the window, and tightening my coat around me.

Reelin has always cared more about me than a person should care about someone else, but somehow, without me noticing, that seems to have changed. He's keeping secrets and telling lies, and I can't understand why. I look at him, and his eyes are already on me, so I look away.

He clears his throat, "Lo, would you like to explain to me why your sister thinks we are keeping secrets from her?" His voice is quiet and steady, and it sends a shiver down my spine.

Lonayla looks at me, confused, then Reelin shifts his weight, "I would just like to understand why she's under the impression that I can't be trusted."

Lo tilts her head at me, "honestly, Rizz, I asked her the same thing."

Reelin turns back to me, with his brows furrowed, "Lailani, care to share?"

The looks on their faces are filled with both annoyance and accusation. It irritates me, because I keep being reminded that they've lied to me so easily. But now, here they are, acting like I'm the problem for not accepting it.

Kieran tries to ease the obvious tension, "ay, y'all, it's all good. Everybody's cool. We finna have a good evening, and we got The Reliving starting tomorrow. It's all good vibes."

Reelin stands taller, crossing his arms, "nah, it doesn't feel like good vibes. What's going on, Lailani?"

His attitude makes my irritation boil over, "well, we can start with why you left me for dead in the pool on Friday, if you want."

"Lailani, YOU left ME!" Reelin's arms gesture to me. His brows are bunched so tight, and his nostrils flare, "I keep fucking telling you that!"

"See? You're a liar. And your little whore from the party? I know you went to see her, today. And I remember her from that night, too. Very vividly, Reelin. She was in YOUR face, right at the fence to Nowhere," I nod my head once, adding emphasis.

Reelin freezes, looking at me like I just spoke a language he doesn't understand, and then I grew a few additional heads.

"Wait, La." Lo steps in front of me, blocking Reelin from my view.

Kieran reaches for my arm, but I pull away, "Lailani, I think you're mistaken."

I step back, looking past them, "I'm not, though. Am I, Reelin?" I raise my chin at him.

Reelin puts his hands on his head, and takes a few steps back. I can see his chest rising and falling through his white hoodie under his coat, like he's focusing on his breaths. Kieran moves towards him.

"Am I mistaken?" I ask again, "did I not see you and that girl? Go ahead, lie again. That seems to be the common theme this weekend."

The salesperson comes over with all of our things folded neatly into three large bags, wishing us a happy holiday. Kieran and Reelin take the bags, as Lo starts for the exit. The guys are waiting for me to go first, but in my heightened emotional state, I don't feel comfortable walking.

"Lonayla!" She turns, and my eyes plead with her. She sighs, comes back, and loops her elbow into mine. She looks for confirmation in my face before we walk out of the store, back into the mall's common area.

We get halfway to the mall entrance, when I hear my name.

"Lailani!" Kieran's voice is a little more aggressive than I care for.

Lo and I look back. Reelin stopped walking a ways back, and he's sitting on a bench, with the bags on the floor, and his head in his hands.

"Damn. This is about to get real dramatic ain't it?" Lo asks.

I frown, and we walk back to the guys.

"Rizz, man, we were just being girls. It's that time of the month for us both, so our emotions are all over the place," Lo plops down on the bench beside him.

Kieran leans against the railing, looking at me, "whatever you think you saw, La, it wasn't that. Ain't no way in hell Rizz would be talking to a bitch with you right there."

I stare down at Reelin, who removes his hands from his head and sighs, "except I was," he looks at Lonayla, then at Kieran, then focuses on his hands, "I *was* talking to someone by the fence to Nowhere. I swore it was after Lailani left the party, though."

I'm disgusted, "oh, you thought I left, so you what? Called some random hoe to the party? Cuz she ain't part of The Reliving program, and I know she didn't go to our school, Reelin. I have never seen her in my life."

Reelin looks over at Kieran, again, then back to his hands.

Lonayla gets up and comes to my side, wrapping her arms around my waist.

My blood is boiling, "so, who the hell is she? And why was she asking me so many questions? Ew, you pillow talk about me? So, this is all a game to you. Because why the hell would one of your little hoes even feel comfortable enough to talk to me, like she knows me? You're sick."

He stands and comes directly in front of me, a look of horror on his face. One hand reaches to my arm, but I yank it away.

"Lailani, what are you talking about? What did she say to you?"

"Save the dramatics, Reelin. A lot of weird shit happened that night, remember? You having some lil' groupie come to the party wasn't the worst part. You leaving me for dead definitely takes the cake."

"La has her ring!" Kieran blurts, and Lo and I look at him in surprise. Reelin freezes, and when I look back at him, his eyes pin me in place.

Kieran continues, "That's why her and Lo were beefing, man. She has her ring back."

"When?" He reaches for me again, and Lonayla loosens her grip a little, but she doesn't let me go.

For some reason, I can't move.

"Lailani?" His face softens, and his eyes look like someone just stirred the richest cup of hot chocolate, and it's still swirling.

He looks at Lonayla, "really?"

She nods, then moves away, letting him place his arms around my waist, he peers into my eyes, and I'm physically unable to push him away. I don't know what's happening right now, but I am not in control.

"Really?" He's looking at me like he's never seen anything so pure in his life. His forehead presses against mine, and then he whispers, "When you're nervous or confused, your eyes turn aquamarine," and then he pulls me in closer.

About a million things cross my mind, and my body doesn't feel like it's mine. I might be holding my breath, but I'm not sure. But I have this hopeful and hopeless liar in my face, breathing me in, like I'm his only source of oxygen. He's holding me like he's trying to fuse our bodies together.

I can see my sister's face, over his shoulder, and she looks so happy, but this is not a happy day. This man is a liar, and so is she. That fact hasn't gone away. And then, I see Kieran. He winks at me, then gives me an excited nod. It's like they all decided that Reelin admitting he was with that other woman, no longer matters, just because of a ring that was returned to me. It does matter. I still want answers.

Reelin whispers in my ear, "I love you so much, Lailani. You have to trust that."

With his hushed tone, that slight rasp wraps around my brain. I can feel his words in my soul. He peppers soft kisses against the crook of my neck, and it's all too much. I think I feel my body tremble, then everything goes black.

*Summer, 1995*

*"I can't do it!" I scream as my four-year-old sister urges me to jump into the pool.*

*"I did it, La! You're five now! You can know how to swim, just like me!" Lo yells from the middle of the three feet.*

*I'm wearing my pink flower one-piece, blue and white arm floaties, and green swim shoes and goggles Daddy got me.*

*"Lailani, you've got it!" Daddy says from the lounge chair. His bare feet are propped up and his guitar is in hand, "you asked to try again, so let's see you do it!" He encourages.*

*My older cousins, Jaimie and Kayla, are in the pool, too. Jaimie is on the C.S. Williams High School swim team, and she convinced her coach to let her teach me and Lonayla to swim here, after the summer practices. Usually, only the bigger kids would be allowed in the pool, but Jaimie is officially a certified lifeguard, and she's her coach's favorite. Daddy came with us today because I told him I could hold my breath under water now. I thought when I dipped my head under to show him, that would be enough. But they all insist I try to face my fears.*

*"I'm right here, La! I'll catch you!" Kayla's smiling, with arms out, and Jaimie stands next to her, looking up at me, nodding her head happily.*

*"But I don't like the water up my nose. It burns!" I whine.*

"Pinch it, like we showed you! Look, watch Lo do it!" Jaimie says, then Lonayla walks to the edge of the pool in her purple and pink striped one-piece with orange goggles and swim shoes.

I watch my sister pinch her nose, and jump into the water. Then she comes up a few feet away.

"Good job, Lo!" Daddy yells from the chair, "La, if you just jump one time, we can go home, okay?"

"But Daddy, the water is too cold!" I say, walking over to him.

"You were just fine sitting on the steps, babygirl." He sets his guitar to the side, then sits up, "you want me to get in with you?" I nod. "Come on!"

Daddy guides me to the water, and he sits on the edge of the three feet. Lonayla walks up the steps and runs around. "Lo, no running!" My sister sits next to daddy and he says to my cousins, "I got it from here, if you want to go further down."

"Daddy, can I go to the deep end?" Lonayla asks with her eyes wide. Her braids with orange and white beads are up in two ponytails with two loose, hanging in the front of her head. She swipes one away from her eye, "I don't even need floaties!"

"Not today, Sweetie. Let's stay over here a few more days," Daddy pinches her cheek lovingly.

Lo nods with a smile, then slides herself back into the water.

"Daddy, I think I don't want to learn to swim. I don't think it's fun," I say, leaning into him.

He hops down into the water, and then reaches for me.

"No! I don't want to!" I pull away.

"I got you, Lailani. It's okay!"

I gasp as daddy pulls me into the pool. I have to hold my breath, even though he keeps me above the water. He leans on his back, and he floats with me in one of his hands beside him, "see? It's not so bad, huh?"

I don't answer, I just watch the water.

*"La, look at this!" Lonayla says, dunking under the water on the other side of daddy, then coming up right in front of me. "I can show you how to do it, too! You don't gotta be scared!"*

*I shake my head, and keep my hands wrapped around daddy's arm.*

*"Uncle Lonnie," Jaimie's coming back to the shallow water. "We have to leave in ten minutes, for the pool cleaners."*

*Kayla climbs out of the pool, then goes for her towel, "La, you spent the whole hour fighting us!"*

*"She'll get the hang of it one of these days," Daddy says, as he sets me back on the edge. "You okay, babygirl?"*

*I frown, and my eyes fill with tears, as I scoot away from the water, watching Lonayla jump in again.*

*"Hey, stop that! It's okay!" Daddy says, as both he and Jamie climb out of the pool.*

*Kayla wraps me in a towel, picking me up, "Stop crying, you're a big girl." She's bouncing me in her arms, trying to calm me down.*

*"Daddy, why is my sister crying?" I hear Lonayla before her head comes around Kayla's back. My braids are up in a side ponytail, and with my head hanging over my cousins shoulder, the hair is covering my eyes. I see green and white beads more than I see my sister.*

*"We'll try again when you're ready, La." I can feel Jaimie rub my back. "The school is going to start swim lessons with groups of kids next year. Maybe you'll like it better with your friends."*

*Daddy takes me from Kayla, "you all better now, kid?"*

*I shake my head.*

*"What if I said mom got things for you and Granny-Gran to bake a cake?"*

*I raise my eyebrows, hiding a smile.*

*Jaimie laughs, "that always gets her. This one just loves being in the kitchen!"*

*We gather all our things, and walk out to the car.*

*"Daddy? I will try swimming again when I'm ten. Okay?" Daddy laughs as he straps me into my seat. Kayla straps Lonayla in, then climbs in between us.*

*"La, if you wait until you're ten, what are you going to do when everyone else is swimming in the summer?" Jaimie asks, putting on her seatbelt.*

*"I'll be your pretty-cookie-passer-outer from outside the water," I declare, and Daddy gets in, starting the car.*

*They all laugh.*

*A very sleepy Lonayla says from her seat, "I want a cookie."*

*"I'm sure La and Granny-Gran will make us something delicious, baby."*

*Daddy turns out of the parking lot, and I watch the clouds in the sky.*

*I'm just so happy I didn't get water up my nose, today.*

# 17 : So Not The Drama

I open my eyes, and the light near my head causes me to close them right back.

"Lailani?" I hear my mom's voice, but it sounds far away, "nurse!"

The world goes dark.

I move my head, and a beep makes my ears hurt. I can feel my face scrunch.

"Oh My God, La!" I think it's Kieran, but I'm not sure.

I hear sniffles, like someone's crying, but I can't take the beeping sound.

Everything disappears again.

I feel a hand on mine, and I try to move, but I can't. I crack open an eye and I see my dad, holding my hand in prayer. I try to make a sound, but nothing comes out. I can't hear anything as Mom comes up behind him. She's yelling something, as my eyes close again.

I feel heat against my body, and I want to move away from it, but nothing happens. I let out a heavy breath, and the heat shifts like a living, breathing thing.

"Lailani?" Some part of my brain reacts to the sound. "Lailani?" the voice is more insistent this time, and it's like something in my head wants me to react to it. Like my mind is urging me to ease the pain laced into the syllables of my name.

"La?" I hear my sister's voice this time.

My chest hurts as I try sucking in a breath.

The heat has moved away, and I feel someone's hand on my forehead, a thumb gently sweeping across my brow. I turn my head into the touch, and hear a whimper.

"La, I'm here," my sister's whisper sounds so sad, "you're gonna be okay."

I concentrate on opening my eyes, and when I do, my sister kisses my forehead, then says her thanks to God. There is a doctor and a resident walking in. A short woman named Dr. Amy Chen, comes closer as the resident, a tall light-skinned man named Domonic Morris, taps on an iPad at the foot of the bed. My sister doesn't move.

"Good to see those sea green eyes," the doctor, says with a smile, reaching into her pocket for a light, turning it on, "mind if I do some quick tests, Miss Grander?"

The resident moves to the side of the bed where Lonayla is. Lo gives me a look, then stands back only a step or two.

"Can you tell me your name, and where you are?"

I get the sense that I'm missing something important, and my eyes sweep across the room. When the resident shifts, I see him—Reelin, putting his phone into his pocket. He's standing near the window in the far corner, and the look on his face is unreadable, so I can't decide if I want it to stay there or not.

It's like the sun is shining for the first time, and it's only on me. It's rays penetrate so deep, the heat goes beyond my body, blanketing the very depths of my soul. I've always known Reelin's existence lives under my skin, permanently part of me, like a tattoo I can't laser away. Even in our years apart, I would wake some days, and it was like I could smell him near me. Sometimes I would feel his gentle touches in the wind, and I could hear that little rasp that chases his voice in every one of my favorite songs. But right now, it feels even deeper than that. Just the sight of him, across this room, makes me feel whole. Every single atom in my body is screaming his name.

The bright light shines into my eye, as the doctor starts her eye reaction tests, making me frown.

"Miss Grander, just your first name is fine," the light moves away.

"Good pupil dilation," she says to the resident, raising her finger in front of me.

"Can you follow my finger, please?" I do.

"Can you stick out your tongue for me?" I do.

The doctor clicks off the light, and I take a breath, "my name is Lailani. I'm in a hospital."

"Good, Lailani," she does soft squeezes down my arms, then puts her pointer fingers in my hands. "Can you squeeze my fingers?" I do. "You're doing great."

She walks to the foot of the bed, raising the sheet, then runs the tip of her pen up my foot, and I bend my toes against it. "Excellent. So, Lailani," she pauses then looks from me to Reelin, then to Lo. Lo looks at Reelin, and so does the resident.

Reelin's face hardens, "I'll be just outside," he dips his chin as he leaves the room.

Once the door closes, the doctor continues, "Lailani, based on the information given by your family, it seems you fainted in the middle of one of your onset rigidity episodes. Based on your previous diagnosis, you have a heightened chance of certain triggers causing much bigger responses when your body feels it needs to protect you."

I don't react, I simply stare. I know all about my illness, so if that's all, then I'm fine because all of this is normal.

"Your sister tells us that you've recently had more trouble breathing, and that you have been vomiting a lot?"

I look over at Lonayla, and she shakes her head, "don't lie, I heard you. Today and yesterday. And every time I turn around, you're trying to catch your breath."

I take in a deep breath, realizing it does indeed feel tighter than it did yesterday. I sigh out my exhale, "I already Googled it. I thought it was secondary drowning, but the internet said that's not a thing, so I just kept it pushing."

The resident is taking notes, but he speaks up, "Miss Grander, while the internet is a great tool, any serious health concerns need to be properly addressed. What some believe to be drownings, or secondary drownings, are referred to as submersion injuries. It's always best to seek immediate medical attention when you believe something like this has occurred."

"I felt fine, for the most part. Just a little uncomfortable, like I always am. I didn't think much of it, because I know my illness is something that can't be predicted, and sometimes I experience new symptoms. I just assumed I was a little more stressed than normal."

"Your sister and parents said that you prefer to pretend that there's no problems, specifically when it comes to your illness and symptoms," he looks at the doctor, who gives him an encouraging nod. "What we would like to know is, have you been feeling more unwell than usual, and maybe been brushing it all off?"

Lonayla responds before I can, "yes. She thinks if she pretends something's not happening, she's fine. My sister can't swim! She nearly drowned when we were kids, and we all thought she died! And yesterday, she woke up in the pool."

The doctor tilts her head, "woke up in a pool?"

I close my eyes, immediately seeing that girl and Reelin at the party on Friday, so I look back at the doctor, "yes, I woke up floating in the pool, after possibly having too much to drink. I got out, looked a mess and went home. No big." I throw a look at Lonayla, who looks like she's about to cry.

The doctor taps her finger to her chin, "I would like to do a chest x-ray, just to make sure there is no pulmonary edema and I would like to run some blood tests, as well." She nods at her resident, then looks back at me, "I would like you to keep the oxygen on until we can rule out any serious complications from your submersion injury. You may be a little tired, but we think that's your body's way of self-soothing after your stress induced syncope. We've been monitoring since your arrival, and while there were no new life-threatening symptoms, you seemed to need sleep. I'm glad you're awake and alert now. With so little knowledge on your disease, and your previous reports of fatigue accompanied by occasional disorientation, we're hopeful that your tiredness is not because of an additional issue. I want to be safe with the labs and scans, so we'll get those completed shortly. Do you have any questions at this time?"

I shake my head, and the doctor and resident head to the door. Lonayla follows them out.

Almost a minute later, Lonayla walks back in and closes the door, "Rizz wants to come in, but I told him we needed a minute. Mom and Dad went with Kieran to get food, but they're on their way back." She sits in the chair beside the bed.

"Last time you were laid up in a hospital bed like this, we were kids, and I was not allowed to say anything about what happened," she looks so sad.

"I'm fine," I reach up to my nose, and frown at the feel of the cannula. When I pull my hand back, I notice my engagement ring.

"Lo?" I ask, staring at my hand.

"It was in your pocket, Mom put it on you," she leans back, wiping her eyes. "La, everything happened so fast! One second everyone is upset, the next, Rizz looks at you like some profit of the Lord, because Kieran decides to blurt out that you had on that stupid ring, and then you just turned into a freaking living statue!"

She stands, tears running down her face, "we didn't even know if we should drive or call 911! But the mall security saw your body drop. Rizz dropped with you, and then everything just happened so fast!" She sits back down. "The medics came and they put you in the ambulance, and I couldn't even think straight sitting in there with you. All I could do was pray. Rizz went to get Mom and Dad, and Kieran followed the ambulance. When we got here, your blood oxygen was so low!" She looks at my face in terror. "Last time you looked like that, we were kids, Lailani. Even with all the appointments about the spasms and falls, and all the late-night stress-induced research and panic attacks that had us in the emergency room, just for your peace of mind over something you found, you ain't looked like that since we were kids! And when Rizz got back with Mom and Dad, you want to know my first thought?" She angrily wipes the tears from her face. "my first fucking thought was that you wouldn't want him to know what's going on, and I would protect your privacy!"

Lonayla looks so angry as she stands, and walks to the end of the bed, beginning to pace. I don't speak. I just look at my hands on my lap, because she's absolutely right.

"La, that man stood outside this room asking so many questions. I asked the doctors not to say anything. The only reason they listened to me, is that I have your same face, and Mommy was crying on my shoulder as soon as they got here."

She comes and stands close, "what are you gonna do when something happens, and it's only Rizz present?" Her voice is softer now. Tears still falling from her eyes.

"Mommy put that ring on your finger after feeling it in your pocket. She was doing the mom thing, and when she looked at it on your hand again, she told Daddy that Rizz deserved to know what was going on. Of course, Daddy said no. When they finally let him in to see you, and he saw that ring, he walked right back out of here. He walked right back out of here." She sits back down, "Kieran said he was saying that he's the reason you were in here. That his excitement about the ring in that moment sent you into shock. Too bad he doesn't know that your body responds in crazy ways to literally anything!" She stands again, pacing across the room, "This is fucked, Lailani! I can't even ima—"

"I'll tell him," I interrupt. Lo whirls around to me, and I give her a half smile, "I'll tell him soon. Not now, but soon." She frowns. "He'll need to know if I'm to be his wife, right?"

Lonayla's eyes widen, and she rushes to the head of the bed, just as our parents walk in.

"Oh, baby! You okay?" Mom says with misty eyes, coming to kiss my forehead.

"Don't be scaring us like that again," my Dad grips my hand, kissing it.

"I'm fine. I just spasmed, stiffened and fainted. You know how it goes."

"We just saw your doctor. Reelin too," Dad says looking at me in question.

"Soon. I promise," I nod.

"She just alluded to being his wife soon, so I'm good with it." Lonayla says, locking elbows with Mom.

"Wait, what about dinner?" I ask.

"Lailani, it's almost 3am," Mom says, before pulling away from Lonayla and walking over to my dad, "let that boy in here."

Lo goes out the door, and Kieran rushes in almost immediately after.

"Oh my God! I hate being outside the loop," he grabs my hand, "you aight?"

I smile at him, then look at the door, "I'm fine. Where's Reelin?"

Just as I say his name, he comes into view, with my sister on his heels. I smile at the sight of him.

"We should go get some coffee or something," Dad suggests, walking Mom to the door. "Kieran, come on, now. Let's give them a minute."

"I just got here!" Kieran whines like a child and Lonayla pulls him by his jacket. "I won't be gone long, Lailani. I know you need me, girl!" They exit the room, closing the door behind them.

Reelin stands so far away, but his eyes are locked on me.

"You just gonna stare?" I ask. "I know I probably look crazy, but it can't be that bad." My chest hurts, as I huff a little at my joke.

Reelin doesn't laugh. He walks over and sits in the chair beside me, never breaking eye contact. He leans onto the side of the bed, placing his head in his hands. I can see his shoulders drop, as he takes a deep breath.

I wait a beat, deciding what to say. "So, it was you—the heat I felt in my sleep. You really are a human furnace," I reach my hand up to his, trying to peel his fingers from his face. "Look at me, Reelin. You're gonna give me a complex, making me think I'm ugly or something."

He pulls his hands down, looking at me with his lips pressed tight. He wraps both of his hands around one of mine, pulling it to his lips, and holding it there. He looks so tired. So sad. So lost. So helpless. So angry. So many things, all at once.

"Lost for words?" I tilt my head.

When those deep dark brown eyes just stare into mine without so much as a blink, I decide to speak instead, "I may have had a submersion injury from waking up in the pool," I say it like it's no big deal. "I may have had some lingering water in my lungs, causing me to have trouble breathing, and because of all the heightened emotions, I fainted." I squeeze my hand around his fingers, and he pulls our hands to his chest. "But I am okay. Reelin. Everything's fine."

"Lailani, they wouldn't even let me see you." He sounds so hurt, I hate it. "I got back here with your parents, and Lo and K stopped me in the hall, telling me I had to wait." His jaw ticks, "I felt so useless, so out of control, so angry. For the first three hours whenever I tried to come into your room, your pops and your sister stopped me, with no reason why. For the next three hours, I sat in the chapel, thinking the worst thoughts. Every terrible thing that could happen crossed my mind, and I felt like I was losing it. For the two hours after that, I sat on the floor by the door, hoping you would wake up and tell them it was crazy to leave me out there."

He closes his eyes and pulls my hand back up to his mouth, running my knuckles across his lips, "when they finally let me in here, the rage of being shut out was gone, and all I felt was fear. I looked at you, helplessly in this bed, for a reason I do not know. I had to go back out to compose myself. I couldn't even come close to you until your dad looked into my eyes, with your eyes. They were so bright and hopeful, Lailani. That sea green is when you're looking forward to something, and he must know I pay attention to the shades, because he definitely knows how to get through to me—the way that he focuses with them. He guided me over to this chair, and told me it was gonna be okay. He had me take up vigil while he and your mom went out. And after sitting here not even ten minutes, you woke up. But then not even five minutes after that, I was sent right back to the outside. Once again, I wasn't able to know anything that was happening with you. Do you have any idea how that feels?"

There's a knock at the door, followed by a nurse who comes to take me for my x-ray.

They do a blood draw, and answer some of my questions about my chest. I ask the nurse if they can check my blood for any substances that could have caused loss of consciousness. I get a breathing treatment once I'm back in the room, because I coughed up a storm at someone's perfume in the hallway. Reelin sits completely still across the room, while they listen to my heart and then check the rest of my vitals again. Once they get me settled, Reelin returns to sit exactly as he was before I left the room. With my hand in his, and a worried look on his face.

Looking at him like this, I know exactly what I want to do.

"I'd like you to take Lo to our house, to pack a few days' worth of clothes for me."

Reelin's face scrunches, and I smile at his confusion, "I'd like to stay with you, if that's cool? Your place, or the dorm. Whichever."

He frowns, "Lailani, there's nothing I want more than to spend every single second I can with you, but are you even sure you're being released? I don't even know how serious all this is."

"I will be, believe me. Please, tell Lo. The sooner you get our things, the sooner we can be in bed. I'm so tired, and it has been a ridiculously draining weekend. Plus, we have school tomorrow." I wink.

"The Reliving can wait. I would much rather know if you're okay, first."

"Fine. Where is my phone?" He levels a look at me, and I nod, "the chart is updated in real time, sir."

He reaches over to the side table just past my head, then hands me my phone.

**Me: I told Reelin we'll stay with them. Come get him from this room.**

**Me: Make sure to pack tampons, since you lied and said we were on our cycles.**

**Sissy: on, freshly off, either way, same thing.**

**Sissy: wait, you serious about staying with them?**

"The app requires all that typing?" Reelin eyes me suspiciously.

"Sometimes." I chirp. I open the app to the loading screen, then flash it at him.

**Me: yep.**

**Sissy: Mommy ain't going for that school shit if that's what you're up to. And you do know there's no way in hell Rizz is letting you go, so don't even try it.**

**Sissy: mom said are they releasing you?**

**Sissy: we're otw up there**

**Me: yes and no**

"You're texting your sister. I'm not stupid."

"Reelin, if you love me, you'll shut up," I huff, and immediately frown at the tightness in my chest. Reelin notices.

"What's wrong?" He sits up higher in his seat.

"Nothing. I need a toothbrush."

**Me: Take mom and dad home, please. Tell them I'm fine.**

**Kieran: Hell nah. We finna be up there**

**Me: Please. You're supposed to be on my side, remember?**

**Kieran: nope**

"I think I want my hair box, so when y'all get to the house, get it for me?"

I sit up higher in the bed, looking at his concerned face, "also, when's the last time you got tested?" His jaw drops in surprise. "I was tested in October again. For obvious reasons, even though I was protected. I still don't want any surprises, you know?"

Mom walks in, "why are you trying to dismiss us?" Lonayla, Dad and Kieran make their way in, too. "There's no hanky-panky in the hospital, you two!" Mom jokes, and I'm glad she's in a good mood.

Dad scrunches his face, Lo gasps, and Kieran just walks over to me, looking at my face like there's something on it.

"What's that white girl movie with the dying sister and the mama who's trying to fix her with the other sister? You look like her all laid up like this."

Kieran's question gets ignored, because it's rude.

"I'll be released within the hour. Did Lo tell y'all we were gonna try the dorms for a few days? I figured all of this was a bit much, and you two deserve a break."

"If you're sure you're fine Lailani, okay," Dad leans against the wall and crosses his arms.

"Lailani, I don't want no shit!" Mom chastises. "Don't let me find out you pretended to be okay, then chased us out of here, and left without being discharged." She looks at Reelin with her lips pursed.

"Ma, who would she leave with? We're all going back to the house—Rizz included." Lonayla says.

"Okay," Mom narrows her eyes at me.

"Lo, you want to just ride with them to get your things?" Reelin asks. "It doesn't really make sense for all of us to go, when we have to come back for Lailani. I'll make sure the doctors clear her, and we can meet you over there."

Lonayla looks at me, "I guess. Whatever."

Kieran squeezes my arm, "I feel like you're trying to pull away from me, Lailani. Trying to get rid of me won't work. We're in this life together forever, sister."

"Kieran, I know that any effort to be rid of you for good, is for naught." I let out a little laugh. "Now get my parents home, it is way past their bedtime."

"Mhmm," he looks at Mom, "You believe this?"

Dad comes and kisses my forehead, "let's go, she wants us gone. I know how to take a hint."

Mom comes and kisses my cheek, then her and Lonayla walk out after Dad. Kieran follows behind them, but before closing the door, he pauses to give me the eye-to-eye gesture. I laugh as the door closes

When I look back at Reelin, he's staring at me, "So?" I ask.

"So?" He counters.

"Tell me something."

The doctor comes in, and looks at me in question. Reelin's entire body stills.

"I told him I had to do tests for a submersion injury." I say, grateful she seems to catch on to not mentioning my other things.

"I think I'm okay with releasing you. I did send an antibiotic to the pharmacy to get ahead of any possible infection, and an inhaler just in case, with your slight difficulty breathing. I would like for you to follow up with your primary care physician in the next week. A nurse will be in with discharge papers shortly. I hope everything goes well for you, Miss Grander. Please feel free to reach out to me, on the portal, when you need to." I nod with a smile, and the doctor walks out.

I focus my attention back on Reelin, "so, are you gonna go downstairs to get tested? Or are you gonna keep sitting there, acting like I didn't already bring it up?"

His eyes widen, "I thought… I—" He pauses, and I find his apprehension funny. "I don't know what I thought."

"The sooner you get tested, the sooner you can share the results. The sooner you share the results…" I nod, widening my eyes, hoping he catches my drift.

"Oh. Yeah. Um. Okay," he stands, and the movement is so awkward, I laugh. "I'll be right back," when he leaves, his face is still in disbelief.

I sit up, looking around the room, then take a deep breath. I'm so thankful the breathing treatment is seeming to do what it's supposed to, because I can feel my lungs expanding more.

I open instagram, and go to Reelin's profile. I scroll his followers and his follows, looking for anyone named "Stacee," and I zoom into every brown-skinned girl-without-a-real-name's profile picture, trying to find any signs of the woman who made Reelin lie to me.

I've already decided I'll focus on my would-be-murder, later. This feels a little more pressing. I'm locked all the way in on Reelin, but one thing I refuse to be, is stupid. I might have a chance to fall all the way in love with this man, and I feel like I should take it. But if someone else is in the picture, that's a problem for me. I won't be sharing, and I won't let someone else make me feel like second choice, ever.

Lailani Grander is one of one. Number one. The only one. And that's on Beyoncé.

# 18 : Put A Ring On It

Much to my dismay, I didn't find anything on Stacee. I can't think too much about it right now, though. I'm on a mission: Operation Give Reelin a Shot.

The discharge nurse just left, and I'm ready to go. I still had on my bra and gray fleece-lined leggings, so I just have to pull on my golden-yellow long sleeve, my socks, and my Dr. Martens.

I sit back down, unlocking my phone to text Reelin, so I can meet him downstairs.

"You ready?" I didn't hear him coming through the open door, and my heart jumps with excitement. I don't know how his voice still does whatever it does after almost 20 years, but when I'm not prepared for it, it's like it attacks my senses, but then soothes me, immediately after.

I smile, "I am." I get up and wrap my gray scarf around my neck, and Reelin walks over with my jacket, holding it open for me. "Thank you."

He grabs his coat off the chair. His nervousness from earlier is gone, but he seems a little preoccupied.

"The nurse said the pharmacy was having issues, so I had them send my prescriptions to the one by the school," I say, walking toward the door.

"Okay. You feeling alright?"

"Yes, sir," I smile, grabbing his hand, and we make our way outside.

It's freezing and I hate it. It doesn't feel like Georgia out here. It feels like the arctic, and I was not built for this. When we get to Reelin's car, I'm so cold, I don't think my knees will bend.

"What's wrong?" Reelin's concern is heavy in his tone.

"I just need a second," I turn to him, wrapping my arms around his neck, stalling for time. "Kiss me?"

He stares into me, with those little wrinkles between his brows deepening, "are you sure you're okay?"

I test my knees, and to my surprise, they bend. Good.

"Yes, I'm fine, worrywart. And you're lucky I'm not offended by you not kissing me when I asked," I pat his chest, then climb into the car. He looks at me with a question he doesn't ask, then closes the door.

When he gets into the car, I'm confused. I just remembered that Kieran drove last night, but Reelin went to get my parents, somehow. "How are we in your car?"

He explains as he pulls out of the hospital parking lot, "Jammy brought it. I took K's car to get your parents, and he followed behind the ambulance in an uber. When I got to your house, your mom was still cooking, and your pops told me to let the kids know dinner was cancelled. I called Kayde from the car, and he was already with Jammy, and she freaked a little. Kayde still had to go get Pooda, so Jammy said she would bring me my car, because they were at Aunt Kira's, where I parked it, and my spare key stays there. They wanted to see you, too."

He takes a quick breath, and I see a hint of frustration in his eyes.

"We didn't know anything, La. Then when I got your parents to the hospital and they wouldn't let me see you, your pops told Lo that the kids were on their way. K intercepted Jammy in the lobby, he told her they would keep them posted, but not to worry. When Kayde and Pooda got here, Lo and Kieran told them they shouldn't even stay. Only reason they listened and left was because Lo told them I couldn't see you, either." He looks over at me, taking my hand in his, and holding it tight, "that didn't stop the worrying."

I bite on my bottom lip. I was really hoping the kids wouldn't have to worry about this. I'll make it up to them.

"I'm sorry I ruined the evening."

"You didn't ruin anything," he stops at a red light, and then looks at me with a frown, "you not being okay, would have ruined everything. But you are, and that's the blessing we're leaving with."

I look down at our joined hands, "you haven't said anything about the ring."

The light turns green. "I don't know what there is to say. I was so happy to know you had it, but then, you were in the hospital. And when I saw it on your finger, I almost lost my mind thinking that you having it, was why you were in this situation. I'm sorry for stressing you out."

"It wasn't the ring. I was overwhelmed with a lot of things, and there were residual side effects from the pool. Your excitement didn't do that. Well, not alone, anyway."

He squeezes my hand.

I almost feel guilty for not wanting to talk about my condition, just yet. Knowing I have an actual problem might ease some of his guilt about what happened. But I know that It could also make things worse, and he'll want to fix me, but he can't. That's the reaction I'm not quite ready for.

He kisses my hand, "I don't know what happened at the party, Lailani. When you said that she spoke to you, I was so confused, because that shouldn't have been possible." He stretches his neck, clearly uncomfortable talking about this. "But I swear to you, I have never slept with that person, nor would that have ever been an option. I don't know her. Not really. She's someone that was around before, but never like what you think."

"Okay."

I don't believe him, but I also don't need this conversation to keep going. I want to know the truth about her, but I want to make the best of The Reliving, first. If Reelin's playing a game, I can play, too. But since he's been back in my life, I've felt all the feels, and I want to give myself a chance to explore them. Even if this girl turns out to be our final end, I won't let her ruin things before I'm ready. These next few weeks, I want to see where we can go. I feel like we're really supposed to try, one more time.

"So, what's the playlist you mentioned?" I ask enthusiastically.

Reelin huffs a laugh, releasing my hand, to pull out his phone, "you really don't check any of the group messages, huh? It was in the Facebook thread."

"Yeah, I don't do those. That's a whole lot going on."

Bow Wow's *"Let Me Hold You"* starts playing, and Reelin smiles so wide, "our song."

I bark out a laugh, "no freaking way this was on there!"

"It's all the songs from freshman year through '09." His smile widens, and it makes my heart happy. "This was our shit, sophomore year."

"You were annoying as hell, thinking you were "box-top Bow Wow," or something" I laugh, turning up the volume.

We vibe out to the music from our past, all the way to the school's campus.

The early college additions to the school are super nice, and everything looks very modern. C.S. Williams sits on so much land, and it's amazing how often they update things. When we were students here, we got the outdoor pool, magnet building, and the new sports complex upgrades to the gym. Since then, they've added an amphitheater, a new stadium, and the early college with its many housing units.

The tech kids now have a completely different building that has more updated resources to further expand their minds. There's also a golf course, a warehouse for creative projects, and the new gym right next to the one we used for the party. The old gym demolition begins in January.

They're leaving the outdoor pool, but turning the old gym into a tranquility center with a green house, sand rooms, sensory rooms and other calming spaces to help promote better mental health practices.

When Reelin opens my door, I struggle to get out, and wobble a little too noticeably.

"What was that?" He's holding my arm with one hand, and his other is on my waist.

"My foot fell asleep, I think," I give him a little nudge. "Relax, I am not made of porcelain."

I think calming thoughts, willing my body to chill. Sometimes, thoughts become things, and I need these thoughts to do the right thing. I'm going to tell him. I am. I would just like to have a good night's sleep, first. I need the conversation to go well. I tell myself I'm safe. That everything's fine, and I need to be okay.

"You look like you're struggling," Reelin moves a hand to my cheek, focusing on my eyes, "Are you sure you're okay? I can't tell, because that hopeful sea green is looking back at me, but your face says something's wrong."

"I'm fine," I insist, pulling away. "Also, my eyes are just green. You think too hard about it, because I literally always just see green." I lean forward, pressing a kiss to his lips, "see? Fine." I widen my eyes, still close enough to feel his breath on me, "see? Green." I chuckle. "Get it? See green? Because you said, 'sea green' is what they are, right now?"

Reelin's hand comes back to my face, then slides from my cheek to my jaw. My breath catches at the shift in his gaze. His hand grips my neck, the other pulls me flush against him.

"Tell me to kiss you, again," he speaks softly against my lips, and I can feel my body responding to him.

"Kiss me."

And he does—like his life depends on it. I can't get enough of how soft and supple his lips are. I release a moan, and he puts his hand inside of my coat, gripping my ass through my leggings. He grips harder, pulling, and it spreads my opening. The friction of my panties sliding back into place when he loosens his grip, sends sparks all through me.

"Ah, boo!" Lonayla's voice comes from behind Reelin, and he pulls away with a tiny groan. "Get a room!"

He turns to Lonayla, releasing me. I steady myself. The cold wind cools me down from the inferno Reelin just sent through me.

"Y'all so nasty. I love it." Lo smiles with all 32 teeth.

Kieran walks over, carrying mine and Lo's Béis weekender bags. I move close to my sister, and Reelin closes the car door, before taking the olive bag from Kieran.

"How you know that's hers?" Lonayla asks.

Reelin's throat makes a sound. He looks at the bags, then back to Lo. "There are two options, and one is green. Be serious." He smiles, gesturing for us to walk ahead.

"How these lil' bags this heavy?" Kieran questions.

"Essentials, baby," Lo shrugs, grabbing my hand, so we can cross the path to the roundabout near the building.

Kieran calls out to us, "go right. Top floor, last one on the left."

I suddenly feel very anxious thinking about walking upstairs. My legs already feel like they're going to walk away from me, any second. I look up, and there are four floors. That means three flights of steps. I inhale slowly. We turn into the opening, and thankfully there's an elevator.

"Oh, thanks be to Jesus!" Lonayla exclaims. I exhale my own thanks. She presses the elevator button, and the door immediately opens, "I was finna tell y'all we had to go home. I wasn't doing the stairs. Especially in the cold."

"Forever Princesses," Kieran laughs, as we step onto the elevator and the doors close. He presses the number 4, and Lonayla releases my hand, taking his.

Reelin moves into my space, staring down at me. My ears and cheeks start to heat. The slow smile that crosses his face is enough to make me collapse. I grab at his waist to steady myself. His deep dark chocolate eyes unravel me to my core, and he's known this since he met me. He smirks and looks away, releasing me from his obvious hypnosis.

The doors open and Lo steps off first. Kieran and Reelin exchange a look I can't read, then Reelin takes the bag from him. I step off before Reelin, reaching for his arm to walk with him, because I don't feel confident enough to walk this outdoor hall by myself. He gives me an appreciative smile, like the closeness is a gift. I always forget how easy he is to please.

We get to the last door on the left, door 416, Kieran unlocks it, then looks back at us with an awkward smile. When he opens the door, the inside is illuminated with a romantic glow.

We walk inside, and there electric candles everywhere. The foyer we step into is about a third from the left of the rectangle shaped space, directly across a hall that leads to the back rooms. There's a kitchen with a breakfast nook to the immediate left, with three huge bouquets of flowers, with tiny pastel orange boxes in front of them. There are white rose petals scattered around it with…

…Actually, wait.

*Lonayla*

We walk into this apartment my man and Rizz got for The Reliving or whatever, and it's decked out real romantic! Candles and rose petals are everywhere! I'm looking all around, trying to see everything at once. I just love how much effort Rizz puts in for my sister, man.

So, I look to the left when we come in the door, and see beaucoup flowers in these big ass arrangements. Its red, orange and pink roses in all of them, but with little added things in each. All different. Probably something symbolic about them for Lailani. They're beautiful as hell, too!

There are tiny flat gift boxes in front of each bouquet, and I'm guessing they're cards with some sweet things on the inside. La is gonna die! She's so weird with romance, but this is so cute! She just told me she was going to be his wife, anyway, so she should love this. They're clearly vibrating on the same frequency, because how the hell he managed this today, I don't know. But hell yeah!

I turn to the rest of the kitchen. On the stove, there's food!

"Rizz, you got my mama to finish the food?" I ask, peeking through one of the clear lids. "Wait! She was making chicken, I thought. This is salmon!" I look over at Rizz and my sister, and he's just smiling like a big dopey kid, and La is just looking around, taking everything in. I wink at Rizz.

I should probably let Lailani look around without me getting into everything first, but as long as I don't touch it, they should be cool. The candles that are everywhere are those cool electronic ones you control with an app, and they're orange right now, so he probably wanted to match the flowers. I walk around the sink, to a large burnt orange box on the middle of the high-top counter, and I can't wait to see what's in it!

When I turn away from the counter, to cross over into the living room area, Rizz walks by me to take our bags to the back. The sectional is cream colored and soft, and there is a little orange box on one of the plush pillows. You've gotta love that man's attention to detail. I walk around the sectional, looking at the coffee table that has a long black box with an orange bow on it. If it's another coat, I'm gonna gag! I turn to my sister, who's by the high-top counter. She's looking at me with the brightest eyes, like she might cry, and I love this for her, real bad.

I smile, walking over to the pool table just beyond the seating area. There's a black album for photos or something on it. It's probably some kind of scrapbook or some shit of all their firsts. Rizz has always loved La out loud, so I just know he's extra sentimental in private.

I turn to look behind me, past Kieran, who's standing like a statue next to the sliding glass door. It's still dark, so I'll go out there in the daytime. There's a phat ass flat screen tv and sound system in the middle of the wall. This is gonna be a cute little spot to stay in. It's simple enough, and cozy.

I walk over to my sister, and I am so excited! She hasn't moved from by the counter, and Rizz is standing by the other end that leads down the hall. He must be waiting for her to take it all in, before he takes her for more in the back. I'd be jealous if it were anyone else, but my sister deserves this kind of shit.

"Um, La!" I urge, "look around!"

She has the biggest eyes, right now. It's so funny seeing my reflection look back at me. Like, she's real cute or whatever. Those misty eyes are so adorable, because one thing my sister's gonna do, is pretend she doesn't have feelings. It's about time she showed some emotion!

"Lonayla, did you even look at everything?" La's eyebrows pull together, "like, really look?"

I'm confused by the question. Rizz walks over, pulling her close to him, and then he looks at me with wide eyes, like I'm missing something.

"Lailani don't be selfish," I say. "Why aren't you opening anything? You don't want us to see, or something?" I turn to look for K, to agree with me, but he's still standing in that corner, looking crazy.

"Lo, look again," I scrunch my face at Rizz's smile.

"I don't need to. Lailani—"

My sister reaches out, grabbing my hand, and we stare at each other for a moment. There's something so sweet in her eyes. She's looking at me like a sweet baby, or a cute puppy. I tilt my head at her, and she just nods. Then I look at Rizz, who has a small smile on his face, then he nods too, gesturing behind me. I turn around, seeing Kieran still standing over there, and I finally realize he's standing in front of something.

I freeze.

"Lonayla," Lailani's voice reminds me to breathe.

When I look back at her, she looks at the flowers, then gestures for me to turn back. I do. I turn in place, looking at everything again.

There's orange, everywhere. Orange. Not green. Is this not for Lailani? I struggle with my thoughts, pretty sure my brain is short-circuiting. Did Kieran do this? There's no fucking way.

I look at Kieran again, and my baby looks so nervous. I take a deep breath, trying to calm my tummy—or my heart, that's in my tummy—I don't know. My man has always physically affected me. He can take me from angry to giddy with just a wink of his brown eyes. He has the most innocent eyes, with long lashes that fan out over them, like a baby doll. He got his hair cut on Friday, so he looks extra handsome with his locs pushed back from his face. I walk over to him.

When I'm in front of him, he reaches a hand to hold mine. I look into his face, and he smiles so sweetly, I choke back a sob. I love this man with everything I am. I often doubt his ability to step up, and that doubt lives under my skin like my Nexplanon. But here he is, doing something so romantic, for me.

"You know I've loved you since I was missing my front teeth, and you was running around with hair beads and bobo's," He looks over to Rizz, then back at me, wiping the tear that falls from my eye, just as Dondria's "You're The One" starts playing quietly behind me. I look over my shoulder and see that there was a tiny speaker next to the album on the pool table.

Kieran continues, "when we were just kids, I would see you and I would feel like the sun started shining, only on you and me. When we would fight, especially over stupid things, I would feel like I couldn't breathe, and the whole world was coming to an end. When you'd come back to me, all my senses would come alive, like it was for the first time."

He releases my hand, pulling the large, thin object from behind him, to in-between us, "Lonayla, my entire world revolves around you. Our kids and you are the only reason I continue fighting so hard for people to become better, because of who you are. All the times you gave me your grace and mercy, then loved me more fiercely than before? I can never repay you for that."

He looks over at my sister and Rizz, "remember when you told me that La's proposal was something you would have died for, and you wanted her exact one, because you felt like satellites was about us?" I nod. "I know you were waiting for me to do the grand proposal, and I just kept asking you in small ways because I ain't wanna come up short, for real. I ain't want you to feel like I was purposely not applying myself. I know that's why you never said yes. It drove me crazy, because while I knew what you deserved, I couldn't fail at giving you exactly what you wanted, but I also didn't want to give you someone else's moment. I wanted to give you your own, because you're the only you there will ever be, and you deserve to feel special. I kept asking without the big strides, anyway, hoping you would just let it be easy. Hoping you'd just say you didn't need a romantic gesture and we could just get married and forget about it. But I'm glad you never settled for that."

He pulls the cloth off of the canvas, and I immediately burst into tears.

Kieran has always been an incredible artist, but most people have no idea. He can draw portraits of people he has only seen in passing from memory alone. On this canvas, he has drawn me, but as if I were the universe herself, sitting atop a sun. The planets and constellations all orbit me, and in my womb, there are what look to be lifelines connecting me to Jazmynn, Payzlie and Kayde, as if they come from me. There are a few scattered clusters of satellites, orbiting me and my kids, with one letter in each of them. I look closer, and see that Kieran Donnell Michaels is spelled out from left to right.

"Those hearts on the kids, Those are the same three rings I have proposed to you with over the last fifteen years. You can remove them, if you ever want to, but I wanted to include them in this. I know I play a lot of games, and I don't always act like it, but I need you to know that you will always mean more to me than materials, fleeting emotions, and my petty insecurities," he moves the canvas back behind him, then grabs my hand, guiding me over to the table.

I look at my sister through my teary eyes and she lets a tear fall too. I'm so glad Rizz is holding her tight.

"These are from our kids," He gestures to the flowers, "the first, is Jammy. Her favorite color is pink, and she chose the carnation to symbolize love and devotion. The second is from Pooda. You know she loves her some yellow, and the lily is meant to represent purity and renewal." I'm sobbing. La passes me a napkin, and I blow my nose. Kieran smiles, then continues, "and big man Kayde chose white. You love his dark skin in white, and now, it's his favorite color. The daisy is for new beginnings, happiness and in his words, a new sibling." I huff out a laugh. "They've actually known this was coming for a while, so we had a few things made for you. Open the boxes."

I open the first box, and there's a gold charm that says 'Jammy' shaped like a heart. I feel my face crumple through my tears.

Kieran says quietly, "flip it over."

I look at the inscription, 'To the mom I choose.' A whimper escapes me. Kieran passes me the second box. The gold charm in the shape of a dress says 'Pooda' and the inscription reads, 'To the mom I believe in.' I have to sit down, because I can't take this. Then Kieran lifts the lid on the third box. The gold charm shaped like a four-leaf clover says, 'Man-Man' and I laugh through my sobs.

"He wanted you to react that way," Kieran's laugh is so soft and sweet, I could die right now. "Read the inscription."

I flip it over. 'To the mom I can never lose.'

I cry harder, and Kieran leans down and kissing the top of my head, "there's more."

"Kieran, I can't! This is too much, and I will explode!" There are literal snot bubbles escaping my nose, and Lailani passes me a few more napkins.

Rizz comes to my left, sliding the box from the counter onto the table. When Kieran lifts the lid, angling the box to me, I gasp. It's the same Burberry coat La got yesterday, and I look up, with my eyes wide.

Kieran laughs with a shrug, "you said I don't buy you nice things. I'm just glad I waited to give it to you until right now." I shrug off my brown trench and excitedly stand. Then Kieran helps me into the new coat. "I don't even know if you noticed it La, but your sleeve has a charm with LA on it." I look at her as she looks at her sleeve, then she lets out a laugh, looking at Rizz. "And yours has LO."

"I want you to always feel special, Lonayla," He pulls a box from his jacket pocket, then drops to one knee. I don't know the sound that escapes me.

"There are more things for you to open, but I can't keep waiting. Lonayla Kristin Grander, light of my life, the mother my kids choose, believe in, and don't want to ever live without, owner of my heart, occupier of my mind, and eternal conqueror of my soul," he opens the box to a beautiful oval cut hidden halo diamond ring, "will you marry me?"

"Absolutely, yes." I say without pause.

Nothing has ever felt more right. Thank you, God!

"I want those boots, too," I laugh, lounging on the couch with Reelin.

Lonayla opened up the rest of her gifts after what was the calmest and easiest 'yes' of her life. There was a charm bracelet with more charms to go with the kids' names, a pair of Burberry saddle boots, and a picture book with portraits Kieran's been drawing of her since we were young, photo memories, personal notes from Kieran, the kids, and even a note from each of Kieran's baby mamas. Apparently that was the important thing Bianca went to his mom's house for, yesterday. Lo cried for almost an hour straight, before dragging Kieran to their room.

"I swore you had those boots already. When we saw them in the store, I felt like I'd seen them before," Reelin's running his knuckles along my arm, as I lay on his shoulder with my knees up, and my body pressed against his.

"Nah, must be one of your other girlfriends," I tease.

"I've never had a girlfriend that wasn't you," his hand moves to under my arm, against my rib cage, "I don't know how to prove to you that you've always been it for me, woman." He kisses my temple.

"Oh, I wouldn't believe you, even with irrefutable evidence," I shrug. "You're a man. Y'all are natural born embarrassments, You'll have someone going through life thinking one thing, then one random day, BOOM! A whole different person, like the other one never existed."

"That's what you think?" He looks at my face, "all men?"

I shake my head, "of course not! Not my daddy. And maybe not Barack Obama."

He shakes his head, "You gon' learn one of these days, Lailani." I move my head closer to his chest, and his words vibrate through me. "The day you realize I've literally never even imagined a life without you, everything will become so much simpler."

"If I give you simple girl vibes, I've clearly not been doing my job. I'm not supposed to be your peace, Reelin. You're supposed to be so stressed all the time, wishing I would release you, so you could enjoy your simple life. Then I'd have to go find a billionaire to pay my bills, and make sure my sister is straight, in case Kieran leaves her, too." I laugh.

"You're dreaming. And nah, you've never been simple," he wraps his arms tightly around me, putting his face into my neck, "and I will never let you go again. Only billionaire in your life will be me, from now on."

His voice mixed with the vibration of him talking against my neck tickles, in the best way.

"You got billions? Dang, you should've told me sooner, I would have married you years ago!"

His laugh rumbles through my entire body, "you've been spoiled all your life so you ain't chasing a bag. I have time to get there. You know I ain't hurting, though. You'll always get what you want, because you deserve to. And I live to make you happy. Clearly. I'm still sitting on this couch because of your crazy no-outside-clothes-in-the-bedroom thing."

He bites my neck, and I giggle, raising my shoulder against him, "the sun is about to come up, then we can take showers. We haven't watched a sunrise together in so long." I kiss his forehead, "I still love rising with the sun, and watching everything around me wake up."

"Me, too," he shifts again, looking at the patio, "you wanna go out there?"

"Immediately, no. It's cold."

I lean further into him, holding him just as tightly as he holds me. It's so comfortable, being with him like this again. It feels like it was always supposed to be this way, and I can't help but wonder what would have happened, if I had just let him love me all those years ago. Who would I be right now? How would our relationship have grown? Would we have kids? Would I be sick? Would I even still be thinking about our inevitable end?

I kiss the top of Reelin's head, letting those thoughts go. There's no sense in thinking about the impossible, and I need to appreciate this moment. I'm safe, in the arms of a man who adores me, and we're surrounded by the rose petals and electric candles from my sister's first real proposal.

Today, I won't worry about a thing. No would-be-murder, no lies the people I'm supposed to trust told me, and no illness that wants to ruin everything. I declare that it's all going to be okay, because it has to be.

# 19 : Okay?

It is now 11 a.m., on the first day of The Reliving, and we're missing it. It was the longest weekend, and my mind is still trying to catch up with the events. Reelin is sprawled across the couch, and I move away from him to check my phone.

**New Message from Dominic Morris, MD: Miss Grander, I understand you wished to have additional drug testing completed, and we've sent the request to the lab. In some cases, certain substances will not appear due to metabolites. Results will always populate in the online portal, once completed. Attached are resources to address any other drug related concerns. linkto.info4u.now**

**Me: Thank you for this! Have a great day!**

I look at Reelin, as he shifts a little in his sleep. Then, I go down the internet rabbit hole I meant to go down when I got home, Saturday morning. I told myself I was leaving this alone, but I'm pretty sure my would-be-murderer drugged me, because there's no way I got into that pool willingly. There has to be an explanation. I saw what I saw, heard what I heard, and woke up in the water fully clothed with my things missing. That was definitely no accident.

"First time waking up to you in more than twelve years," Reelin's voice reaches me mid scroll through benzos on drugs.com. I look at him as he sits up high, stretching his arms over his head. "Though waking up to you fully clothed on a foreign couch was not what I was hoping for, I guess the rose petals and candles give it a nice touch."

I huff a laugh, locking my phone screen, "sir, I know you didn't think you were getting any this morning."

"Of course not," he comes around the coffee table, pressing a kiss to my forehead, then walks to the kitchen, "did you know the fridge was fully stocked? K went a little crazy with the groceries. He was very excited about this."

"I love the effort he put into everything," I smile, looking around the room, "I especially love that he made it happen so fast! When did he even have time? He just said he was doing it yesterday."

Reelin laughs, "that was his way of telling you without telling you. He wanted you to know, but because our first engagement was kept from Lo—"

"First engagement?" I interrupt.

"Yes, first. As I was saying, he had to keep it from you because our first engagement had to be kept from Lo. The man got caught up in his emotions, when he tried to tell you, but he had planned to do this yesterday no matter what. He wanted to make sure she was his fiancée for the first day of school." Reelin comes to sit near me, on the edge of the sectional, handing me a bottle of water, and then he takes a sip of his own.

"Where'd the food come from?" I'm having trouble opening the water, but don't want to make it obvious, so I set it on the table, "those are my mama's dishes."

"Your mom prepped all the food on Thursday, and wrote instructions down for how to finish it. K had all this in here, so after church, he just had to put everything in the oven, really." Reelin stretches again, then relaxes, looking past me, through the sliding glass door.

"When we were at the church, your parents were apologizing to him, because Lo had made other plans. I was gonna try to get out of it, but I couldn't make up a legitimate reason fast enough. The kids knew about all this, so they thought plans just switched to family dinner, and with Lo being in the group, no one could act like there were other plans. I know K was panicking, but the kids held it together. Jammy had him on FaceTime the whole time he was waiting to surprise Lo at the church, keeping his nerves under control. He tried to ignore the group, but Lo would've asked where he was, and it could've started a fight. So they all just acted like they didn't know he was there," Reelin shakes his head with a chuckle.

"They could've fooled me," I bite my cheek, looking at the water, thinking to ask him to open it. "Wait, so Lonayla was the one who wanted the family dinner? Not my mom?" I laugh, "she's funny. Wait till she finds out she almost derailed her own engagement!"

Reelin laughs, "It worked out, though. Jammy and Pooda came here while we were at the hospital, to finish the food. Kieran had a feeling you'd wanna switch up and stay here. He decorated and everything after brunch. When Lo switched plans, he was just gonna do the family dinner and ask her at dessert. If she said no, your pops was gonna suggest they discuss it alone, and K was gonna bring her here. If she said yes, they were probably coming here anyway," he winks, chugging the rest of his water.

"Why does Lo think you don't want to be around your parents? She had already told K you wouldn't want to go home when you were released from the hospital, then out of nowhere, you told me you wanted to come here."

"Mom and Dad are old, Reelin." I want this water bad, I give in and pass it to him to open, "I don't need them worrying about me. If I left with you, they wouldn't."

He passes back the water and I chug savoring the way it feels going down my throat.

"Well, I'm glad they trust me with you."

**New Message from Sissy: it wasn't a dream!**

**Me: NOPE!**

**Sissy: Please tell me you had Rizz touch you on the inside**

**Me: LMAO! Not a chance**

"It's Lonayla. Guess they're awake," I say.

Reelin grabs his own phone off the coffee table, "I'm sure they've been awake," He chuckles.

**Sissy: Boo! You suck!**

**Me: I don't, but I know you do, lol**

**Sissy: Yes, Yes I do. And very well, might I add.**

**Me: We missed school today. There's still time to make it after lunch!**

**Sissy: Telling mom you're really on drugs**

**Sissy: No way in hell I could be in a classroom today**

**Sissy: Why does everything feel so different?**

**Me: because it is, my darling sister. You're a Feyoncé!**

**Sissy: I am! He liked it and he put a ring on it! This is crazy!**

**Me: It's beautiful**

**Sissy: We have so much to do! Like, so much! Get ready!**

**Me: Whenever you're ready, babe**

"I think we're gonna have a bridezilla on our hands. She's gonna want all the things." I laugh to Reelin, who's looking at his phone with a scrunched-up face.

"I wouldn't expect anything less," he says, without looking up.

**New Alert from Health Portal Now: Two (2) New prescriptions are ready for pickup.**

"Oh, shit. I forgot I have prescriptions," I furrow my brows, "Lo was supposed to have Mom's car. I completely forgot."

"I'll go. You relax," Reelin stands, "get comfortable, shower, and have something to eat. I'll be back soon," he walks to the back room.

"You sure?" I call after him, feeling like I should go too.

He comes out of the room with his jacket, "I'm sure. You need anything else?"

I shake my head, as he grabs his keys, then leaves. I feel a little odd about his sudden change in demeanor, but I decide not to let it stress me, because I hear Lo calling my name.

"La?" She comes into view, fully dressed with Kieran at her heels, "we'll be back, you need anything?"

I shake my head, "no. Where are you going?"

Kieran is looking at his phone while Lo puts on her coat.

"Just to run a quick errand. Be back!" Lo says, as they go out the door, too.

"What the hell was that all about?" I frown, looking around.

Guess I can shower and eat something. I didn't expect to be here by myself, but I have more research to do, anyway.

**Apple ID Sign In Requested**

**lkgrander@granderthings.me**

**Your apple ID is being used to sign in to a device near Atlanta, GA**

**Don't Allow          Allow**

I roll my eyes and press don't allow, then lay back, to stretch my body. I was sitting still for way too long, so a hot shower will do me just right.

I walk into the back room that has my things in it, and go straight into the connecting bathroom. I look at my reflection, glad my eyes almost look normal, and not hollowed out like they have been. The sleep I got in the hospital was probably exactly what I needed. I straightened my hair yesterday, but my edges are a little puffy from sleeping on them, so I need to make sure I wrap it before I even think about turning on the shower.

I turn around to take in the nicely sized bedroom. It's decorated in neutral grays and whites. There's a queen-sized bed made with white sheets and a gray comforter, with a gray headboard and footboard pushed into the corner. A white nightstand on the left of the bed houses a lamp with a gray lampshade, and my coat lays over a light gray reading chair that sits a few inches over. There's a decent sized window about a foot past the end of the bed, with a white bookshelf beside it, containing only a welcome card to "Miss Lailani Grander" on the school letterhead, sitting atop a little plushie of a python—the school's mascot. The wall adjacent to that has a small gray table with two matching chairs, and there's a long white dresser under a 40inch flatscreen tv. Just beyond that is the bedroom door, which is at the corner of the wall leading into this room's bathroom. And then just past the bathroom door, to my left, is another small white dresser with three drawers, where my bag sits.

"I thought I told them to bring my hair box," I say to myself, reaching into my bag, pull out the comb, brush, satin scarf, and bonnet Lonayla thankfully packed for me.

I don't know where the three of them had to run off to so quickly, but I can't let myself panic. I spent the weekend questioning everything, and I really just want to ease up on the over-thinking, so I don't stress myself into another ridiculous episode.

I open the group thread for The Reliving, and scroll to the playlist link. I look at the list of songs, and smile, pressing shuffle, and the first song to play is Chingy's "Pullin' Me Back." I guess this is a sign.

I sing along while I wrap my hair, then get undressed and into the shower.

# Part iii : Flash Memory Overload

# 20 : Moments In Time

*Reelin.*

*Lonayla.*

*Kyler turns up the heat.*

*Kieran.*

*Reelin.*

*Monica's speech.*

*People jumping in the pool.*

*The initial tree.*

*Maliah bellyflops.*

*Reelin.*

*Our initials.*

*Reelin professes his love again.*

*Kieran gloats.*

*Lonayla gives me a drink.*

*Jessy's honey bun machine.*

*Reelin's laugh.*

*Kassidy asking to work in my shop.*

*Gabe's kids' photos.*

*Reelin's eyes.*

*Random chick.*

Lonayla laughing at me.

Spray-paint.

Monica's pregnant.

Kieran's laugh.

Random chick and Reelin in heated conversation.

Lonayla.

The initial tree.

A cake.

Karaoke.

Reelin and the random chick by the initial tree.

Kieran teasing me.

Pineapple on the grill.

Reelin's smile.

Lonayla's passing out shots.

People popping balloons.

Random chick and Kieran.

Kia asks for my number.

Reelin.

My bag and coat in the chair.

Lonayla gives me another drink.

A honey bun.

Reelin.

My reflection in the bathroom mirror.

Kieran.

*Classmates cheering.*

*Random chick talking to me.*

*The woods to nowhere.*

*Laughing.*

*Reelin.*

*Random chick with Reelin.*

*Reelin's blank stare.*

*Warm water envelops me.*

*Darkness.*

# 21 : Last Tuesday

"Lonayla?" I shout.

I'm standing in the mirror, trying to decide if I'm going to wear pantyhose or not, when Lo comes into my room.

I turn to her, "sheer or opaque?"

"Sheer. You sure you don't want to wear the red?" She sits on my bed, "I'm sure Rizz will like both, but the red gives seductress, and that's what you need."

I laugh, and pull off my silver sequined dress, tossing it on the stool by my bathroom door, "I don't need to seduce Reelin. I don't even plan to let him see me naked while I'm here, thank you."

I toss Lo a sly smile, and walk into my closet, "I thought I had more party clothes here."

"I gave you at least six options, while I packed your bags. You're the one who insisted you didn't need anything." I look out as Lo checks her phone, smiling, "I'm wearing that one leopard cover up. The sheer dress I got like, a month ago from that online place you've been working with. Kieran hasn't seen it yet. He loves me in animal print, so he's welcome."

"I'm shocked you haven't let him see you, yet." I walk out of my closet with three more dresses and a jumpsuit in my hands. "Is he mad you're making him wait until Friday?"

"Nah," Lo gets up, taking the clothes from my hand, to lay across my bed. "He said he understands. He knows Rizz won't see you until the party, and I didn't want to make him feel any kind of way. You gotta tell him soon, La."

"I will."

I bite my lip, standing near the bottom of my bed, looking at my outfit options. "Lo, try on the green."

"You tired, already?" She frowns, but takes off her robe, "you take your medicine?"

"I will."

I won't. I just need her off my back. I sit in my reading chair, and pick up my computer to check on my fulfillment correspondences for my store.

"I just need a little break, and you love playing dress up, so this works."

Lo laughs, stepping into my deep green leather mini dress, "This one is gonna be perfect, actually. Especially with your alligator pumps."

I look up from my email, and Lo lifts up on her tip toes, doing a little spin. I beckon her over, "let me clasp the neck." She comes over and squats down, then hops back up when I'm done. "God, I miss being able to move freely."

"It's okay. I'll be your personal body double whenever you need me to, sissy." She gives a sweet smile, then poses, "So what are we thinking? Devil-in-a-green-dress, or nah?"

I chuckle, looking from the high neck to the perfectly placed thigh slit. The dress is backless, and drops low enough to show the top of my ass, and I have a gold body chain in mind for it.

"I like it. It's a contender. You mind trying the zebra?"

"La, I love this dress so much, let me have it."

"Girl, no,"

I turn my attention back to my email, while Lo changes into the zebra-print jumpsuit, "I have to call Lacey, about the delivery from today."

I FaceTime Lacey from my computer. She answers from behind the counter, at Grander Things.

"Hey, boss!" She smiles, walking to the back, "what's up?"

"Is it super busy?"

"Not too bad, actually. Having fun?" She smiles, sitting in one of the black chairs in the break room.

"I've been asleep mostly," I smile, opening my calendar in another window.

"So, I was looking at my emails, and there were three deliveries scheduled this week—I had them on the shop calendar. I see one was supposed to be done today at 7 a.m., and I had you as the designated receiver, but I don't see any notices for the delivery?"

"Oh, yeah! They came. I forgot to send the message, my bad," she gets up, moving to the computer, "I have the invoice here. I'll scan it in."

"Okay, great. I appreciate it. I know we didn't open until 11, and when I checked my email, I was almost worried we missed it. With it being the holiday season, I don't want that hassle."

"Of course! I'm sorry about that," Lacey's email arrives.

"It's cool, Lace. I'm glad it was done. Thursday has two mid-day deliveries, so you won't have to worry about getting there early. Thank you for being a team player."

"La, you deserve a break! I was happy to do it. It worked well for me, actually. I went to the gym and everything, before we opened. Got to flirt with my lil' gym bae," she chuckles, looking toward the showroom. "Boss, Jaleah's up front by herself, and it looks like a group of people just walked in."

"Of course, babe. Thanks again! Y'all take care," I smile, ending the call.

When I look up, Lonayla is staring at me in the loose-fit, strapless zebra jumpsuit.

"Turn around."

She frowns, "this ain't it, La. It's a pool party. This gives old-lady-brunch at best."

I laugh, "fine. So, the green or the silver."

Lo steps out of the jumpsuit, putting on her robe again, "I still prefer the red." She shrugs, looking at her phone, "Kieran does, too."

"Kieran would agree with whatever you say, even if he hates it," I put my computer down, and stand to stretch, "I think the red is just a little too naked. It's winter, Lo. I should wear tights, or boots, and neither can work with that little scrap of mesh fabric. I'm almost positive that dress was meant to be lingerie."

"Girl, Rizz will eat his heart out!" She smiles, plopping onto my bed, "and then, he can eat you," she winks.

"I think the heart attack he'll have when I show up basically naked, to a social event with all the men we knew in high school, would get in the way." Mom knocks on my open door, pulling our attention.

"Hey, Mommy,"

"Hey, naked girl," she chuckles, setting two covered plates on my dresser, "I brought y'all up some dinner. Your dad made tuna casserole."

"Yes! I'm starving! Thank you," Lonayla hurries over to grab one of the plates.

I put on my gray robe, "Ma you want to watch a movie?"

"Maybe later, I'm working on a dress for Jaimie's baby's christening," Mom smiles, and walks out.

"La, lets watch Love Island. I miss Serena and Kordell on my screen, real bad," Lonayla takes a bite of her food, "Mmm, Daddy gotta stop trying to make us fat. It's been two days, and we've eaten enough for a week, already!"

I laugh, "I'm pretty sure I'll need to fast Thursday and Friday to look good in any of these dresses, so I agree."

"You'll literally look the same, bomb as fuck. Rizz will just have more cushion for the pushin'," Lo humps the air, then takes another bite.

"Shut your whore mouth!" I laugh, "let's go to the TV room."

I grab my plate, and we go to watch our show.

My sister and I are sprawled across the couch, watching Love Island USA, Season 6. Our dad brought us two bottles of wine, with a bowl of fruit and cheese, before he went out to his music studio, about an hour ago.

**New Message from Reelin Houldover Jr.: Hey, you up?**

**Me: Yeah. How was your day?**

**Reelin: Busy. One of my counselors said she has covid, so we had to inform all the parents and make sure we got everyone tested. I think I might have to close the center the rest of the week.**

**Me: Damn, I hate that covid is still a thing.**

**Reelin: Yeah**

**Reelin: You busy rn?**

**Me: Watching tv with Lo**

**Reelin: Call me when you're free?**

**Me: Okay.**

**Me: we can text.**

**Reelin: I'm finna work out. I wanted to talk to you while I hit these weights.**

**Me: Sorry. Talk later. 💚**

**Reelin: I look forward to it**

"La, Kieran said they might close the youth center. I guess one of the counselors been up there saying she had bad allergies, but it was covid. Ain't that some shit?" Lonayla asks.

"Yeah, Reelin just told me."

"So, we can probably see them before Friday then, since Rizz ain't gonna be busy anymore."

I raise an eyebrow at her, "not if they have covid."

"Oh, shit. You're right. Damn, I ain't even think about that," Lo frowns. "Damn, Friday's still a little too close, if they do."

"Yep."

I look back at the screen. It's been a few hours of our binge-a-thon and that weird girl, who yapped all over the clock app after being sent home, just came in.

"They can never make me like her," I say, scrunching my face.

"Neither of them, because what was that face when Leah made it to the final four? Jealousy is crazy," Lonayla pauses the TV.

"La, you gotta tell Rizz. What if they do have Rona? He can't see you for what, ten days? How are you gonna explain that?"

"I'll just tell him I can't get sick. I think that's a very normal response."

"But not a normal situation, Lailani. You literally can't get sick. That means I can't see them, either. How would that be normal? How would we explain that it's not as simple as you not wanting the sniffles?"

"Stop frowning, I'm sure it's fine. Worst comes to worse, I'll skip the party, and ask them to get another test done. If anything, you can stay with Kieran, and I can miss the first few days of The Reliving, under the guise of being sick."

Lo scrunches her face at me "because you are sick, and no one knows. This feels so wrong, La."

"I'll tell them, Lonayla. I told you—in my own time."

"K's gonna be so pissed at me, when he finds out."

"I'll make sure he understands. Please, Lo. I have to be the one to share this. I'm the one who will have to accept the behavior changes and their worries. Let me decide when I do this."

She shrugs, huffing a breath through her nose, "fine."

"Thank you," I pull the heated throw closer to my chest and slide further into the couch cushion.

"I think we should skip the recoupling, I don't care for this," Lonayla says, going to the episode list. "What happened with PPG while ol' girl was there? Do we need those?"

"I mean, we can skip to the casa recoupling, if you want."

Lonayla skips episodes, and I can't help thinking about how Reelin will react to not seeing me for longer than he anticipated, if he does have covid. The last time we had to be apart for something, and I stayed away longer than he expected, the boy nearly lost his marbles.

*Summer, 2009*

*My parents surprised Lonayla and I with a trip to Greece, to celebrate Lonayla's high school graduation. Mom woke us up in the middle of the night with new luggage, and told us we had an hour to pack before we needed to leave for the airport. Naturally, I was stressed, because I needed more time, an itinerary, and a destination, so I'd know how to pack, but it was still exciting.*

*When we arrived at our gate, and found out where we were going, Lonayla nearly fainted. She talked about going to Greece for her 18th birthday from the ages of 12– 15. Once she started spending more time with Kieran's kids, she pretty much decided it was a lost dream, and said she would just take the kids when they got older, instead. On her actual birthday, back in March, she had a little staycation in Athens, Georgia. Not quite the Athens she wanted, but she found it adorable that Kieran at least attempted to humor her with it.*

"Oh my God, the kids!" Lonayla exclaims, dropping her duffel.

"It's taken care of, Lo." Dad laughs, "they do have mothers, you know."

Lo gives Dad an annoyed stare.

He laughs harder, "oh, come on! Don't get upset! They do!"

Mom suppresses her laugh, pulling Lonayla into a half hug, "leave her alone, Lonnell. She loves those babies."

"We all do! But they can't always come first, Lai. They do have other parents." He looks at Lonayla, "Is that better? I said, 'other' that time."

"Whatever. I know they have moms," Lonayla sits back and puts in her earbuds.

I yawn, "Greece is gonna be so pretty. I'm excited."

"Me, too," Mom smiles.

I look at my phone, checking the time. It's way too early to call Reelin, but I know if I wait until we land, I'll have a million freaked out voicemails from him. I send him a text.

**Me: Off to Greece on a surprise trip from mom and dad. I'll call when we land.** 🧡

**Reelin: I know. See you on the 15th.**

**Me: Why am I not surprised you already know?**

**Reelin: I couldn't tell you, but your parents told us a week ago when they were making arrangements for the kids. Kennedi was mad as hell she had to be a mom this week, but K's doing summer school and I'm going to Texas tomorrow.**

**Me: I didn't know you were going home. That's nice.**

**Reelin: I'm only going because you won't be here. Mom dukes called, then guilted me into it with Aunt Kira as her backup.**

*Me: I hate that you don't like being with your family. Especially because when your parents come to Atlanta, you have such a good time with them.*

*Reelin: My parents aren't the problem. It's everyone else. It's cool, though. I'll get my visit in, then I won't have to see any of those people for another few years.*

*Me: when do I get to meet "those people" anyway?*

*Me: You met everyone at our reunion three whole years ago, but you never even let me hear about your family.*

*Reelin: If I can help it, you'll never meet anyone else.*

*Reelin: Before you ask, they're not important, La. You've met everyone that matters. Besides, you are my family*

*Reelin: and we'll build our own family soon.*

*Me: You wouldn't want your kids to meet your family?*

*Reelin: no. now please, leave it alone.*

*Me: *blank bubble**

*Reelin: I'll take your blank bubble as "yes, babe. I understand. Can't wait to see you when I get back, and then we can practice making our family for the rest of the summer."*

*Me: lol. It's 5am. So your foolishness means you clearly need to go back to sleep.*

*Reelin: Jammy's right here with me, wide awake. Ain't no sleep. It's cartoons and cereal time.*

*Me: Well, we're about to board, so I gotta go.*

*Reelin: okay. Have a safe flight, baby. I love you.*

*Me: I love you, too. I'll call you when I land, if it's not too late.*

*Reelin: it's never too late. Call me.*

**_Me: okay. Ttyl._**

*When we arrive in Greece, it's a little before 1 a.m. the next day, 6 p.m. yesterday, Atlanta time.*

**_Me: Landed. Might fall asleep, so I'll call when I wake up. Daddy said he'll pay for the phones, but I can't text like that because of the roaming. The hotel is gorgeous, the rooms are huge, and Lonayla is the happiest girl in the world. Love you._**

**_Reelin: Okay. Glad you're safe. I love you, too._**

*We ate literally everything, took pictures of everything, and enjoyed a cool wine tasting, while Mom and Dad rested for the first day. Day two, we shopped, ate, then shopped some more. We visited museums, saw gorgeous views, and had a super cute beach dinner. Lo cried her eyes out every time she looked out at the water, remembering where we were. We took a short flight from Athens to Mykonos for two days, then ferried from Mykonos to Santorini for two days, then went back to Athens for our final night.*

*When we were packing our bags to head to the airport, our dad came in to say he and Mom would go home, and they would extend mine and Lonayla's trip, if we wanted to stay a little longer. He said he hadn't seen either of us so happy or relaxed in a while, and that we deserved to enjoy our young and free selves for as long as we could. With my first year of college being so busy, and Lonayla taking on so much responsibility, we both considered it.*

*After a little more than an hour of talking through it, we decided to stay, as long as the kids were taken care of. Lonayla called Kieran to tell him, and he thought it was a fantastic idea, but I couldn't get Reelin on the phone. I didn't bother sending him a text, because I knew Kieran would let him know for me. Kieran took it so well, I expected Reelin to do the same.*

*He did not.*

*I woke up to Lonayla on the hotel phone, cursing someone out.*

*"I don't give a shit about any of that!" I get out of my bed, and sit on Lonayla's with my brows raised. She just looks at me, rolling her eyes, "I said, no! My sister is not even like that, and I can't believe you would fix your mou—"*

*I take the phone, "hello?"*

*"Why the fuck was I not informed that you were staying in Greece, Lailani?" Reelin's voice both vibrates through my eardrums, and sets my teeth on edge.*

*"I tried to call you." I look at Lonayla as she lays back, exasperated, "were you just arguing with my sister?"*

*"No, we weren't arguing. I asked her why you didn't call me, and she said you did, but you didn't tell me shit, Lailani."*

*"Um, I did call you, though," I look at my sister again, "I called twice, actually."*

*"Boy had the nerve to ask me if you were staying here because you met someone!" Lonayla says.*

*"You thought my parents were just gonna fund an international fling for me and my sister?" I scrunch my nose, not believing the question I'm having to ask.*

*"That's not what I said. Lo don't listen!" Reelin sighs, "I asked her what was out there to make you want to stay and not tell me, then she went on about how you don't have to explain yourself to me. I only asked her if it was more important than you coming home. Lonayla took it to being there with someone else."*

*"Well, I don't have to explain myself, but also, it was our dad's idea for us to stay."*

*"I made plans for us, Lailani," he says, his voice straining.*

*"Then you should've answered your phone."*

*"When are you coming back?"*

*"We're only staying three more days," I say, laying back by my sister.*

*"Aight," he hangs up.*

*"Did he just hang up on you?" Lonayla asks.*

*I pass her the phone, "yep."*

*She chuckles, "you know he tatted you this week?"*

*"Please tell me you're lying."*

*"Nope. K told me, just before Rizz got there. That man is in love love."*

*"I hope it's a joke," I get up and go back to my own bed.*


*Three days later, when Lonayla and I got back home, Reelin was waiting in the driveway. He greeted my dad, then offered to carry in our bags.*

*After Lonayla and I greeted our mom, I looked at Reelin, then nodded my head to the back door. We walked over to the lemon tree, our favorite place to sit.*

*"Show me this tattoo."*

*He smiles and turning his head. My name is in cursive right behind his left ear.*

*"It's cute and small, so I'm good with it. If it was obnoxious, I was gonna be so pissed."*

*"I know. I know you hate when people tattoo each other," he scoots closer on the little black bench. "I missed you. I was slick angry when you stayed away longer."*

*"I know. Why, though?" I ask with a frown.*

*"I hate being away from you. I already hated being in Texas, and when I came back home, you were supposed to be here the next day. Then K tells me I had to wait, and that shit bugged me. But I think I was madder he knew and I didn't. I would've booked a flight if it was any longer, honestly." He kisses my temple.*

*"You're so dramatic," I shake my head, smiling.*

*"Yeah, well. You make me that way."*

*"No. I have no control over your ridiculousness, sir."*

*"I'm only ridiculous because I love you."*

*"I love you too, Reelin," I get up, "But I need to shower."*

*He stands, pulling me closer, "want to go to my place? We can shower together, and I'll show you my other tattoo."*

*When he smiles, it oozes through my core, like hot lava.*

*"It better not be big and ugly."*

*His laugh makes my lady bits hum, "you gotta come with me to see. Plus, we're supposed to practice making our own family, remember?"*

*"No kids till after I graduate law school—maybe a year after I open my bakery— then you can put a bun in the oven," I press a kiss to his lips, "but yes, we can go to your place. Let me tell my parents."*

*Reelin smiles, then we go back inside.*

*That night, I learned that he was so annoyed, I was staying away longer, he got another tattoo just to feel close to me. It made absolutely no sense, but he claims it was the best angry decision he's ever made.*

*He's lucky it was cute.*

# 22 : Last Thursday

"Ma, we're going to the mall. You wanna come?" I ask Mom, when she emerges from her sewing room.

"No, you feeling okay? Every time I came to your room yesterday, you were asleep," she comes to put her hand on my forehead, checking for a temperature.

"Yeah, I was just tired. I never get to just rest, and since I didn't have to check any invoices or anything at the shop, I gave myself permission to relax."

Lonayla walks in, and kisses Mom's cheek, "hey, Ma. You've been sewing all day."

"Yeah, I've been in the zone."

"I think I want to go do a grocery run, too. I want to get some ginger ale and stuff," I say.

"Okay, well get those frozen fruit bars your dad likes, too. I have to finish altering your Aunt Ivy's suit, and your dad wants me to make him a pair of pants for the city ceremony next week." Mom turns to Lo, "you get the thread I asked for?"

"Yes, ma'am. It's in the bag by the stairs," Lo goes to get the bag.

"If I had time, I'd make your party dress, La. I'm sorry I'm so swamped," Mom says, squeezing my shoulder.

"It's fine, Ma. I thought I had something to wear, but I don't like anything in my closet. I'm just going to look around, and if I can't find anything, I'll wear something simple."

Lo walks back into the kitchen and hands Mom the bag of thread, "we can bring you back food."

"Oh, no. I told you, I'm prepping a meal for a very special project later, so I'll eat some of that before it gets picked up," she looks at her watch, "I should probably get started on that, actually. You girls be safe."

Mom smiles, then disappears back into her sewing room, then Lonayla and I leave.

"I'm so glad they tested negative, man," Lo says, as we pull into the mall parking lot, "I was gonna be so pissed if this weekend was ruined. Tomorrow is gonna be legendary."

"I think I'm finally getting excited, too. Reelin called this morning, and he wants to go to eat first. He called it 'our first new date,' and asked to pick me up."

"Please, I can't! That's adorable," Lo squeals as we get out of the car.

"Yeah, I think I've missed him more than I care to admit."

"Lailani, it's okay to still love him. You two were meant to be!"

We walk into the mall, to Lonayla's favorite store for party dresses.

"I can't know if I love him, though. We haven't spent actual time together, yet. It'll take some time."

"It was instant the first time, it can be instant now," Lo shrugs.

"It wasn't instant! It took at least…" I pause, trying to think about it.

"It was so instant! Instant anything else was slower than how instant your instant was," Lo laughs, "bro, you were so stuck on stupid, with big ol' bug-eyes every time he spoke to you! It was so adorable. I had never seen you like that before. He was all in immediately, too! The way he claimed you in front of everyone, just to make sure you didn't think he was talking to someone else? Please, La. You two were very much instant."

Lo's right. I was genuinely stunned when he told Maliah I was his girlfriend in the middle of the hall that day. Then everyone in school knew about it before our class let out. I tried to deny it at first, because I would never let a boy stake his claim on me, but Reelin was so sweet and chivalrous. He stayed after school that day, because I had volleyball practice, and afterwards, he waited for my dad to pick me up. When I got to school the next day, he was waiting out front with a cranberry juice, a chocolate muffin and a blueberry one. Mom thought it was the cutest thing, ever.

He went on like this for two weeks before finally asking me to be his girlfriend, for real. He asked instead of insisting I was, and I thought it was worth it to give him a chance.

On a day when neither of us had practice, we sat out by the bleachers, talking about the sky. He started listing cloud types, and told me that a cloud weighed more than a million pounds, and I was mind-blown. A few days later, he asked me on our first date, and I found out that he asked my dad for permission at his football game the week before. By the end of that night, I was a smitten kitten.

"La, you should wear that one bikini with the snakeskin cover up, now that I think about it. That'll be so fire!" Lonayla says, shifting through a rack of dresses.

"I don't want to wear a swimsuit, because I don't want anyone to think they can play with me and that pool," I pull out a red dress with a mesh middle, then put it back. "I don't need anyone getting crazy, and assuming that with me in a swimsuit, they can throw me in."

"I feel it. But everyone knows you don't swim."

"It's been 16 years, and people might not think about it. I will not be anywhere near the water."

Lo pulls out a gold dress, "you want to be a trophy?"

I laugh, "no. Whatever I wear, I'm wearing it to dinner, too. I have to look at least semi-appropriate."

"I think whatever you wear will be appropriate."

"I think I don't want to look like a streetwalker, in case it's a nice restaurant or something." I huff a laugh, "I don't wanna have him looking like he had to pay-for-play, then set him off when people stare at me like a piece of meat."

"Yeah, that man don't play about you."

It feels like we've looked at every dress in the store, before I decide to just wear something in my closet. When we get outside, Lonayla is on the phone with Kieran, telling him about some message about Kayde from his school.

"I want to go to the hair store," I say to Lo, as she starts the car.

"Where y'all at? I can come to you," Kieran's on speaker.

"No, we're doing girl things. Check on your son. Make sure that lady ain't playing with my baby," Lonayla says, and I can hear the annoyance in her voice.

"Aight. I'll call you later. Love you."

"Love you too," she hangs up.

"That raggedy bitch Kayde has for his lit class claims he didn't turn in his midterm. It's fucking December, and that hoe is JUST NOW trying to say he won't pass her class because he owes her a paper. That bitch is irritating as fuck, and I know for a fact Man-Man did that paper, because he called YOU about it."

"The one on why he loves Atlanta?" I ask, recalling a paper I edited for Kayde, back in October. "Yeah, I thought he got an A on that paper?"

"Yes! Exactly!" Lo's hands tighten on the steering wheel, "you know my kids are good kids, La. Even if he did forget to turn in a paper, why would you wait until the literal last fucking day to say something? The semester officially ended yesterday! This bitch…"

Lo glances at her phone screen, "hold on."

She answers her phone on speaker, "hello?"

"I talked to Ms. G. She said I gotta resubmit my paper, and she'll give me half credit," Kayde sighs, "I turned that paper in, I swear."

"Hold on, baby. La, do me a favor, and check your email. Man-Man, you sent your submitted paper to Auntie La, right?"

"Yes, ma'am."

I scroll through my inbox, and open the messages from Kayde, then show the one about his paper to Lo.

"Exactly what the fuck I'm talking about!" She nods her head, "you sent the screenshot of your grade to Auntie La. Send that to that bitch, and call your dad, right now."

"I forgot all about that! Thank you, I will. I'll call you back. I love you."

"I love you too, baby. Get it done," she hangs up.

"La, I don't play about my kids."

"Oh, I know."

I can see the stress leaving her shoulders, "you want to get something to eat?"

Lo smiles, "you know I do. Let's do that one Mexican spot that had the bomb ass birria."

"Okay. I still want to go to the hair store first, though."

Lo nods.

We pull up to the Mexican spot first, and I have to laugh.

"What? It was closer! You don't even like every hair store, and why pass the food joint?" My sister laughs, getting out the car to go inside.

When I get out of the car, I can't move, "wait, Lo, I'm stuck!"

Lo jogs back for me, grabbling my arm, "where's your cane?"

"I don't think I need it. I just need to take it slow. It's so cold, it keeps throwing me off," I frown, finally able to move my legs to go inside.

We walk into the restaurant, and the smell of fried tortillas and cilantro makes my stomach happy. Lonayla walks me over to a table, and takes off her coat, before going to the counter. We always get the same thing, here: four quesabirrias con consomé y carne asada fries.

I look out the window, up at the sky, thinking about seeing Reelin for the first time tomorrow. I haven't thought much about it since we started talking again, because it was easy to keep him away. He's been so intentional about respecting my boundaries, so he hasn't pressed too hard about seeing me. When I landed on Sunday, I sent him a selfie from the airport, with a message saying, "I came to give life to The Reliving. Everybody's welcome," and he called almost immediately, asking to pick me up.

Reelin's been very busy with work, and he was adamant about not attending The Reliving without me, so he didn't make necessary arrangements to be away. When I told him I wanted to sleep this week, and that he should handle his business, he was so conflicted. He knew I was right, but he wanted to see me more than anything. I negotiated with him, though. My daddy taught me how to make something seem more appealing than it really is, when I need something to go my way, and I really need him to stay focused on what's important. Plus, I really did want to sleep.

I told him we should use this week to build the anticipation. If we knew exactly when we were going to see each other, and we had to focus on everything else until then, it would make it more exciting. He had to make sure he could be away from the youth center for the next two weeks, so he had a lot of things to wrap up, and I was going to be catching up on family time, sleep, and making sure my shop was running this week. So, we wouldn't have been able to spend much time together, anyway. I made it sound like those little moments wouldn't be worth it, and waiting until the kick-off would be super special.

He finally agreed, but mostly because he really had to lock in with his work. Reelin runs the youth center full time, but he's also a licensed medical doctor of psychiatry, and he still sees patients. That was his dream since he was a kid, and he made it happen. All week, he has been making sure his schedule works enough to be away. So far, only two families have not confirmed their appointment changes, and one of the counselors at the youth center may be unavailable to switch days. Worst case scenario: Reelin has to leave for a few hours next Thursday and come the second half of the day the following Monday. It works out much better than not attending at all, though.

"What you over here thinking about?" Lonayla sits across from me, in the red booth.

"The Reliving. It's gonna be so weird being students on a schedule with people we were students with, nearly two decades ago," I finally shrug off my coat, "I think it's cool they want to test the curriculum with us, though. Real life necessities for the human experience, is such an undervalued concept in this world we live in."

"Hell yeah, so much evil for no reason. People taking lives just for the hell of it, people hating you based on your personal preferences or shit you can't change, like your race or who you love. People can't even live comfortably in their own skin without someone trying to tell them they're doing it wrong and going to hell, or worse, trying to force them into their boxes, just because they don't understand."

"It's sick, really."

Lo nods, looking at her phone, "La, I think I need to take a pregnancy test."

I look up in complete shock, "I thought you had the implant?"

"I do, but I may or may not have missed the renewal date by like, a week or three," her face scrunches, "or a year."

"Oh my God, Lonayla."

"I know! I didn't think about it, La. I literally thought I did it last year, but I checked, and I definitely didn't. This is why I wanted to switch to a doctor in Miami, I was so busy with other things, I just completely spaced on the gyno."

I blow out a breath, "well, Mama Lo, you could be a bio-mama soon." My eyes widen, "Kieran know?"

"Immediately, no. He probably knows I forgot and has been trying to get me pregnant," she leans back against the seat. "I need to find out, and if it's a mess, we gotta handle that before it can't get handled. No babies until marriage. You of all people know that."

Indeed, I do. I had a situation once, and I swore I wouldn't let it happen again.

*November 3, 2009*

*Reelin's 20th birthday.*

*I just got out of class, and my mom asked me to take a garment bag to a client of hers, who works in the health center just around the corner from campus. While I wait for the lady to come out, I flip through one of the magazines on the table, and hear a couple talking across from me. When I look up, the woman waves. I give her a smile, then look back at the magazine.*

*"Excuse me?" the pretty pale-skinned woman says to me.*

*I look up again, "yes?"*

*"I saw you walk in here, and I was telling my boyfriend that you had the prettiest eyes," she smiles, leaning her head on the man's shoulder. He's tall and average looking with a brown beard, and skin nearly as pale as hers. He smiles, then looks*

*down at her large bump. "Joey says his granny had green eyes, too. Green eyes ain't so common. I hope our baby gets green eyes."*

*The lady has crystal blue eyes that sparkle in the light. They're literally so pretty, I pause looking at them.*

*"Yeah, my dad has green eyes, so he passed them down. His came from nowhere, it seems. But your eyes are incredible."*

*"Blue eyes are ridiculously common, though. I want my baby to have something unique. Part of me wishes I had got knocked up by a black man, so I don't have some average looking little white kid."*

*The man, Joey, looks extremely uncomfortable. He shifts, but she doesn't even seem to care.*

*I give her a small smile, then look back at the magazine. That lady is bold as hell. A minute later, I hear Joey clear his throat, like he wants my attention.*

*I look up again, "yes?" I can feel the frown on my face.*

*"Just like she wants a black baby, I'd like one, too."*

*I look around, wondering if anyone else is hearing this shit.*

*"Excuse me?"*

*"Well, we noticed you was here alone, and Brittknee and I would like a black baby."*

*The lady adds, "and with your green eyes, I would just die!"*

*"I'm not pregnant, and that's insane," I sit up higher in the seat, crossing my leg over the other. "You don't just ask people for their babies. That's out of line."*

*"We didn't mean to offend you." Brittknee's eyes mist over. "We just... Well, we thought..."*

*"I get what you thought, and it's still insane. Please leave me alone," I look at the clock on the wall, then at the receptionist, who clearly heard that nonsense, and is just as embarrassed and disgusted as me. She nods, getting up to go find Miss Janice, my mom's client.*

*"So why you here alone?" Joey asks. "Where's your husband?"*

*I look at him, and I can feel the rage building in my gut, "If you say another word to me, he'll be behind you, with one foot up your ass, and the other standing on the teeth he'll knock out, for you disrespecting me."*

*"He doesn't mean it in a bad way! He means, why are you in this alone? Someone should be here with you," the Brittknee girl rubs her belly, and I look between them realizing that no matter what I say, they're not hearing me.*

*Miss Janice finally comes to the door. I get up, and carry over the garment bag.*

*Then I hear Brittknee say, "they're always so embarrassed about being someone's baby mama. It's okay, not all of us believe in marriage."*

*When I reach the door, and hand over the clothes, Miss Janice hugs me, then looks closely at my face, "Lailani, you're glowing."*

*"I'm not glowing, I'm simmering. That couple over there asked to take my non-existent green-eyed, Black baby.*

*Miss Janice looks horrified, "Come back here. What you mean?" She takes me to her office, and hands me a bottle of water.*

*"It was insane!"*

*I finish recapping what just happened, and Miss Janice shakes her head in disgust.*

*"I have to go, though. It's my boyfriend's birthday, and I'm cooking him dinner," I give her a small smile and stand.*

*"Lailani, I don't mean to be in your business, but you really are glowing." Her smile and the pointed look makes my stomach flutter. "Have you—"*

*"No, ma'am," I interrupt.*

*She raises her hands in defense, "okay, I was just asking."*

*"I'm not even thinking about children until after college," I walk to the door, "but thank you for giving me a moment to calm down." I smile, and she walks me out.*

*"Of course! Tell your mom thank you for me! Be safe, my love."*

*Thankfully, when I walk through the lobby, those weirdos aren't there. I sigh, and wave at the receptionist, then walk out to my car. I look at my phone calendar to make sure I remember the date of my last cycle, and I panic when I realize I'm late. I have to call Lonayla.*

*"Hello?"*

*"Lo, It's an emergency! Where are you?" I try not to sound panicked.*

*"I just got out of class, what's up?"*

*"You have any kids tonight?" I start the car, and pull out of the lot.*

*"No. Mama Kira has Jammy today, because we're doing adult dinner for Rizz, remember?"*

*"Yes, I remember. Where's Kieran at?"*

*"He has class until five, then he'll meet us at Rizz's. What's wrong?"*

*"Can you meet me at Kieran's? I need you to help me with something before we go to Reelin's." I can hear the panic slipping into my voice.*

*"Yeah, I can be there in 20. How close are you?"*

*"I have to make a quick stop, but I can get there right around then, too. So, I'll see you in a few."*

*I hang up, tossing my phone into the passenger's seat, "shit! Shit! SHIT!"*

*I pull into the CVS, and buy every pregnancy test on the shelf, with a gallon of water. When I pull up to Kieran's campus apartment, I say a quick prayer, then rush to his door, knocking like a mad woman.*

*Lonayla yanks the door open, "bitch, what the fuck?"*

*I shove past her, "Lo, I'm late!" The tears I've been holding in come out like a dam burst open, "How am I late? Why would I be late?"*

*Lonayla reaches for me, pulling me into a hug, "La, it's okay! It's okay! We just have to calm down, and think about this!"*

*"I don't want to think, Lo! A stupid white lady and her stupid boyfriend started telling me they wanted my baby, then Miss Janice said I was glowing, and now?*

NOW I'M LATE, AND I HAVE TO COOK DINNER FOR THE MAN WHO MADE THIS HAPPEN!" I cry harder.

Lonayla looks inside the CVS bag, "okay, La. Okay. Let's at least figure this out before panicking. You've been very stressed lately. It could be nothing!"

I swipe angrily at my face, nodding my head. I let the last few sniffles calm, then reach for the water, and start chugging. Lonayla is reading the directions on one of the boxes, when Kieran walks in.

"I thought you had class?" Lo says, putting the box behind her back.

"I do. I left my flash drive," he squints, and cocks his head. "What are you hiding?"

"Nothing." I take the box from her, and she holds her hands out, "see?"

"Yeah, I see," he pockets the flash drive that was on the counter, then walks over to us on the couch. Lo is standing in front of me, and he places his hands on her waist, moving her away. He sees the bag full of pregnancy tests, and looks back at Lo, "we pregnant?"

"God, no!" She answers too quickly.

"Then what is this? Why else would you be taking all these tests?" He picks up the bag, "you thought you were, but you're not? Why didn't you tell me so we could do this together?"

"I'm not pregnant, so it doesn't matter."

"It does matter, Lonayla. Why not tell me?"

"Don't you have class?" She sits next to me, "you should go."

Kieran's face twists, "nah, no class today. You clearly wanna fight, so let's fight. Why would you keep this from me, then come in here and take all these tests? Were you gonna tell me at all?"

"It's not time to fight, Kieran. Go to class," Lo groans, plopping her body against the back of the couch, "I don't have time to fight with you, right now. So, please. Go."

I look at Kieran, and I already know he's not letting this go.

*'Nah this is MY shit! You came over here because you thought I wouldn't be here! That shit's fucked up, Lonayla! If you were pregnant, would you have killed my baby? Huh? Is that why you were sneaking?"*

*"Yes."*

*I know the moment the word leaves her mouth, Kieran's going to blow.*

*"ARE YOU FUCKING SERIOUS RIGHT NOW? YO, I CAN'T BELIEVE YOU JUST SAID THAT SHIT! WHA—"*

*"Stop," Lonayla interrupts without yelling back, "It literally doesn't matter. Go to class, Kieran. I'll see you at dinner."*

*Kieran pulls on his baby dreads. I can't let Lonayla have a fight that's for no reason.*

*"Kieran, she's not pregnant."*

*He knows not to start that screaming shit with me, so before he responds, he takes a breath, calming himself, "La, I heard that part. I want to know is…" When his eyes focus on me, he shifts his weight to his other leg, then he squats down in front of me, looking at my face, "oh, shit."*

*Lo sits up, "I told you I wasn't pregnant." She pats my knee, and Kieran's face softens.*

*I shake my head violently, and the tears come again, "I can't do this, Kieran."*

*He wraps his arms around me, "hey, yes you can! You can literally do anything. Everyone knows you're gonna be the best mom, Lailani. Don't cry. Don't cry."*

*He rocks me back and forth while I sob. "Lo, does Rizz know?"*

*Lo scoffs, "would we be here, if he did?"*

*That's a fair question. Of course not. It makes me cry harder.*

*Lonayla rubs my back, "La, we gotta at least find out before you cry yourself into the grave."*

*Kieran pulls back, and takes my hands in his, "let's figure this out. We got a birthday boy who would love nothing more than to be here with you for this."*

*"I can't tell him. I need to know before I tell him, because I have to know how I feel about it first."*

*Lo sits back with a deep sigh, and Kieran shakes his head at me, "La, keeping this from him won't change it, no matter what these tests say. Whatever it is, it is. But it is half his, if it's something. He would hate not being able to support you through this. You know that."*

*I know Kieran's right. I take a deep breath, reaching for the water again, "Okay."*

*Kieran stands and calls Reelin, telling him to come to his place as soon as he gets out of class. When Reelin knocks on the door less than thirty minutes later, I feel the tears starting to fight their way to the surface again.*

*"What's wrong?" He rushes straight over to me, squatting down. Lonayla moves from the couch to the kitchen with Kieran, and they watch us.*

*He looks like he was worrying his way over here. "I—"*

*"Lo said it was an emergency, and that you needed me," he interrupts.*

*I look at Lonayla.*

*"I texted him that we were here too, because K only told him to come here. I didn't want him thinking you were at his place already, and to go there first," she shrugs.*

*"What's wrong?" Reelin pushes my hair from my face behind my ear, "are you okay?"*

*I release a breath through my nose, "I'm late."*

*"Okay," Reelin's confused expression would be cute, if I wasn't so freaked out, "late for what? I'm supposed to be in class, so not dinner…"*

*"No, Reelin. My period is late."*

*He doesn't look away from my face. His eyes burn into mine, and I know he's seeing something beautiful happening. Something like the planets aligning, and trees growing from seeds to giant canopies over a beautiful house, with a white picket fence and children frolicking. But I'm not ready for this.*

*"Hey?"*

*He blinks, and when his face softens, I feel myself calm down.*

*I look down at the bag, and he follows my gaze, "you bought the whole store, huh?"*

*I have to laugh, "I was in a panic. I didn't want to go back to the clinic for those people to ask for my baby again."*

*His face jerks to me, "who?"*

*I shake my head, "I'll tell you later."*

*Reelin stands, helping me up, then leads me to the bathroom. Kieran brings us a plastic cup, and I feel the room spin. Reelin starts pulling the tests from the bag, and the room spins faster. I grab ahold of his arm, to steady myself. I think the ground is turning fluid, and I can't decide if I should sit down, or run away.*

*"Lailani, you okay?" Reelin's voice usually calms me, but not now. "Lailani?"*

*"Stop talking."*

*"La, Wha—"*

*"Reelin! STOP TALKING!" I begin to hyperventilate. I feel like the walls are closing in around me, and I close my eyes, trying to think steadying thoughts.*

*"La?" I smack my hand against his mouth.*

*After a moment, I bend at the waist, "Lonayla!"*

*She comes around the corner, "what's wrong?"*

*I look up at her and shake my head, before I move my hand from Reelin's mouth, and slide down the wall to the floor.*

*"K! Bring me some water! Hurry!"*

*Kieran comes with my gallon.*

*"Here, La. Drink." Lo sits next to me. Reelin hasn't moved, and Kieran is standing in the door frame.*

*I feel myself calming.*

*"Lailani?" Reelin interrupts my calm, and I feel my heart trying to speed up again. "You—"*

*"Reelin, I swear, if you say another word, I will die," I look up at him, and his face is twisted into the saddest frown.*

*Lonayla waves the guys away, "hey, give her a minute."*

*"Reelin, I don't want to do this today," I breathe out. He opens his mouth to speak, but I raise my hand to stop him, "I'm sorry, but I can't take your voice right now. Give me a minute. Please." He nods, and I have to look away from how sad his face is.*

*When Reelin and Kieran are out of earshot, Lo leans her head against the wall, and watches me for a few minutes.*

*She finally breaks the silence, "you know, I would normally say we should make a run for it, but it feels a little evil on the man's birthday." She scrunches her nose.*

*I smile, and blow out a breath, "I don't want to ruin his day. I don't want to do this today."*

*"So, we won't."*

*"Tell him that," I give her a knowing look.*

*"Rizz, Lailani wants you to enjoy today, and to leave her alone about your maybe baby!" Lo yells.*

*Kieran yells back, "he said ain't no way in hell, because Kieran wants to know, now!" Lo and I both laugh. "He said is it safe to speak?"*

*I nod. "You may speak!" Lo yells back.*

*A moment later, Reelin appears in the doorway, "Lailani, you know I'll do anything you want to do. No matter what that is, I'm in this with you. You know that, right?"*

*"Yes, Reelin. I know."*

*"So, what do you want to do?" Lo gets up, letting him join me on the floor. "I'm with you."*

*I look into his perfect brown eyes, and I can feel my heart bursting with every loving emotion that could exist, and then some.*

*"I want to go make your dinner."*

*"And I want you to make my dinner." His smile could bring on world peace.*

*I kiss him. I kiss him like his lips are the key to every unsolved mystery in the world, and I'm seeking every ounce of knowledge there is.*

*"That's how y'all got in this mess to begin with," Kieran shakes his head, and we laugh. "I want you to make his dinner too, so can we go? Since niggas skipped class for this, and no one wants me to know if I'm gonna be an uncle or not, today?"*

*Reelin helps me up, and we leave.*

*He loved his dinner, and he was actually surprised by his cake. Outside of the dramatics with the pregnancy tests, it was a good day.*

*That Saturday, we took a test with my parents, Kieran and Lonayla in the other room.*

*It was positive.*

"Where'd you go?" Lonayla's voice snaps me out of my thoughts. Our food has arrived.

I sigh, "my pregnancy thing."

"Oh." She doesn't say anything else.

I try not to think about it as we eat, but Reelin makes it hard.

**New Message from Reelin Houldover Jr.: I told you about the girl K brought to the center to mentor with the newborn?**

**Me: yeah.**

**Reelin: She brought the baby up here. He has green eyes.**

"La, please." When I look up, Lonayla is looking at me. "Kieran just told me, too. The baby at the youth center?" My eyes mist over. "I know it's hitting you at the craziest moment, but it's okay."

I take a deep breath, "I know."

**Me: You okay?**

**Reelin: No**

**Reelin: I've never seen a green-eyed baby before.**

**Me: Maybe you'll see another someday.**

I push my plate away, and look at Lonayla.

She sighs, "Kieran said the baby is so sweet. He said Rizz wouldn't hold him, though."

Lo frowns, and I look out the window again. It's crazy that I was already thinking about this, but now everyone else is, too.

# 23 : Oh, That's A Bit Much

November 7, 2009

"We should schedule an ultrasound and  get you some prenatals, La." Mom says, sitting next to me on the couch in the family room.

Everyone was so excited to see the positive results. Everyone but me.

As soon as the second line appeared, I lost it. I couldn't even take a second test. I knocked over the cup, then wailed like a banshee. I was literally devastated. Reelin was so confused by my reaction, but he let me react. I carried on for almost an hour before I lost my voice, and even then, I sobbed and sobbed.

Reelin never said a word.

Now, I'm laying on the couch, exhausted, and all cried out. It's been five hours.

"I hope it dies," I whisper, "I hope it knows I don't want it, and it just… dies."

My dad sighs, and walks into the other room, calling my therapist. I've had the same therapist since I was ten, but I rarely see her.

Reelin is staying quiet, but Kieran and Lonayla aren't going to accept my behavior.

"La, don't talk like that!" Lo brushes my hair from my face, and my mom pulls my feet onto her lap.

I look at Kieran, and I can see the words he wants to say in his eyes. Before he can speak them, I croak, "I don't care what I said to you back then. I was young and dumb. I mean it, I hope it dies." I lace so much venom into the word, it hurts.

"Lailani, you're just in shock. You don't mean it," Kieran squats down so he's eye level with me, "and just like you told me, I'm here with you. I got you."

I sit up, "what don't you get? I said I hope it DIES, Kieran! I don't care about you being here! You can vanish from the planet, and I won't care! Unless you're gonna help me figure out the quickest way to get rid of a baby, I want you to leave. If you can't give me a solution in the next ten seconds, I want you GONE! You made mistakes, and you had babies you didn't plan for—we know. But I am not YOU. I don't make mistakes like that. I am smarter than that."

The screechy voice leaving me sounds so far removed from my body. Kieran walks into the kitchen, and I hear him go through the back door. Lonayla goes after him. I look over at Reelin's blank face, and I realize I've been expressing my regret, and he hasn't said a single word about it.

"It's been hours, Reelin. Don't you want to chime in?"

He doesn't say anything, and I'm grateful, because as soon as I move again, I have to vomit. Mom helps me lean over, Reelin brings the small trash can from by the TV, and my dad looks around the corner in concern.

"I hate my life," I cry. "I can't believe I was dumb enough to get pregnant. I hate this so much, Mommy." I sit up, and Reelin sits beside me, using his sleeve to wipe my mouth. I'm so weak and exhausted from all the flailing and screaming I did, that I let him lay me onto him. Mom rubs soft circles on my back, and I continue to sob, "I hate this. I hate it so much. I hate myself for letting this happen. I hate it so bad it hurts, Mommy! Please, tell me how to fix it."

My dad comes into the living room, and squats down in front of Reelin's legs, "Lailani, Dr. Howard will be here first thing tomorrow. I also called Dr. Kantz to schedule an appointment for you."

"Daddy, I'm so sorry. I'm so sorry I was so stupid. Please, help me, I don't want this. I promise I will never let it happen again, but I can't let it happen right now." I'm full-on snot bubbling and Reelin's shirt is drenched. He doesn't seem to care, though. Dad looks at him, then stands. Before I realize what's happening, my dad is carrying me out of the room.

"Please, Daddy. I don't want to be a mom. I don't want to do this."

My dad doesn't say anything. He carries me up to my room, placing me onto my bed, then brushes my hair out of my face, and lays with me, letting me cry myself to sleep.

*I never believed in abortion for consensual sex. Knowing how hard and how long my parents tried to get pregnant, I couldn't Imagine ending a little life, knowing there were people who couldn't create one. I also knew I didn't want to have babies until I was finished with school, and my bakery was open. At the very least, I wanted to be older than 21, and to be a wife. I was careful with my birth control. I couldn't grasp how I could possibly be pregnant, I never missed one day.*

*I wake up the next morning, and my throat hurts so bad. I look across my room, and see Lonayla fast asleep in my reading chair, and Kieran at her feet. I turn over to Reelin's eyes staring at me. I feel my cheeks and ears heat, and I'm reminded by his missing shirt, that I may have gone overboard in my screaming fit, yesterday.*

*"My parents know you knocked me up, and let you sleep in my bed?" I say, shifting to face him, then frown at my morning breath, "God, no one was gonna make me brush my teeth before bed?"*

*Lonayla's voice answers, "we were on suicide watch, not hygiene duty."*

*I get up. "Ha, ha. I was upset, not stupid," I see the look on Kieran's face as he sits up, and choose to ignore it, while I walk into my bathroom. "I'm alive. Your job is done." I start brushing my teeth, and there's a knock at my door.*

*Mom comes in with a tray of bagels, fruit and cream cheese, followed by Dad with a tea kettle and all the fixings.*

*"Lonnell," Mom tilts her head to me, "I told you she was gonna wake up and ask why they let her sleep without her routine."*

*I huff a laugh, "they had one job."*

*I turn off my bathroom light, and return to sit at the head of my bed, where Reelin is now propped up on the pillows.*

*"Y'all let him back in my bed, and I think it's time we discuss your parenting," I joke.*

*"So, you're in a better mood?" Dad asks, standing by the door, his green eyes are blazing with the sun rays coming in from the window across the room. "I thought I was gonna have to chain you up, but figured he was the better option," Dad winks*

*at Reelin, then looks at Lonayla and Kieran, "I couldn't keep them out of here, though. Jammy and Pooda are down in our room."*

*I look at Kieran again, and he just stares back at me. "When did your girls arrive?"*

*Mom replies, "about ten minutes after your screams stopped, thank God." I frown. "We're gonna get Man-Man this afternoon, then we're going to the zoo."*

*"Lailani, Dr. Howard is here. I told her I'd have you downstairs in ten. Dr. Kantz can see you first thing tomorrow."*

*"Okay," I shift uncomfortably, "I—"*

*"We know. You don't want this," Mom interrupts, "get yourself together and get downstairs, please. She's in the kitchen."*

*"You three, eat. When the doctor leaves, you can come down. Let La have time to talk alone," Dad says to Lo, Kieran and Reelin, then he and Mom leave my room.*

*"Any chance you wanna do my therapy, Lo?"*

*"Not a chance in the hell of hell's hell, La," she's running her hand through Kieran's baby dreads, and he continues staring at me with a blank expression.*

*I look over at Reelin and his face is still blank, too. "You okay?" He doesn't say anything. I get up, running my fingers through my hair, trying to smooth it down. "You're giving me the silent treatment?" He doesn't respond. "Okay, well by the time my voice is fully back, I expect you to have expressed your feelings about all this. I say it should be about an hour or so before the silence pisses me off, though."*

*I go downstairs, and let Dr. Howard try to talk to me about my feelings. By the time she leaves, two hours later, I feel even more solid in what I need. My mind has not changed. My parents sat in for the last half hour, and I could tell my mom hated how sure I was. She tried to hide it, but her face gives everything away. The sadness in her eyes was palpable.*

*"I'm going to let Kieran and Lonayla get the kids ready so we can go." Mom says when Dad walks Dr. Howard out.*

*"Okay. I'll be right here, living in my mistake until it either rights itself, or someone helps me figure out what to do." I shrug, making sure not to look at her as she leaves the room.*

*"Lailani, you need to talk to Reelin," Dad sits across from me, "you need to let him talk about his feelings, too. Even if they differ from yours, you need to hear him."*

*"I asked him what he had to say, and he didn't say anything. He hasn't spoken a word this whole time, has he?"*

*"He and I spoke, yes. And you need to hear what he has to say," Dad gets up, just as Kieran and Lonayla walk in. Dad kisses my head, and Lo sits down next to me. "I'll be in the room with the babies." Dad leaves.*

*"Where's Reelin?" I ask.*

*Kieran shakes his head, sitting down across from me.*

*I sigh, "you want to say something Kieran? Go ahead, tell me how I'm a hypocrite. Tell me I'm a terrible person, and how disappointed you are! Go ahead. I'm waiting."*

*He cocks his head to the side, "you know, I was hurt when you wished death on the child you created in love. It wasn't hurt for me or your hypocrisy, though. It was hurt for my cousin, because he had to hear you speak about yourself like you were nothing, and he couldn't comfort you. He couldn't fix the problem for you, and I knew he would beat himself up over it. He has this need to make everything okay for you, but this thing? He's part of the reason it exists, and he can't reverse time. He sat and watched you go through hours and hours of self-loathing, and he couldn't even help. He was hating himself for putting you in this situation. He was hating himself because in loving you, he caused you so much pain, and you looked like you were ready to leave this life. I wasn't hurt because you said some hurtful things to me, or that you took back your words from when it was me in your shoes, because I love my kids, and I'm grateful they exist every day."*

*Kieran gets up and stands close to me, "you, though? You only said you wanted your baby to die because you couldn't believe this happened. You aren't in control, and that's the part you hate. You lashed out because you need to have the power. God decided to gift you and the man you love with a child, and you will never be more powerful than God, Lailani. No matter how anal you are about control." He kisses* the top of my head, "I'm going to get my daughters ready to have a fun day with their Grandys. You just remember you're not the only one without control here. There's someone with even less than you, sitting up in your room, hating himself more than you ever could."

With that, he leaves Lo, and I try to process everything he just said, but I can only think about that last sentence.

"La, I'm sorry," Lonayla's voice seems so small, "you know they're like brothers."

I get up, "yeah, I'll go talk to him."


I walk into my room, and Reelin's on his phone, standing by my window. I climb onto my bed to wait, but when I move a pillow behind me, I knock my phone off my nightstand. Reelin looks back, and I give him a half smile, then he walks over picking up my phone, and handing it to me.

"Yeah, I will," he nods, looking at my face, "Okay, thank you," he hangs up and sets his phone onto the nightstand, then walks to the end of my bed, looking at me like he doesn't know what to do.

I clear my throat, "I think your hour is up. My voice needs a few days, I think. That's even better for you, because I can't really interrupt, so you'd definitely win in an argument," I smile, pulling my knees to my chest, "so, say all the things. I'm all ears."

Reelin turns to my dresser behind him, and pours some of the hot water into a mug. I'm surprised it's still steaming, but then I see the hot plate under it. He fixes a chamomile tea with lemon and honey, and puts half a bagel with apple butter on a saucer with some fruit, then brings it over to me.

"Thank you," I take the mug, and he sets the saucer on the nightstand. Then he steps back, watching me.

"You're really not gonna say anything?" I blow into the mug before tasting the tea. "Nothing? No yelling. No disappointing soliloquy, or a haiku about love and babies?" His jaw quirks. "Ah, you do want to say something. I saw that." I smile, taking another sip of the tea, then set the mug down, picking up the bagel. I tear a piece off and put it in my mouth, talking around it, "don't worry, Kieran probably *already said everything you're thinking. He made sure to humble me and everything. Made sure I know to never try out-controlling God again." I shake my head, putting another piece of the bagel in my mouth, "he definitely ripped me a new one. And he didn't even curse, I don't think. Made sure that I—"*

*Reelin rushes over to my window, looking out, then he walks out the door. I'm stunned, sitting with my mouth open, mid-chew. I set the bagel down, lick my fingers, and climb out of bed to rush after him.*

*"Reelin?" I pass my doorway, "Reelin? Where ar—" I stop short at the top of the stairs as the front door closes behind him. I turn back to my room, because I'm not about to be the crazy pregnant lady chasing after her baby daddy.*

*I plop back down on my bed and look around, unsure of how I feel, "what the hell just happened?"*

*A moment later, my bedroom door opens, and I look up in surprise. Reelin walks in with a duffel bag, and closes the door. I tilt my head in question, but he just walks over to my closet and sets the bag inside, then turns his back to it, placing his hands on top of his head with a deep breath.*

*"I—"*

*"I'm sorry, Lailani," he leans against my closet door, closing it, "I did this to you, and now, I can't make it right."*

*I want to tell him it's okay, but it's not. I think about what to say, but nothing feels right. I chew on my bottom lip, watching him take deep breaths with his eyes closed. I don't know how much time passes, but I finally speak.*

*"You didn't do anything to me." He opens his eyes, and frowns. "Okay, you did, but you didn't force anything on me, so you're not to blame."*

*He takes a deep breath, and walks over to my window, "I should have been more careful. I honestly didn't care about anything. I knew you were on the pill, but even if you weren't, I didn't care." He turns to me. "I wanted this, Lailani. I wanted this, and it happened, and I never thought to ask you what you wanted."*

*I can feel my face twist, even as I try to keep my cool, "you knew I didn't want to be a teen mom."*

*"You're 19."*

*"Yes, emphasis on teen. You knew I didn't want kids until after law school an—"*

*"Yeah, and after your bakery was open for a year. I know," he sighs, sitting on the ottoman to my reading chair, elbows on his knees, "I didn't care."*

*I stare at him in bewilderment. This is what my dad and Kieran thought I needed to know? This was supposed to make everything better? Or was the point to make me feel worse?*

*"Even so, you couldn't just make a baby by yourself," I stand and pace my bed, "I can't even be mad at you for wanting it, because I let this happen."*

*His releases a very pained sigh, "I need you to be upset with me, La." I stop pacing, to stare at him. "I need you to be upset at me, because at least then, you won't blame yourself and leave this earth because of this."*

*"Boy, what—"*

*"You remember I told you about my sister?" He stands, "how she killed herself?"*

*"Reelin, I wo—"*

*"She was pregnant, Lailani. She killed herself because she was pregnant."*

*I sit back down. I knew suicide was always a touchy subject for him. It's the reason he wants to be a psychiatrist. He told me his sister killed herself when he was in the fifth grade. He never said how or why and he rarely brought up his family. When Reelin came to our school in tenth grade, he said he had some family issues, but he wouldn't elaborate. That Christmas break, he told me about the sister who killed herself, because he was going home to Texas to surprise his mom. He knew the holidays would be hard for her, because he was away for the first time.*

*"She got pregnant right after she left for college. She was afraid to tell our folks, because she wasn't married, and she felt like she let them down. She left a note saying how much she hated herself for it, and that she wished she could fix it, but this was the only way."*

*Reelin sits on the side of my bed, and his voice lowers, "I need you to not hate yourself, Lailani."*

"I'm just a little bit dramatic. I wouldn't hurt myself," I say, moving closer to him.

"Leesa would probably say that, too. But then she did."

I feel my eyes prickle, "I mean it, though. You know me. I'm a little too selfish for that. I don't even like doing those home wax kits, because I don't like pulling away the paper."

When he looks at me, his eyes are so sad, I can feel my heart break. "I don't know if I could survive losing you. I don't think I could live on this earth without you in it."

A tear falls. His or mine—not sure which—because I climb onto his lap, and we're both crying. His phone rings, and I try to move away from him so he could answer, but he holds me tighter, shaking his head.

After a while, I pull my face out of his neck, "I don't HATE the idea of being a mom. I just hate that I couldn't plan it."

"I hate that you couldn't plan it too," the little wrinkle between his eyebrows deepens. "I promise, next time, you can plan the whole thing. Down to my haircut before we do it."

I bark a laugh, "your hair cut is probably how we got here in the first place."

"I hope it's a little girl that looks just like you."

"I want a boy, so that's out. He can look just like my daddy, and we can name him Lonnell Jr.," I smile, then I realize my hand's on my stomach, and frown, "he heard me say that I want him gone."

"He doesn't have ears, so you get a pass." Reelin smiles, and I could fall into the look in his eyes a million times, and never get tired of it. "But we gotta talk about his name."

"What's wrong with my daddy's name?" I act fake offended.

"Lonnell Houldover?" Reelin squints.

"No, Lonnell Grander Jr. Duh. My daddy has no sons! Who else will carry on his name?"

"You're gonna have a different last name than our kid?"

"No, I'm keeping my name," I pat his face gently, "shouldn't have gone out of order, mister. Baby carriage first? Yeah, you skipped marriage already. We can just be boyfriend and girlfriend until we're done."

"You wish," he smirks.

"I promise you, you'll be very disappointed if you propose to me, so I suggest you don't."

Reelin gently bites my shoulder, and I laugh, trying to pull away from him. He lays me on the bed, playfully biting and tickling me.

"Okay, okay! Reelin Grander is my final offer!" I laugh out.

"Okay. I'll take it," he pulls me against him, and we lay silently for a while.

"What was that hideous bag you put in my closet?" I ask.

"Your dad had Aunt Kira bring some clothes for me. He knew I'd want to make sure you were okay."

"We really have to do something about their parenting. One daughter has three kids she didn't birth, and the other is a teenage baby mama," I say, and Reelin snorts.

I look into his eyes, and I want him to feel as safe as he always makes me feel. I want him to know he can always open up to me, "you wanna talk about her?"

He freezes, then moves his arm from around me. He looks sad again, "La, my family will never be an important topic. I never need to talk about any of those people. They don't matter. Outside of my parents, the only people you need to know are the ones you talk to. Aunt Kira, Kieran, his kids, and whoever else you know through them. Forget that I have a family."

I nod, then turn over. He puts his arm around me again, and it makes me smile. "Wanna talk about him, then?"

Reelin kisses the back of my head, "he'll have your eyes, and I will love him more than I could ever explain."

We fantasized about our son for the rest of the day. We wrote down things we wanted to say to him, hopes and dreams, and we settled on him being Reelin III.

*When my parents got home that night, we talked to them about him too. Mom cried tears of joy at my acceptance, and explained how much of a blessing this is for us. Lonayla and Kieran had all three kids that night, and we slumber partied in the TV room. Reelin and me were the last ones awake, and we couldn't stop talking about our future. It was a beautiful fantasy. We were so happy living in all of these ideas.*

*When morning came, it was like my fit from Saturday never happened. Reelin woke up with me to watch the sun rise, and we had our little baby notebook half-filled with what life would be.*

*And then, my period came. The sadness hit almost as heavy as the devastation two days before. Only this time, everyone felt the exact same.*

Lonayla and I take our food to go, and we're getting back into the car.

Lonayla looks over at me, "I'm sorry I might have this dumb ass situation that brought you back to your own. I'm sorry I wasn't more responsible."

"Lonayla, You've managed to not get pregnant before now. You're for sure the more responsible one," I give her a half smile. "While we don't know if it was real or not, it was a possibility for me, when I was young. I was the foolish one. You're grown and in love. Whatever happens, it's gonna be beautiful."

Lo smile, then asks me, "Hair store?"

"Yes, ma'am. I think I want to go blonde for the party."

"Oh, this the type of time I was hoping you'd be on. Let's fucking go!" Lo bounces in her seat turning on the playlist she's been listening to since we got home. Christina Milian's *Dip it Low* starts playing. "Ex-fucking-Xactly!" Lo turns up the volume.

"Yes. Immediately, yes!" I smile, and start singing along.

# 24 : Ready For Love

Lo and I just got back to the house, and I want to go to my dad's studio to see what he's working on. Lo goes upstairs to finish binging *The Wire*, like she's done most of the week.

"Hey Ma, it smells good in here." I set my computer on the island, "you need help?"

"No, I'm actually done. Someone's picking up here, shortly."

"Let me find out you're a caterer, now!" I smile, and wink at her, "I'm gonna go bother your husband," I grab my computer, and tighten my long coat around me to walk outside.

"It's windy, La. Use those walking poles, please." I try not to roll my eyes. "I mean it!" Mom demands, when I open the back door.

"Yes, ma'am."

When I walk into the studio, I'm immediately grateful for the warmth. While it has heat, having to walk outside to come in here, has never been my favorite thing. I look around the room, leaning the walking poles against the wall. My dad has changed everything in here.

"Daddy?" He turns, and smiles, pulling off his headphones. "When did you add these?" I gesture to my right.

There are beautiful portraits of my mom, my sister and I, where his guitar wall used to be. Beside the images is a staircase that leads up to a small platform above the recording booth, that now houses his guitars. My dad is sitting in the middle of the room, at the mixer, and I can tell he wasn't expecting to be interrupted. I walk to my left, and sit on the navy couch.

"Kieran gifted me those Christmas of '21, I wanna say. I forgot you hadn't seen them. I kept them wrapped all this time, because the platform was being built, and then I got a distracted for a while. I just got them put up a few months ago. Since we started decluttering, I had a lot of things I needed to clear out."

He laughs, setting his guitar down, "what's up, babygirl?"

I smile, opening my computer, "I just wanted to come in here with you. You know I play a lot of your songs in my mix at the shop, but I wanted to see what else you might have for me."

"I actually laid down the melody to a new song. It's a special request, and it's gonna be something. I can't give you the words," he winks, "but I can let you hear what it sounds like so far. He turns to the computer.

"I want the words, too! I won't tell," I get up, and sit in the chair beside him, "I love that you know how to work all this. I just know Mommy would hate to even try."

"Your mother can do a whole lotta things most people can't. These computers ain't worth the extra stress, when she can create things they never can," I smile at his smile, "and it's music, baby. You know I'll always figure out a way to have my music."

"Oh, I know," I lean back in the chair, and Daddy presses play.

Two acoustic guitars layer into each other, like they're doing some sort of dance. It kinda feels like the notes are floating in and out, but together. It's sweet and smooth, and it raises the hairs on my arms.

After about 90 seconds, he stops it, and I nod in excitement, "oh, that's nice."

Daddy's smile is so precious, "glad you like it, kid. I have to have it finished soon. I don't know when it's going to be used, but I can't wait to know how it's received."


My dad's first love, besides my mother, has always been music. He plays six instruments, but he favors the guitar. When my dad decided to pursue law, he skipped out on an opportunity to tour with Ms. Patti LaBelle, and Mom has always said he was insane for that. Daddy said that building a family with her was what mattered most, so he was solid in his choice. He would write and record background for artists when he had the time, but it wasn't his top priority. Some of his best music came from when he and Mom were going through their saddest times, when trying to conceive. To cope with his feelings of failure, he would write songs as his release.

Two years into starting his private practice, Dad had more time for his music. He would shop around his sound, and the record execs ate it up. Artists wanted sad songs to add layers to their public personas, and Lonnell Grander had plenty to give. Dad's a lot older now, and with the way a lot of music has lost the heart and soul of sharing true human emotion, he still gets to write from time to time. He loves doing fun songs with upbeat dance grooves, but his ultimate joy, is when he can take a person's story, and turn it into a vulnerable serenade.

"Everything you write is magic, Daddy."

"I love to create, so I would hope so," Dad picks up his guitar, "I'm probably adding a third layer and some keys to this one. I have to really think about it."

He pauses, then looks at me intently, "you were asleep all day yesterday. Are you okay?"

I get up to grab my computer, "yeah, I was just resting. I don't have a lot of days to just sleep."

"You're welcome to always come home for rest, Lailani. That shop will never matter more than your health."

"I know. I'll start scheduling a few days to relax soon, I promise."

I pull up my music app, "I need to download every song you have on here, so I can mix them into my playlists. I want everything."

"How long until we have Reelin over for dinner?"

I'm surprised by the question, "I don't know. Where did that even come from?"

"I'm just saying, he's back in your life, and you've been home all week, but we've not seen him. Are you making us wait until the ceremony to see you together?"

"I never took him from you guys. I love that you respected my choice, but just like Lo, y'all could always talk to and spend time with him. I'm not so selfish that I would take him away from everyone else. I just needed him away from me."

Dad looks into my eyes, and I feel like I'm in trouble. I shift in my seat, closing my laptop. "Lailani, have you two discussed where you go from here? Have you talked about what happened, and what your plans are? We need to know how to move forward with him, too."

"I don't really know. We'll find out in the next few weeks, while we navigate being in each other's spaces, again."

"I'm hopeful for you. I really am."

"Me, too," I give a half smile.

My dad starts playing India Irie's *Ready For Love* on his guitar, and I sit back, with a huge smile. Then I can't help but to sing along. I actually used to sing with him all the time. My musical gifts are my best kept secret. Right after Lonayla's sixteenth birthday party, Reelin heard me sing for the first time, and it was such a special moment. It was actually this exact song, too.

*March 17, 2007*

*Lonayla's Sweet Sixteen*

*"Kieran, I need you to be serious!" I shout, standing in the kitchen, "I need this to be just right, so stop laughing!"*

*I went a little overboard with the cake for Lonayla's party. The leprechaun I made nearly toppled off the display tray, when Kieran couldn't stop laughing when we tried to move it.*

*"La, you know it looked like lil' turds! That's why you're fixing it!" He's still laughing, and I want to plunge the nearest knife into his throat, but my sister would be devastated.*

*"Okay, excuse me for using the wrong tip. I thought it looked more like kinky hair, but I can see why the stubble is the better choice," I shake my head, piping small chocolate dots onto the leprechauns face.*

*"Where is Reelin with the gold coins? My mom should be back with Lo soon, and I need to spread them out."*

*"He's here," Dad says, coming over to look at my work, "you changed the turds. Good."*

*Kieran bursts out laughing again, "see? Everyone knew it!"*

*I roll my eyes, "okay, so what is he doing?" I ask my dad.*

*"I sent him around back, I didn't know you were still in here."*

*Dad walks back around the island, and stands beside Kieran, "get those giggles out, because La might kill us if this cake falls."*

*"That's literally exactly what almost happened," I frown, setting down the piping bag, then step back to make sure the cake looks good, "Daddy, please help Kieran get this outside. Wait, actually, I'll ask Reelin to help you. Kieran can't be trusted."*

*I turn around just as Reelin comes into the back door.*

*"Hi. I put those chocolate coins on the gift table. Did you want them in here?" He looks so handsome, today. He cut off the box-top, and his tapered fade is so mature.*

*"No, I need you to help my dad move the cake, though."*

*"I got the cake!" Kieran groans.*

*"Well, you two can move the cake, Lailani can do whatever she was doing, and I'll just go sit down until the guests start arriving," Dad suggests, then walks out of the kitchen.*

"That cake is crazy, La," Reelin smiles, walking over to get a closer look, "you did yo thang. I don't know how I'm always surprised when you do something like this."

"She don't do nothing else, so she better be fye at it," Kieran chuckles.

I squint my eyes at him, "aren't you supposed to be getting dressed?"

"Gotta move the cake, first," he shrugs, then frowns, "Kennedi said she was invited?"

I roll my eyes, "all three of your baby mamas were invited. Mom insisted. Bianca has work and Alexa said she has a big paper due. I told Mom that Kennedi would only want to come, just to get under Lo's skin, but Mom said I had to be nice, because Lonayla is."

"My mama has Jazmynn, so Kennedi has no reason to come here. If you ain't with my kid—the only reason you got an invite—then why you think you should be here?"

"Probably because you literally picked a fight with Lonayla last year, ON her birthday, then hung out with Kennedi, claiming it was for your daughter," I scrunch my face.

"We were in a tough spot last year," Kieran's shrug almost sets me off.

"That's minimizing it, bruh," Reelin says, before I can say something out of line, "You were playing crazy last year, and your baby mamas played right along with you."

"Exactly. It was literally a weekend full of nonsense!" I add, then start ticking off my fingers, "Friday, piss off Lo to hang out with Kennedi. Saturday, Alexa's pregnant. Sunday, Bianca can't let Alexa think she's the only one, so BOOM! She's pregnant too. Yuck! They were so excited to break the news on Lonayla's birthday weekend."

Kieran's face hardens, "I don't really want to talk about that, Lailani."

"Well, maybe you need to stop acting like you don't understand how your dumb decisions are the reasons these girls are doing weird things to set off my sister," I turn around and storm outside, to keep from letting the thoughts of my sister's heartbreak ruin my mood for the night.

*I walk over to the table designated for gifts, and take the chocolate gold coins to spread them across the food tables. The caterers are almost finished setting up, and the decorations are beautiful. Lonayla's birthday being St. Patty's Day was always my favorite thing because my favorite color is green, so there were always things she had that I could make mine. This year, she's going to be so surprised to find that all of her decorations are orange.*

*I have turned the backyard into Party Central. There's a raised stage for surprise musical guests, and large light-up letters that spell "Lonayla's Sweet 16" in front. There are massive balloon arches of orange, brown and white, with Lonayla's photos on some of the balloons that frame the dance floor my dad had brought in. Lo has been obsessed with Philly cheesesteaks this past year, so Mom brought out a crew from Geno's in Philly, to cater. There's a candy bar, a soda bar, an ice cream stand and a temporary tattoo booth with real tattoo artists who do semi-permanent designs with black henna. I couldn't let the Irish thing go completely, so there are white four-leaf clovers as chairs beneath brown tables. I went with orange and white tablecloths, and added centerpieces made into little white four-leaf clover shapes, holding disposable cameras for everyone to use, and Lo to have developed for an album.*

*I turn to see Reelin and Kieran walking out the door to bring out the cake. The cake is a two-and-a-half-foot tall leprechaun with brown skin and green eyes. He had a full hanging beard, but now, it's more of a close trim. His mustache and eyebrows are perfectly bushy, framing his button nose, plump lips and round cheeks. He's wearing a black pin-striped suit with an orange shirt and an orange and green paisley tie. He's holding a pipe in one hand, the other in his pocket. His shoes are shiny and black, with gold buckles. His hat matches his shoes and there's a green feather in it. He is so cute, I don't care what anyone says.*

*"Careful," Dad says, guiding them to the table, "Lailani, you need to get dressed," he says to me. I nod, but watch the cake until it's on the table.*

*When I can release a breath, because the cake is okay, I walk to the back door, and Reelin catches me, "hey, I have something for you."*

*I smile, "I'm Lailani—the not-birthday girl."*

*His little laugh could send me into the next universe, "I know who you are, and I know what day it is. I got her something, too."*

*"Okay. Well, save if for after Lo opens her presents."*

*"Cool. Remind me. It's in my trunk," he kisses my cheek, "your pops put me on guest duty, and I think it's about that time. I'll see you in a little bit, I'm gonna walk around front."*

*"Okay," I watch him walk over to my dad, and the two of them go around to wait for the guests.*

*"Lo's gonna love this, La. You did ya thang," Kieran comes up to me, putting his arm around my shoulder, "you look a mess with these rollers in your hair, though."*

*"Shut up!" I swat at him, and go inside.*

*Thirty minutes later, I walk outside to all of our people. The DJ is playing some mix that has all the boys being ridiculous. Lonayla and Mom come around from the front, and Lo looks gorgeous. They spent the night at an away spa, so I could get the party together. Lo didn't care to go out, probably because she was expecting the same green everything, but I slaved over the cake, and the details for two days, and it was so worth it. We partied our hearts out.*

*As people left, and the excitement died down, Reelin helped to get Jessy and Kia home, because they were both high out of their minds after someone snuck in weed brownies. Mom had two of the brownies, so she was definitely fun to party with, before she went to sleep. Kieran was supposed to help with clean up, but he found his way to the tv room, and fell asleep. Lo decided to go up with him, before the last of the guests even made their exit.*

*I sit by my dad, on the edge of the stage with his guitar in hand. He looks like one of the people from those old movies, who sing about getting the girl, with the last of the party lights on, strumming a sweet tune.*

*"It's just us on clean up. Play me something, old man. I didn't get to perform earlier."*

*He switches his tunes, and I begin to sing, "I am ready for looooooovvvvveeeeeee. Why are you hiding, from meee?" I close my eyes, singing like I can relate. I feel my dad shift, but I don't pay much attention to it, because I'm in the moment.*

*After the last note, I open my eyes to my dad smiling in front of me. I'm immediately confused, because I still feel him at my side. I jerk my head right. It's Reelin.*

*"We can clean up tomorrow. Goodnight, you two," Dad smiles, bowing his head, then places his guitar on the chair, before he walks inside.*

*I feel like my heart is beating out of my chest, like in those cartoons, "I thought you left?"*

*"I did," his voice plays a note in my head that gives me a rush I can never stop chasing, "but now, I'm back."*

*I feel like the earth shifted on its axis, then flipped over to make sure I felt it.*

*"Party's over."*

*His smile pulls my intestines out through my bellybutton, "Why do you like to hide yourself from me? When were you gonna tell me you sing?"*

*"I don't. I can, yes. But I don't."*

*"Will you sing for me?" He stands, and picks up my dad's guitar.*

*"What are you doing?" I laugh, but he just looks into me from three feet away, and starts playing the song again. I'm stunned.*

*"When were you gonna tell me that you play!"*

*I stand, and he smiles again, moving closer. I really can see my life in his eyes.*

*"I don't. I can, yes. But I don't. You're not gonna sing?" I shake my head. He huffs a small laugh, and if I thought the world shifted before, imagine my surprise when he starts to sing, "I will learn what you teach, and do the best that I can."*

*Seriously, this boy is not real. He can't be. I back up, sitting on the stage to catch my breath. He stops playing, sets the guitar back down, and comes to sit beside me.*

*"We'll touch on hidden talents another time," he pulls out a little green box, "I told you I got you something."*

*I take the box and open it up to a gold charm bracelet with four charms on it. I pull it out to inspect the charms. There's a little cloud, a letter R, a heart, and an infinity symbol with a tiny letter M.*

*"An M?" I look at him, confused.*

*He takes the bracelet to put on my wrist, "mine forever."*

*"You know—"*

*He kisses me before I can finish. When he pulls back, he presses his forehead against mine, "stop thinking about the end. You have to just enjoy life's moments, Lailani."*

*I don't say anything. I just sit with him, enjoying all of this.*

I smile as my daddy finishes the song, "you played that for me, huh?"

"You always had that boy's nose wide open."

I still can't understand when he was able to take lessons from you, without me knowing. I didn't even know him when he came here, but he knew you. That will always be crazy to me."

Dad laughs, getting up, "life has a funny way of bringing the people we're supposed to have around, no matter the circumstances," he kisses my head, then walks to the door, "I don't know how to do that download stuff, so you're on your own. Lock the door when you come back in, please."

When my dad leaves, I think about how cute it was to learn that little Reelin was one of my dad's private students, when he visited for the summers. I still don't remember him, but apparently we hung out for weeks at a time every summer since kindergarten. Kieran had so many cousins that visited, I couldn't keep up. Orientation day for tenth grade, I saw Reelin talking to my dad, but I thought my dad was just being friendly. Reelin picked up his private lessons again, around then. We had known each other a whole year and a half by Lonayla's sweet sixteen, but

Reelin was too shy to tell me before that day. Little boys are so weird. Lonayla only knew Kieran could draw because I was always in his class, and I knew. He would never show her, though. It's weird that they keep secrets like that.

I laugh at the thought, then sing to myself, "I am ready… for loooooovvvvveeeeeee…"

# 25 : Last Friday

*The morning of the party.*

I wake up to my phone ringing on my nightstand. I reach over to see who it is, but it stops, so I turn over and try to go back to sleep, only for my phone to start ringing again.

I catch it this time.

**Incoming Facetime Call from Reelin Houldover Jr.:** "Wake up, sleepy head"

"Didn't anyone tell you that double calling is serial killer energy?" I groan, wiping my eyes.

"I think you told me that a time or two. But you've told me everything I do was serial killer energy, since the tenth grade," Reelin's chuckle zings into my brain, and I suddenly feel like I just took a shot of caffeine. Awake.

"You have some questionable creepiness to you," I sit up, yawning, and I can see he's sitting outside with over-the-ear headphones on. "What are you doing waking me up on vacation?"

"Today's the day!" his smile is so sweet, "I finally get to see you, touch you, smell you…" he raises an eyebrow, and I laugh. "I know I get to hear you every day, but to hear you while I taste you?"

"Okay, simmer down. I told you I'm not even on that type of time," I lean against my headboard, "It's too soon, Reelin. We have to give it some time to know if this is what we both want, for real."

"I've always known exactly what I want."

"Yes, but things are different now. We're different," I frown, trying to pull my knees towards my chest, and it's too hard, without using my hands to help. "I don't even know how to use my own body anymore." I don't realize what I'm saying, until I say it.

"What does that mean?" His nose wrinkles, and he uses his shirt to wipe sweat from his face, "use your body like how?"

I have to think quick, "well, last I recall, you and I were very much… athletic. But I'm not anymore. I'm pretty sedentary, if I'm being honest."

He smiles shyly, "oh, it's gonna be fun working certain muscles again," he licks his lips and stands. I can see the track behind him now, "and I'm positive I still know your body better than you do, too."

As if she heard him, the little lady that lives between my thighs, blooms to life.

"Trust me, you don't," I shift a little against my excited eavesdropper.

Reelin's expression darkens, "trust me." his eyes feel like they're right in front of me, instead of on the screen. How the hell am I going to handle being near him, when I'm falling off the bone with just a look? "and you know I like to talk you through it."

For someone who hates large bodies of water, I risk creating one and drowning myself, with just the thought of this man all over me. He really took his time learning what I liked, and I've always appreciated his attention to detail. I was never left needing more. He would take things at whatever pace my body needed, without me having to say a word. Whether it was both of us reaching our peaks, or just him, pleasuring me—I was left completely spent. Every. Single. Time.

I don't even realize my hand has moved downwards until I shift again, and he smiles like he knows, "don't you dare. Not when I'm this close," he bites his lower lip.

"See? Serial killer. I wasn't even doing anything," I turn onto my side.

"I'm just at the school. I can come get you right now, to calm that urge."

"Reelin, I'm not sleeping with you today."

"Who said anything about sleep?" I see him get into his car, "we never have to do anything you don't want to. Just let me come get you, and we'll go from there."

I think about it for a minute, and I can see him hoping I agree to this. My body wants him so bad, I fear I might jump on him the moment he's in my face. His post workout glow? The pheromones? I can't. I should just rub one out and make him wait until dinner to see me, like we planned.

"Okay."

Wow, am I pathetic.

"I'll be there in a few."

"Okay," I hang up, and I feel my heart jump out of my body.

"Lonayla!" I yell. I don't hear anything. I check my phone for the time. It's just after eight, so she might still be asleep.

I climb out of my bed, and walk into my bathroom. My lady bits are calmed down, and I need to brush my teeth and everything. When I finish my skincare, I take off my bonnet, and my hair is a disaster. I shake it, tug at it, finger through and all, but it doesn't even try to cooperate. I walk back into my room, then to my closet, and I feel myself panicking. I'm really about see Reelin in the flesh for the first time in twelve and a half years.

I walk over to my window, just in time to see his chocolate brown Benz pull up.

"Shit," I feel my back stiffen, because I'm close to freaking out, and I have no idea how to explain it. I shuffle over to my bed, and call him.

"Hey, I'm—"

"Don't hate me," I sit on the edge of my bed and set my phone down, on speaker.

"You don't want to see me."

Not a question. He sounds like he knew it was coming.

I press Facetime, and his face appears on the screen, "what's wrong?"

"I just…" I pause, because I feel so ridiculous, "I want to be pretty when I see you."

"You're beautiful."

"Yeah, but I want to feel it too," I frown, looking down at my phone, "I have to do my hair, and I still have no idea what I'm wearing to the party tonight. Plus, we're supposed to go to dinner, so I want to make sure I look decent, you know?"

"I understand," he leans back in his seat, "believe it or not, I was nervous about seeing you, too."

"Stop it."

"I'm serious. I need a haircut, and I went to the school to run the track because my barber stays down the street, so I was hoping for a house call. I was so busy all week, I didn't even think about it until this morning. It's only been a week, but my lining still needs a touch up before our date."

I pick up my phone, "is it crazy that I let you see me looking like a raggamuffin on Facetime?"

"You're the cutest raggamuffin I ever did see, so nah," we both laugh.

Lonayla walks into my room, "Rizz is outside."

"Hey, Lo," Reelin laughs, and I turn the screen to her.

"Boy, what the hell? Why are y'all on the phone, when you're here?" She sits on my bed, "why are you not in this bed, weirdo?"

"I was having a moment of weakness, trying to get to your sister before it was time. This is our current compromise."

"Crazy," Lonayla's phone rings, "there's ya boy, see you later!" And she leaves.

"My barber just texted me. He can get me in at 10," Reelin sits up in his seat, and starts his car, "I should go to my house and bring my stuff back over here to Aunt Kira's. I'ma get ready over there, so I'm close."

"Okay. I have to do mine and Lonayla's hair, and I don't know how long that will take," I lay back on my bed, "I'm going for a completely different vibe tonight. It'll be like day and night from now until then"

"The sky any time of day has nothing on the beauty that is you," I can see his car is moving now, "whatever you wear, and whatever you do to your hair, will be perfect."

I chuckle, "you're such a schmoozer."

"The schmooziest, for you," he smiles, and I want so badly to take up residence in his dimples for the rest of the year.

"Get off facetime while you drive. I'll see you later," I sit up again.

"I was thinking I'll come get you around 4:30."

"Party starts at eight, and it's a nighttime cookout, so we don't need to go crazy. How long are you planning on eating?"

"If I'm eating you, we might not make it to the party at all," he smirks.

"Stop."

Please, for the love of God.

"Okay, if you feel like that's too early, just let me know when you're ready. I'll be close."

"Okay, I will," I get up, and walk out of my room, so I can make some tea.

"I love you, Lailani."

"Goodbye, Reelin," I hang up, smiling to myself, "that boy, that boy, that boy..."

It's a well after 2 p.m., and I'm just finishing with Lonayla's hair. We both decided to wear wigs for the party tonight. We went to the hair store and she fell in love with this 40-inch chocolate colored wig, and she asked me to cut layers and bangs into it.

"Lo, I need you to come put it back on, so I can see if these curls fall right!" I shout from the TV room, "if you look a mess, that's on you!"

Lonayla comes in on the phone, "no, she hasn't even decided what she's wearing! She won't wear the red or the green," she frowns, and sits between my legs on the floor, "let me call you back when she finishes my hair."

When she hangs up, I place the frontal on her forehead, "Kieran?"

"Of course. He likes the green the best, so you should wear that," she holds the front in place, while I fit the wig over her head, "he said Rizz is wearing some leather situation."

"He better the hell not. Leather what?" I frown, picturing something ridiculous.

"I think they have matching outfits, girl," I can hear that she's frowning, too, "they're gonna look like some 90s duo, and I just hope it's in a sexy way, and not a cheesy one."

"Ain't no way in hell, hold on," I text Reelin.

**Me: Leather?!!!**

**Reelin: LMAO it's not what it sounds like**

**Me:** 😰

"Oh my God, it sounds like he is," I say to Lo.

"I couldn't see what they actually got, but when Rizz got to the house, Kieran told him they were 'both wearing the leather,' and I just think it can't be good."

**Reelin: trust me, you'll like this**

**Me: Twinning with Kieran, though?**

**Reelin: type shit. Not like that but like that**

**Me: don't be looking a fool, Reelin**

**Reelin: and risk you pretending you don't know me? Never**

"I guess we just have to wait and see. Leather to a pool party sounds insane. Turn to face me, so I can make sure your face is framed right."

Lo turns on her knees, and I check the curls, running my fingers through them.

"La, I know we're the fashion girlies and all, but I swear if Kieran shows up here looking like some fool, I'm gonna be pissed. Does it look good?"

"Absolutely," I lean back, and tilt her head side to side, making sure everything moves right, "I love it."

Lonayla smiles, and goes to the mirror on the other end of the couch, "oh, yes. I love that my sister can do literally anything, because baby, you took this cheap ass wig and made it look like I went to get my hair done, for real," she sways her head side to side, then turns to check how the back falls again. "Bitch, the v-cut falls exactly right! Oh, I gotta get dressed!"

"Girl, it's too early!" I laugh.

"I'm gonna get some flicks for the Gram. I look too good!" She smiles walking out, then rushes back in, "La! Your hair! Is it still in the sink?"

"No, it's over there," I nod to the stool by the mirror with my damp wig on top, "I'm gonna get started in a minute,"

"I didn't even see it. All this chocolate goodness was in the way. You need me to do anything?"

"Nah, I'm gonna finish everything with it on my head. I'll do your eyebrows and stuff first, though."

Lonayla comes back over to the couch, "I love you, man. Thank you for keeping me together," I can see her eyes mist over.

"Ew, Lo. I think we should take that test. You're being mushy," I chuckle.

"Oh, wow. That hurts, La," she frowns, then leaves the room.

I lean back on the couch cushion, and stretch my legs on the coffee table. My body is not as sore as it could be, but I should probably do some stretches, heat my torso, and prep my legs to be out for the night. I go to my room for my heating pad and the jet boots my mom got me.

When I walk back into the tv room, Lonayla follows me, "let me do your braid down, so we can go to the store, because I think you're right," she frowns.

I look down at the heating pad and leg sleeves, then at the mirror with my hair supplies beside it, "better idea: blow dry my wig while I sit with these. I'll do two braids in my hair, and when I finish, you can lay on my lap, and I'll do your brows. That way, it'll give me time to stimulate my muscles."

"Okay, perfect."


Thirty minutes later, my hair is prepped, Lo's brows are done, and I'm fitting my wig on my head, "I'll style it when we get back, but I think it'll work. Let's make this run. I need to grab some gel inserts for my boots."

"You thinking about what you're gonna wear?" Lonayla's looking at herself in the mirror again, "I still think the red or the green."

"I might do the green, but I just thought about that little black dress Mommy made for me a few years ago, for that one boat party thing?"

Lonayla's freshly done eyebrows shoot straight up, "oh, miss girl! I forgot about that! That's perfect! You never even wore it, right? Where is it?"

"In the garage, in one of the garment bags, I think. Will you help me pull it out when we get back, please?"

"Yeah, Daddy said he's ready to finally move all that stuff into the back in here, so their cars can go in the garage again, too. Hopefully it's easy to find, and not lost in his jumble. You know they've been decluttering?"

"Yeah, I went in there when we got here, just to see if my old jeans were out there, but I didn't feel like searching. I'm almost sure I saw the rack with my dresses, though."

I shrug and get up, walking out the TV room, "let's go! I don't want anyone seeing my hair until it's done, so let me grab a hat. I'll meet you downstairs."

"Okay," Lonayla goes down, and I continue to my room, calling Reelin.

"I was just thinking about you," I can hear his smile, so I smile.

"I was just calling to ask your opinion on seemingly naked dresses in public."

"Will people see things they don't need to see?"

"Of course not," I say, pulling on a yellow bucket hat in my bathroom mirror.

"Then I say I love seemingly naked dresses, especially when it'll make it easier for you to sit on my face."

I feel like my body just short-circuited, "stop it, or I'm wearing a pantsuit," I joke.

"I'll get that off you with expert ease too," his voice is dripping with sex, and I'm not ready. "If that's what you want, of course.

"I don't. Not yet," I can feel the lie on my lips, but I can't give in to him this fast, "we have to figure some things out."

"What if it's the end of the world though?"

"If I die tomorrow, it doesn't even matter, does it?"

He lets out a small hum, as I'm walking down the stairs. If I weren't holding on, I would have rolled the rest of the way down at that sound. "So let me give you everything you need. Are you almost ready for me to come get you?"

I look at my phone screen for the time, "It's barely 3 o'clock. I haven't even finished my hair, and I just figured out what I'm wearing, so I have to pull it out and make sure I can wear it. I'm not even almost ready," I put on my coat to walk outside.

"Okay. Well, I'm waiting. I've been waiting."

"I'll see you, soon. I gotta go."

"I love you."

"I know," I hang up, and go outside to the car.

Lonayla and I just got back to the house, and it's already 4:30.

"I can't believe we had to go so far! Why the hell would they close the lingerie store?" Lo complains as we walk into the garage.

"I don't know. I still don't get why you needed those specific pasties, when you're wearing a bikini under the cover up," I walk over to one of the hanging racks filled with garment bags, to look for my dress.

"I told you, I might not wear the top, but I don't want my nipples to be out."

"It's a pool party, and you'll most likely be in the pool. Wear the top," I pull out three bags with black dresses, and hold up the first one, "this dress is cute, too."

"I have my heart set on the other one already. And I don't know if I want to get in with this hair. I feel too cute to ruin it."

"You know I won't be near the water, so I feel that," I shrug, then see the dress I was looking for, "got it!"

"Perfect. Also, I think I'll wear your little red dress," Lonayla smiles, taking the dress from me.

We walk inside, and our mom is coming around the stairs, "I told your dad I heard the garage, but he said I was being crazy," She looks at Lonayla's hands, "I remember that little dress. You wearing that?"

"Nah, La is. I'll be much more naked," Lo smiles, as I walk into the small bathroom to wash my hands.

"I bet you will. I like your hair!"

"Thanks, Ma. La's finna be a blonde bombshell, and she has her first date in a few, so we gotta get ready. You better hurry, Lailani!" Lo starts up the stairs, just as I come out of the bathroom.

I look at my mom, she's smiling at me, "I'm really happy for you. Bring him in here, Lailani," she squints her eyes, then walks down the hall, to her room.

I laugh, and go up the stairs to get ready.


When I get upstairs, Lonayla's waiting by my door, "I don't think I can pee on the stick, La."

"Okay. You have to know though, right?" I walk past her into my bathroom, removing the hat from my head, and shaking out my wig, "I think I'll style it up, tonight."

Lonayla walks into my bathroom, setting the pregnancy test on the counter. She leans against the wall behind me, looking at herself in the mirror, "how am I gonna be a mom, La?"

I stare back at her reflection, "you've been a mom since you were fourteen," I turn to face her directly, "what's this really about?"

Her eyes water, and she takes a deep breath, "I can't let him have his way, La. I can't let him just make me his fourth baby mama. I can't be one of them. I refuse to be one of them."

"Lonayla, you will never be minimized to just a baby mama. You might become a mother to his baby, but you won't be—"

"I'm not a wife, Lailani. He doesn't love or respect me enough to marry me. Why the hell would I just have a baby for a man who doesn't care about what I want?"

"He's been asking you to marry him since your high school graduation, Lo."

She scoffs, "no. He's been trying to stop me from being with anyone else by pretending to propose to me. Not once has he done it right. Not once have I felt like he's serious," she takes a deep breath, and wipes her eyes, "you know what, let's just take this test so I can know how much more to drink tonight. Ain't no way I'm fucking keeping it, so let's do this. Let me get something to drink, and a cup to pee."

Lonayla walks out of my room, and I pull my phone out of my pocket, to text Kieran.

**Me: How long until you grow up?**

**Kieran: prolly like five years. 40 sounds like a good time.**

**Kieran: What's up?**

**Me: I want to plan a wedding.**

**Kieran: okay? plan one**

**Me: don't piss me off**

**Kieran: You tell that boy Rizz you wanna to get married today, you'll be married today**

**Me: no**

**Kieran: I'm gonna tell him**

## Me: bye

"Lo?" I shout, just as she walks back into my room.

"I don't have to pee yet. Give me a minute," she chugs a bottle of water, and walks over to my reading chair.

I pull out my rattail comb, a brush, hair gel, bobby pins, scrunchies, and my hairspray to get started on styling my hair.

Lonayla's phone rings, and she answers on speaker, "what?"

"No 'what' girl, what's wrong with you?"

It's Reelin. I poke my head out the door.

"Nothing. What's up?"

"I just wanted to know if you wanted to come to dinner tonight, to keep your sister comfortable. I don't want her feeling like I'm pushing too hard, and I kinda been saying stupid shit to her."

"You're fine, Reelin," I shout, tightening my ponytail, "if I wanted to go as a group, I'd have told you that."

He's silent for a moment, "I wasn't expecting you to be on the phone. I'm sorry."

I walk over to sit on the ottoman, "what's wrong? Why do you sound like that?"

"Nothing's wrong. K said I was being pushy, and I didn't want to fuck shit up."

I laugh, "you've always been pushy, Reelin. What's with the nerves?"

Lo chimes in, "don't listen to Kieran, he doesn't know a damn thing."

"Are you sure, Lailani?"

"I won't even wear panties," I joke, and Lo laughs, but Reelin doesn't respond.

"Or I can wear pants. You know we'll only go as far as you want to, sweetheart."

Reelin huffs a small laugh, "aight, aight. Enough of that. Okay, I was a little nervous."

"Don't be. We'll figure all this out, nerves be damned. I'll let you know when I'm ready," I go back into my bathroom.

"Cool. I love you."

"Love you too, bro," Lonayla responds, before hanging up and rushing into the bathroom, "okay, I gotta pee."

I'm standing by the sink, while my sister pees in a cup, and all I can think about is how Kieran would hate not knowing what's happening right now. When I went through this, he made it clear how important it was for Reelin to be present to support me, and I feel like I should at least try to give him the same courtesy.

"Lo, you should let Kieran know."

"If I'm pregnant, he'll try to make me keep it, La. We just went over this. I don't want his baby."

"I'm pretty sure he'll support your choices."

"Did he support yours?" She sets the cup on the floor, then sits beside it, prepping the test, "he loves being a dad, Lailani. He has asked me to have his babies since the day we found out about Jammy coming."

"I actually think he would have supported my decision. He was just stuck on Reelin's pain, because of his sister's situation. I don't think me aborting was what he feared. It was me doing something to harm myself, like she did. I'm pretty sure he's not that kinda guy. We've known him our entire life. He'd support you, Lonayla."

Lonayla takes a deep breath, "take the picture." I look at her in question. "Me, right here like this. Take the picture."

I take the picture, and text it to Kieran. He calls me immediately.

"She okay, what's going on?"

"She just filled the little chamber, and now we wait."

"I can be there in five."

"NO!" Lo and I both say.

"No, we just thought you should be a part of this," I look at my sister's worried face, "Kieran, she doesn't want a baby right now."

"I will support whatever she wants, La," he takes a deep breath, and then I hear him pull the phone away to tell Reelin what's going on, "can she hear me?"

"Yes, I can," Lonayla responds.

"I'm with you. Whatever happens."

Lonayla starts to cry, and we all wait in silence.

I don't realize I'm holding my breath until Lonayla shoots up off the ground, "shots for everyone!" She picks up the test, and spins around, "Oh my God, THANKS BE TO JESUS!"

I laugh at her excitement as she runs out of my room, "hello? You still there?"

"Yeah, so she's happy. That's good," I can hear the slight disappointment in his tone.

"Kieran, she wants this to happen, just not right now," I reassure him.

"Yeah, I know."

Lo runs back in with a bottle of whiskey in one hand, and a bottle of tequila in the other, "pick your poison, bitch! We're finna turn the fuck up!"

"Yeah, we'll see y'all later. Have fun," Kieran hangs up.

"Lo, you could at least pretend to care that he wants kids with you."

"We have three, remember? Now be happy for me! Whiskey or tequila?"

I shake my head, "whiskey."

Lo pours our shots, and throws out all the evidence of the test, dancing to a made-up song the entire time, "no babies, no babies, no crazies, oh yeah!"

I go back to my hair, and wrap my satin scarf on tight. Lo sits in my room, and talks to Kieran about why she doesn't want a baby right now. The conversation started out crazy, but it sounds like they're in a calmer place. I look at the clock—5:03pm, and I have to get in the shower.

When I finish my full hygiene routine, I put on little lacy black underwear, and sheer pantyhose with an oversized white t-shirt, so I can add finishing touches to my hair. I walk into the TV room, and Lonayla is sitting on the end of the couch with a bottle of Sir Davis in her hand.

"Shot-o-clock!" She smiles, raising the two shot glasses, "gotta get you loose, missy."

I know what she means. My sister wants me to be a very freaky girl, but I actually need to loosen my body, because of the stiffness in the cold.

"Okay, pour me up!"

She smiles, and presses play on the music. Gucci Mane's *Freaky Gurl* starts playing.

"Ha! I get it, Lonayla!" I laugh, taking the bottle from her, and filling the shot glasses.

"Let's have the best night of our lives!" She smiles as we cheers, "like it's the last night, La! There is no tomorrow!" I walk over and sit in front of the mirror, plugging in my flat iron.

Lonayla dances around the room while she gets ready, and we sing along to her playlist of all of our favorite songs from high school. I finish my hair, and we go back and forth with whether I should wear pumps and pantyhose, or bare legs and my boots. The boots win, because I feel more confident on my legs in them. I fill in my brows, and put on strip lashes and just a little wing of liner, because I want to keep it simple. While I line my lips, Lonayla 's phone rings. I look at the time, and it's 5:58pm.

She answers, "hey."

"Yo, y'all still not ready?" Kieran's voice comes through the speakers.

"We are, just adding finishing touches," she passes me my earrings from the couch, and while I put them on, she smiles at me, "La looks the fuck good!"

"I bet she does. Rizz looks like he models for Rick Owens or some shit."

I smile, "he better look good, is all I know."

Kieran laughs, "Now La, you know we don't play them looking-a-mess games. You ready to party like it's your last night alive?"

"Why is everyone saying that? Y'all hoping I die, or something?"

All three of them have said something like this today.

"No, La." Lo rolls her eyes, "it's just a saying, damn."

I shrug, then Kieran adds, "Yeah. Rizz just walked in."

"What's up, Lo?" I smile, hearing his voice. "Where's your sister?"

"I'm right here."

"Hey, baby. You ready?"

"Yeah."

"Say less, I'm on the way."

Lonayla pours another shot, "okay! See y'all in a few! K, we still going to grab food?"

"Yeah. I already rolled up, too."

"Perfect! See you soon!" She hands me the shot glass, and we toast, "to the end of the world!"

I don't know why, but that statement makes me feel a little anxious.

# 26 : And We're Back



*Now.*

I stare at my reflection in the mirror.

*Reelin. Lonayla. Kieran. Reelin. The initial tree. Reelin professes his love again. Random chick. Kieran gloats. Lonayla gives me a drink. Random chick's smile. Lonayla laughing at me. Spray-paint. Kieran's laugh. Random chick and Reelin in a heated conversation. Lonayla. Reelin and the random chick by the initial tree. Kieran teasing me. Reelin's smile. Lonayla passing out shots. Random chick and Kieran. Reelin. Lonayla gives me another drink. Reelin. Kieran. Random chick talking to me. The woods to nowhere. Lonayla. Reelin. Random chick with Reelin. Reelin's blank stare. Random chick with Reelin. Random chick with Reelin. Reelin's blank stare. Warm water envelops me. Darkness.*

I gasp, as the memories fade away. Memories are usually such a nice thing for me, but the ones from Friday night only give me negative feelings.

That hot shower was so good on my body, but not so much on my mind. I feel like every time I let my mind wander too long, I either see things that confuse me further, or more of the beautiful, brown-skinned girl from the party. Who the hell is she? Is she that person named Stacee? When Reelin mentioned her on the way here from the hospital, he said "that person" but not her name. So, is it a different girl? How can I be sure? I told myself to leave this alone, but here I am, coming back to it.

Reelin raced out of here with a weird energy after checking his phone. Even if I wanted to think he wasn't going to her, I can't help but feel like that's exactly where he went. When he admitted he was with someone at the party, Kieran changed the subject, so I couldn't demand answers. Was he protecting him? Was Kieran keeping me from learning about her because she's not just some random person? I want to think it's just a coincidence, but then Lonayla and Kieran left almost immediately after Reelin did, and no one made it clear as to where they were going. Does

Lonayla know this girl, too? And if she does, why are they keeping her from me? Is it serious? I really hate not trusting them. It makes me feel like I'm losing my mind.

I throw on a pair of black sweats, and a white oversized off-the-shoulder sweatshirt, thankful my sister packed my black slippers. I run my fingers through my hair, letting it fall around my face and shoulders, then I walk into the kitchen to find something to eat.

I want to let myself be in the moment, I do. And I want to believe it's just my internal fears of wasting my time that are making me think these thoughts. I want to feel like the feelings Reelin has sparked inside of me, are supposed to be here. I want things to be okay, so things have to be okay.

I text my sister.

**Me: Marco**

**Sissy: Polo**

**Me: Where are you?**

**Sissy: out. be back.**

Okay, dismissive. I text Reelin.

**Me: Hey, the pharmacy giving you trouble?**

I've already eaten a yogurt and some fruit. Now, I'm sipping on an apple juice, looking out the sliding glass door, at the ugly day. I don't want to eat Lonayla's engagement meal without her being here, because that feels rude. I also don't feel up to cooking, so I walk back into the kitchen to get some cookies. It's been almost 20 minutes, and Reelin still hasn't replied, which is weird. He could be driving, so I guess I shouldn't overreact.

I hear the door.

"Honey, I'm home!" It's Lonayla.

"Where the hell did you go?" I plop onto the couch.

"K wanted to run by his mom's, then I went to the house to get the car," she takes off her coat and walks over to the kitchen, "Rizz said you wanted your hair box, so it's in the car. Also, I want to show K the youth center situation. I think if there's any time to do it, it's now."

"Yeah, he's going to be so happy, Lo."

"Yeah, I hope so," she sits on the couch, fruit snacks in hand.

"Where did Kieran go?" I ask, as she pours the whole pouch into her mouth.

Lo just shrugs as she chews, pulling her phone out of her pocket.

I text Reelin again.

**Me: Did you die?**

"Kieran said he had to go do something. I didn't get a chance to ask, because Mom was still gushing over the plans she apparently knew about—and let me ruin, when he left. She also hadn't seen the ring."

Lo turns her phone to me, showing me a picture of Mom, Dad, and the kids, "the kids spent the night with them. They went over there while we were at the hospital. They said they wanted to be there for support. Mom said call the house when you feel up to it."

"I love that." I look at my phone again, checking my messages. Still seeing nothing from Reelin.

"I want to start looking at dresses, but I also want Mommy to design mine," Lonayla's scrolling on her phone, "she said she had a bunch of mockups for you, but I don't even remember all the choices, and she didn't know where they were."

"I have them. They're at the house. I think all the stuff from when I was engaged is in a box in the tv room, actually."

**Me: Reelin? What the fuck?**

**Reelin: omw**

**Me: ???**

# Reelin: omw

"La, you never picked a venue, right?" Lonayla asks me, getting up, and going to the kitchen.

"Has Kieran mentioned anyone named Stacee to you?" I can feel my heart racing.

"No, why?" she asks, coming back with more fruit snacks.

I shift, then look at my phone again, "just wondering."

"When do you think we should look for your wedding box? You gotta start planning again, too! Daddy said he knows it ain't a double wedding, but the fact that we're both engaged is making his wallet sad."

"I'm not engaged, Lonayla. I'm simply wearing jewelry that was gifted to me," I snuggle up on the couch, pulling the throw blanket over me.

"Yeah. Okay, girl," Lo snorts.

I look at my phone, and go back to drugs.com, then think about my sister's errands.

"Lo, when did Reelin tell you I wanted my hair box?"

"When we left," she's so focused on her phone, I can't tell if she realizes that she said, 'they left,' like they left together.

"Where did y'all go?" I can't help but ask.

"I told you, Lailani," she cuddles up with one of the throw pillows, and continues her scrolling.

Now I'm feeling more annoyed than I would like to, watching my sister scroll, looking so peaceful. She's so blissfully happy, but I'm sitting here thinking about the weirdness, and the lies that have been going on around me. I don't like that I have to question every little thing, but if it looks like a duck…

I hate that she's clearly not concerned with anything but her own stuff, and I need to have that same energy. I need to think of a plan, and not focus on the little lies that keep appearing in front of me.

Step 1: find the drug they used

Step 2: cross reference with the doctors, and my test results

Step 3: confront the culprit, make them explain, then decide where to go from there.

I open Google to return to my rabbit hole, but my mind takes me to the last time Lonayla kept something about Reelin from me.


*Christmas Eve, 2021*

### ***Incoming call from Kieran Michaels:***

*"Bro, it's barely 9 a.m., what's up?" I answer on speaker, while in my parents' kitchen, in my floury disaster.*

*"La, I need your help," Kieran sounds stressed.*

*"Okay, what's up?" Lonayla walks in, and looks at my phone curiously.*

*A pause, "It's Rizz," Kieran's tone is strange, "Lo ain't answering, an—"*

*"Call me. Now," my sister interrupts, "right now," then she hangs up my phone.*

*"Why'd you hang up?" I ask her, while I grease my cake pans.*

*She looks at me with a clenched jaw, "be serious, Lailani," her phone rings, and she steps outside.*

*I'm busy making cakes and cupcakes for our house, Kieran's house, my cousin Jaimie's family, and for the church, so I don't think too much about my sister not wanting me to hear whatever's going on with Reelin. It's not really any of my business. Plus, if I really want to know, I'll always have access to the man.*

*Lonayla walks back in, "I'll be back. You want me to bring back anything?" I shake my head, and she leaves.*

*The look on her face was so weird, but she and Kieran are always beefing, so I decide it's that, and I keep working.*

It's been more than eight hours, and I've finished all the baked goods. I thought Lonayla would be back by now. I call her but she declines, so I text her.

**Me: Lo, you're supposed to help with drop off, remember? It's almost 6.**

**Sissy: Can daddy help you? I'm a little busy.**

**Me: daddy isn't here. He and mom went to that music thing, remember?**

**Sissy: shit, La. I forgot. Okay, give me a minute, I'll be otw**

I finish stacking the boxes, and move them to the end of the island, preparing to take them to the car. I get to the last three boxes of cupcakes, and my body locks up. I fall like a plank—the wind knocked out of me. This is the third time this has happened in the last two months, but I'm almost sure it's just my anxiety. I take a few deep breaths, trying to get my heart to calm, then roll over to stand.

The cupcakes are still okay, thankfully, but I have to fix the icing on a dozen or so of them. I can't stop shaking, and this is not the time to have my body reacting like this. I look at the time—6:27 p.m. I don't know how, when it was literally just ten till. Where the hell did that time go? I set the cupcake boxes on the counter one by one, with shaky hands, then go into the fridge for the leftover icing, thankful it hasn't gotten too cold.

"La?" Lonayla is standing right next to me, "what the fuck?"

I blink, looking at her, "what?" I look at my hands, holding semi-warm icing, and an empty piping bag, "when did you get here?" I begin filling the bag.

"Just now. Were you daydreaming? What happened to the cupcakes?" She points at the boxes.

"I dropped them. It's fine, I just need a minute."

*"Sure," Lonayla looks at me with an unasked question, "should I start loading the car?"*

*I nod, and Lo goes to the other boxes, taking a few to walk outside. I look at the clock—6:59 p.m. What the hell? I lost time again. I finish the cupcakes as quickly as I can, and Lonayla carries the boxes to the car. I'm still feeling way too shaky, and it's actually making me more anxious.*

*"I need you to drive, please," I tell her, "I think I'm too tired."*

*"Cool," Lonayla gets into the driver's seat, and I struggle with lifting my leg to get into the car, "La, what are you doing?"*

*"I think my body is having a panic attack, Lo. I don't know," I fight back tears, and take a deep breath, forcing myself into the car.*

*"These anxiety attacks have been more and more often, Lailani. I think you need to slow down at the shop," Lonayla looks annoyed.*

*"I will. Next year is the ten-year anniversary. I'll slow down, after that," I focus on my breathing, and we head out to drop off the goodies.*

*Kieran's house is the first stop. Kayde comes to grab their cakes and cupcakes from the car, so we can get to the church to meet with Ms. Patty before she leaves. Ms. Patty's nephews take in their load, which is most of the goodies. They have four cakes and five boxes of cupcakes. After the church, we head to Jaimie's. She asks us to come inside, but I'm not feeling it, so we tell her we'll visit tomorrow after brunch, then we head home.*

*Mom and Dad pull into the garage just as we pull up, and I feel like there are cinder blocks in my limbs, as I climb out of the car.*

*"Y'all get the church their stuff in time?" Mom yells, after Dad opens her door for her to get out.*

*I close my car door, and Lonayla moves around the car towards Mom and Dad, and then I realize I can't move.*

*"Yeah, just in time, too," Lo says, then looks back at me, "Lailani?"*

*I see my sister's face twist. Mom's shouting something, and Dad is running towards me, but the world fades to black.*

"Stop," I say to my sister, who's saying something over and over.

"Lailani, sweetie, the ambulance is on the way," I hear Mom before I open my eyes to see her, "you fainted, honey," she has tears in her eyes.

"La, are you hurt?" Dad asks with a soft, but insistent voice.

"No. I'm fine."

I move, trying to sit up, "stop, Lonayla."

My sister, who was repeating, "Don't die" over and over, says it two more times before stopping.

"I don't need an ambulance, I need a hot bath."

Dad helps me to stand.

"No, La. You fell like a board. It was inhuman. You're going to the hospital," Mom insists, as Dad nods.

"I promise, I'm fine. I am not spending Christmas in the hospital, for them to just tell me to double my Prozac," I shake my head, "I just need a hot tea, a hot bath, and a good night's sleep. I will be fine."

I hear the ambulance coming, and Dad shrugs, looking at Mom, "you know she won't go if she doesn't want to."

I tell the medics my sister panicked, and called without thinking. They check my vitals, and make sure I have no signs of a concussion before leaving. I promise my parents and sister I'll see the doctors first thing Monday. Mom makes my tea, and Lonayla walks me upstairs.

After my bath, I lay in my bed, and I hear a knock at my door.

*"Come in,"* I'm scrolling WebMD about lost time, because I've noticed that happening more often, lately.

Lonayla comes and sits on my bed, *"La, I don't think I have ever seen a human body stop moving like that. You were just standing one second, then a statue the next."* She sounds worried, *"you hit the ground like something that wasn't real!"*

*"I've been a little stiff. It's probably because I was baking all day without a break. We can just do some yoga tomorrow,"* I shrug, *"we're getting old, girly."*

*"Okay,"* she lays next to me, *"can I sleep in here?"*

I look at her with a furrowed brow, *"why?"*

*"It was a shitty day already, and then you just made it shittier,"* Lonayla's frown makes me sad.

*"What happened today? With Reelin?"* I ask, actually caring to know.

*"Nothing. It's fine."*

She looks me in my eyes, *"Lailani, I will do whatever I can for you, you know that, right?"* I nod, *"but I need you to understand that no matter how you feel about Rizz, no matter how much you pretend he doesn't exist, he's part of my family, too. I'll protect him, just like if he were you."*

With that, Lonayla pulls the covers up to her chin, and closes her eyes. I stare at the worry lines in her forehead. She's really stressed about something, but she's not sharing Reelin's business with me. I'll respect her decision, of course.

**Me: Hey, what happened today?**

**Kieran: Did you go to the hospital?**

**Kieran: I already talked to Lo, and I know something happened**

**Me: I just needed to relax, I'm good. What happened with Reelin?**

**Kieran: It's cool. When are you going to the doctor?**

**Me: Monday. Tell me what happened.**

**Kieran: I want to go with you.**

*Me: it's not that deep*

*Kieran: it is to me.*

*Kieran: I'm coming with you*

*Me: don't be dramatic. Tell me what happened.*

*Kieran: Ask him for yourself. Goodnight Lailani. Merry Christmas.*

# 27 : Do You Remember

I wake to Reelin kissing my forehead, and I look around, confused.

"What took you so long?" I ask him, seeing Kieran and Lonayla in hushed conversation in the kitchen.

"I'm sorry, I had to swing by my house to get some clothes. I didn't know I was staying here, remember?" He moves my legs, to sit under them.

"It's been hours," I look at my phone, "it's been four hours, and you weren't responding to my messages. What took you so long?" I narrow my eyes at him, then immediately stop, because I don't want to hear anything about my eyes turning whatever color when I'm suspicious, or something.

"You know the ceremony is tomorrow," he shifts a little, looking over to Kieran and Lo, then tries to change the subject, "y'all know what you're wearing tomorrow?"

"I don't care if they go naked," I respond, before they can. Everyone looks at me, and Reelin's eyes widen.

I repeat my question, "what took you so long?"

Kieran walks over to the couch, "La, the committee is hosting a banquet tonight for the honorees, and he had to tell them he won't make it."

"You knew this man wasn't leaving you for a dinner," Lonayla adds.

"While I appreciate the peanut gallery answering for a fully grown, fully capable man, I would like him to answer my questions. Thank you," I crinkle my nose.

Reelin just reaches for the prescription bag on the coffee table, and asks Lonayla, "can you bring your sister something to drink, please?"

This man has some gumption, I'll tell you that. I try to pull away my legs, but he holds them in place.

"Let me go, Reelin."

Lonayla hands him a bottle of water, and he takes it with his other hand, then looks at me with a look I know means he's annoyed, but I don't care.

"Answer my question."

"I went to my house. After my house, I went to meet with a lawyer about a continuing situation. After that, I came back here," he hands me the water, using his forearms to tighten his grip on my legs, he opens the prescription bottle, then passes me one of the tablets.

"Then why are your little protectors trying to make me think you went to cancel a banquet appearance?" I tilt my head at Lonayla and Kieran, "which is it?"

"It's all of the above," he nods at my hand, then waits for me to take the medicine, before loosening his grip on my legs, "I've never known you to be so suspicious."

"I have never died before either, Reelin," I move my legs off him, "and you could've saved me, but didn't. So, I guess we're both out of character these days, aren't we?"

I get up with my phone and the water, then walk back to the bedroom, rolling my eyes at Lonayla and Kieran as I pass them.

I lay on the bed, and look up at the ceiling, seething at the secrets and lies that are coming left and right. I feel like I'm going to lose my mind. I hear the front door open and close, and then some hushed conversation on the other side of this door. I roll over, and scream into the pillow.

Lonayla walks in, "what the fuck, Lailani?"

*She's* mad at *me*? There's no fucking way.

"Who the fuck knows you're here?"

I turn my head, then sit up when I see a black box with a red bow in her hand. I tilt my head in curiosity, and Lo places the box beside me, waiting expectantly.

The note on the package reads:

**_For Lailani, the only girl in your world_**

"Is this a joke?" I say looking at the label again, "what does this even mean"

Reelin walks in with Kieran behind him. He says nothing as he leans against the wall by the bathroom, staring straight at me. Kieran looks at me like I've done something wrong, and Lonayla crosses her arms with a frown. I'm confused as to how I'm suddenly the problem.

"Outside of our parents, the only people who know I'm here, are in this room," I widen my eyes, and shake my head in a very obvious manner, "so, stop looking at me like I did something to y'all,"

"Open the box, La," Kieran says, moving to Lonayla, and putting his arm around her waist.

Reelin is staring through me, at this point.

I pull the lid off the box and immediately want to vomit. There—in this box that smells like cigarettes and mildew—is my original Burberry coat that went missing on Friday night, with a note that reads:

**_Since you're still living._**

**_Stay warm, Sweets._**

Reelin moves to me quicker than I can process. He shoves the box away, and grabs me, pulling me to him. I feel myself shaking, but I can't put my thoughts together fast enough to form words. The note was clearly meant to let me know that I'm not losing my mind. I did in fact die by someone's hand. This is the proof that it was intentional.

I try to pull away from Reelin, but he won't let me go.

I'm getting hot, and I can't see through my eyes that are now filled with tears, and whatever the three of them are saying, I can't hear.

I feel my spine go rigid, and I try harder to pull away, but Reelin just holds me tighter.

I know they're speaking, but all I hear are harsh muffles.

And then, I can't stop it. I vomit all over Reelin's chest, arm and shoulder.

"GET IT THE FUCK OUT OF HERE!" Reelin shouts. He loosens his grip, and I bend over his arm, hurling again. He doesn't let me go, and he's rubbing small circles on my back.

I lift to my full height, wiping my mouth with my sleeve, and try pulling away again. Reelin is covered in my vomit, but he makes no move to fully release me.

"Please, I need to sit," I plead, "let me sit."

He assists me back to the edge of the bed, twisting to sit beside me, keeping me in his arms. Kieran walks back into the room, and turns into the bathroom for a towel, and Lonayla rushes out.

"Fuck, man," Kieran says, trying to hand Reelin the towel, but he doesn't take it.

Lonayla comes back in with a ginger ale, holding it out to me. Reelin grabs it, pops it open, and tries offering it to me. I shake my head, watching Kieran use a towel to get the vomit off the floor. Lonayla puts her hair up in a bun, and then rushes into the bathroom for another towel, and my Dr. Bronner's baby soap, then comes over to me, squatting down, so I can see her face.

"La, I need you to let me take off your shirt," my sister is looking at me like a lost puppy she's trying to rescue. She looks to my right, "Rizz?"

Reelin says nothing, but he loosens his grip a little. Lonayla stands, setting down the towel and soap, then takes the other hair tie off her wrist, to collect my hair.

I look up at her, "where did you guys go?"

She pauses to look at me, then to Reelin, who still has his body loosely around mine. I grab his hands, pulling myself away, and stand. I look at Kieran, who has just finished wiping the rest of my chunks off the gray imitation wood floor. His expression is pained. I look back at Reelin, who is sitting on the edge of the bed, covered in vomit. He has no expression on his face at all. And then I focus on my sister again, as she moves in front of me, so that she is the only thing that I see.

"Do you know what color my eyes turn when I'm unsure, Lonayla?" I ask, while I try to focus on her eyes, "because I don't. Just like I don't know what color yours turn when you're lying to my face. Because you keep doing it, and you always look the same."

"La, what are you talking about?" She acts offended.

"What is going on, Lonayla?" I try to back further away, but the dresser is behind me.

Kieran takes a step closer, "La, what's wrong?"

"Don't," I shake my head, slowly trying to move to the door, "you all think I haven't noticed the small things. The hushed conversations, and answering for each other when things don't add up?" I move again. "The random things appearing, like my lip gloss that you *hate*," I emphasize that word to Lonayla, "there was no reason for you to have it. And it's only when I'm alone, just after being around y'all, that someone is trying to get into my iCloud. The secrets and lies I keep catching you all in… I—"

"Lailani," Lonayla's hands are up, like she's trying to keep them in my vision. As if I'm the person to be feared, here. "What are you talking about?"

I look at Reelin, and he's still staring at me, with his blank face, "do they know?"

Lonayla steps closer to me, "know what, Lailani?"

I'm almost past the dresser, and then I can make a run for it.

"What are you talking about?"

I look at her again, then at Kieran's pleading face. Then my eyes are drawn back to Reelin.

"Do they know that you watched me drown? That you had the same exact expression as you do right now, as I took what you thought was my last breath?" I feel the tears falling from my eyes, but I reach the door, and I turn to run.

Only my body won't let me, and Kieran catches me, "Lailani, stop!" He shouts, as I fight against him. "Stop! You don't understand!"

"La, please!" My sister has the nerve to cry, and I can see her lying face.

"How could you know that him and little whore tried to kill me, and just act like everything is okay?" I'm full-on sobbing, still fighting against Kieran, "how, Lonayla? How?"

She straightens, and her face twists, before it goes blank, "oh my God, you're losing it."

"No! I remember!"

I finally hit Kieran in his nose hard enough for him to let me go, so I can back away. As he falls, Reelin comes into view behind Lonayla. Their blank expressions send terror through me.

I place my hand on the wall, inching my way down the hall on stiff legs. Lonayla drops to her knees beside Kieran, who's holding his bloodied nose. Reelin walks closer to them, still staring at me. I notice the tears in his eyes, and it sets my teeth on edge. The audacity of *him*, to cry in this moment.

"Lailani, please," Kieran says through the blood-soaked hand covering his nose, "you really don't understand."

"I don't want to," I want to turn to see how far the door is, but I can't let myself look away from them.

"I don't understand," Lonayla sobs, "what the fuck is she talking about?" she asks Kieran, then looks behind her, to Reelin, "Rizz, what is happening?"

He doesn't speak. He just continues his murderous crybaby stare.

"So, I take it Stacee knows I survived, huh? That's why my coat arrived in this place that only the three of you knew I came to?" I feel like my legs are going to give out, but I keep inching away, "I watched you watch me, with not a single feeling—knowing I would die," I wipe at my face with one hand, then place it back on the wall, to keep myself steady.

"It's not what you think," Kieran stands, "it's so much more complicated than that."

Lonayla looks at Kieran in disgust, registering his words, then backs away from him, "what the fuck are you talking about?" She comes closer to me, but I can't move anymore, "what do you mean it's complicated, Kieran?" She looks between the two men, then puts her arm in front of me, defensively, "you actually tried to kill my sister?"

There's a ring behind me, and I'm startled stiff. Lonayla grabs me, looking at the box that's a few feet away, in front of door. The ringing stops, then starts again.

"Don't answer it," Kieran says to Lonayla, as she shifts around me, against the wall.

Reelin moves quicker than I can process. He passes us, going straight to the box, dumping it out. My old phone falls out, and he clicks to answer, not saying anything, putting it on speaker.

"Hey, Sweets. Remember me, yet?" A female voice says.

Reelin's entire body goes almost as rigid as my own. Kieran rushes over to him, "Stacee, this isn't a fucking game! What the fuck is wro—"

"Aw, KK, don't be that way. I told you and Matty I wanted her gone," Stacee purrs.

"Who the fuck is Matty?" Lonayla asks.

I stare at Reelin, who is focused on me.

"Yikes, the love of your life uses that kind of language? That tone? How gross. I really hate those green-eyed demons."

"What do you want, Stacee," Kieran's asking her like this some sort of normal situation, and she's simply annoying him and not alluding to my attempted murder.

"I want the last 25 years of my life back!" She yells, "I want her to know what it means to ruin a life, just because you can!"

A gasp escapes me, and I am suddenly so sure of exactly who Stacee is. I lift off the wall, and Lonayla stays with me, as I move closer to them. Kieran moves from in front of Reelin, who just watches me, as I look into his eyes.

Those deep brown eyes that have always affected me. They stared into my soul before I even remembered. Not until this very moment.

"It got really quiet over there," Stacee croons, "having a moment, are we?"

I reach for the phone, keeping my eyes on Reelin, "Stacee?"

"Remember me, now?" She laughs, and it zaps through me.

Reelin is still covered in vomit, unmoving as we stare at each other. I cup his wet cheek with my other hand, "you're Matthew?" I ask, without needing to. "Stacee, from the pool. Summer Stacee. Stacee is your sister."

Reelin's face crumples, and he closes his eyes.

# Epilogue

*Sophomore Year*

## Reelin

It's the first day of 10th grade, and I've officially moved to Atlanta. Since I'm still a minor, and my family circumstances are changing, I get to live with Aunt Kira to finish high school.

I haven't been this excited to see anyone in my life.

The last time I saw her, she was being taken away in an ambulance. It sometimes feels like yesterday, when we all thought she was dead. When we all thought my sister killed her.

That was five years ago.

I'm the youngest of ten siblings, but I grew up like an only child. My sisters always joked that I was an accident, because they were all close in age. My parents slipped up and had me after a seven-year gap. Stacee was the closest to me in age. She was 17 when I was 10.

We were visiting our Aunt Kira and cousin Kieran, for the opening of Aunt Kira's beauty salon that summer. My mom would usually only let me spend two weeks in Atlanta, but Kieran and I begged her to let me stay with them for the whole summer. Mom didn't want it to be too much trouble, but we did the cousin thing, and asked in front of everybody.

"MJ can always stay here," Aunt Kira says.

"I'm staying to help with Matty, too!" Stacee reassures.

Mom was fine as long as I was, and with Stacee here, Mom and Dad didn't have anyone home with them all summer. I know that made her happy.

Stacee worked in Aunt Kira's salon most of the time, and when she could, she would come to the pool with us at C.S. Williams High. She had a crush on one of the Grander cousins, Kayla.

Kayla and her sister, Jaimie, had a really cool relationship with the swim coach, and we got to use the school pool for fun, as long as one of them was present.

The last day of summer vacation, before fifth grade, Stacee asked why we were playing video games instead of at the pool. Kieran told her the older Grander girls weren't home, so we weren't allowed. Stacee didn't like that. She said Kayla was probably lying, because she knew that Kayla's boyfriend was back in town. Stacee went outside, and we went back to playing our game.

A few minutes later, Stacee came back in, telling Kieran and me she got permission to take us to the pool. She said to invite all our friends—especially the younger Grander girls, since she knew we liked them, and we deserved a fun final day of summer break.

Everything started off so normal. Everyone but Lailani Grander got in to swim, and I kept close to the side making sure she was having a good time.

I remember every second. Every blink. Every little thing.

*Summer 2000*

*"You okay over here, La?" I ask her for the third time. She never seems annoyed by the amount of times I ask her. She always smiles like it's the first time.*

*"I'm having a great time, Matthew. How about you?" She smiles with her eyes. They're the prettiest green, like green water taffy.*

"*I always have the best time when I'm around you,*" I lift out of the water to sit beside her.

*Lailani caps her marker, and puts her coloring book down, before asking me, "are you excited to go back to Texas?"*

*I shake my head, "no. I wish I could stay here, forever."*

*"Forever doesn't exist for people, Matthew," her eyes widen, "If it did, nothing would end. You don't truly know if you like something until it's over."*

*I love how she speaks, even when it makes me a little sad, "I don't think we wait until the end, though. I think you have to like things in the moment."*

*"I think most people think that, but that's why they always have sad days," she looks at me thoughtfully, "do you have a lot of sad days, Matthew?"*

*"I don't know," I say, trying not to look too pathetic. Then I slide back into the water, "I'll have a lot of sad days when I can't see you every day."*

*Lailani smiles, "just come back next year! It was so cool that you came the whole summer, this time! Do it again."*

*I have to tell her how I feel.*

*"I want to tell you something no one else knows," I move closer to her legs that are dangling in the water.*

*"What is it?" She crosses her legs, like she didn't want me to touch them.*

*"Matt is just my nickname," I whisper.*

*She makes a face like she already knows, "duh, it's short for Matthew."*

*"Yes, but Matthew is not my first name, either," I smile, and look around to make sure no one else hears. Lailani leans her head closer, so I go for it, "I'll tell you my real name, if you become my girlfriend."*

*She scrunches her nose, "I don't want a boyfriend."*

*I tilt my head, "but you said I was special, that's why you don't call me MJ like everyone else."*

*She shakes her head, "I said—"*

"What are you two talking about?" Stacee interrupts from the chair behind us.

"Nothing," I'm on the verge of tears, because La is looking at me like I mean nothing, but I care so much about her. Am I really not special, to her?

"Matty, why do you look like you're gonna cry?" Stacee asks in her annoyingly overprotective big sister way.

"Are you okay?" Lailani asks in a sweet voice, and I can tell she really wants to know." I didn't mean—"

"Nope!" Stacee interrupts her, giving her a mean look, before she shouts, "everyone out of the pool! We're gonna play a little game!"

When we all get out, Stacee walks to the edge of the pool, and turns to La, who twists to look at her. Lonayla and Kieran sit beside Lailani, and Kieran's arm on Lo's shoulder.

"Your cousin paged me, Sweets. She should be here soon. Don't you want to show her you can swim, after all these years?

"No," Lailani answers, without a second thought.

"I heard you told her you would learn when you were ten," Stacee tilts her head in question, "aren't you ten? I haven't even seen you try at all this summer."

"I don't want to learn, and no one can make me," La says calmly.

Stacee smiles at her, then says to everyone else, "Lailani here just got an attitude with me! Remember kids, I am your elder, and you have to respect me."

She looks back at La, "I don't like how you act all better than everyone else, because you don't want to get your hair wet."

Before anyone can do anything, Stacee grabs Lailani's waist, carrying her to the deep end.

Everyone is shouting. Everyone except me, because I'm frozen in terror.

"Look at you, you're doing it! See, you know how to swim! You just have to do it under the water, not in the air, silly!" Stacee teases La as she kicks and screams in her arms, "you can do it!" Stacee yells, then she throws Lailani into the eight feet.

*Everyone goes silent. No one moves.*

*The first time she comes up for air, the scream she lets out rings through my whole body. It feels like she's been screaming and splashing forever. I think time might have stopped.*

*Kayla and Jaimie rush into the gym, and immediately start screaming. Kayla runs to the phones, and Jaimie dives into the pool, fully clothed.*

*Stacee doesn't say anything. She just winks at me, with an evil smile on her face.*

*I feel like I can't breathe, and I don't want to until I know that Lailani is okay.*

I walk over to where the most beautiful girl I have ever seen is talking to Kieran and her sister on the bleachers, after our morning conditioning.

I hear her say, "I've never seen that boy in my life. What's his name?"

"My name is Reelin." She turns to me, and I'm stunned by how she looks both exactly the same, and completely different than the last time I saw her. "You can call me Rizz, though."

I'm trying to memorize every new thing about her through the perfectly preserved things from before. Her eyes are the most beautiful green— like a paradise sea. I remember that they change shades, and I can't wait to learn what this one means.

"Rizz? Like that singer, Ralph Tresvant? Are you a fan?" Lonayla laughs similar to Lailani. They were always almost mirror images.

"Nah, Rizz is because my sisters said I have a lot of charisma. It just stuck with me from middle school," I do my best to sound cool. I can't even think about the fact that I'm all sweaty, and I probably stink.

I had hoped I would finally talk to her for the first time in class, with my normal clothes on. When she walked out here, and sat on the bleachers, I could barely focus on anything else. I saw her immediately, like my mind and body felt her before my eyes could see. Coach pulled me aside after practice to tell me to tighten up, or I wouldn't be starting this year. I can't even care, really. Because here she is, right here and right now, in the flesh. I've missed being able to be close to her, and I'll do anything to never have to think about a day when she's not near me again.

I knew it before, but it feels more real now.

Lailani is alive, and she will be mine.

I will do everything I can to protect her. I Promise. Forever.

To Be Continued...

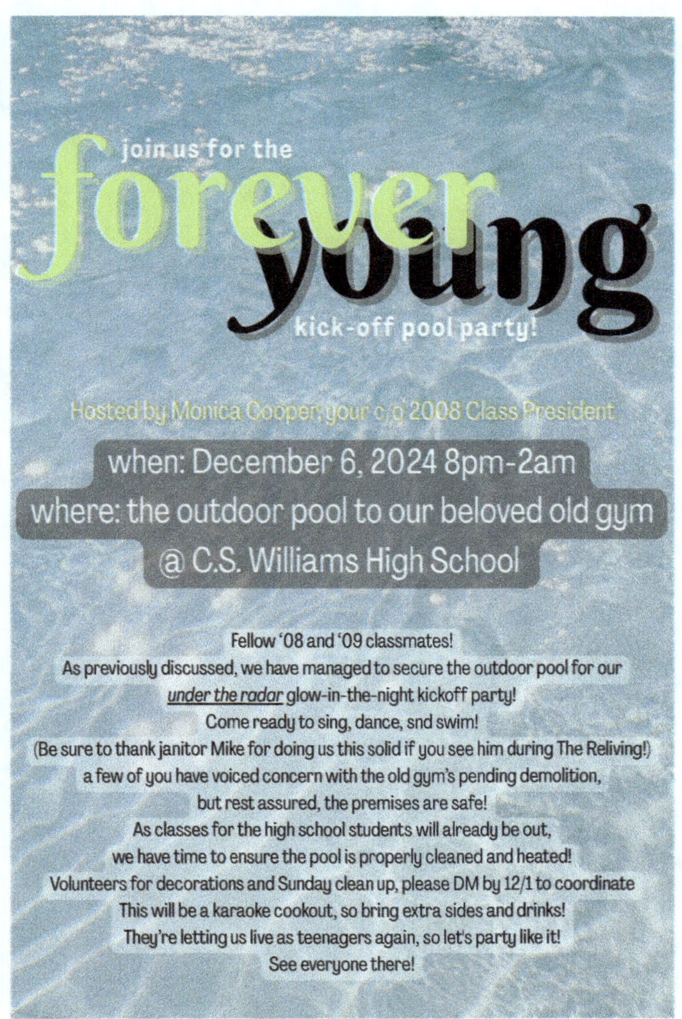


Learn what really happened the night of the epic "Forever Young party" and why, in End's Beginning. *Coming Soon!*

# About Fool's End

I loved writing this story. I loved it so much, I could've made it 400,000,000 pages, and still would have had more to say. That's what's so fun about creating things—you can literally create more. The flashbacks in tandem with the present-day experience, make the possibilities feel so endless for me. I love my characters so much, I want to write every single person an entire lifetime, just because I can. I might put out little novellas, just for the little things. If you can guess my favorite character, you get… I dunno… brownie points!

I am so detailed, and I wasn't sure other people would appreciate the little things, so it took me almost three weeks to comb through and remove unnecessary specifics. I am also ridiculously long-winded, so these characters always have so much to say. When recording my audiobook, a lot of those specifics came back, but it's only because it came naturally, and my final edits were completed while listening to my audio. If you listened to the audio, I'm sorry about my lisp. I tried my best to dull it down, and while most people never notice it, I hear it so strongly, always. I would have had someone else record it, but I really wanted to do this entire project by myself. I hope it was worth the time.

I've been working on so many stories, but I've never thought about thriller or suspense, because I wasn't sure I could execute it well. Then, I woke up on a random day in March 2025, and literally said, "I'm gonna write a whodunnit, but I'm gonna make her live, and have to figure out the reason why." Now, I'm not sure if I've ever heard of a murder mystery where the victim survives, and the story basically continues as a romance—or if that even makes sense—but I decided to write it, because why the hell not? If I ever tell the original thought behind how this story was actually supposed to end, people might think I'm crazy.

The title of the book actually came to me while writing the first chapter. I knew what I was going to make the story into, and with the pool being a large part of it, I first thought to call it "Off The Deep End," but because my FMC was going to be struggling with trust and constantly feeling foolish, me being born on April Fools' Day made "Fool's End" sound better. At least it does in my head. Lol.

After waking up in that pool, Lailani had to navigate so many things that ultimately made her appreciate her relationships more. Struggling with her need for control, trust issues, health scares, her need for detachment, looking forward to the end of everything, and letting others be there for her, Lailani  has to learn to grow in love, by simply living in it. It's not always as simple as what you see, and things can become more beautiful when you just let them be. I hope it came across the way it was meant to.

This was always going to be a duology, and book one was actually supposed to include the scene with the attempt on Lailani's life, but I decided not to do that just yet. I want to break down the entire scene of the crime, adding depth that would have possibly extended the story way too far for one book. I'm a fantasy reader, so 1,000+ pages is normal to me, but I know people like to get to the point these days, and in the romance and thriller genres, I hear the shorter, the better. I tried, I swear.

The Reliving is actually something I have thought about for years, and never truly figured out how to bring to fruition. I will definitely expand on the program in the story, because it feels necessary in real life. Who knows, maybe my mind can create something great and make this world a better place. We have way too much hatred, and not enough positive representation. I see negativity spread more than anything, and that has to change.

While I never outlined this story, I had an idea and kept it going. I didn't want to put myself in the headspace of having to follow a preconceived guideline, so I just let my words flow. When I break down the "why" of it all, it will hopefully give even more to the love story, and make sense of just how deep love can go. You'll get to experience the story from Reelin's perspective, when the story continues. You've gotten a sneak peek at that, and at Lonayla's already. Kieran's POV is also coming of course, and Lailani will still be dealing with the realization of life being unpredictable, no matter how much she fights for control.

I hope you'll continue the journey with me.

Little things you'll notice in my writing, is the way the Blackness and disability are not shared in any way that categorizes them as lesser experiences. I am a proud Black woman, so there will always be black themes, and including disability somewhere in the story, is because it is something that should be normalized. Disabled persons are just as important as anyone else, so we have to release the weird stigma around them. Every life is precious, no matter how they were born. Learn to accept people's uncontrollable differences. Learn to understand that some illnesses are invisible, but those that aren't, are still not one size fits all. It would be irresponsible of me to not provide representation for everyone. (Except racists, rapists, abusers, and cold-blooded murderers. You get nothing from me.) It has always been so important to me to make sure that good people feel seen. Let go of judgement, and spread love—it makes life better.

Ashleigh Woodward has always been a creative. No matter the art form, it's likely that at some point in her life, she has tried—and possibly been good at—most morally acceptable things. She enjoys anything that assists in her escape from reality, because that's how she learned to cope with uncomfortable situations from a very young age.

Ashleigh was born in Denver, Colorado and raised in Atlanta, Georgia. So she's a Southern Belle, who only likes the idea of snow when she doesn't have to experience the cold.

In her late 20s, Ashleigh was diagnosed with a rare disease, and told she didn't have long to live. She never subscribed to that thought process, though. While it took her a while to remove the self-doubt and insecurity, she's determined to live life on her own terms.

As a business owner, a coach, and an eldest daughter, Ashleigh's need to make the world a better place, is stronger than anything. Venturing into the things she's only dreamed of doing before, her hope is to inspire others to be their best selves, spread more love, and to live in gratitude. Life is meant to be lived, so let it be beautiful.

9 798999 256133